DAMAGED!

by
Bernadette Y. Connor

Waverly House Publishing
PO Box 1053
Glenside, PA
1-800-858-2253

Published by:
Waverly House Publishers
P.O. Box 1053
Glenside, Pa. 19038

Library of Congress Catalog Card Number: 98-61432

ISBN: 0-9650970-2-1

Cover design and illustration:
Kirk Gaines
Gaines Production and Associates

Printed in the United States of America
First Edition

Acknowledgements

First, I must thank and give honor to God for selecting this vessel to deliver "*Damaged!*"

My next heartfelt thank yous must go to Sharon Edwards and Clarence E. Barnhill, the two people who, after supporting me through some of the most difficult situations life can produce, helped me focus on my literary goals.

Knowing my financial circumstances couldn't support a hobby of collecting discarded raisins, there was one person who loved and believed in me enough to take on the role of benefactor and easily adapted to the role of my most avid reader, my beloved big sister, Martha J. Patterson.

A young man in pursuit of his own dream fulfilled mine by directing me to Waverly House Publishing. Thanks and much love, Maurice G. Smith.

Thank you to my editor at Waverly House, Nora Wright, who professionally performed her job and remained my respected friend and colleague, which was no easy task.

There are so many others to be thanked who listened to my whining and continued to encourage me, and those who answered tough technical and professional questions. They include: Blanche Day, Raymond Patterson, Eros L. Connor, Erica L. Connor, Richard E. Patterson, Vera LaRue, Eleanor Davis, Edna Cole, Joyce Day, Mary Barnes, Trudy Robinson, Janis Miller, Renette Townsend, Mary Otey, and Joseph L. DiTomo, Jr., Esq. If I've missed anyone, please know it was not intentional.

Dedicated

to the memories of my beloved

mother, Inez Patterson
father, Richard O. Smith
son, Edsel L. Connor, Jr.
first love, Kenneth A. James
dearest friend, Harold Burnside

and

to the greatly anticipated futures of my beloved

son, Eros L. Connor
daughter, Erica L. Connor
grandchildren:
Johnnie Barnes
Emanuel L. Connor
Natasha L. Connor
Ky Aryana Connor-Watts
nephew, Richard E. Patterson

Chapter One

The flawless, milk chocolate beauty of the young lady could only be regarded as exceedingly pleasing to the eye. Her long, coarse, pitch-black hair was pulled back severely into a ponytail which dangled loosely between her shoulder blades. The exotic slope of her almond-shaped, dark brown eyes gave the illusion of a perpetual smile. Although still in her teens, she had an exquisitely proportioned body and the promise of blossoming into a truly memorable woman. Her low, slightly raspy voice foretold a future of wonderfully intimate conversations.

In fact, Adrena Reynolds possessed every superficial physical element necessary to fulfill the yearnings of a healthy young woman; moreover, a pool of intelligence to be envied bubbled vibrantly beneath her stunning exterior.

Unfortunately, deeply-scarring emotional experiences had forced Adrena to grow up practically in seclusion. Happy thoughts of teenage girls the world over seldom, if ever, entered her mind. On the sofa of psychiatrist Dr. Vivian Matthews, Adrena had been revealing her life, real and imagined, since she was ten years old - state-assigned.

The years of discovery and growth shared by Adrena and Dr. Matthews had produced a relationship which surmounted all barriers to intimacy and, as a result, was more binding than one between a therapist and patient should be. Perhaps, if Adrena had not been Dr. Matthews' very first patient, it would have been different. If only there had been one other person in the world Adrena could have turned to - a mother, grandmother, or an aunt. If she had not been so young, so physically and emotionally savaged . . . so vulnerable and needy.

Or perhaps if the state had placed Adrena with a foster mother, as Dr. Matthews had recommended, and not with couples. In their therapy sessions, Dr. Matthews had learned of Adrena's deep-seated distrust of couples. Adrena believed all women were born with minds of their own, but she also believed that the mind of a woman would be devoured by the man she loved, as payment for loving him. Only recently had Dr. Matthews been able to make any progress in altering Adrena's ideas of the dynamics of male-female relationships.

Over the past six years, Adrena had been placed with seven foster families. During that time, there had been two separate incidents in which Adrena set fire to the house while her foster parents slept, after one of them did or said something which she deemed unacceptable! Fortunately, there had been no loss of life. The first incident, which occurred when Adrena was eleven, was shared with Dr. Matthews, but the doctor had simply refused to believe that the beautiful, soft-spoken little girl could be capable of such a vicious act and insisted that the fire wasn't Adrena's fault - after all, with children, it was sometimes impossible to discern truth from imagination. On the second occasion, Adrena made it clear to Dr. Matthews that she was in fact the arsonist.

There were other tales Adrena did not share with Dr. Matthews. Nearing her twelfth birthday, Adrena was living in the foster home of Mr. and Mrs. Kevin Rose. There were five children in the Rose household - three natural children and two foster children. Adrena was the oldest and the only female.

Occasionally, Adrena's conspicuously developing body held the attention of Kevin Rose. Of course, he would never have admitted to wanting to take his attention any further than admiration - and, in fact, he never did. Kevin Rose was, for all intents and purposes, a good foster father. He spoke with such melodic clarity that he could help a child with phonetic spelling from way across the room. He could give math the kind of rhythmic spin that made it a wonder to the youthful mind.

Adrena saw how Mrs. Rose's angry eyes traveled constantly from her lusting husband to Adrena. However, Mrs. Rose never said a word to her husband; her only response was to send Adrena to the store or on some other unnecessary errand. Hadn't Adrena seen her own mother give her stepfather that same impotent look of defeated disgust on more than one occasion?

Taking matters into her own hands, Adrena began to give serious thought to stopping Mr. Rose from giving her that look only men seemed to deliver so well. As Adrena washed dishes after dinner one evening, the answer came to her while cleaning and preparing the coffeepot for Mr. Rose's morning cup. Adrena dabbed dishwashing liquid onto a paper towel, wiped the inside of the filter tray of the coffee machine, replaced it, and smiled.

No one questioned Adrena about Mr. Rose's heinous bout of nausea and diarrhea that forced him to leave work early the next day and spend the evening in bed. In the weeks that followed, no one questioned Adrena about Mr. Rose's sudden burst of manic energy after drinking Ritalin residue or about his deep, unrelenting, Benadryl-induced evening naps. Dr. Matthews removed her from the Rose household only after Adrena began to complain about the other children.

The next foster family in Adrena's life only lasted two days. Mr. Jacobs made the mistake of innocently stroking Adrena's arm in greeting the first day. Then he allowed his hand to flow down her back the second day, and Adrena's reaction to his familiarity was immediate and violent. As Mrs. Jacobs frantically dialed for the police, Mr. Jacobs fought valiantly with Adrena, suffering deep scratches, dark bruises, and a vicious bite. He knew he had done something to provoke Adrena, but didn't know exactly what it was. He pressed no charges. Dr. Matthews retrieved Adrena from the police station and confined her patient in the medical wing of the orphanage for six months for further observation.

Adrena would waltz into Dr. Matthews' office for her scheduled visits and calmly admit to most of her despicable deeds. By observing Dr. Matthews' responses to certain revelations, Adrena developed enough of a survival instinct to know exactly which facts to filter out. Medications administered to unwitting foster parents were never discussed. Only fresh anger compelled Adrena to divulge the occasional indiscretion involving a human being; however, she told Dr. Matthews everything about the atrocities she committed against animals. Dr. Matthews would fervently admonish Adrena for acting out and threaten to institutionalize her if she couldn't rein in her more violent behavior. Then they would discuss Adrena's unacceptable activities, how she felt about them afterward, and what appropriate responses could have been made.

No matter how horrendous Adrena's behavior, the remarkable little girl appealed to Dr. Matthews' unfulfilled maternal instincts. Taking on the extra responsibility of encouraging Adrena to reach up, rather than lash out at the world, was not originally an act of love for Dr. Matthews - it was simply humane. How anyone could see a child in desperate need, have a little time, intelligence, patience and a few extra dollars, and not share them was beyond the young doctor's comprehension. Dr. Matthews could tell no one exactly when the lines between doctor and patient became blurred . . . nor could she tell anyone the exact day she began to love Adrena as if she were her very own child.

Adrena's strikingly attractive features were all that were noticed by most people. Her behavior, in average situations, could only be viewed as normal, but in a stressful or intimate scenario one would begin to see Adrena's flaws. Dr. Matthews, however, didn't see them as flaws; she saw Adrena's reactions as perfectly appropriate under the circumstances. Adrena was striking back at a world that had, until the age of ten, violently abused and neglected her. As a matter of fact, Dr. Matthews saw Adrena's self-protective reactions as progress, for a child who once had lain passively catatonic, unless touched, for seven months and had not been able to speak for a year. Her entire existence had revolved around loneliness and fear. She feared everyone. And every painful step Adrena made from that state of being was not only a personal victory for her, but for Dr. Matthews, too . . . as were her missteps, regressions and failures.

After many long, gratifying hours of individual tutoring by Dr. Matthews and staff members, Adrena left the life of institutions and entered the world of real schools. Because

Adrena would become sulky and belligerent if anyone other than Dr. Matthews entered school on her behalf, Dr. Matthews remained deeply involved in her school life. She always collected and signed all of Adrena's assignments, projects, and report cards. Dr. Matthews also doled out the appropriate feedback. She applauded wildly at every piano recital. So too was Dr. Matthews involved in every other aspect of Adrena's life. She wept and frantically paced the hospital corridor when Adrena's appendix ruptured. She expressed disappointment when Adrena disobeyed her foster parents. It was also Dr. Matthews who tried desperately, through therapy, hypnosis and drugs, to give Adrena a glimpse of normalcy.

♦   ♦   ♦

Today, Dr. Matthews' precious, slightly imperfect, doll had taken a giant step backward. Adrena, with her uniquely impish but angelic smile, sat across from Dr. Matthews in the comfortably appointed office and shared her latest terroristic act. Life experiences from the ages of three to ten had robbed Adrena of any genuinely reliable emotions - hot or cold. Now, at sixteen, her richly seductive voice was a contradiction to her matter-of-fact manner of speaking.

"Doc, they've told me I can't come back to school for three days."

"Why, Adrena?"

In a breathless, but somehow unconcerned rush, Adrena said, "I really need to get back before then. I have a final on Friday. Can't you do something, Doc?"

"You haven't told me why."

With a barely perceptible tilt of her head, she said, "There was an incident in chemistry class today."

"Involving what and whom?"

"Involving a little liquid acid and Harvey."

Fighting an overwhelming parental urge to yell, Dr. Matthews asked, "Adrena, what happened to Harvey?"

Without emotion, Adrena began her story. "This morning, in homeroom, Harvey flicked his tongue at me. I

ignored him, like you told me to, Doc. He sits behind me in
English. Anyway, he kept leaning forward, panting like a
dog, and making sickening, sucking sounds in my ear. I
ignored him.

"During lunch, he came over to my table and stared. He
picked up my ice cream cup, pulled the lid off, and licked the
ice cream. Then, he closed it and put it back on my tray. I
took a deep breath and ignored him. Just like you told me to.

"Everything was fine, until seventh period, Doc. That's
chemistry. We were all working on erosion experiments.
The teacher gave us each tiny vials of acid to do simulations.

"Harvey got up and headed in my direction. He walked
right up to my seat, reached down, and that slimy bastard
touched my ass. He squeezed it, Doc. I closed my eyes, took
a deep breath, and tried to ignore him. When Harvey came
back, he did the same thing again. A couple of the kids
laughed. I don't know why. Do you?"

Speaking therapeutically, Dr. Matthews said, "Some of
the children were sexually excited. Others were nervous.
Giggling was the only acceptable response they could exhibit
and remain a part of the group. It's typical adolescent
behavior, Adrena - as basic and old as time. They think of it
as part of the mating ritual. As usual, they're wrong. What
Harvey did to you, Adrena, was not acceptable behavior. Go
on with your story. Did you continue ignoring him?"

Irritated by Dr. Matthews' detached reaction to the
obvious sexual assault, Adrena responded sharply, "Doc, I
tried. He wouldn't leave me alone. He kept touching me. I
tried!"

"I believe you tried, Adrena. Just take a deep breath, calm
down, and tell me what happened."

As always, Adrena followed the doctor's instructions to
the letter. She took a deep breath, composed herself, and
continued. "Breathing didn't work the second time Harvey
touched me. I didn't blow up, Doc. Really. I raised my hand
and asked Mrs. Marshall if I could refill my vial. She told me
I could, if I didn't put too much in it and promised to be
careful. I promised.

"I took the long route around the room, walked over to the cabinet and filled the vial to the top - carefully, the way Mrs. Marshall said. Without looking, I knew Harvey had spun completely around on his stool to watch me. He probably wiggled his legs in that disgusting way of his the entire time. If not exactly that, I know he did something because some of the kids were laughing and pointing in his direction. I didn't put the lid on the vial for my return trip.

"When I got close, Harvey grinned. I knew he intended to touch me again, Doc. I didn't try to duck him, either. Just like I expected, Harvey put his hand out and ran it over my ass again. Before he could squeeze, I turned and tipped the vial. That acid landed right where I wanted it to - all over the fly of his baggy jeans! I should have aimed higher though."

Adrena stopped her storytelling and smiled at the recollection before continuing, "I stood there just long enough to see the puff of smoke and the little holes flare out in Harvey's pants. Then, I walked on. I was in my seat when Harvey started screaming like a little girl.

"Mrs. Marshall took Harvey's jeans and underwear off right there in class in front of everybody. He kept yelling, 'Adrena! Adrena!' I didn't care what he yelled. Mrs. Marshall didn't say a word to me until after the emergency medics took Harvey's bare ass off on a stretcher.

"I told Mrs. Marshall it was an accident. Harvey had pushed me. Two other people saw Harvey's hand. They told Mrs. Marshall it looked like he pushed me, too."

Mimicking Mrs. Marshall's words and mannerisms, Adrena said, "Adrena, you could have ruined Harvey's entire life with your carelessness. If you had simply followed instructions and put the lid on securely, the entire incident would have been avoided."

Resuming her own persona, Adrena continued, "She recommended a three-day suspension, Doc, and the principal agreed. Can't you talk to them, Doc? I really need to take that test. They may try to penalize my grade for taking it late."

"Adrena, I can't do that. What you did was wrong. You have to understand there are penalties."

"So what, if what I did was wrong? What he did was wrong. We were both wrong."

"That's right. Still, two wrongs didn't make it right, Adrena."

"What's so exciting about being right, Doc?"

"You'll be the one on the outside of the bars. Is that exciting enough for you?"

"His shit accelerated as the day went on, Doc! I ignored him! Was I supposed to just let him keep going? If he tore my clothes off, was I supposed to take a deep breath and continue to ignore him? When would it have been cool for me to pour the acid, Doc?"

"Actually, never, Adrena. Retribution should be handled by the proper authorities."

"I wasn't there for the vote, Doc."

Unable to avoid the smile creeping across her face, Dr. Matthews said, "I wasn't there either, but I abide by that decision. It's the law, Adrena. What you did wouldn't even be considered self-defense. It's called vigilantism. The authorities do not look kindly on it. Degrees of wrong are seldom weighed in courts of law. You were both wrong."

"His trip to the hospital made it right for me . . . for now. The best burns were on his thighs. Only a few drops landed where I wanted them to. If you talk to the principal, he'll believe it was an accident, Doc."

"Perhaps he would, Adrena. I won't tell him that though. My participation would only mean I condone your behavior. I don't. If losing a few points is the penalty, you'll pay it. Didn't you see any other alternative responses to Harvey's misbehavior?"

Obviously agitated, Adrena barked, "No!"

"Why didn't you tell Mrs. Marshall that Harvey was touching you?"

Adrena asked, her voice dripping with sarcasm, "Why didn't Harvey tell Mrs. Marshall he was going to touch me? Besides, you should know by now that the only woman I depend on to save me, is me."

"I don't question the fact that you were provoked, Adrena, but I would be shirking my responsibility to you if I didn't help you find alternative responses. Socially acceptable responses. Non-criminal behavior. Mrs. Marshall isn't your mother, Adrena. Mrs. Marshall might actually have done something constructive."

"Look, Doc, I know Mrs. Marshall's not my mother. If she was Mildred, I wouldn't have wasted a drop of acid on Harvey's sorry ass. A big stick would have sent him off to the hospital, too. I like Mrs. Marshall. She's a real nice lady. Sort of reminds me of you. I talk to you, but I don't expect you to rescue me from the Harveys of the world, Doc. All women do is talk. It sounds nice, but men don't understand talk. They understand fear, pain, death, acid. Real things."

"Adrena, if you continue to act out, you're going to destroy everything you're working so hard to accomplish. Straight A's and a scholarship all down the drain for one impulsive act."

"I never act impulsively, Doc. I know exactly what I'm doing, when I do it."

"There's not one flicker of remorse for causing Harvey that much pain, Adrena?"

"Not a flicker, Doc. Since you're not going to talk to the principal, let's talk about something else."

"Okay. Your mother will be here for your next visit. How do you feel about that?"

There was a slight tilt of Adrena's head and a pause before she responded, "I don't feel anything about that either, Doc. My mother's dead. She married good old Bartholomew. Remember?"

"Well, your mother's ghost will be here. She has something to tell you."

Adrena closed her elegant eyes and said dreamily, "Adrena, my dearest daughter, Mama's got a terminal illness. She'll be dying soon. Of course, there will be a great deal of suffering beforehand. Will you be there for me?"

There was the briefest of pauses before she said, "Oh Mama, I wouldn't miss your suffering for anything in the world. When does it start? I'd like to have refreshments on hand!"

Moaning audibly, Dr. Matthews said, "Adrena, that's cruel."

"Hey, Doc, we're talking about the woman who sat in the room and watched her husband tie up and rape her own ten-year-old daughter. The woman who knew he intended to sell me to every sick junkie in the city, all for the price of getting high. My suffering didn't pull one drop of motherly love from her, and her suffering won't get a drop from me either. The colder and deader the slut is, the better I'll like it. If you're really hoping to mend those fences, Doc, save it for somebody else. My mother and her husband are the owners of my final emotion."

"Is hate your final emotion, Adrena?"

"It's deeper than hate, Doc. Darker. Colder. More like hate's great, great, great-granddaddy."

"Adrena, hatred will consume you. Destroy you. There has to be some other emotion you're not acknowledging."

Adrena closed her eyes again. She slowly rocked her head from side to side, mimicking an internal audit. She opened her eyes and said frankly, "Nope. Can't find another emotion worth mentioning, Doc."

"How do you feel about me, Adrena?"

A faint smile touched Adrena's sensual lips before she said, "I like you better than any other human on this planet. I would die for you, Doc. Now, I bet you want to to know why."

Dr. Matthews said, "Yes, I'd like to know why."

As if she were reading the ingredients on a cake box, Adrena said, "Because, somehow, I know you would die for me. At first, I thought you were throwing me pity parties. Doing things for the poor, little, homeless, emotional idiot. I told you the very worst things I could think of. Most of it true, by the way. Very few lies. You would shrug and tell me I was on the wrong track. Then, you would cross your arms and tell me one or two other ways I should react in the future. When my session was over, you would give me a gift for some special occasion.

"Doc, I don't know why you do, but you love me in spite of the fact that I can't love you back. I know the state doesn't pay you for all of the sessions I have. They never paid you for visiting my schools or the hospital. You never forget my birthday, Valentine's Day, Easter, or Christmas. Every Halloween costume I've ever had came from you. Every special dress. Extra shoes. Money for class trips. Gym clothes. Piano lessons. You're the molder of all the happiness I've known. Led me to the only peaceful corner in my mind. If there is one iota of good in me, and I sincerely hope there is for your sake, you are its mother. Just remember, I didn't say there was."

"Adrena, there is no greater love than laying down one's life for another. You're saying you love me."

"No, I'm not. I'm stating facts."

"Okay, young lady, your time's up. No more crimes at school. You're not too old, pretty, or intelligent for another confinement trip to the orphanage. Is there a note or anything I need to sign for school? A call I have to make?"

"No note. You have to be with me when I show up on Monday morning though. The principal wants to speak to you. Personally, I think he likes looking at you, Doc."

"He's not my type, Adrena. Okay. I'll pick you up at seven-thirty. Continue your breathing and concentration in adverse situations. If anything else happens, call me before you retaliate. Take your medication. I don't know what your mother has up her sleeve, so be prepared for your next session. If you need to talk before then, call me."

As Dr. Matthews watched Adrena proudly prance in the direction of the elevators, her final goal for Adrena crystallized in her mind. More than anything in the world, she really wanted to hear Adrena say she loved someone. Dr. Matthews would settle for her admitting she loved *something*, but Dr. Matthews' ultimate goal was to hear Adrena admit to loving *someone* . . . just once!

Chapter Two

There were only two people in the world Adrena would admit to having some regard for - Dr. Matthews and Mrs. Stanley, her foster mother. Thanks to the intervention of Dr. Matthews, Adrena had managed to live with the Stanleys for two years, which was a record for Adrena. Other couples had given up on her and called the authorities after one or two unpleasant events. The key to the present successful union was Mrs. Stanley. She always contacted Dr. Matthews in emergencies or if the couple had any concerns.

Dr. Matthews had visited with the Stanleys before Adrena moved into their home and given them a complete rundown of Adrena's habits and peculiarities, assuring them that as long as Adrena took her medication and did not feel threatened, she would be a most pleasant houseguest. As is commonly practiced when placing emotionally troubled children, Dr. Matthews had not gone into Adrena's mental or physical history or conveyed a diagnosis.

Upon Adrena's arrival at the Stanleys', she was the only foster child living with them, and Dr. Matthews suggested it stay that way until Adrena bonded with the couple. Being the only child in her biological family and not having attended school until she was ten had deprived Adrena of the socialization skills required to cope with living with other children. Wanting nothing more than to provide a good home for Adrena, the Stanleys followed Dr. Matthews' lead.

Mr. Stanley's normally quiet, non-aggressive behavior made him the perfect man to have in Adrena's company. He spent most of his time tending the plants in his hothouse. A year would pass before Adrena felt secure enough in his presence to ask questions. Mr. Stanley was so soft-spoken, Adrena strained to hear his answers. This, coupled with the fact that Mr. Stanley seemed almost as disinterested in

Adrena as she was in him, made him appear to be much less threatening to her than other men.

Adrena and Mr. Stanley had long talks about plants. He told her they were not only beautiful, but that many of them held power over life in their precious petals. Even with these conversations under his belt, Mr. Stanley never assumed the barriers were down. He never addressed Adrena directly. Mr. Stanley was sensitive enough to know Adrena had to initiate conversations or contact, or there would be problems.

It was Mrs. Stanley who interacted with Adrena most of the time. Knowing how fiercely protective all foster children are of their limited privacy, she seldom entered Adrena's space without permission. In Adrena's presence, Dr. Matthews had insisted Mrs. Stanley monitor all of Adrena's on-hand medications. This gesture from the only person in the world Adrena trusted made Mrs. Stanley's requests to inspect her room, or to check her supply of Zoloft, Ativan and Benadryl, less threatening. From time to time, Adrena even sat and talked with Mrs. Stanley in her bedroom. They discussed school, teenage grooming woes, and Adrena's refusal to make friends with girls or boys.

In time, Mrs. Stanley could tell when Adrena was overdue for medication. Familiar with Adrena's unusual sensitivity to tones of voice, Mrs. Stanley would calmly say, "Adrena, you're a little anxious. What time did you take your medicine? Should you take the Ativan?"

Unperturbed by this request, Adrena would take a quick glance at the clock and say, "Wow! You're right again. My whole life revolves around taking pills. I wish I didn't have to take them anymore."

"I know, honey. But, the Doctor thinks it's best for now, and she hasn't steered you wrong yet. Has she?"

A little sulkily, Adrena would respond, "No, ma'am."

"Well, go to it, girlie."

Adrena would leave and take her medication. Her levels were well-maintained and monitored in Dr. Matthews' office every week, but it didn't take much of a lapse to tilt those levels. Dr. Matthews had experimented with several antidepressants, before finding one which gave Adrena a functioning balance. Only once, in the two years Adrena had been with the Stanleys, had she waited too long to take her medication. On that occasion, Adrena did not move after Mrs. Stanley reminded her about taking it. Adrena's stillness and the light film of perspiration coating her top lip alarmed Mrs. Stanley, and she softly told Mr. Stanley to call Dr. Matthews. He left his wife and Adrena in the living room and made the call in the kitchen.

Adrena's behavior slowly swayed from still, quiet, and lightly perspiring, to a minor neck tick, to paranoid questions, and accusations. "I know what's going on. Where did he go? If that old bastard thinks he's going to touch me, he just might die doing it! It won't happen to me twice, old lady!"

Remaining calm, Mrs. Stanley tried to reassure her. "He's going to call Dr. Matthews, Adrena. You didn't take your medicine. Something is going wrong with you. What do you think Mr. Stanley is going to do to you? He wouldn't ever hurt you, honey. You know that."

Mr. Stanley returned and stood silently in the doorway, poised to pounce if Adrena made a threatening move on his wife or on herself. The moment Mrs. Stanley moved, Adrena's fears swelled, and she yelled them all at the Stanleys. "You thought I didn't know what the two of you were up to, didn't you?! You thought I would fall asleep! Then you would sit there knitting, while he did whatever he felt like doing! Didn't you?! Or, did you plan to join him in some little sex game you two cooked up just for me?! You don't fool me, you old biddy! Men who don't talk do the same shit as the ones who do! I know that old bastard's running this show! You're just his stupid mouthpiece to get to me! I'm telling you now, I'll kill you both before I let anybody do anything else to me!"

Getting her first glimpse into the true depths of the damage that had been done to Adrena made tears sting Mrs. Stanley's eyes. Gritting her teeth and rallying her emotions quickly, Mrs. Stanley said adamantly, "Adrena, no one will ever hurt you under this roof. Not me. Not Mr. Stanley. Nobody. If they do, I'll help you kill them."

Unable to process this response amid her rapidly scattering thoughts, Adrena stopped momentarily. Fleetingly, Adrena wanted to grab what Mrs. Stanley said, hold on and hide behind it, but before she could, thoughts of past betrayals quickly hustled those thoughts out of her range of consciousness. The venomous ranting continued and escalated.

"Touch me! Come on, you old, dried-up bastard, touch me! Which part would you like to touch first, you sorry old fuck?! If you think that old babe can help you hold me, think again! What I won't break hasn't been named yet!"

A half-hour elapsed before Dr. Matthews arrived. Adrena was well on her way to being out of control, and the web of anxiety and paranoia made giving Adrena a shot almost impossible for three people. After all, to do it, she had to be touched.

Dr. Matthews had held Adrena's drugged, sweat-drenched body in her arms, rocked her and whispered reassurances. The moment the fight left Adrena's body, the doctor insisted she get the antidepressant medication down her throat. If Adrena fell asleep without taking the antidepressant, a devastating depression would loom larger than life for her when she woke. That would trigger another violent episode. If that happened, a trip to Huntingdon Psychiatric Center might be required to stabilize her, and Dr. Matthews would do anything to prevent another stay at Huntingdon for Adrena. Convincing an adult patient that commission to a psychiatric facility didn't mean they were insane was an arduous task. Convincing a teenager was much closer to impossible.

Like most patients tethered to medications, Adrena wanted desperately not to have to take them. Her mother's dependency on street drugs had motivated Adrena's need to be free of them. She refused to accept the fact that her sanity was being held hostage by drugs, and she found herself experimenting with longer and longer lapses between doses. The withdrawal episode, however, had frightened Adrena. She gained a respect and fear for medicine when, for the first time, she experienced the true effects of addiction . . . and the

Stanleys came to realize that Adrena's self-control could
never be taken for granted.

♦   ♦   ♦

After relating the Harvey incident to Dr. Matthews,
Adrena returned home to the Stanleys. Although Adrena only
mumbled a greeting, the Stanleys found nothing out of the
ordinary. They were used to her occasional mood swings and
didn't notice the steam seeping around the rim of Adrena's
normally tightly sealed self-control. However, the Stanleys
did notice when Adrena slammed her bedroom door. That
was something new and demanded investigating.

Mrs. Stanley followed Adrena upstairs to see if everything
was all right. She knocked on Adrena's door. There was no
response. Mrs. Stanley knocked again.

With a tinge of anger, Adrena responded, "Yes?"

"Are you okay, honey?"

"I'm fine. Just got a headache. I'm going to take an
aspirin and lie down."

"May I come in for a minute?"

"For what? I told you I have a headache. Why do you
want to come in?"

Not bothering to lie, Mrs. Stanley said, "I'd like to come
in to take a look at you, for my own peace of mind. As grown
as you think you are, you're still a child, Adrena. You may be
overlooking something."

Taking a moment to compose herself, Adrena wiped the
perspiration from her upper lip and said, "Okay."

An obviously concerned Mrs. Stanley rushed into the
bedroom. She held Adrena's face in her hand and looked into
the beautiful brown eyes. She ran her hand over Adrena's
brow and neck, and asked anxiously, "Has your stomach been
upset or anything?"

Submitting to Mrs. Stanley's ministrations because she
knew the lady meant well, Adrena answered, "No. My
stomach is fine, Mrs. Stanley. I have a headache. You fuss
over me like I'm a baby."

"Well, that's my prerogative, Miss Adrena. Is your medicine giving you a headache again? Did you tell Dr. Matthews about it when you were there?"

In disgust, Adrena spat, "It's not my medication. It's my mother."

This puzzled Mrs. Stanley. Adrena had never mentioned her mother before. "What about your mother?"

"She's coming to see me next week."

"What are you talking about, child? She's not coming here. I don't care what Social Services says - if you don't want to see her, you don't have to. Nobody told me about it. How did you find out?"

"She's not coming here, Mrs. Stanley. She's coming to Dr. Matthews' office."

"Oh . . . well, if Dr. Matthews agrees with it, Adrena, maybe it's not such a bad idea. The doctor always has your best interest at heart. There's no telling where you would be, or what condition you would be in, if not for Dr. Matthews. She will be there with you, won't she?"

Adrena answered with growing agitation, "Yes, Ma'am. Neither one of us knows what she wants, though. I haven't seen her in six years. She called me a few times, but I refused to talk to her. I have nothing to say to the woman, and I don't want to hear her voice."

"Okay, Adrena. You calm yourself down now. We'll see you through this some way. The doctor will be there with you in her office, and I'll be here when you get home. Nothing's changing. Don't stress yourself. Come down and eat your dinner. Take your regular medicine and that Ativan. Get some sleep and face each day as it comes."

A wan smile touched Adrena's lips. She said, "Okay, Mrs. Stanley. I'll be down in a few minutes. I promise."

Mrs. Stanley left Adrena sitting on the side of her bed. Adrena's hatred held much more venom than Mrs. Stanley could ever imagine. There were so many unusual scars on the child. Most were obviously surgical. Still, there were some with no explanations. Mrs. Stanley's mind would never be able to sink low enough to gather all of the pieces of Adrena's puzzle on her own. The best she could hope was that Adrena would share it with her someday.

Adrena sat quietly on her bed. The sweat film returned to her top lip. Familiar pictures and fragrances filled Adrena's senses. Her mother's dirty scarf, with the thick, greasy knot in the back and huge, suffocating clouds of cigarette smoke. The stench of unclean bodies, blatant sex, and filth. Blackened fingers, empty liquor and soda bottles, and an array of drug wrappers on the floor. Roaches scampering. A McDonald's bag thrown here and there.

The parade of filthy, disgusting men coming in. Her mother performing one sickening sexual act after another with them. The men either paid or argued over the price with her stepfather - no one caring that there was a five-year-old crouched in the corner of the room.

One memorable night from the past began to unfold before Adrena's mind's eye. She saw herself as a five-year-old, sitting in the middle of the dismal, one-room living space she shared with her mother, stepfather, and two other women to whom Adrena could never assign a role. Adrena heard the approach of people arguing. Recognizing her stepfather's voice in the crowd, she knew they would be coming to their room.

Grabbing her imaginary doll, Adrena shuffled herself toward a corner. As usual, Adrena's tiny frame wasn't buried deep enough into the corner to satisfy her stepfather, Bart. He rushed over and gave the little girl a hard kick with his big, ragged, sneakered foot. To make sure she wouldn't turn around anytime soon, Bart gave her several extra kicks. This was the only way Bart ever touched Adrena, and he never spoke to the child. All communications passed from Bart to her mother, Mildred, to Adrena. Food dwindled down the same way.

With Adrena out of the way, Bart turned to Mildred and grunted, "Do it now."

Sounding drunk, Mildred slurred her response, "Why can't one of them do it?"

"You do it! You do it now! If I have to tell you one more time, your ass will be out! Out of everything! Got it?!"

A strange man's voice said, "C'mon, baby. I ain't dat bad. We can work this. C'mon. This is jus' a li'l freak show." One of the women with no names said, "Yeah, jump to it, ho'. We ain't got all night." There was a loud slap, a yelp, and scuffling. Frightened to look and worried someone would fall on her, Adrena dared to take a peek. Bart held Mildred by the neck and forced her down on her knees in front of one of the four men in the room. Adrena heard the man unzip his pants. Saw him fumble, retrieve his goods and present them to Mildred's tightly clenched lips. Bart squeezed Mildred's neck until she opened her mouth. Hoping her mother wouldn't have to do that again and not wanting to see it, Adrena closed her eyes.

Every time Adrena peeked, the vulgarity of acts had accelerated. At the height of the atrocities, her mother and one of the other women sexually serviced all four men at one time. The extra woman tried to persuade Bart to do something with her. He turned her down for a while; then he let her drop down on her knees for him, too.

Finished with the two men she had been with, Mildred saw what Bart and the woman were doing. Clad in nothing but a tee shirt, Mildred ran over and dragged the woman's face from Bart's crotch. Mildred drew her fist back and slammed it into the woman's face so hard a tooth hit Adrena in the corner. Bart's laughter mingled with that of the other men in the room. The two near-naked women tussled viciously. When Bart tired of the entertainment, he moved to separate them and said, "Now, you two kiss and make up."

One of the men said in an excited rush, "Hell, yeah! Make 'em kiss and make up, Bart, man! Yeah!" He lit a joint and leaned on the wall.

The glitter of the knife Mildred produced from thin air changed the tone of excitement. Bart gave her his lethal stare and attempted to take the knife from Mildred's hand. She sliced his arm open from the elbow down to his wrist. As soon as she realized she had cut her beloved Bart, and seeing her high going down the drain, Mildred started babbling an apology, "Baby, I'm sorry. You know I can't stand to see you with no other woman. You know I love you, baby. Don't be

mad at me. They'll give you some good shit for the pain
when you go to the hospital, baby. Shit you like. C'mon, I'll
go with you."

Bart grabbed his arm and spun in a circle. Blood dripped
and flew around the room. It ran down Mildred's dirty tee
shirt when Bart clamped his arm around her neck. Bart
squeezed Mildred's neck in the fold of his wounded arm, until
her eyes bulged and saliva ran from her mouth and mixed
with his blood. He let Mildred's nearly nude body slide down
to the floor and kicked her toward Adrena's corner. Bart
kicked Mildred over and over, harder and harder, until she
was in the corner with Adrena.

Out of spite for what Mildred had done to him, Bart
wrapped a filthy shirt around his bleeding arm, sat on the bed,
popped a few bright orange capsules into his mouth, lit a
joint, and opened a bottle of Jack Daniels. He glared
hatefully at the huddled, whimpering mother and daughter in
the corner and took a big gulp.

Needing to join in on the alcohol and drug festivities,
Mildred absentmindedly stroked Adrena's face with her
blood-soaked hand and begged for Bart's forgiveness. The
texture and smell of the blood, semen, marijuana, and alcohol
made Adrena retch. If she had eaten anything at all that day,
it would have been splattered all over herself and Mildred,
too. Adrena tried to wiggle away from her mother's rancid
and bloody touch. Everything about the woman revolted the
little girl.

Mildred continued to whine and beg until Bart lay down
on the bed and that same woman climbed up and lay on top of
him. Mildred crawled around the room, shoving drug-dozing
people out of her way, as she searched for her knife. With
that knife in her hand, Mildred dragged the woman from the
bed and sliced her face up one side and down the other. In his
drugged stupor, the injured Bart was no match for an angry
knife-wielding Mildred, and the battle raged in slow motion.

On her bed in her pretty room at the Stanleys', Adrena
could see and hear Bart and Mildred screaming at each other
over women, drugs, alcohol, and money. She cringed at the
loud, cracking sound of Bart's hand slapping her mother, the

countless thuds of Mildred hitting walls, radiators and floors. And after Mildred stabbed Bart, his loud vulgar curses.

Their voices camouflaged Mrs. Stanley's calls. Memories of being cold, hungry, frightened, kicked, and terrorized completely enveloped Adrena. Sweat poured down her face. Trembling, Adrena clenched the bedspread in her fists.

Moments later, Adrena didn't see Mrs. Stanley standing in her doorway. She flinched violently when Mrs. Stanley pressed the Ativan on her. Mindlessly, she swallowed the tiny pill without water.

Mrs. Stanley's prayers somehow blended into the pictures and sounds that flipped from her mother and Bart, to Harvey, to Dr. Matthews. Adrena couldn't distinguish who had done what to her. Before drifting off, Adrena only had one clear thought. "They will all pay."

Chapter Three

At five-thirty, Dr. Vivian Matthews walked out of the perfectly air-conditioned, hermetically sealed Chambers Building and into the blinding sunlight. Vivian's soft, buttered-brown complexion glowed, as her body quickly thawed in the heat of the day. She leisurely strolled the one block to the garage with her shoulder-length, sleekly waved black hair and full hips swinging in unison. There was a healthy bounce to her ample bosom. Vivian's long, shapely legs afforded her a generous stride; she'd been told they made her outfits sing. No one was fooled by the tailored, eggplant purple suit. It only appeared professional while Vivian sat behind her desk. The shortness of her skirt hinted heavily of the playful and sensuous side of the good doctor.

Male heads swiveled in appreciation of the drop-dead gorgeous woman passing. This always alternately repulsed and reassured Vivian . . . and it kept good old Howard Shaw, the great love of her life, on his toes, too.

At the garage, Vivian waved to the attendant and climbed into her white Maxima. She sang along with the radio as she pulled out of the garage and into traffic. Howard would be waiting for her at the restaurant. They had designated Wednesday evenings as their night out, and it always began with dinner at the Board Room. After dinner, activities varied - movies, theatre, shows, dancing. The night always drifted off with them entwined in each other's arms. Vivian loved the way Howard asked, "Flowers or stripes?" - his way of determining whether they would be sleeping in his bed or hers.

Howard's business partner, Clayton, spotted Vivian entering the lounge before Howard did and greeted Vivian with a hug and kiss that drove his watchful partner nuts. Clayton loved irritating Howard, but, although handsome and charming, Clayton was not Vivian's type at all. Any commitment, outside the stock market, frightened him to death. He'd ask half jokingly, on many occasions, "Why can't I commit, Dr. Viv? Didn't my mother wean me properly?"

Vivian's response would always be, "She weaned you just fine, Clayton. She forgot to worm you though. You'll commit when you run up on the right hydrant. Don't worry."

Together, Howard and Clayton formed the brokerage firm of Williams and Shaw. They belonged together. Clayton was flamboyant, suave, and free-flowing. Howard was conservative, calm, and borderline obsessive. Their clients usually loved one, hated the other, and after reading the growing bottom line of their investment statements, highly respected both.

Howard approached with a smile for Vivian. After turning and giving Clayton a scowl, he wrapped his arms around Vivian, kissed her leisurely, and said, "Hi, sweetheart. Is this man bothering you?"

Shaking her head in playful, coquettish innocence, Vivian responded, "No, dear. You know I'm not into tall, dark and handsome."

With a mock frown, Howard said, "I'm afraid to ask, but I have to know. Exactly what kind are you into?"

Still securely wrapped in his arms, Vivian replied slowly, "Tall, dark, handsome, intelligent, sensitive, and sexy with substance."

Howard looked Clayton in the eye, shrugged, and said, "I knew she liked me better. I wasn't worried."

Clayton smirked and said, "Yeah, sure, man. You're secure. That's why you always swell up and get that murderous glow going in your eyes when somebody looks at her."

Howard said calmly, "Say what you will, she's mine. Are you joining us for dinner?"

"No, Howard. I'm going hydrant hunting tonight. And, when I find it . . ."

They all said together, "After you sniff it a few times, you're gonna piss on it and move on."

The threesome howled with laughter. It was probably the first time that day any of them had felt free enough to truly express themselves. When the laughter died down, Howard and Vivian excused themselves. Their table was ready, so they bypassed the bar and ordered drinks there.

As Vivian sipped her Manhattan, Howard silently played with her fingers on the table. He stroked, caressed, and flicked them one at a time, always beginning with the thumb and working his way to Vivian's little finger. He loosely interlocked his fingers with hers for a few moments and began again. There were times when Howard studied Vivian's hair, ears, knees, nipples, or navel with that same intensity. A year ago, it bothered her. When asked why he was . studying one of her body parts with such rapt intensity, Howard would always respond sweetly, "Because it's yours, Viv."

To break the spell, Vivian asked, "How was your day, Howard?"

After a quick bite of his bottom lip, he said, "Fine. A little too quiet. I could actually hear Clayton's business and personal conversations most of the day. Does he talk in his sleep, Viv?"

"How would I know? I've never slept with him, Howard."

"Am I confusing psychiatry with mysticism again?"

"That, or you're implying I've slept with your partner."

"Well, I know that hasn't happened. Clayton wouldn't be able to wait to get to the office to share that with me. He'd stop at a phone booth in the middle of the night, call me at home, and gloat over every detail."

Laughing at his obviously feigned irritation, Vivian asked, "Howard, if Clayton upsets you so, why did you go into business with him?"

"He reminds me of my oldest brother. They get some kind of sick kick out of precariously holding me by my thumbs and dangling me over a cliff. They both excite, frighten, and irritate the shit out of me. Still, I love and admire them. Go figure, Doc. That's enough about that numbnut. How was your day?"

From long-established habit, Vivian referred to her patients as "they," or by their diagnosis. No names, ages, or genders. Vivian couldn't risk anyone ever being able to say she broke the doctor-patient oath of confidentiality. Keeping the secrets of the clinically depressed could be depressing, but to do otherwise was perhaps the most common way that psychiatrists lost their practices and even their licenses. If they discussed a patient's problems with foster parents or school officials, it could create an unnecessarily prejudicial environment for the patient. Even to law enforcement, psychiatrists couldn't reveal information given them by a patient. In fact, keeping the secrets of a psychopath had driven many wiser than Vivian to suicide.

"My day was good, Howard. Only one rattled my cage a little. They suffer from post-traumatic stress disorder and exhibit socio and psychopathic behaviors. Seems like old demons may be gearing up. If I don't handle it properly, someone could really get hurt."

"Can't you just crank up their medication?"

"You have to be very careful when medicating a non-institutionalized, potential psychopath, sweetheart. If you short circuit the don't do it switch, there will be corpses everywhere."

"Has this person ever actually killed anyone, Viv?"

"Not that I know of, but they claim to have killed some pets. I can only guess if they're telling me the truth, but the way they described how they did it makes me think it's true. They are such a highly intelligent, devious person - the type that can go undetected for an entire lifetime."

"How did they do it?"

Lost in thought, Vivian didn't know what Howard was asking. She gave him a puzzled frown.

"How does this person kill pets, Viv?"

"Oh. Lures them away from home, preferably to a wooded area - then removes the tags, poisons them, watches them die, buries the tags, goes home and reports an injured animal at the location to the SPCA. They hang up before anyone has a chance to ask any questions. The SPCA comes out and finds the poor thing dead, with no identification. They take it in and incinerate it. At best, they'll only take a guess at what killed the dog. The owner thinks Buffy ran away from home. If any questions are asked, no one has any answers anyway."

"Viv, what about the voice of the caller? Wouldn't that give them a clue?"

"Nothing concrete. Voice interpretation varies from person to person. How many times have you misinterpreted a voice? Thought the person was this or that. Thought their age to be this or that. Black or white. Saw them and been completely wrong?"

With a sniff of indignation, Howard said, "I usually get the sex right."

"Have you ever gotten it wrong?"

"Only once, Viv. She sure did sound like a guy though. On the phone and in person."

"Can't convict on a sound-like, Howard. The person who called could have been a concerned citizen. Innocent people call the police every day to report things they don't want to get involved in."

Howard continued to question Vivian, trying in vain to figure out some way that the authorities could find out about the patient Vivian was treating without her revealing it herself.

"Even if you connected all the dots, Howard, all you'd have is a line - you wouldn't have any proof," Vivian told him.

Howard asked, "Has this person done this more than once?"

"Yes, dear. Several times. Just never in or near the same place. Poisoned one right in the owner's yard. Sat in theirs and watched the thing twitch until it was dead, too. No one ever suspected this person actually did anything to the dog. It just somehow got into something that killed it."

Howard was really disturbed by the callousness of Vivian's patient and said, "You should report them to the authorities yourself, Vivian."

"I can't do that for obvious reasons, Howard. You ever heard of doctor-patient confidentiality? I wouldn't have a patient if I snitched on one of them. Nor would I have a license to practice."

"I don't like this person, Vivian. Do you have to treat them?"

"Don't be silly. Of course, I have to treat them."

"Please be careful then."

"Oh, I will. I'm the only one who knows what this person is truly capable of doing."

Howard gave Vivian one last look of concern and changed the subject. "What are we doing after dinner tonight?"

Feeling tension of the day in her shoulders, Vivian groaned miserably and said, "If you don't have any definite plans in mind, I'd like you to take me home, give me a massage, and hold me for the rest of the night."

With a grimace, Howard asked, "Just hold you?"

Vivian purred, "Oh, you know how grateful I can be when you hold me right, Howard. Are you saying you're not up to the challenge?"

"You're in luck. I happened to bring both of my arms with me today, sweetheart. All you have to tell me now is stripes or flowers."

Stripes meant Howard's house. Flowers meant Vivian's. Really wanting to unwind, Vivian said, "Flowers."

"Did you remember to pick my shirts up from the laundry? If not, I'll have to stop first."

"I remembered."

"When a woman remembers your shirts, you have to give her flowers."

"Thank you. Can you call the waiter now? I'm starving."

While Howard ordered dinner, Vivian thought about Adrena. If Howard had known how much that young lady really meant to Vivian, he would have fallen flat on the restaurant floor. If he knew Vivian was glad they hadn't been able to link Adrena to any of those dogs, he would have insisted she see a shrink, too.

And Vivian couldn't imagine how Howard would handle what Adrena had done to poor Harvey. He would probably want to know why Vivian hadn't committed her. Men are particularly sensitive to those types of injuries. They all draw up, wince, and groan at the thought of a groin injury. Collective penis consciousness.

Harvey had stirred Adrena's pain pool. He was lucky that
was all she had done to him. The fact that Adrena had said,
"For now," haunted Vivian. Adrena seldom made empty
remarks. That one meant she fully intended to do something
else to Harvey. If Vivian could get into her head, maybe
Adrena would tell her what it was. If not, Vivian would
have to persuade Adrena to temper her anger toward
Harvey. Sometimes that worked. Sometimes not. This is
where Vivian wished there were a pill for what ailed
Adrena.

Howard and Vivian ate dinner and talked about
insignificant things. Howard told her he had tickets for the
Jazz Festival. Vivian told him she wanted to go to the art
show on Saturday. Finally, they talked a little about their
families and then headed for home.

Snow greeted Howard and Vivian at the front door. She
was the first gift Howard had ever given Vivian. A pure
white Persian cat. Not being an animal lover, Vivian had put
a bright red collar with a bow and bell on Snow. According
to Vivian, Snow would scare the crap out of her otherwise.

Snow only tolerated Vivian, but she was truly fond of
Howard. In fact, Vivian had to fight Snow for her spot on the
sofa sometimes. Snow would leap up and curl up on
Howard's lap the moment he sat down, look up at Vivian and
roll her exquisite green eyes. Vivian dismissed Snow and
drew the line at her bedroom door.

Howard and Snow headed for the kitchen. He cuddled,
kissed, and fed her. She purred loudly and lapped it all up.
Sort of the way Vivian did when Howard cuddled, kissed, and
fed her. Vivian understood Snow perfectly. She just didn't
like her.

Vivian played her messages and thanked God there was
nothing pressing. A few friends and an invitation to dinner on
Sunday from Howard's sister, Talia. Of course, they would
go. Vivian got along well with all of Howard's siblings,
except his oldest sister, Lula. Lula was suspicious of every
woman in any of her brother's lives. She thought they were
all gold diggers. Lula was known to go to great lengths to get
rid of them, too. So far, she'd failed with Vivian.

Howard yelled from the kitchen, "You want me to bring you anything while I'm in here, Viv?"

"No. Are you going to play with that cat all night?"

"Is that jealousy I hear in your voice?"

"Could be."

"She's a cat, Vivian."

"Does she have your undivided attention, Howard?"

"Momentarily."

"Well, then she's competition. Jealousy is not necessarily a species-specific phenomenon."

"What?!"

"Leave the damn cat alone and get in here. That's what."

With jacket in hand and a devilish smile on his deep brown, incredibly handsome face, Howard sauntered into the living room. Six-feet-tall, lean, and muscular, Howard moved with smooth, feline precision. His white shirt with crisply-starched collar and cuffs provided the perfect accent to his black suit pants, full-cut charcoal vest, and red tie. He had a straight, broad nose and gleaming, white teeth, with close-cut hair, black and wavy. His heavily lidded bedroom eyes and magnificent smile had broken more female hearts than he would ever know. Now Howard stood in front of Vivian, slid his arms around her waist, and gave her a generous, warm kiss. Vivian purred deep in her throat to show her appreciation. Howard giggled.

Barely taking his lips away from Vivian's, Howard announced, "I'm all yours now."

Sighing and pouting, Vivian said, "It's about time."

There were a series of small kisses. Then, one long, hot, wet and sensuous one. Tongues danced from one mouth to the other. Their bodies strained to be closer. Hands roamed, stroking, and caressing. Thoughts fell away. Sensations ran rampant.

Suddenly, something foreign, ever so softly, brushed Vivian's ankle. She shuddered and jumped away from Howard. It was Snow. Vivian had to get a bigger bell. She hadn't heard one ting that time.

Thinking it very funny, Howard chuckled and said, "It's just the cat, sweetheart. Why are you so nervous?"

Perturbed with Howard and the cat now, Vivian snapped, "I'm not normally nervous. It's just when varmints creep up and barely touch me, that I get wound up."

Still grinning, Howard said, "Snow only wants to be loved too, Vivian."

"Tell her to stay away from my leg! Go find her own man or cat! She gives me the willies when she does that!"

Separating Vivian and Snow, Howard took Vivian by the hand and led the way upstairs to her bedroom. Of course, Snow followed. Seeing her, Howard gently picked the cat up, put her down outside the bedroom door, and hurriedly shut it. Snow started meowing immediately. In a matter of moments she sounded like a baby in distress. The frown on Vivian's face deepened. In defeat, Howard threw up his hands, flopped down on the bed, and reached for the remote control. Vivian left him there; she had to use the bathroom.

Vivian undressed, freshened up, and put on a nightgown while she was in there. When she came out, Vivian found Howard leaning on one elbow, flicking stations, as only a man would bother doing.

She slid down next to him and said, "Howard, choose a station and leave it there, or turn it off."

His eyes darted from the television screen to Vivian's face. The flicking slowed. She stared at him. Suddenly, the screen went black. The remote control flew through the air and landed on the pillows. Howard pounced on Vivian, tickling and poking. He smothered her with tiny, wet kisses. Laughing and screeching, Vivian couldn't return his kisses.

Breathlessly giggling, Vivian said, "Howard, you promised to give me a massage and to hold me. This is not what I had in mind."

Howard stopped abruptly. "Oh, that's right. I forgot."

Giving her one last peck on the nose, Howard got up and started to undress. Vivian made a mad dash for the door. He asked, "Where are you going?"

Over her shoulder, she yelled, "I'll be right back!"

Almost stepping on Snow, Vivian mumbled angrily, "Get out of my way, cat."

Vivian returned with two chilled glasses of white wine. She put them down on her night table and threw Snow out again, nowhere near as carefully as Howard had done. She flipped on the radio, dropped down onto the bed, sipped, and watched.

It was Vivian's turn to lean on her elbow. Howard had a magnificent body. The fact that he always undressed slowly, carefully folding and hanging his clothes, made it seem more like a program. Completely nude, except for his socks, he sat down on the bed to pull them off. This show always ended the exact same way. Howard, meticulously rolling and tucking those socks into his left shoe. If he ever tucked them into his right shoe, Vivian would be asking the most mindboggling questions he'd ever heard for hours.

Howard slid back, took a sip from Vivian's glass, leaned down, and tenderly kissed her. Vivian closed her eyes and enjoyed the sensation of Howard's wine-cooled lips warming up on hers. Taking the glass out of Vivian's hand and setting it on the table, Howard moved closer and wrapped his long arms around her. The heat from his body was intoxicating. He began to firmly stroke and massage her back and hips. It felt so good, Vivian sighed audibly.

As the tension left her body, Vivian's head dangled back. Howard nuzzled and nibbled her neck. He slid the tiny straps of her gown down and exposed the tops of her breasts. His hands went back to stroking and massaging Vivian's back, while his nuzzling and nibbling moved down slowly. With little effort, Howard worked Vivian's entire gown down around her waist and devoured her breasts, never interrupting the motion of his hands on her back.

With a parting kiss on the tip of Vivian's nipple, Howard rolled Vivian onto her back. Looking deeply into her eyes, he lay on top of her. His lips descended onto hers. Howard's warm, wet kiss was so passionate, Vivian gripped his sides tightly. He moaned.

Without breaking the mood of his kiss, Howard began to make the most delicious nibbling motion with his mouth, gradually working his way down to Vivian's navel. She felt completely adored when Howard kissed and caressed her that way.

Vivian's gown disappeared. Howard's lips and tongue danced and darted over every part of her anatomy. Howard teased and taunted Vivian's body until she didn't know whether to pull his hair out or her own.

On Howard's return trip, he comfortably slid into Vivian, and she arched her hips to receive him. Panted, pinched, and moaned. As Vivian met Howard's thrusts, he told her how much he loved her. Asked if she loved him.

In the midst of tiny, trembling explosions, Vivian groaned, "Oh, yes."

Never breaking his stride, Howard asked, "Are you going to marry me and have my babies, Vivian?"

"Oh, yes."

"When?"

"Whenever you're ready."

As Howard's pace quickened, he moaned, "I'm ready, Vivian. Oh, God, I'm ready!"

One thrilling physical eruption after another made Vivian squeal, screech, pinch, and claw. That just made Howard work harder. Finally, he shuddered, groaned, and squeezed the pillow.

Howard rolled onto his side and started snoring immediately. If it wasn't early and Vivian didn't know he would wake up again, she would have been upset. Instead, she cuddled up close, kissed Howard's sleeping lips, and dozed off, too. Still, the final echo in her mind was Adrena's, "For now."

Chapter Four

The next morning, Vivian gave Howard a passionate, "have a nice day" kiss at her front door. She growled at Snow, locked the door and headed for the Huntingdon Psychiatric Facility. Her Tuesday and Thursday patients all resided there. Huntingdon wasn't a bad place. It was a necessary place. Some people really needed to be there. Still, God knows, Vivian hated admitting anyone.

Vivian only had three patients residing in Huntingdon. They exhibited harmful behavior either toward themselves or others, or they refused to stay on prescribed medications to control their psychotic or neurotic episodes. She usually persuaded the frustrated family members of patients with lesser problems to find other alternatives for them. An unnecessary week in a locked facility could give a salvageable case the final push off the cliff and cause irreparable harm.

Unlike some of her colleagues, Vivian never kept a patient institutionalized a moment longer than she felt necessary. In her professional and personal opinion, no one really got well in a place like Huntingdon. It merely provided a secure environment for patients to let go and begin the long journey back to stability . . . if they were coming back. In Vivian's six years of experience, the best she could hope for were stable periods. Let them languish there one day too long, and you're back at square one.

While clean and functional, as mental facilities go, Huntingdon couldn't be described as anything more than dismal. Someone had done a study and decided colors provoked thought. They obviously found substantial evidence that vivid colors wreaked havoc on the unbalanced mind. The Huntingdon Board of Directors took the report literally. Every room had off-white walls, dead-green carpeting, and colorless, childproof furnishings. Posters and paintings also evidently instigated thought and were forbidden.

Vivian defied anyone to name one of the tunes on the muted, lifeless, piped-in music. Everything, down to the solemn, dark, massive desks and chairs in the doctors' offices were exactly the same. Even the plants Vivian brought in to cheer the place up seemed bored to death.

Some of the doctors saw Huntingdon patients as guaranteed income. Insurance companies more readily picked up the tab for in-house care. The minute they stopped paying, the patient's mental health miraculously improved. Most families were completely unaware of the dwindling coverage phenomenon.

A few of the doctors played what Vivian called "the mind game" - overmedicating to cause patients to drag limbs, drool, hallucinate, and slur their speech. This effect frightened the hell out of family members who were so glad the deterioration didn't take place at home that they gleefully gave the doctor carte blanche when it came to the patient's care. However, if the family did ask too many questions, they were given doubletalk. If they disagreed with the diagnosis, took the patient home and stopped the medication, the patient snapped. If they took the patient to another facility and another doctor prescribed a different medication, the patient snapped. Either way, the patient lost.

The two days a week Vivian spent in this antiquated asylum were all she could take. Her own mental health was jeopardized. No amount of training prepares you for insanity day after day. Unshed tears often threatened to choke Vivian the moment her eyes rested on some of the long-suffering souls.

The everyday sounds of Huntingdon crept into Vivian's sleep at night. Incoherent mumbling and shuffling, the constant rattle of medication cups, the unexpected and thunderous roar of huge psychiatric attendants as they ran to subdue an out-of-control patient. Followed by the disturbing thumps and thuds of battle. The bone-chilling screams and cries of the jacketed and strapped. Howling patients, whose minds refused to come to grips with their circumstances. The incessant, muffled screams emanating from the padded isolation rooms. In the midst of all the madness, one obsessive patient repeating the same mundane phrase over and over. "Food in a bag stinks."

Two of Vivian's patients were severely chemically depressed. One showed improvement with her medication. The other slipped further and further away, no matter what Vivian tried. This patient's silent, comatose stare bore a hole through Vivian's soul. While the re-emerging popularity of lithium and electroshock treatments didn't impress Vivian, her field of choices had grown narrow.

Her third patient was a depressed agoraphobic, a doctor of science, by profession. Sometimes his conversation was intelligent, stimulating, and witty. Other times, he didn't know anything. He wanted to die all of the time. The things that managed to penetrate his melancholy fugue frightened him. Every shift change disturbed him so much he hyperventilated until the nurse sedated him, or he passed out on his own.

Vivian visited each patient and spent the required hour with them. The best patient of the day, Vivian saw last. She was glad to see that this depressed patient, who had shown improvement on the new medication, was finally beginning to level out emotionally. Their conversation was positive and upbeat. Vivian would see that this patient got her walking papers in the near future.

Vivian had spent most of her life taking care of, or dealing with, the mentally and emotionally challenged. Her mother, lovingly referred to as Connie by her husband, had been diagnosed as an acute depressive personality when Vivian was five years old. Connie cried from sun up 'til sun down, every day of her adult life. Vivian could only remember seeing her mother's smile in photographs.

Vance Matthews, Vivian's father, did everything he could to make his wife happy. They moved away from family and friends Connie insisted were disturbing her. Vance painted rooms numerous times, changed fixtures, moved furniture and bought new furniture to please his beautiful, young wife.

Absolutely nothing worked. Many doctors suggested he put her away. After one visit to a psychiatric facility, Vance refused to discuss it.

All of the neighbors were afraid of Vivian's mother. Connie would pace the length of the fence around their property every afternoon for hours. If a passerby innocently touched the fence or dropped something on the sidewalk, she would scream at them and shake the fence threateningly. To avoid the pretty lady, whose behavior they didn't understand, they would leap out into the street.

Connie and the driver of a car that had stopped in the middle of the street and honked his horn for one of the neighbors got into a particularly vicious argument. He jumped out of his car to make his point clear to the yelling woman. She lunged at him fearlessly. Another passing car brushed him. The dirt from the fender smeared his clothing. He jumped back into his car and sped away.

Vance, Vivian and her sister, Maxine, were all Connie had. They knew all of her moods, likes, and dislikes. Vivian and Maxine loved their mother from a distance. Vance was the only person Connie allowed to touch her on a consistent basis. Never having given up hope that her condition would somehow correct itself, they were all truly devastated the day that Connie committed suicide.

Vivian dedicated her life to helping anyone who suffered the way her mother had. Maxine thought the problem lay in some malady of the brain tissue. Once found and corrected, there would be no need for institutions or drugs. She became a surgeon.

Soon after Vivian and Maxine (whom everyone called Max) went off to college, Vance remarried - a perfectly normal woman with whom he had one son and two delightful little girls whom Maxine and Vivian seldom saw. Vance was happy, and his elder daughters were happy for him. He worked as a heavy equipment driver and had few worries. As far as he was concerned, the equipment on the job could be stolen or burn up - it wasn't his, and he could care less as long as his paycheck was there every Friday. Truthfully, Vivian envied the rewarding simplicity of Vance's present life.

In many ways, Vivian was now reliving Vance's former life with Connie. In Vivian's subconscious mind, Adrena was Connie. Like Vance, Vivian would do anything to make life more bearable for Adrena. Vivian's education and instincts assured her there was no hope of ever curing Adrena. Patching up Adrena's ragged foundation, keeping her emotionally stable and socially functional meant Vivian was doing all that could be done for a child damaged the way Adrena had been. The thought of committing her to Huntingdon repulsed Vivian, as it had Vance so many years ago. What was left of the child's sanity would surely drown in that sea of madness.

Vivian made it a short day at Huntingdon and before leaving for home, she called her office to check for messages. There were none. A deep, soul-cleansing sigh of relief always signaled the end of Vivian's days at Huntingdon, and today was no exception. She even thought that after a day of talking to, and at, her institutionalized patients, Snow would be considered a good companion. She might even let the feline diva sleep on her lap - of course, Snow would not jump up on Vivian unless completely convinced that Howard wouldn't be coming.

The moment Vivian got in and made herself comfortable on the sofa, with a cup of tea and the snoozing kitty, the telephone rang. Not in the mood to go back out, Vivian groaned and answered. Millie, Vivian's secretary, patched through a patient who was feeling a little unsure. Vivian listened to the woman's complaints and hearing no rumble of impending doom, assured her everything would be fine and hung up.

While readjusting her tea, kitty and magazine, Vivian's telephone rang again. Vivian's sharp hello relayed the irritation she felt.

Howard's sense of humor kicked in with, "Hi, sweetheart. Bad day at the bat farm?"

A small smile crept across Vivian's face as she said, "No, Howard, it wasn't a bad day. I'm just feeling a tad burned out these days. Wondering if I chose the right profession - if I'm really being as effective as I should be."

"Have you considered taking a sabbatical, Vivian? Sounds like you need one."

"What would I do on a sabbatical, Howard?"

"You could travel, relax, marry me, have a baby."

"What is it with you and having babies lately?"

"Excuse me, but we're not getting any younger. A few years from now, you'll say you're too old to have a baby."

Vivian laughed a little and said, "A few years from now, I will be too old. I'm thirty-two now."

"Right. Like I said, you could travel, relax, marry me, have a baby. Or, do you think someone you're more compatible with is coming along?"

Vivian laughed so loud this time, an irritated Snow looked up at her. "No. I know a perfect fit when I have one, Howard. If there's anyone else coming along, he can just keep going."

"Right. Like I said . . ."

Vivian groaned, "I know . . . I could travel, relax, marry you, and have a baby!"

"Exactly! You prefer a summer or winter wedding?"

"This is the first time you've asked when you weren't firmly in the grips of passion. Are you serious?"

Slightly put out, Howard said, "I've meant it every time I asked, Vivian. Whenever I asked. I thought you meant yes when you said it, too."

"If you really meant it, Howard, why haven't you ever asked me with your clothes on? Over dinner? After dinner? Anytime, when I could take you serious?" There was a long pause. "Well?"

"Hold on a second, Vivian. I'm trying to write this all down. I've only been asking once a week, for the past six months. Maybe I'll get a real answer now that I'm getting the proper proposal instructions."

Cruising smoothly into Howard's mood, Vivian said, "Oh, you're writing it down? Let me be more specific then. I want dinner, flowers, dancing, champagne. You, on one knee, looking me in the eye when you ask, and a ring that takes my breath away."

"Can you swear I won't have any problems, if I meet your demands, Miss?"

"I don't swear, Howard."

"If I've got to do all that to get an answer to a question I've been asking for six months, you've got to swear today, Viv."

"Are you really that insecure, Howard?"

"No. I just never saw you as a purely traditional, sentimental woman."

"Exactly what type of woman do you think I am?"

Without pause, Howard said, "Beautiful, intelligent, strong, independent, understanding and compassionate. A caring woman, who doesn't smother, strangle or bewilder. I think you trust me. I know I trust you. The only negative I'm aware of is you can't cook."

Vivian screamed with laughter. Frightened, Snow jumped down and darted into the kitchen. Vivian sputtered, "Okay. I can't cook. Have no interest in learning either."

"How do you plan to feed your family, if you're not interested in learning?"

"I'm not interested. But . . . I'm willing if the cause is good enough. And I never thought I would have a family to feed anyway, Howard."

"Really? Never mind. Did I mention that you were sexy and passionate?"

"Not today."

"Okay, that too. How about beautiful?"

"I think you said that first."

"Good. Can't leave that out."

"Does that mean when I'm no longer beautiful, you're running for the hills?"

"Vivian, by the time you're not beautiful anymore, I won't be so hot myself. We might be racing each other to the hills."

Vivian laughed again. Howard's sense of humor was definitely a great drawing point. At the end of a day of tension, pain and grief, he always said or did something that made Vivian laugh. She loved him for lots of other reasons, too. Dependability held top honors. If she needed him for anything, he was there. Right behind that, trustworthy. Vivian had never caught Howard in a lie. If he wasn't right

beside her at the end of the day, he was on the telephone with
her - not always understanding what she talked about, but
willing to listen. Vivian appreciated that.

Feeling a little lonely, Vivian asked, "Will I be seeing you
later on tonight?"

"I don't think so, Vivian. This is some list I've got to
work on. If you'd like to reconsider and just take me the way
I am, perhaps I could find time to get over there."

"Oh, well, since I won't be seeing you tonight, will you at
least call?"

"Of course I will."

"Oh, Howard, did I mention Talia wanted us over for
dinner on Sunday?"

Sarcastically, Howard said, "If you love me, Vivian, you
won't mention that again until Sunday afternoon."

"Oh . . . well, I definitely love you, so Sunday afternoon
it is, Howard."

"Good. I'll call you when I get in. I've got to make sure
the market doesn't fall before I fill this list."

Chapter Five

In Vivian's office on Friday morning, Millie buzzed and said, "Mrs. Stanley is holding on one. She's frantic, Vivian."

Vivian quickly pressed the button and asked, "Mrs. Stanley? What's the matter? Is Adrena in a crisis?"

On the verge of yelling, Mrs. Stanley said, "No. She's pretty close, though. I've had to shove Ativan down her throat two nights in a row, Dr. Matthews. She only got an eighty on a test she thought she should have gotten a hundred on. You know how seriously that child takes her grades. Since she came back from your office on Wednesday, she's had one long headache. Nothing's relieving it.

"Now, I don't get into your business with Adrena, Dr. Matthews, but I have to this time. You told her about her mother coming next week, and she's not handling it well. If you could cancel it, I would appreciate it."

Taking a deep breath, Vivian asked, "Where is Adrena now, Mrs. Stanley?"

"She's upstairs in her room sleeping."

"Okay. Please listen to me, Mrs. Stanley. I know Adrena is upset about facing her mother for the first time in six years, but she has to. Not just for therapeutic reasons. There are possible legal problems we have to discuss. Adrena doesn't know it, but her mother has been trying to regain custody. I don't know, for a fact, that's what she wants, but I'm certain it will be mentioned."

Mrs. Stanley lost control and yelled, "For what?! I don't know what she did to Adrena, but she's not getting her back! That girl broke out in a cold sweat at the thought of sitting in a room with her! You'll have to get a bed for her at that hospital if she has to go back now, Doc!"

"That's why I agreed to the meeting. Perhaps, if Adrena tells her mother she doesn't want to come back, she'll drop the issue. I'll have to see what condition her mother is in when she gets here. If she's anything like she was three years ago, we should be able to sidestep her request easily. If not, I may be left with no other alternative than committing Adrena, to keep her out of her mother's clutches. To tell the truth, Mrs. Stanley, I can't believe the state is even entertaining the notion of returning Adrena. They think blood ties mean family. Adrena has never had a family."

Calming down a little, Mrs. Stanley asked, "What do you want me to do? She's gearing up for a nervous breakdown."

"I want you to give Adrena Benadryl capsules twice a day. One in the morning, the other in the evening. If she's still complaining about a headache, or agitated at bedtime, give her the Ativan. You can start the regime this morning as soon as Adrena wakes up. Has she been sleeping?"

"I think so. I can't be sure though. She looks tired and haggard when she comes down for breakfast."

"I'll call in a prescription for something to help her get some rest. Give it to her instead of the Ativan."

Like a mother about to lose her child, Mrs. Stanley asked, "Dr. Matthews, do you really think you'll have to commit her? Adrena's a little strange, but she's not crazy by a long shot."

"I sincerely hope not. We won't build any unnecessary bridges, Mrs. Stanley. We'll just cross them as they appear."

"Yeah . . . Adrena will have to pay the tolls though."

"Not if I can do anything to stop it. How is she doing otherwise?"

Perking up a little, Mrs. Stanley responded, "Oh, she's doing just fine. Since she's been home on suspension, she helps me cook and clean. Helps my husband in his hothouse. I even saw her talking to the girl next door a few times. Other than that, she studies and plays the piano. Really, Dr. Matthews, Adrena is no trouble at all. I love having her around."

Vivian's buzzer sounded again, so she said, "My first patient is here, Mrs. Stanley. If you have any problems with Adrena this weekend, please call me immediately. If she wants to talk to me, have her call. You do have my home number, don't you? Remind her that I will be taking her to school at seven-thirty on Monday morning."

"Yes. Thank you, Dr. Matthews. Goodbye."

"Goodbye."

For the remainder of the day, Vivian barely heard a word her patients said. Every time the buzzer sounded, Vivian jumped. She was afraid Mrs. Stanley would be calling to tell her Adrena had done something drastic. Vivian wished she had pressed Adrena a little harder for her true feelings about the upcoming reunion. She might have been able to hash out some of her pent-up hostility - at least, diffuse some of her fear. If Adrena made it through the weekend, Vivian felt she would be all right. She thanked God for making Adrena a survivor and finished her day.

Before leaving her office for the day, Vivian felt a desperate need to make two telephone calls, the first to Adrena, and the second to Howard. If the first went badly, the second would be her Band-Aid.

Mrs. Stanley answered on the first ring and called Adrena to the telephone. Adrena sounded emotionally drained, but coherent.

Vivian said as cheerfully as possible, "Hi, Adrena. Are you feeling any better?"

"Hi, Doc. I'm okay. Mrs. Stanley is just a worrier."

"People who care do that, Adrena. What about your headache?"

"It's still hanging in there. Maybe the Benadryl will relieve it if I take a nap."

Glad to hear her natural resilience wasn't wavering, Vivian said, "I hope so. You're not to worry about your next appointment, Adrena. You're not ten years old anymore. And you won't be facing her alone."

"Hey, Doc, don't you know I'll spit in both of that hag's eyes if she says the wrong thing? I'm not afraid of what she'll do either. It's all about what she's already done, Doc. Pictures keep jumping up in front of me. All kinds of sick, creepy stuff about Mildred and Bart that I want to forget. Will they ever go away?"

Hating to have to say it, Vivian responded, "Adrena, I will not lie to you. From time to time, those sick, creepy memories will come back. One day, you'll find yourself in a place where you will be able to cope with them, without becoming physically ill though, sweetie. That's what we've been working on all this time, and I'm really proud of the way you're handling this. You're developing a brand new set of coping skills. The day will come when those awful memories won't have enough power to completely terrorize you anymore. I honestly believe you will get there. Facing this demon may very well be your first test."

In an unfamiliar tone of voice, Adrena said, "For you, I'll try, Doc. I know how important my passing that test is to you."

"Not for me, Adrena. For you. This is all for you. I'm here for you. Mr. and Mrs. Stanley are here for you. When you face the demon and strip its power, it has to be for you, too. You have to learn to love yourself as much as we love you."

Without saying another word, Adrena put the telephone down on the counter and left the room. Mrs. Stanley picked it up and asked, "What did you say, Doc? She went upstairs. She's got tears in her eyes. Should I go check on her?"

"No, she's fine. I told her she has to learn to love herself as much as we love her. She has never felt loved, Mrs. Stanley. It frightens her. Loving means someone has to be degraded or get hurt in Adrena's mind. Don't worry. We'll get her through this . . . somehow."

"Okay, Doc. Thanks for calling."

"You don't have to thank me, Mrs. Stanley. I called for my own peace of mind."

Vivian dialed Howard's office and was completely caught off guard when Clayton answered.

In a rather bored tone of voice, he said, "Good afternoon. Williams and Shaw. Williams speaking."

Vivian couldn't resist asking, "Did the market crash, Clayton?"

Recognizing her voice immediately, Clayton said, "Not yet, Dr. Viv. But, I must admit, it's nowhere near as reliable or predictable as the loon business."

"E-ew. We do get testy when we're left to answer the phones, don't we?"

"Yes, we do."

"Where is everyone, Clayton?"

"If I said Barb and Howard were in his office, completely naked and wrapped in each other's arms, would you dump him?"

"Probably not without the benefit of video. I'm too far gone to give up on your word. Where are they really?"

"Truthfully, I don't know. Howard called from the floor two hours ago and asked Barb to meet him somewhere at three. Your guess is as good as mine what they're up to. Kevin and Marty are even missing this afternoon. I'm here all alone. Buying, selling, and answering the telephones."

"If he calls in, tell him I've gone home."

"I'll do that. Have a nice weekend. Oh, I'll see you at Talia's on Sunday."

"Good. See you then."

Vivian hung up and called Jessica. Maybe she felt like coming over for an afterwork drink and a pizza. Being alone was beginning to bother Vivian more and more these days. Jessica agreed, and she brought her sister, Eunice. Adding to Vivian's surprise, her sister, Maxine, dropped by, too. The calendar fell back fifteen years when the four of them were together.

By seven they were all wound up, having graduated from a sophisticated white wine to drinks of choice. Open pizza boxes were scattered all over the living room. Already-modeled new outfits lay thrown aside. The music blasted, and they laughed and talked over it the way they had done all their lives. Eunice had brought a strawberry cheesecake. They devoured it in no time.

Vivian asked, "Eunice, why did you bring this cake in here? None of us needs it."

Obviously intoxicated, Eunice winked and said, "Vivian, honey. Don't you know life ain't worth livin', if all you get is what you need? Cheesecake, pound cake, German chocolate cake, and Godiva chocolates have blessed me with the sweetest big hips in town."

Maxine asked, "Is she telling the truth, Jessica? If she is, I'm throwing that damned Stairmaster in the trash."

Rolling her eyes, Jessica said, "Go on and throw it away, girl. It's sad, but true. Peter literally drools every time she sways into the room. And, as depressing as this may sound, he's not the only one. I think the entire thin movement was a hoax. Nobody, and I do mean nobody, looks at me that way. I'm willing to pay somebody to do it now - just to see what it feels like."

Vivian said, "Don't do that, Jessica. It's too pitiful. Haven't you run into Clayton lately? He'll do it for free."

Jessica ran her hand over her face miserably and moaned, "Please don't mention that man's name to me. He has stood me up more times than my Mama did trying to teach me to walk."

Maxine yelled, "You too?! I thought that clown saved that routine just for me."

Jessica asked, "Why haven't you latched onto one of those nice, well-paid doctors at the hospital, Maxine? I saw one over there a few months ago, to die for. I'd take him home, without a paycheck."

Maxine said matter-of-factly, "And, you'd dress in disguise when you brought him back. He's gay, dear."

In shocked disbelief, Jessica groaned, "Oh, no, Max. Not him. Are you sure we're talking about the same one? He works in the emergency room. Tall, amber, wide shoulders, great ass, green eyes, curly black hair, deep sexy voice?"

Maxine said, "Yup. That's him. He's a fraud. Manipulates women to get what he wants, knowing he's not the least bit interested in them."

Confused, Vivian asked, "Do they play that game, too? I had a patient who married one. Devastated when she found out. I always hoped that was a fluke."

Maxine looked her older sister in the eyes and said, "Vivian, stop being so damned naive. If men knew there was a market for sap, they would sweet talk trees. There is not a doubt in my mind that the doctor Jessica is referring to fully intends to hoodwink some poor soul into marrying him. It's about image, Viv. Homophobia is alive and well. It can keep him working the graveyard shift in the emergency room for the remainder of his career. Guaranteed short-term burnout. So, he spends every free moment in one woman's face or another. Smiling, flirting and stroking. Better to be known as a Casanova than gay. Hell, I would have taken him seriously, if I hadn't caught him in a luscious liplock with some guy in the lounge."

The laughter was so loud, Vivian barely heard the telephone ring. Not wanting to miss any of the conversation, Vivian briefly decided to let the answering machine get it, but thought about Adrena and answered instead. She had to stick her finger in her ear to hear.

Howard asked, "What's going on over there, Vivian?"

Grinning drunkenly, Vivian said, "The gang's here."

"It sounds like they've been there for a while. I guess it's safe to say you haven't missed me."

"No, it's not. Where have you been all day anyway? Where are you now?"

"I've been very busy today, Vivian. Had a few things to find. I'm at home now. I thought about coming by, but since you have lots of company, I'll see you tomorrow."

"Are we going to the art show tomorrow, or did you forget?"

Howard moaned, "Oh, sweetheart, I completely forgot. What time does it start?"

Disappointed, Vivian said, "It starts at two. If you have something else to do, don't worry about it. Maybe one of the girls will go with me."

Howard hurriedly said, "No. I should be able to do what I have to do by one. I'll be there no later than two. Will it be all right if we're a few minutes late?"

Not used to Howard putting anything ahead of her, except pressing business, Vivian pouted and said, "I guess so. Where did you and Barb go today?"

"Who says Barb went anywhere with me today?"

"Clayton."

"Oh, him. He just told you that because he was left in the office by himself today. We didn't go anywhere together. I was on the trading floor most of the day. Barb asked if she

could leave early, and I told her I didn't see any problem with
it. Clayton's upset because no one consulted him."

Vivian didn't know who to believe at this point and asked,
"Are you sure, Howard?"

"I'm sure. You go back to your company now. Tell them all
I said hello. I'll see you between one and two tomorrow. Okay?"

Angry, without really knowing why, Vivian said sharply,
"No, it's not okay."

"Why not, Vivian?"

The only thing she could think of to say was, "Because I
don't want to spend the rest of the night with them. I wanted
to spend it with you."

"That's really sweet of you to say, sweetheart. I'd rather
spend it with you, too, but you have company, and I have a
few things to do early in the morning. We'll be together for
the rest of the weekend. I promise."

Mumbling like a spoiled child, Vivian said, "Okay,
Howard."

She heard the smile in his voice when he said, "I love you,
Vivian."

"I love you too, Howard."

She hung up the telephone, and a chorus of "I love you
too, Howard" echoed behind her, followed by a lot of eye
batting and kissing sounds.

Laughing, Vivian flagged the silly women and said,
"Howard asked me to tell you all hello."

Jessica asked, "When is that handsome fool going to
marry you, Vivian?"

Maxine chimed in, "Yeah. When is he? You've been
playing with Howard for almost two years."

Eunice said, "Leave Vivian alone. Play with that fine
devil as long as you want to, Vivian. If you listen to the can't
find one, ain't had none sisters, you'll regret it. Let those two
keep dieting, stairstepping, and pumping iron."

Vivian said in a lofty tone, "For your information, Jessica
and Maxine, Howard has been asking me to marry him once
a week for the last six months."

Maxine asked, "Well, what the hell's the problem?"

"He's not asking at the right time."

Maxine, Jessica, and Eunice looked at each other and shrugged. Eunice finally said, "Okay, Vivian. You've stumped me with that one. When is he asking? And when is the right time?"

Maxine snapped, "Yeah! If the man is right, the time is always right. Did Daddy waste a lot of money sending you to school? What's the matter with you, Vivian? Hell, I haven't heard the wedding march in so long, I've forgotten how it goes."

Thinking they would understand, Vivian said, "He only asks when we're making love."

Again, they all looked at each other. This time there were confused frowns and shrugs. In unison, they asked, "And what's wrong with that?"

"I want him to ask when his head is clear. After dinner. On his knees."

Maxine walked over to Vivian. Took a tiny flashlight out of her pocketliner, turned it on and said, "Follow this with your eyes, Vivian."

Following her sister's instructions, Vivian asked, "What am I doing this for?"

Maxine said, "Sis, I'm hoping whatever is wrong with you is physical. A tumor. Something I can drill a hole, pluck out, and patch up before the man gets away."

Vivian batted the light down. Jessica and Eunice screamed with laughter. Not discouraged, Maxine asked, "What if he never asks on his knee, Vivian?"

"You won't be hearing the wedding march anytime soon, Max. I want him on his knee."

Jessica frowned and said, "Vivian, you're talking body parts. Back, stomach, knees. Why does it matter what he's leaning or lying on?"

Eunice jumped in with, "Wait a minute. Vivian, you know I love you like a sister. You know I'm not just asking this to get into your business. I can only guess Howard's not too bad in bed. You've been with him a while now. When the two of you are in the middle of whatever, and he asks you to marry him, what is your response?"

Vivian whispered, "Yes."

Eunice asked, "Just yes?"

With a truly dumb expression on her face, Vivian expanded her response to, "*Oh*, yes."

"Excuse me, but did you say, '*Oh*, yes?'"

Grimacing, Vivian nodded.

Turning to Max, Eunice said, "Maxine, go git the drill and scalpel. We'll hold her down. She's got the man by his best parts. He's begging, and she's having some kind of Lana Turner, Doris Day flashbacks."

For the rest of the evening, they took turns shaking their heads at Vivian. She didn't care. Vivian had waited thirty-two years to be asked. She could wait a little longer for knees if she wanted to. If Howard really refused to get down there, Vivian would be severely heartbroken.

Chapter Six

The next day, running a little behind schedule, Howard arrived at Vivian's house at five minutes after two. He let himself in. Vivian hadn't heard the door, but she heard him carrying on with Snow. Vivian thought, "One day, he might actually get to me first . . . maybe if I run and jump into his arms the way that shameless cat does!"

She continued making the bed and waited for Howard to come upstairs. Still a little put out with his secretive, missing-in-action routine, Vivian was determined to ignore him.

Obviously in no rush to get upstairs, Howard played with Snow for quite a while before making his way up the stairs. Vivian glanced up at him briefly, as she put the finishing touches on the comforter and pillows. However, she couldn't miss Howard's warm smile, as he crossed his arms, leaned his tall frame in the doorway, and watched her. Howard was dressed in khaki-colored slacks and a cream collarless shirt. To Vivian, he looked so handsome and relaxed. He didn't look good enough to make her forget he hadn't been around lately though, and she never verbally acknowledged his presence.

Without a greeting, Howard asked, "Vivian, are you upset with me about something?"

She answered sarcastically, "Yes, I am. Where have you been, Howard? What are you doing that you can't tell me? Are we going to start keeping secrets and staying home now? I hope you know two can play that dumb game."

Like most people when they are lying, Howard answered her questions with a question. "What do you mean, where have I been? I haven't been anywhere worth mentioning. And I'm not keeping any secrets."

"You're lying, Howard Shaw. Not well, either."

Howard's handsome face twisted into a painful scowl, before he said, "I am not lying. Do you want to go to the art show or argue?"

"I'm not going anywhere with you until you tell me where you've been for the last two evenings."

"Are you going to force me to say it's none of your business, Vivian?"

Shocked, Vivian asked, "Is that what you're saying, Howard?"

"Sort of. I thought you trusted me. I've only been missing two evenings. Didn't I call?"

Anger building, she said stiffly, "Yes, you called. What's that supposed to mean? I'm not going to play games with you, Howard. If you have something you'd like to do better, you run right along and do it."

"Vivian, what's wrong with you? This is not the first time I haven't come over two evenings in a row. I've never had to deal with any insecurities before. Why now?"

"I am not insecure! I'm not stupid either! If I were to disappear, the way you have, then you'd see insecurity in its purest form!"

Without flinching, Howard said, "You are absolutely right, Vivian. I admit to my insecurities, without reservation. I'm not a liar though. Now, let's go to the art show. You'll find out what I've been doing soon enough."

With a full head of steam, Vivian said, "I'd better."

"You will."

Uncharacteristically, without any exchange of affection, Howard and Vivian left for the art show. They didn't indulge in any frivolous conversation during the ride, either. At the show, a sophisticated and contemplative crowd milled around the paintings and sculptures. Several black artists had work on display, but Vivian didn't buy anything.

Howard saw something he wanted to think about. A bronze statue of a nude father, mother, and newborn. Vivian wondered why they always depicted entire families in the nude in artwork. When were fathers ever openly nude? After the delivery of a baby, Vivian couldn't recall anyone ever mentioning the father being nude, too. So, when Howard asked for her opinion, of course, she had none.

Vivian's head hurt something awful. Too much of a good time with the girls the night before. Drinking, laughing and screaming always gave her a headache. Vivian's sister, Maxine, almost always gave her a headache, too. According to Max, Vivian never responded correctly to anything.

In the car, Howard asked, "Are you feeling okay? Did you eat breakfast?" Before she could answer, he reached over, touched her forehead, and asked, "Are you catching something?"

"No. I just need lunch, two aspirins, and a nap."

"What do you want to eat?"

"I'll get something when I get home. It doesn't matter what it is."

At home, Vivian made them both lunch. Tuna sandwiches, pickles and chips. As long as she didn't have to turn on the stove, Vivian was fine in the kitchen. They sat and ate in silence.

"Howard, I'm going to lie down now. If you decide to leave, just lock the door behind you."

Vivian left Howard at the kitchen table, lovingly stroking Snow. In her bedroom, Vivian tossed two aspirins and some water down her throat, looked at herself in the bathroom mirror, and agreed with Howard. She really did look like she was coming down with something. Sighing heavily, Vivian undressed and crawled into bed. In Vivian's next moment of conscious awareness, Howard was sitting on the side of the bed calling her name.

"Vivian. Vivian. Are you feeling any better? It's time for dinner."

Vivian moaned groggily, "I'm not hungry. What time is it?"

"Yes, you are hungry. It's a little past eight. Get up and get dressed. Dinner's ready."

Completely confused, she asked, "You cooked?"

"Sort of. Why do you ask like that? I cook better than you," Howard responded, as if insulted.

Vivian said apologetically, "You're right, Howard. I'll get up if you massage my shoulders. They feel like they're stuck in the wrong places."

Howard's long, strong fingers kneaded the kinks out of her neck and shoulders. He kissed the nape of Vivian's neck and ran his hand down her back. She moaned her pleasure. Then he gave her a sharp whack on the butt and said, "Get up and get dressed, Vivian."

"Formally, or informally?"

"Any way you want. Your dinner's going to get cold."

Howard left the moment Vivian was upright. She sat on the side of the bed for a few more minutes, mumbling, "Why do I have to get up? So he made dinner. Only made it because he knows he's in trouble. A meal won't erase the fact that he's not telling me where he's been for the past two evenings. And, let's not forget the half day at work."

Vivian quieted and wondered momentarily what she would put on. Should she throw on a robe and slippers, or something that said she cared what he thought? Sighing, she admonished herself for even entertaining the notion that she didn't care what Howard thought. Who the hell was she fooling? Howard and all of his insecurities meant the world to her.

She dressed in a flowered, flowing lounge set, combed her hair and put on lipstick. Even dabbed a little of Howard's favorite fragrance in a few of his favorite places.

As Vivian descended the stairs, all of the lights were off in the living room. Eerie shadows flickered on the walls. Standing at the bottom of the stairs, Vivian called out, "Howard, why are the lights off? Where are you? If this is a joke, I'm really not going to like it. You know I hate jokes played in the dark."

Howard said, "Don't turn them on either. It's not dark in the dining room, Vivian. Stop being a crybaby and come on."

"Where's Snow? If she touches me in the dark, I'll kill her."

Laughing, Howard said, "I don't know where she is. Come on. Face your fears like a brave, intelligent, sane, reasoning woman."

Making her way through the living room, looking for Snow in the dark, Vivian mumbled, "Very funny."

In the dining room, she saw Howard sitting at the table. Candlelight danced in his smiling eyes. He stood when Vivian came in. The table was impeccably set . . . but those were not her dishes. The floral arrangement in the center of the table wasn't familiar either.

Out of the corner of Vivian's eye, she saw movement. Fleetingly, she thought it was Snow. Then Vivian realized it couldn't be. The figure, dressed in black and white, stood taller than she. It moved toward the table, pulled out the chair and said, "Welcome to dinner, Dr. Matthews."

Vivian gasped, squealed, and jumped, poised to run. Howard's laughter broke the spell. She stood still long enough to realize the figure was a waiter. What was he doing in her dining room?

Shaking visibly, Vivian asked, "What's going on here, Howard?"

With a stupid grin on his face, Howard said, "Dinner."

Looking distrustingly at the man in black and white, Vivian asked, "In my dining room? With a waiter?"

"Yes, Vivian. Catered, in your dining room, with your favorite waiter. Don't you recognize him?"

Finally, getting a mental picture of what was going on, Vivian looked at the waiter again and asked, "Is that you, Paul?"

Paul smiled broadly and said, "Yes, it's me, Dr. Matthews. Mr. Shaw didn't tell me you would be terrified. He said you would merely be surprised."

"Well, I am surprised, Paul. And, terrified. What's going on?"

Paul said, "If you take your seat, I will serve your dinner. All other explanations have to come from Mr. Shaw."

Vivian checked under the table for Snow, before sitting down. Still laughing like a loon, Howard sat with her. Vivian kicked him under the table. He tried to stop laughing, but he couldn't.

With Paul in the kitchen, Vivian asked, "Okay, Howard, what are you doing?"

Before he answered, Paul came in with wine. The moment he poured, Vivian's absolutely favorite song, *Teach Me Tonight*, wafted out of nowhere. The nearness and clarity of the music caused a shocked Vivian to clutch the tablecloth. It was a live band playing softly in Vivian's office which was right off the hallway. Howard and Paul laughed hysterically at her reaction.

Holding her head, Vivian said, "Howard, please tell me what you're doing, before my heart stops beating."

"I'm following your instructions to the letter."

Confused, Vivian asked, "What instructions?"

"Your proposal instructions."

"I don't recall saying anything about frightening me to death."

"No, you didn't. That was my idea. I thought you might appreciate a little stimulation, combined with some levity. You've been preoccupied and irritable lately."

"Oh, really?"

"Yes. Now, calm down, drink your wine, and have a wonderfully intimate dinner. Enjoy the music and the remainder of the evening."

"Not until you tell me there's no one else in my house."

Trying to don a serious bearing, Howard said, "Vivian, there is no one else here. Me, you, Paul, the five guys playing in your office, and Snow. Atmosphere and dinner, catered by your favorite restaurant."

Howard had chosen the menu carefully. Seafood. Everything he knew Vivian loved. Shrimp appetizers, followed by a delicate salad, sprinkled generously with fresh crabmeat. A lobster entree, with tiny broiled potatoes, broccoli, and a side dish of mussels. Everything buttered, cheesed, and parsleyed to perfection. They drank an entire bottle of wine with the meal.

Paul cleared the dinner dishes and promptly brought out two huge wedges of chocolate cake. A single, ripe, red strawberry languished on top of each. Eunice's sweet hips remark came back to Vivian, and she laughed as if she were hearing it for the very first time. Howard and Paul looked at each other and shrugged.

Howard and Vivian leisurely ate cake and made small talk. There were no more accusations or lies. Vivian almost mentioned his sister's dinner again, but remembered she wasn't supposed to until Sunday afternoon. With nothing else to talk about, Vivian asked, "What else was on my list, Howard?"

"Flowers."

"Well, where are they?"

Howard reached under the table and produced a long silver box, with a large red bow. Ceremoniously, he handed it to Vivian. Paul appeared with a vase and placed it on the table. Then he disappeared again. Vivian slid the bow off and lifted the lid. Two dozen, long-stemmed, flawless, peach-and-white roses, complete with baby's breath, lay elegantly inside. The card read:

To Vivian . . . the woman I've grown to love more and more every day. The woman whose smile means more to me than she will ever know. The woman I hope to spend the rest of my life loving and being loved by.

Love, Howard

Vivian smiled and cooed, "Oh, they're beautiful, Howard. Thank you."

She leaned over to kiss him. As soon as their lips touched, Paul appeared again and asked, "May I help you with the flowers, Dr. Matthews?"

Handing the flowers to Paul, Vivian asked, "Howard, is there anything else on the list?"

"Dancing."

Howard stood and extended his hand. Vivian took it, and he led her off to the darkened living room. Paul brought in the candles and placed them on the mantle. Howard held her close as they danced to tunes like *Days of Wine and Roses* and *Moon River*.

Everyone close to Vivian knew of her passion for old movies and music. Fred and Ginger took her breath away as they glided, strolled, and paused with precision. Vivian loved rhythm and blues, too. But, when it came to romance, the old standards gave it a whimsical, wonderful quality. Old movies and music stimulated her dreams.

Howard and Vivian were kissing when Paul appeared in the living room doorway. That was a signal. Howard stopped dancing and kissing, ran his hands down Vivian's back and sighed. He said, "It looks like the evening's drawing to a close, sweetheart."

Frowning, Vivian whined, "Already?"

Howard led her over to the sofa and said sadly, "I'm afraid so. But, before it all ends, I have to complete the list."

Vivian sat down. Howard got down on one knee, reached under the sofa and produced a tiny black box. It seemed to take forever for him to get the top off. Then, he didn't let Vivian see it. The suspense was killing her. She couldn't believe how much trouble he had taken to orchestrate all of this. Paul appeared, disappeared, and the band began to play the *Moonlight Sonata*.

Howard smiled, looked into her eyes, and said, "Vivian, I know I've asked this question about a hundred times, and I know you've answered it a hundred times. For me, tonight is no different. All of the love and passion I felt for you on those occasions, I feel now. I've taken my time searching for just the right woman for me. I'm sure I've found her. Will you marry me?"

In the flickering candlelight, Vivian studied Howard's face. There was only one question she had to ask herself. "Have I found just the right man?" There was only one answer, and she gave it softly, with happy, satisfied tears blurring her vision. "Yes, Howard."

After removing the ring from the box, Howard picked up Vivian's left hand and slipped it onto her finger. Finally, there it was. A large, emerald-cut diamond, set high in the center, with two graduated baguettes stepping down on both sides. Blue highlights winked at her in the candlelight. Howard had fulfilled Vivian's request. The ring had actually taken her breath away.

Howard kissed Vivian tenderly. His lips refused to leave hers until the band played the last note of the sonata. Playfully, rubbing his nose against Vivian's, he asked, "Did I miss anything, sweetheart?"

Overcome with emotion, Vivian whispered, "No, Howard. You didn't miss a thing."

"Good. I was sure you would leave me before I got this off the ground. You are truly an untrusting woman."

"Only when you're missing."

He gave Vivian a quick peck on the tip of her nose, got up, and went toward the kitchen. Vivian took the opportunity to openly admire her ring. She wondered what the girls would have to say about this! She had won. He got down on that knee. With his clothes on!

Howard concluded his business with Paul and the band and released Snow from wherever he had her pent up. She meowed her complaints. The band members all congratulated Vivian on their way out. She thanked them and told them how much she enjoyed the music. Vivian received an enthusiastic congratulations hug and kiss from Paul. Vivian assured Paul they had all done an absolutely wonderful job, after scaring her half to death.

With them out of the way, Howard asked pitifully, "Would it be sacrilegious to listen to some music recorded after 1950?"

Happy as a clam, Vivian said, "You can listen to anything you want now. Jimmy Jam, Ice Cube, Iced Tea, Frosted Flakes and the Bananas. Anything."

"Thank you. Are those real artists, or did you make them up, Viv?"

She shrugged.

Howard turned the radio to the jazz station. He came over, plopped down on the sofa, stretched out and laid his head in her lap. Automatically, Vivian kissed him and caressed his chest. Looping his long arm over her head, he pulled her closer.

Groaning, Vivian said, "Howard, you're breaking my back. Maybe I should stretch out next to you."

"I'm sorry, sweetheart."

Howard sat up, and Vivian lay down next to him. Not liking that arrangement, Howard pulled her up, so he could lie on the outside.

"Why are we doing all of this, Howard?"

"Oh, you don't remember the last time you were on the outside of this sofa?"

Laughing hysterically, Vivian said, "That's right. You let me fall on the floor."

To himself, Howard said, "I did not." Out loud, he said, "If you say so, Vivian. You didn't talk to me for three days after that little fiasco."

"Well, you shouldn't have laughed until you choked. It wasn't that funny."

Howard thought, "From my vantage point it was." Out loud, he said, "No, it wasn't that funny, sweetheart. You didn't tell me how you felt about the ring. Did it take your breath away?"

All snuggled up in the arms of the man she could never have created in any of her wildest fantasies, and loved as much as humanly possible, Vivian's new ring was almost forgotten. Holding it up, so they could both see it, she said, "Oh, yes, Howard. It's stunning. I love it."

"Good. I love you, Vivian. If you're not happy, neither am I."

"I'm happy, Howard. And I love you, too."

Howard lowered his warm lips to Vivian's. She received them gladly and ran her newly ringed hand down the most desirable male body she had ever known. Every inch of him felt good to Vivian. Howard's tongue danced sweetly around Vivian's mouth. Inside and out. She felt the familiar tingle of desire in her stomach as Howard's hands moved and massaged. Their bodies naturally moved in sync.

The moment Howard's hand slid under Vivian's blouse, Snow jumped up on their legs and Vivian screamed. Howard groaned and said, "Don't move, I'll take care of her."

Vivian silently thanked God she wasn't on the outside of the sofa. Howard would be in stitches, and she would be pissed. The delicious mood would be shattered and the most memorable, romantic evening of her life, destroyed by a cat.

Howard came back and extended his hand for Vivian. She gave him her hand. He only wanted her to sit up so he could easily remove her top. Vivian pulled Howard down to his knees, unbuttoned his shirt and slid it off of his shoulders. The entire time, Howard gently massaged her exposed breasts. He only relinquished them long enough to shake the shirt off, freeing his hands.

Vivian lay back. Howard joined her. She enjoyed the smooth, sensual touch and taste of his bare skin. A master at disrobing her, Howard had the bottom of Vivian's suit off with the flick of his wrist. With the warmth and tenderness of Howard's hands and mouth propelling her excitement, Vivian's head dropped back and lolled. She alternately gasped and moaned deep in her throat. Howard didn't give up until she begged, "Sweetheart, please stop."

Howard's lips finally came to rest on Vivian's neck. Still quivering, she managed to maneuver her way to a sitting position. She straddled his legs and fumbled with his pants. He gave her very little assistance, but Vivian finally got them off. Howard lay back like a big lazy lion, with his hands folded behind his head, watching Vivian, as if her every move fascinated him.

It was Vivian's turn to devour Howard. He maintained his cool, relaxed demeanor, until her hot, wet tongue touched his navel. The rapid, agonized contractions of his stomach muscles told Vivian he was beginning to have difficulty maintaining control of his mounting excitement. Vivian teased his navel with her tongue until one of Howard's arms came down. Then, Vivian took her attentions down his groin to his thigh. She gave it a long, moist kiss. Then, she bit it. Not hard. A nibble.

Howard popped up and said, "Vivian, sweetheart. Please be careful."

Licking her lips leisurely, Vivian said slowly, "Lie back, Howard. Stop being such a crybaby. Act like a big, strong, sexy, sane, reasoning man."

A big grin parted his face when he said, "Okay."

Howard lay back, closed his eyes, and tried to relax. Vivian massaged his thigh and erection at the same time. She gave his other thigh a long, moist kiss. Knowing Howard had braced himself, anticipating her bite, Vivian abandoned the game and closed her hot, smooth lips over the pulsing head of his erection. The violent contraction of Howard's stomach muscles and his tiny whine told her she had made her point. Now it was Howard's head that lolled, as he groaned and gripped the side and back of the sofa. It didn't take long to make Howard beg.

"Vivian. Vivian. Sweetheart, please."

She popped up and asked, "Please what, Howard?"

Barely able to speak, Howard said, "Please, stop. If you don't stop, you're going to be real pissed with me while you're waiting for it to reload."

Like a little girl, Vivian asked wickedly, "You wouldn't do a thing like that tonight, would you, Howard?"

"Sweetheart, I'm trying real hard to give your needs priority tonight."

"That's another one of the reasons why I love you. I'll stop if you promise not to pull any more tricks on me."

Howard didn't respond until Vivian moved to resume her previous activity. He said quickly, "I promise. I promise."

Grinning, as if she had won a real victory, Vivian slid up and straddled Howard's legs. Now, it was her turn to kiss him. The motion of their bodies fell into sync. Vivian raised up and lowered herself onto him. Howard raised his hips to meet her. He slid his hands along her long, smooth thighs, coming to rest on her perfectly rounded hips. Then, he proceeded, in more than one position, to make Vivian beg, pant, plead, and squeal with delight. Somehow, she managed to be back on top when they reached the great finale.

Vivian lay on top of Howard, sweating and breathing like she'd run a marathon. She played in the puddles of perspiration on Howard's chest with the tip of her nose and tasted them with her tongue. Thinking Howard had fallen asleep, the rumble of his voice startled her.

"You don't have to drink sweat, sweetheart. There's an unopened bottle of champagne chilling in the dining room.

Of course, you forgot that was on your list. You wouldn't have remembered until we had another fight either."

Exhausted, Vivian asked, "Do I have to get it?"

With a sigh, Howard said, "No. Tonight's on me. Remember?"

Rolling onto her side, Vivian grinned and said, "That's so very nice of you, sweetheart."

Howard sat up and winced.

Vivian asked, "What's the matter?"

Rubbing his side, Howard said, "You wounded me with that ring. I'll probably need a kidney transplant before you get used to wearing it."

"I'm sorry, Howard. I'll take it off next time."

Shaking his head, he said, "Oh, no, you won't. I don't ever want to see your hand without that ring on it, Vivian."

That order didn't fluster her one bit. She said enthusiastically, "Yes, sir!"

Howard opened the champagne in the dining room and brought it into the living room. On his second trip, he brought back two glasses and a book. Before pouring the champagne, he handed Vivian the book and said, "That's your assignment. Be able to make something out of it before the wedding. Oh, by the way, when is the wedding?"

Vivian looked at the book, back at Howard, and said, "This is a cookbook, Howard."

"I know that, Vivian. Just find something you like and take a crack at it. When's the wedding?"

Still studying the cookbook, as if it were a genuine moonrock, Vivian answered, "Whenever you want, Howard."

Surprised by her response, Howard asked, "Really?"

"Yes. As long as it's here. Just our families and a few close friends."

Without a thought, Howard said, "One month from today."

Vivian frowned.

He said, "That's it. You left it up to me."

That's the way it would be. On Saturday, July thirteenth, Vivian would happily become Mrs. Vivian Matthews-Shaw, better known as Dr. Vivian Matthews-Shaw.

Chapter Seven

Sunday morning sunshine flooded the small, beautifully-furnished bedroom in the Stanley household. Adrena Reynolds opened her eyes and breathed her first headache-free breath in three days. She lay in bed waiting for a tormenting picture or voice from the past. None came. The haunting memories of Mildred and Bart had finally stopped. Adrena's selective, conscious thought processes were functioning, and her thoughts flowed easily to Dr. Matthews, her savior from that night of horrors. Memories of how she had entered Adrena's shattered life six years ago now pushed the hideous remnants to the rear of her mind and soothed her, as only thoughts of Dr. Matthews could.

Reliving that day in her mind, Adrena saw the most beautiful woman she had ever seen, through a mist of pain and medication. Of course, the little girl thought she was dreaming. Dr. Matthews stood close to Adrena's bed and looked down on her new patient. In Adrena's condition, the doctor seemed much taller than she actually was. Adrena could still remember the clean, sweet smell of her perfume and hear the genuine compassion in her every word. There was no pity. As Adrena surfaced from her catatonic state, she appreciated the way Dr. Matthews refrained from physically touching her after recognizing the revulsion in Adrena's eyes. Instead, Dr. Matthews stroked and comforted Adrena with words and deeds. For Adrena, Dr. Matthews represented the first person who respected her feelings and space.

Dr. Matthews did not try to hide her contempt when she came to tell Adrena that Bart was being held in jail for child molestation, abuse, and endangering a minor. Her mother's charges were child abuse, neglect, and endangering. Because Adrena had been removed from the dwelling, Mildred was released on her own recognizance, and the court issued a restraining order prohibiting her from coming anywhere near the hospital.

It was an extremely nervous Dr. Matthews who tried to explain to the wounded, frail, and frightened ten-year-old that she would have to go to a psychiatric facility for observation. Adrena couldn't respond, if she were inclined to, because she had no idea what it was. At the time, Dr. Matthews didn't know Adrena hadn't been to a doctor since she was three years old, and most of what Dr. Matthews said fell into an abyss of ignorance, but Adrena loved the sound of the pretty woman's voice. Adrena had never held a conversation with anyone other than her mother and the nice old lady named Mrs. Townsend, who lived next door.

Mrs. Townsend would see Adrena sitting on the stoop all day and long into the night. She often pleaded with the child to let her help. When it was bitter cold out, and she was unable to witness it another minute, Mrs. Townsend would physically drag Adrena into her warm, cozy apartment. She occasionally bathed and fed Adrena. Mrs. Townsend literally introduced the little girl to fresh fruit. She washed and pressed clothes collected from others and dressed Adrena, combed her hair, and tied colorful ribbons on her ponytails. Adrena loved watching Mrs. Townsend's television and eating sandwiches and cookies in a litter-free environment. Televisions rapidly came and went from Adrena's one-room dwelling before she ever knew if they worked. Mildred and Bart sold them for drug money.

Mrs. Townsend never knew Adrena was whipped every time after she dolled her up. Like junkies the world over, Mildred and Bart were paranoid about being caught at something they forgot or hadn't given any thought to. Mildred insisted Adrena was spreading their business all over the neighborhood, and especially with the old woman next door. Adrena was forbidden to talk to anyone, child or adult. No one was supposed to notice the little girl who sat on the stoop three-quarters of the day, every day, no matter what the weather, invariably improperly dressed.

Many times, Mrs. Townsend threatened to call the authorities on Mildred and Bart for not sending Adrena to school. She never did though. Like elderly people the world over, Mrs. Townsend was afraid of the repercussions of junkies. Overnight, they could make her life hell. If they didn't beat her to death or make her too afraid to open her front door, they would steal everything in her apartment and try to sell it back to her real cheap. Hearing Adrena's seemingly neverending, tormented screams, Mrs. Townsend finally mustered the courage to call the police the night of the rape.

The authorities did a lot in Adrena's case. They hospitalized Adrena to take care of her physical damages. They institutionalized her to take care of her mental anguish. They assigned her to what they thought were wholesome, nourishing family environments to learn and grow in.

The doctors at the hospital did all they could with Adrena's body. A broken arm and collarbone and a dislocated hip were Adrena's minor injuries. Both her uterus and colon were perforated during the assault. At ten years old, Adrena endured a hysterectomy, colon resection surgeries, and reluctantly learned the intimate workings of a temporary colostomy.

She spent three months in the hospital. The tiny medical facility of the Rhawnhurst Orphanage was what Adrena called home during the next six months of her therapy. Left alone, Adrena lay silently in a catatonic haze day after day. The child never responded to anything said around her. She never reacted to any alarms or panic-stricken staff running past in the hallway in response to emergency cases. When touched for any reason at all, Adrena screamed, scratched, bit, and spit until she puked every time. The nurses resorted to sedating Adrena intravenously to take her temperature. They increased the sedation to make her sleep through the night. Nightmares caused Adrena to screech, squirm and flail her one good arm for hours on end. In a matter of moments, the ward would be reduced to a howling insane asylum filled with frightened children.

Adrena's next stop was Huntingdon Psychiatric Facility. That's where Adrena saw Dr. Matthews for two hours every day. Dr. Matthews had been visiting Adrena a few times a

week at the hospital and Rhawnhurst. She had brought
Adrena puzzles, books, and a doll. Adrena couldn't read and
had never seen a puzzle before, but she treasured them just the
same. The gift that Adrena prized most was the doll. In her
short life, Adrena could only recall having an imaginary doll.
While the mute Adrena lay listening, Dr. Matthews read those
books to her and showed her how to put a puzzle together
at Huntingdon. Dr. Matthews also arranged for a tutor
to teach Adrena and asked the staff to help whenever
possible. They knew some of what they were teaching was
getting through to the silent girl, because Adrena's eyes
followed their every move and rested on their faces when she
didn't understand.

Initially, Dr. Matthews never spoke of Adrena's mother
and Bart. Making Adrena comfortable and getting to know
her came first. Dr. Matthews talked about her own childhood
and family to the silent, acutely paranoid child most of the
time. Adrena felt she knew Doc's family well, but especially
Dr. Matthews' sister, Maxine. Would know her if she passed
her on the street. Adrena loved hearing stories about how
Max would ferociously look out for Vivian. Adrena had often
wished for a brother or sister during those awful days and
nights with Mildred and Bart. Someone to huddle and hold
on to when Bart yelled and brutally kicked her into a corner
with the trash and roaches.

Remembering the many times Dr. Matthews actually
rescued her forced a smile to Adrena's face. If anyone upset
Adrena, they had to explain why they had done so to Doc. If
Adrena came down with a fever, cold, stomach ache, or a
reaction to her medication, the Doc came running. The doctor
was never satisfied with the reports of others who might not
be doing a competent job.

Doc never let Adrena's silence get the best of her. She
talked, laughed, and smiled, as if the one-way conversations
were two-way. Recognizing Doc's back-and-forth banter,
Adrena thought the Doc must have perfected such
conversations as a very young child just like her. Adrena had
often talked to herself or her imaginary doll because there was
never anyone to talk to when she lived with Mildred and Bart.

Responding to her own questions on behalf of the imaginary doll came as instinctively as breathing.

The memory of her own first words to Doc made Adrena laugh out loud. It was questionable which one of them was most surprised. After a year of only speaking within her mind, Adrena didn't even recognize her own voice.

That day, Adrena was recovering from one of her many reconstructive surgeries, and the orderly wheeled her down to Doc's office. In her customary, muted silence, Adrena sat clutching the books Doc had given her, and without hesitation, Doc cheerfully chattered away.

Everything was fine until Adrena's doll crossed her mind. She searched her lap and the crevices of the wheelchair. No doll. Doc watched, but kept talking. Adrena's search escalated. She tried to scoot forward in the seat. Maybe the doll was behind her. The books fell to the floor.

Doc addressed Adrena directly, when she saw how frantically the child was searching. "Adrena, what are you looking for?"

Without looking up, Adrena spoke for the first time in a long time. "Where's Max?"

Doc was stunned, but delighted, and managed to reply, "She's probably operating on somebody about now. Why?"

Adrena looked at Dr. Matthews as if she'd lost her mind and said, "My Max. Not yours."

Astonished by the information, Doc asked, "You have a Max, too?"

"Yes."

"Oh. What does she look like?"

"You know what she looks like. You gave her to me."

Shaking her head, Doc asked, "I gave her to you?"

"Yeah. She's always with me when I come down here. I have to go back to get her."

Doc was so glad to hear Adrena speak, she forgot they were in a mental institution. She smiled and said cheerfully, "Well, you're here now, and you're fine. You can get Max after we talk for a little bit. That wouldn't be so bad, would it?"

Adrena's hot gaze singed Doc's professional veneer when she spat, "No! I want to go back to get Max now!"

Dr. Matthews stuttered a bit. "Uh . . . I'm sure she's fine, Adrena. She's waiting for you in your room."

"You don't know that! I don't know where she is, and she's mine! I want to go get her now!"

"If I call upstairs and ask them to look for Max and bring her down, will you calm down?"

Adrena screamed hysterically, "No! I don't want anybody touching her! She's mine! Take me back to get her! Somebody could be touching her right now! Stealing her! Selling her to strangers!"

Doc jumped up, picked up Adrena's books, and started pushing that wheelchair as fast as she could. The entire time she kept saying, "Okay, sweetheart. We'll go find Max. If anyone's got her, we'll get her back right now."

Of course, Max was lying on Adrena's bed when they got there. Adrena smiled in front of Doc for the first time. Relief flooded the good Doc. She had to sit down on the bed and cover her face to regain her composure. That was when their conversations graduated to two-way.

Now, Adrena's gaze rested on Max's pretty, malt brown plastic face, as she lay on her bed in Mrs. Stanley's home. Max's fixed smile allowed Adrena to imagine the doll was in sync with her thoughts of Dr. Matthews. At sixteen, Adrena's best friend and bedmate was still Max.

The day Adrena's mother and Bart were sentenced, Dr. Matthews came to Huntingdon to give the news to Adrena personally. Mildred Hanover had been sentenced to six months of actual prison time, five years probation, and temporary loss of custody. Bartholomew Hanover had been sentenced to eighteen months of actual prison time and five years probation.

With no real concept of time measurement, Adrena asked, "Is that a long time, Doc?"

Dr. Matthews spat angrily, "Not very long at all, Adrena. Not for what they did to you. They'll both be free before your physical rehabilitation is done. Neither one of them should

ever walk the street as free people again. They're too
irresponsible and cruel to be free."

"What does temporary loss of custody mean?"

Growing visibly angrier by the minute, Dr. Matthews
said, "That means she has the legal right, as your mother, to
get you back, Adrena."

Still confused, Adrena asked, "Do you mean I have to go
back to live with them again? After what they did?"

With tears in her eyes, Doc replied helplessly, "Yes."

Adrena felt fear, rage, and hysteria creep into her soul.
Her head shook from side to side as she screamed, "I'll never
go back! Nobody can make me! I don't care what they say!
They don't know, Doc! Make them know I can't go back!
They hate me! I hate them! They'll sell me, Doc! Please,
don't let them sell me!"

That was the first time Adrena touched Dr. Matthews.
Adrena painfully hobbled over to the doctor, clasped and
clung to her tightly. Adrena wept and pleaded uncontrollably.
Two alarmed staff members came running, one with a
sedative syringe in hand. Dr. Matthews waved them away.
She refused to medicate Adrena for every tear, the way the
other doctors did their patients. Instead, Dr. Matthews held
Adrena, like the wounded child she was. She quietly
reassured Adrena she would do everything in her power to see
that Mildred and Bart never got their hands on her again and
rocked Adrena to sleep. Indeed, Dr. Matthews' diligent care
and Adrena's ignorance had rescued the fledgling remnants
of Adrena's sanity.

True to her word, Dr. Matthews' reports to the court on
Adrena's progress kept her mother at bay. Mildred's rare
telephone calls to Adrena were never taken. Adrena had not
actually heard her mother's voice since that night and never
wanted to hear it again. She felt that this upcoming meeting
must have been forced on Doc - that Doc would never have
allowed it otherwise. Adrena knew there were limits to what
Dr. Matthews could do to protect her from Mildred. Unlike
her wicked, lawless mother, Doc would never dream of doing
anything outside the system. It was going to have to be up to
Adrena to stop Mildred and Bart from interfering in her life.

The system was obviously too confused for Adrena to depend on them to protect her.

While Adrena lay on her crisp, clean sheets in the Stanley's well-adjusted household, an evil smile crept across her pretty face as she mapped out a course of action. She knew exactly how to dispense of Mildred and Bart. A good time. They loved good times more than anything in the world. Adrena would throw them a going away party. Somehow, she would send them up and out of the picture.

Mrs. Stanley was pleased and surprised to see the smile on Adrena's face when she came down for breakfast. The Stanleys exchanged apprehensive glances, but said nothing to each other. Adrena's bubbly conversation was infectious, and they fell right into it. She offered to help Mr. Stanley in the hothouse. He had promised to show her how to extract and preserve seeds from plants, especially the ones that were used for medicinal purposes. Mr. Stanley had no idea how interesting this would be to Adrena.

Chapter Eight

On Sunday, at two in the afternoon, Howard and Vivian sat side by side in his gleaming, silver Jaguar. In silent stillness, they sat there for a long time. Doom permeated the air. Vivian waited patiently for Howard to say whatever was on his mind or start the car. He looked as if he were on his way to the guillotine, instead of a family dinner at his sister Talia's.

Finally, sighing heavily, Howard asked, "Vivian, do you know Lula's going to be there today?"

"Yes, I know she'll be there. Why? Is there a problem I should know about?"

Miserably, Howard ran his hand over his face and said, "You know how she feels about you, Vivian. She's not going to be thrilled to hear we're engaged. I have a gut-wrenching feeling Lula is going to try to start something. She seldom surprises me or any of the rest of the family with her antics. It's just outsiders who can't believe what she's done."

"Like what, Howard? What can Lula start with me?"

"God only knows, Vivian. Promise me you won't let anything she says or does upset you. The moment she starts, we're leaving."

"Anything you say, Howard. As long as you feed me before the evening is over."

Starting the car, Howard said, "Okay. Let's get this over with."

Their ride to Talia's was relatively quiet. Lost in admiration of her engagement ring in the sunlight almost the entire time, Vivian hardly noticed.

If news of the engagement didn't upset Lula, the ring certainly would. Not knowing very much about the prices of jewelry, even Vivian could see Howard had paid a pretty penny for this bauble. Vivian loved her ring and Howard.

And, Vivian loved Howard enough to put up with his wicked witch of a sister - at least she thought so.

All of Lula's early attempts to bring an abrupt end to their relationship had failed. Still, she insisted on making life as miserable as possible for Howard and Vivian. Knowing Howard spent every Wednesday evening with Vivian, Lula had feigned a different life-threatening illness every other Wednesday for months. When Howard showed up with Vivian in tow, Lula would whisk him off to her bedroom and hold him hostage for hours. If she knew they had plans for the weekend, Lula would attempt to assign him ridiculous, menial tasks. She would call Howard's house, or Vivian's, at ungodly hours of the morning to invite him to breakfast. Lula did it all to prove her power in Howard's life. She tested any woman's mettle, and Vivian was no exception.

Howard's youngest sister, Talia, lived in a pretty, gray-and-white rancher, set all alone on a rolling acre of plush green grass. She told Vivian her husband, Teddy, pulled every weed by hand. Teddy's love of his lawn showed. Each tree and bush was pruned to perfection, and his flowers bloomed on cue. A kaleidoscope of vivid, vibrant colors displayed Teddy's precision landscaping skills. Nothing lay on the ground that shouldn't be there.

As Howard and Vivian pulled up and parked on Talia and Teddy's tree-lined street, the first person they saw was Teddy. His eleven-month-old son trailed behind. The little fellow had just begun to walk, and it showed. Howard came around and opened the car door for Vivian. She got out, took a deep breath, and they walked, hand in hand, over to Teddy and the baby. Vivian couldn't resist picking the little guy up. Howard and Teddy greeted each other warmly, and Teddy gave Vivian a hug and kiss.

With a proud smile on his face, Teddy said, "Vivian, T.J.'s in the biting stage. Be careful."

Vivian looked at the happy little cherub and asked, "Would you bite me, T.J.?"

T.J. gave her a wide grin, showing four brand-new, front teeth. That was her answer.

The four of them joined the rest of the group. There were about fifteen people around picnic tables set under the trees out back. Lula wasn't among them, but Clayton was. Everyone shook hands, hugged, and yelled excited greetings. The Shaws didn't get to see much of each other these days. They all had demanding jobs, homes, and families. Howard would be the last of the five Shaws to get married.

Howard's oldest brother, Sheldon, and Clayton stood together under a tree on a hill away from the main crowd. They were talking about things they didn't want anyone to hear - especially Sheldon's wife. Howard gave Vivian a quick squeeze and peck before whispering, "I'm off to the torture chamber."

The moment Howard joined Clayton and Sheldon, there was a lot of laughing, backslapping, and handshaking. Teddy collected T.J. from Vivian and headed for the group. Gary, Howard's middle brother, soon followed.

During the baby exchange, Talia caught a glimpse of Vivian's ring and asked breathlessly, "Vivian, is that what I think it is?"

"Is what, what you think it is?"

With hands on hips, Talia said sarcastically, "That rock on your finger, Sweetie. Don't play dumb with me."

Vivian waved her hand nonchalantly and said, "Oh, this old thing. Howard asked me to marry him and gave this to me last night. Do you like it?"

Talia hollered, "He did! Let me see it!"

The entire female crowd swarmed around Vivian, admiring the ring and congratulating her.

Talia yelled, "Howard, you didn't tell me you were going to propose to Vivian! I thought we were tight!"

Grinning, Howard yelled back, "We are, baby sister! I didn't want to be embarrassed if she said no!"

Talia said, "Yeah. Fat chance. She's put up with you for over a year. How bad can you be for the rest of her life?"

Before Howard could respond, Lula, her husband Bruce, and a woman Vivian didn't recognize walked up. All of the festive conversation and activity ceased, and the procession was watched with such reverence that Vivian expected everyone to bow at any moment. Talia broke the silence when she walked over to her sister, gave her a solemn hug and said, "Hi, Lula. Bruce. Lydia."

In response, they all nodded in a non-committal and regal way.

Some of the others began to make their way over to greet them in a more familiar fashion. The men under the tree held their positions and, for some reason, were all solemnly shaking their heads in unison. Vivian stayed where she was, too. Lula didn't like her, and Vivian didn't care much for her either.

Talia handled the introductions.   She said loudly, "Everyone, this is Lydia. Lydia, this is everyone." Looking in Vivian's direction, Talia added deliberately, "And this is Vivian. She's Howard's fiancé."

Obviously unprepared for the announcement, Lula frowned sourly and asked, "What did you say?"

Talia said happily, "Howard proposed to Vivian last night. She's got a rock that'll choke a horse to prove it. So, whatever you had in mind, Lula, forget it."

Lula waved her massive hand and said, "I don't have to forget a thing, Talia. Asking and doing are two entirely different things. Nothing's done yet."

Talia's eyes rolled around in their sockets, as Lula bypassed Vivian without a glance and headed toward the men. Bruce and Lydia followed quietly. Gary and Teddy nodded politely and retreated when Lula and her entourage reached the group. Flanking Howard, Sheldon and Clayton stood firm.

Without acknowledging anyone, Lula asked with indignation, "Howard, is what Talia said true?"

Howard nodded his head and said, "Yes, Lula."

Sounding like an angry, abandoned mother, Lula asked, "When were you going to tell me?"

"Today."

"Do you think that was wise?"

"What do you mean, do I think that was wise?"

Lula glanced briefly at Lydia and said, "Take a guess."

Howard looked at Lydia with a frown and said angrily, "I don't have to take a guess about anything. If you think that by bringing Lydia here today, you're going to change anything, you're wrong, Lula. I'm marrying Vivian, and that's that."

Lula smiled wickedly and said, "Don't be so quick to declare a victory. The day is young, baby brother."

Sheldon snapped, "Not as young as you think it is, Lula. Why can't you ever mind your own business? I hope you don't think I'm going to stand by and let you ruin Talia's dinner. I'll lock you, your husband and your uninvited guest in the basement if I have to." Pointing at Lydia, Sheldon continued, "This kind of thing is childish and uncalled for, Lula. You are way too old for this nonsense."

Lula hissed, "Who addressed you, Sheldon Shaw? There's a little surprise on the burner for you, too."

"I just bet there is. Your day wouldn't be complete if you didn't aggravate me. Not that I care, but who did you dig up for me?"

"Don't worry, you'll find out soon enough."

"You're spending too much time in the graveyard, darling. Digging up old girlfriends should be beneath you. If you spent half as much time working on your own marriage as you do trying to drive wedges between everybody else, your husband might stop drinking."

Completely disregarding the fact that Bruce was just behind her, Lula said, "You don't understand, Sheldon - I find Bruce a lot easier to take a little drunk than stone sober!"

Obviously embarrassed by the exchange, Bruce stepped forward and said sternly, "Lula, that's enough."

Lula looked Bruce up and down contemptuously, started to speak and decided against it. Instead, she turned and walked toward the crowd. Lula took a seat at the table and didn't say anything else for quite a while. Lydia followed her. Bruce stayed under the tree with the men.

Vivian studied Lydia. She must have been someone special in Howard's life. She definitely had the look. Statuesque. Great figure. A full head of dyed blonde hair, teased feverishly to achieve the tousled look. Golden brown skin that was very similar to Vivian's, magnificent hazel eyes and beautifully dressed.

With all of that going for Lydia, there was not a drop of envy in Vivian's heart for her. Howard loved Vivian, and she knew this beyond a doubt. As long as Lydia stayed in Howard's past, Vivian had no problem with her being here.

Talia came over to where Vivian was standing and asked, "Vivian, can you help me in the kitchen?"

"Sure."

As soon as they were inside the house, Talia grabbed Vivian's hand and dragged her off to the bedroom. Breathlessly, she said, "Vivian, Lula's up to no good. Has Howard ever mentioned Lydia to you?"

Unexcited, Vivian replied, "No, Talia. Should he have?"

Talia gave a tiny shrug before saying, "When you have a vicious sister like Lula, you should empty your closet and check it before inviting any company. Anyway, Lydia was the woman in Howard's life before you. They dated off and on for a year. She's pretty, but there's no one home. Lula tricked her out of the relationship without much creativity at all."

Vivian held up her hand to stop Talia and said, "Okay, I get the picture. Lula's not getting a rise out of me, Talia, don't worry. She may get one out of Howard, though. He's easy. I'll try to keep his lid on until after dinner. Okay?"

Still looking a little concerned, Talia said, "Okay, Vivian. I'm really happy for you and Howard. You're right for him. He seems to be right for you, too. Please don't let Lula have her way. She's my big sister, and I love her, but she can be a giant pain in the ass. One day I'll tell you the long story of why Teddy and I had to elope."

Vivian said calmly, "She won't change our plans, Talia. Now, what are we taking out to eat? I'm starving. We didn't get up early enough for breakfast."

Talia flashed a satisfied smile and said, "Let's get those salads out there then. The vegetables are already warming. There's corn on the grill. Teddy cooked the meat early this morning. It's in the warmer."

Talia and Vivian made several trips to get everything outside. Talia's friends and sisters-in-law pitched in. Lula sat regally still. Howard had been lured away from the group by Lydia, in Vivian's brief absence. Vivian wasn't surprised or amused. Not wanting Lula to be mistaken about the way Howard felt about her, Vivian let them have the moment.

Once all the food was out, Vivian went to retrieve her fiancé. Every eye followed the scene. Howard spun around with a miserable expression on his face, and Lydia hurriedly wiped at her face in a gesture of unease. It was easy to see Lula had placed both of them in an awkward situation.

Vivian wondered what conversation had just taken place between Howard and Lydia and hoped that nothing of substance had evolved. Smiling, she slid her arm around Howard's waist, stroked his back firmly and said, "It's time to eat, Howard."

In a barely audible whisper, Howard responded, "Okay, sweetheart."

He looked at Lydia and said, "Lydia, this is the woman I'm going to marry. I don't know what my sister told you. I don't know how, or why, she convinced you to come here today. Believe me, Lydia, I did not ask her to bring you."

Lydia sniffed and said, "Yeah, sure, Howard." Turning to Vivian, she said, "I hope my appearance hasn't upset you. Lula led me to believe Howard was unattached. Anyway, congratulations."

A fixed smile was Vivian's only reply. She knew how to play the game, but she couldn't trust her tongue to cooperate.

Lydia turned and walked toward the tables. Everyone pretended not to be watching . . . everyone except Lula. Her stare never wavered. Vivian couldn't help noticing how gorgeous Lydia was as she walked away, and a flash of jealousy ran through her - but that was how Lula wanted her to react, and she quickly dismissed it.

Howard wrapped his arms around Vivian and asked, "Are you all right?"

Still smiling, Vivian said, "I'm fine. Maybe I should be asking if you're all right. The two of you had a pretty involved conversation going on."

"I'm fine, too. Lydia's the one who's confused. She lied about not knowing about us, Vivian. Clayton ran into her a week ago. He told her I had been with you for over a year. Vivian, Clayton slept with Lydia a week ago. Even if I were alone, I wouldn't want her after that. She honestly thought I would reassess my situation if I saw her here. The woman's no brighter now than she was when I dated her. I hate games, Vivian."

"Well, I'll never play games with you, Howard."

Howard snapped back to being the man Vivian knew only too well. He shook his head and said, "Oh, no. I like the games you play, Vivian. Don't ever stop playing."

"I just don't want to start out on the wrong foot."

Howard tightened his grip on her waist and said, "You can start on either one of your feet, sweetheart. I love both of them."

Blushing, Vivian said, "I'm certainly glad to hear you say that. Now, are you going to eat? Or, are you going to smolder some more?"

"I'll eat if you give me a kiss first."

Vivian let her head dangle, closed her eyes and waited for Howard's warm mouth to cover hers. As she tasted Howard's moist, sweet tongue, Vivian moved closer. His embrace tightened a little more, and their familiar, synchronized rocking began. The sudden applause reminded them they were being closely observed. Howard gave Vivian a tiny peck, filled with promise, and released her. They walked, hand in hand, back to the gathering.

Everyone's grin said the family was pleased as punch with the way things turned out. Everyone, except Lula and Lydia. Lula's eyes rolled like no others Vivian had ever seen. Lydia couldn't make herself look in their direction.

When Clayton came over and gave Vivian a hug and kiss on the cheek, Lydia looked physically ill. When he admired Vivian's ring and enthusiastically congratulated her, Vivian thought Lydia was going to cry. Sheldon, Gary, and Bruce followed suit. Lula's stare was brutal.

They all ate, drank, danced, sang old songs and played several vigorous games of volleyball. T.J. and another little fellow were trampled twice. The adult participants wiped them off, applied Band-Aids where needed and released them again. Without hesitation, the two toddlers went back to the volleyball court. No one could say Shaw children weren't durable.

The day was turning out to be a little better than tolerable. Lydia tried to corner Howard a couple more times, but he expertly avoided her. Howard playfully punched Clayton and Sheldon for staring at Vivian's rear end and making remarks every time she bent over. Privately, he admonished her for wearing what he called a revealing outfit. Vivian asked what she should have worn for an outdoor activity. They both had on shorts. That's when Vivian knew, for sure, the world was normal again.

The only moment of uncertainty came later in the evening when Lydia purposely brushed Howard in a most inappropriately familiar manner. They exchanged a few heated words, and Lula piped in, "Oh please, Howard. You and Lydia have shared more intimate moments than a leg bump and a stroke. Don't act ugly because your fiancé is next to you."

Howard's eyes were slits when he said, "Lula, you have created all the turmoil in my day you're going to. Do us all a favor and back off. I don't want to forget you're my oldest sister - that you raised me and did a damned good job, too. But, let go, Lula. That's all I have to say. Let go and take your game-playing friend with you."

Bruce hid his face in his hand and chuckled silently. Clayton laughed out loud and said, "Amen! The man's thirty-six years old. Give him a break. Please."

Lula growled, "Mind your own business, Clayton."

"For your information, Lula, Howard is half of my business. He's happy. I'm happy. His only problem is he looks at you like you're his mother. I don't. I see you as the bossy control freak you are. If we were alone, I would be more than happy to explain to you exactly where you lost control. Let's just say there are a few things you can't do for Howard. Lydia had her chance and couldn't handle the job. Now, Dr. Viv is obviously taking very good care of him.

That ring says she's doing a bang up job of it, too. Back off, Lula. You're not funny anymore. You're starting to get on my nerves, and I'm not sensitive."

"Dr. Viv is looking for a free meal ticket, just like every other woman in town, Clayton. The day after my stupid brother says, 'I do,' she'll suddenly come down with some affliction that can't be corrected. She's not completely stupid, so she'll throw in a baby or two for good measure. That'll guarantee her an income for the next twenty years easily. If I'm so wrong, why don't you have a wife, Clayton?"

"I haven't found anyone as unlovingly distrusting as you, sweetheart. I'm so impressed with your open hostility toward people who have never done one thing to you, that all I'm waiting for is a woman just like you, Lula."

There was some commotion beginning near the house. As promised, Lula had managed to thoroughly disturb Sheldon's wife, Charlene, and things didn't look very good. After assuring himself that there would be no violence, Howard returned and said, "That's it, Vivian. It's time to go."

For once, Vivian didn't argue with him. Howard gave Talia a hug and kiss and thanked her and Teddy for inviting them. Talia insisted on making plates for them to take home, and Vivian helped her make them quickly. Everyone could hear Sheldon and Charlene arguing the entire time. There was no denying it, Vivian was shaken. She could no longer dismiss Lula as just an inconvenient obstacle. Vivian now knew exactly how Lula felt about her, approximately how far she would go to have her way, and that as far as Lula was concerned, the marriage was out of the question.

Chapter Nine

At exactly seven-thirty on Monday morning, Dr. Vivian Matthews sat in her car at the curb of the home of the Stanleys. Before she turned off the engine, a vibrantly healthy Adrena Reynolds bounced out of the pretty, blue-and-white structure and down the porch stairs. As Adrena climbed into the Maxima, they exchanged huge smiles. Both Adrena and Dr. Matthews were happy that morning for different reasons.

Dr. Matthews beamed on her patient-protegee and said, "Don't you look wonderful this morning, Miss Reynolds? I take it your headache didn't ruin your entire weekend?"

Strapping herself in with the seatbelt, Adrena responded, "It backed off yesterday, Doc." Then, Adrena paused and studied her hands before asking plaintively, "Doc, are you going to tell the principal I poured that acid on Harvey on purpose? I promise I won't do anything like it again, if you don't. They might refuse to let me go to school there, if they think I'll maim the students."

"Well, I'm certainly glad to hear that you're concerned, even if it is only in a self-serving vein. No, Adrena, I couldn't tell the principal that even if I wanted to. It's considered privileged information. Will you be apologizing for it this morning?"

A look of uncertainty crossed Adrena's pretty brow before she asked, "Will I have to apologize to Harvey, Doc?"

"I don't know, Adrena. If you have to apologize to Harvey, will you?"

"I'll apologize to the principal for doing it on school property. I'll even apologize to Mrs. Marshall for doing it in her class, but Harvey's out of the question, Doc."

"What if he apologizes to you first, Adrena?"

Wickedly rolling her expressive eyes, Adrena said, "Let Harvey pour his apology on his burned pecker. If it heals that, I'll consider accepting it."

Dr. Matthews gave Adrena a severely disapproving look.

The meeting with the principal went remarkably well, and to Adrena's surprise, once the principal learned all the details of the incident, he said that Harvey would be suspended also. The principal and Mrs. Marshall concluded that the accident occurred because of Adrena's negligence and Harvey's raging hormones. Adrena's apologies to Mrs. Marshall and the principal were accepted, and she was sent off to class. Adrena never noticed Dr. Matthews' engagement ring, and Dr. Matthews never mentioned it to her.

The moment Vivian arrived at her office, Millie yelled, jumped, squeezed, and held on to her hand for at least five minutes, intermittently gazing at the magnificent engagement ring. Vivian finally got Maxine on the telephone at eleven. Maxine screeched her unbridled excitement into Vivian's ear for ten minutes and ended it all with a promise of coming to see the ring the moment she got a break. Jessica and Eunice met Vivian for lunch. They howled their excited appreciation of the beauty of it all through the entire hour.

Every patient noticed the ring. They talked more about Vivian's engagement and impending wedding than their own problems. As the week progressed, Vivian considered putting the ring in her purse, but what Howard had said about never wanting to see her hand without it again made her abandon that idea.

By Wednesday, Vivian and Howard had begun their wedding plans, but they were deadlocked on where to go for a honeymoon and how long they would stay. Howard wanted two weeks. Vivian felt one week was sufficient. Howard wanted to go somewhere cold. Vivian thought the islands alluring. Howard thought the wedding should be held at his house; it was bigger. Vivian wanted it at her house; it was brighter and more comfortable.

Howard proposed that whichever house they married in, they would live in the other. Vivian had never given a thought to giving up her house. All she knew for sure was that if they lived in Howard's house, those stripes would have to go! They made her feel as if she were incarcerated.

They agreed to agree before Friday. Vivian needed to place an order for invitations -- not that they really needed them -- they would only be inviting family and a few friends. Howard promised to emphasize to Lula that there should be no uninvited guests. Having performed so well for the proposal, Paul was chosen to handle the catering. Their blood tests would be done early Friday morning, and the application for a marriage license would be filed the following Wednesday.

Vivian hadn't seen Howard since he brought her home Sunday night. Five minutes after they had lain down that night, Sheldon called. Charlene had thrown him out, and he had been Howard's houseguest since then. The thought of leaving Sheldon alone in his home for any extended period of time frightened Howard.

If Howard hadn't known better, he would have thought Sheldon had been born in the lap of luxury. The truth was Sheldon was used to Charlene picking up after him. Sheldon made a sandwich and destroyed the entire kitchen. He left beer bottles and snack wrappers everywhere. They played tennis after work, and his racquet lay on the foyer floor until Howard tripped over it the next morning.

Howard was so angry his teeth were grinding together when he spoke to Vivian about his brother. Howard had to clean up before the cleaning lady came because he didn't want her to see all the mess and quit.

♦   ♦   ♦

Although Adrena's mother was not due until three-thirty, Adrena came into the office promptly at three on Wednesday afternoon because Dr. Matthews wanted to talk to Adrena about the meeting first. Most of all, she wanted Adrena to know that past issues would not be discussed today and to reassure her that the meeting would be terminated if anyone got out of hand. Just for insurance, Dr. Matthews had arranged for a psych tech from Huntingdon to be present in the waiting room.

Millie and Adrena exchanged chatter before Millie buzzed the doctor. When Adrena strolled into the office, Dr. Matthews was pleasantly surprised to see how relaxed she appeared to be. Lights sparkled in Adrena's elegant eyes, as she flashed her warm smile at the Doc. A perfectly pressed, pink shirt-and-short set flattered Adrena's figure, and her ponytail bounced with every move.

Adrena said buoyantly, "Hi, Doc."

"Hi, Adrena. You look fabulous."

With one hand on her hip and the other patting her hair, Adrena said, "Oh yeah. I look good, Doc. Way too good to spend the afternoon with my shrink. Even if she does look better than I'll ever be able to dream of."

Dr. Matthews waved her down and said, "Oh, go on, girl. I wish I could still compete with a sixteen-year-old."

The dramatic movement of Dr. Matthews' hand attracted Adrena's attention to the ring. She saw the smile fall from Adrena's face and heard her breathing grow shallow. Adrena stiffly walked over and nervously picked up Dr. Matthews' hand.

The tremble alarmed the doctor. Calmly, she asked, "What's the matter, Adrena?"

A tear splattered onto the back of Dr. Matthews' hand. Then, another. She couldn't imagine what had so drastically changed Adrena's mood. She lifted Adrena's tear-stained face and asked with mounting concern, "What's the matter?"

Choking on her tears, Adrena managed to say, "That's an engagement ring, Doc. You're getting married."

"Yes, it is, Adrena. Aren't you happy for me?"

Adrena's head shook slowly from side to side. An onlooker would have thought Dr. Matthews had just told the child she was dying.

Dr. Matthews asked sadly, "Why not? I'm not getting any younger you know. You don't want me to be alone forever, do you, Adrena?"

In a misery-racked whisper, Adrena said, "He'll hurt you, Doc."

"No, he won't, Adrena. He loves me, sweetheart."

With her voice climbing from a whisper to a yell, and finally ending in a loud, gut-wrenching plea, Adrena said, "He loves you. He'll change. He'll change! He'll yell at you, for absolutely no reason! When he's tired of yelling, he'll slap you so hard you can't hear! Choke the shit out of you! He'll punch you! Twist your arm 'til your hand touches the back of your head! Knock you down! Kick you! Yes, he will kick you until you pee on yourself! Over and over! Slam your head into things! When he's done whipping your ass, he'll snatch you up, say he's sorry and make you cook for him! He'll make you do things that'll make you wish you were dead, Doc! Please . . . please, don't do it!"

Dr. Matthews put her arms around Adrena and fought back her own tears. Adrena had just described her mother's relationship with Bart. Adrena still could not believe other men didn't all treat their women that way -- not even after living in the peaceful, loving environment of the Stanleys.

Speaking softly into Adrena's hair, the doctor said, "No, Adrena. Howard won't do any of those things to me. I won't let him. I love Vivian first. I love Howard second. If he disrespects me, I'll leave long before any of that happens."

"No, you won't. You love him. You'll stay. Try to understand him. Try to fix it. In the end, you'll learn to live with it. A few drinks and a joint might get you through the beginning of the week. You'll take the more serious dope to get through the weekends if you have to. You'll hide what he's doing from everybody. You'll do anything to make him happy. To keep him. Why, Doc? Because you love him."

Dr. Matthews lifted the tormented child's face, so she could look into her eyes and said, "Adrena, I promise you, I will never let him hurt me. He's a very nice man, sweetheart."

All of Adrena's anger surfaced when she said, "He'd better not hurt you, Doc. I'll make him sorry the thought ever crossed his fucking mind."

Hoping to circumvent or extinguish some of Adrena's anger, Dr. Matthews asked, "Would you like to come to the wedding, Adrena? That way, you can see him for yourself. You'll see he's a great guy, and I'm a lucky woman."

"I don't want to see him, Doc! He's a man, isn't he?!"

"Yes, he is a man, Adrena. He's a nice man. One that I can depend on to love me. A man who will take care of me if I get sick. He'll hold my hand if I'm scared. We'll have dinner together. Maybe even take turns cooking. Marriage is not a man who pimps his woman for drug money and abuses her child, Adrena. It's not. You live with Mr. and Mrs. Stanley every day, sweetheart. Does he do that to her?"

"No. Mrs. Stanley wouldn't stand for him mistreating her. She's a strong old lady, Doc. Besides, you really can't count him. Mr. Stanley is one in a million. He puts insects outside to keep from killing them. He plugs up every hole the mice and squirrels chew in his hothouse so they won't be poisoned. Mr. Stanley would stop traffic while the damned varmints crossed the street, if they could tell him they wanted to cross."

Adrena fell silent for a moment and then began to retreat by saying, "I can't go to your wedding, Doc. I wouldn't know what to wear, or how to act in a room filled with rich people. Besides, I've never been to a wedding before."

Wanting desperately to help Adrena cross yet another chasm created by Mildred and Bart, Dr. Matthews offered, "If I buy you a new outfit and get your hair done, will you come?"

A deep frown creased Adrena's beautiful face. She asked, "Why would you do that, Doc? I'm just a patient. Is my approval of this guy really that important to you?"

With genuine sincerity, the good doctor said, "You're much more than a patient, Adrena. We're friends. And, yes indeed, your opinion counts, too. Please come."

"How does Max feel about him, Doc?"

"She loves him. She wishes she had seen him first, but don't ever tell her I said that." Dr. Matthews smiled conspiratorially.

Still pouting, Adrena said, "I won't know anyone except you. They'll all know I'm your patient."

Dr. Matthews said sternly, "Let's get one thing straight, Adrena. You don't have mental patient stenciled on your forehead. No one will think any such thing. Besides, Max will be there. You'll get to meet her, too."

Lights blazed in Adrena's eyes at the mention of meeting Max. She knew Doc loved her sister more than anyone in the world. To finally see her thoroughly excited Adrena. Maxine was the warrior. No one bothered Doc with Max around.

Adrena often daydreamed about what life would have been like if she'd had Max with her. After Dr. Matthews assured her Maxine knew none of her circumstances, Adrena agreed.

Unfortunately, Dr. Matthews only had enough time to tell Adrena there would be no discussion of past issues and to ask if she was ready for her mother's visit, when Millie buzzed and announced Mrs. Hanover's arrival. Dr. Matthews asked if Ward, the psych tech, had arrived.

Millie said, "He's here, and he's packed," which meant he had brought restraining tools.

Dr. Matthews told her to send Mrs. Hanover in.

A composed Adrena sat on the sofa, with her head up and hands loosely clasped in her lap. Dr. Matthews sat in her wing chair, until Mrs. Hanover entered the room. She stood to greet her.

Mildred Hanover looked both better and worse than the last time the doctor had seen her. The woman was barely skin and bone three years ago. Incredibly, she was smaller now. Her clothes, while clean, were ill-fitting. Her hair had been cut short, pressed hard, and brushed flat to cover missing patches. Clearly dilated pupils revealed she hadn't completely given up drugs, and the slight tremor in her icy-cold handshake said she might be needing them soon. Dr. Matthews was sure none of this would escape Adrena's attention either.

Dr. Matthews smiled as warmly as she could and said, "Good afternoon, Mrs. Hanover."

Mildred Hanover, speaking in a raspy, sarcastic tone of voice, said, "Good afternoon, Dr. Matthews. Is that my Adrena? Look how big she is. God, you grew up pretty, girl. Stand up, so I can see you."

Adrena stared blandly at her mother. Her silence was deafening. Dr. Matthews assumed from Adrena's mute response that standing for her mother's examination was out of the question.

To break the silence, Dr. Matthews said, "Let's just sit down and talk for a while, Mrs. Hanover. Perhaps the ice will break if you'll explain your visit."

Seated and looking only at the doctor, Mildred nervously began her story, "It's like this, Dr. Matthews. My mother has been sick for the past two years. She's had a heart attack and a bunch of small strokes. Mama's completely paralyzed on her left side now. Can't see nothin' out of one eye. The other one is going. She has high blood pressure and diabetes.

"They've done all they can do for her at the hospital. Now they want to send her to a hospice. You know. To make her comfortable until she dies - which won't be long, 'cause Mama won't do a damn thing they tell her. Anyway, Mama don't want to go to the hospice. She wants to go home."

Mildred paused and looked at Adrena. Adrena's impassive stare amply communicated her feelings about Mildred's story. Dr. Matthews saw that none of it mattered to Adrena. Looking from one to the other, she noticed the resemblance. This wretched woman had once looked exactly like Adrena. Men, alcohol, and drugs had taken a hell of a lot from her. Dr. Matthews could only wonder if Mildred had any idea how much . . . if she even cared.

Adrena spoke for the first time, when she asked her mother, "Why are you staring at me?"

Defensively, Mildred said, "Don't get huffy with me, Adrena. I haven't seen you in six years. Can't I look at my own kid?"

Adrena rolled her eyes hatefully and said, "Yeah, sure you can. As a matter of fact, that's what you were doing the last time I saw you - just looking."

Obviously uncomfortable with the change of subject, Mildred turned to Dr. Matthews and said nervously, "I thought that subject was off limits. Why is she bringing it up?"

"She's merely saying what's on her mind, Mrs. Hanover." Turning to Adrena, Dr. Matthews said, "Let's hear her out, Adrena. There will be time for hashing out those things at another time. Not today."

Adrena took a deep breath, turned to her mother, and said sarcastically, "Well, you've seen me. You want to tell me what good old Granny's failing health has to do with me? It can't be because you thought I would care. She never gave a damn about me. Let you drag me up and down the street in

all kinds of weather. Refused to feed me, when you begged
her to. Walked past me on the street, without so much as a
glance of recognition. So she's dying. What else?"

In an attempt to explain her mother's behavior, Mildred
began by saying, "Adrena, Mama was struggling herself. She
couldn't take on a child."

"Did she have a roof, Mildred? Did she have an extra
slice of bread? A glass of milk. A fuckin' smile?! She
couldn't share a smile with me? I was her own flesh and
blood. Just tell me what you want and get the fuck out of my
face, Mildred. Save your excuses for the Lord. Maybe He's
interested."

"Mama wouldn't help you because of me, Adrena. She
thought I would come to my senses once I realized you were
being neglected. She didn't know the power drugs hold over
people. Don't hold what I did against her, Adrena. She needs
you now. She's dying. Tell her how it is, Dr. Matthews."

"I beg your pardon, Mrs. Hanover? I don't know how it is."

Mildred shot back angrily, "I thought you fixed her.
Explained how things like that happen. Why people act the
way they do."

"I wasn't there, Mrs. Hanover. Adrena was. I can't tell
her how to feel. Adrena has come a long way, over a virtual
mountain of damages. Physical and emotional. Explanations
of a disaster are as helpful as an umbrella in a tornado to
the victim. You wanted to talk to her. There she is. Talk to
her."

Adrena asked, "What do you mean, she needs me?"

Mildred glared hatefully at Dr. Matthews and said, "She
needs you to take care of her for a while. Mama can't do
anything for herself."

"Me?! I'm not taking care of anybody! Nobody took care
of me! I couldn't do a thing for myself either! What's wrong
with you doing it?! She's your mother! Where's your damn
sister?!"

Anger was building in Mildred's eyes when she said,
"Antoinette won't come anywhere near my mother. They've
hated each other since we were kids. Mama won't let me in
her house, Adrena. Not even to take care of her. Thinks I'm

gonna steal things. I'll go to jail if I let my foot rest on her sidewalk. She had a lawyer see to that."

"Let's get this all straight, Mildred. I'm supposed to take care of your mother because she hates your sister and wouldn't trust you with the sidewalk? Right?"

"That's right. Mama needs one of us now, and she doesn't want anybody in her house but you, Adrena."

Adrena said nonchalantly, "Sounds like Mama's on her way to the hospice. I'm not doing it, Mildred."

"You'll do it, Adrena! Or, I'll snatch your pretty ass out of that nice little life you're living so fast you won't know what hit you! If you think I'm lying, I've got the papers right here in my pocket! Don't test me! The state's tired of taking care of you, honey. You're sixteen, and they don't give a damn if I'm still strung out. Now, Dr. Matthews, break that down so that this slut's pretty brain soaks it up."

Dr. Matthews was as close to asking someone to leave her office as she thought she would ever be when she said, "I can't explain something I totally disagree with, Mrs. Hanover. Adrena will never have to come back to live with you. She's in a stable, loving home, with people who will fight you for her. By the time they're done tying up your application, Adrena will be eighteen. Of course, I'll vehemently object to your having custody of her. Now, if you'd like to continue your appeal, I suggest you do it without the threats. They're hollow, Mrs. Hanover. Adrena will not fall through the cracks of the system."

Mildred spat, "Why?"

"Because I'm the putty."

The room fell quiet after that exchange. In the silence, the wheels in Dr. Matthews' mind spun. She wanted nothing more than to snatch this drug-ravaged little weasel by the throat and yell in her face, "Bitch, if you come anywhere near Adrena, I will snap your pathetic neck and dangle your head out the window!"

Suddenly, Adrena said something that sent shock waves through the entire room. She said, "Okay. I'll do it."

Dr. Matthews screamed, "What?! What did you say?! Why, Adrena?! You don't have to do that! She can't make you!"

Thinking she finally had the upper hand on Dr. Matthews, Mildred sneered cockily, "I thought you said you couldn't tell her what to think. Well, she's thinking on her own now. Deal with it, lady."

Attempting to console her doctor, Adrena said, "Don't worry, Doc. I can handle it. I don't want her to hassle you and the Stanleys. Besides, Mrs. Stanley is only an inch away from slapping the fire out of Mildred for causing the headache I had last week. If Granny's on her way out, it probably won't take long." Then, looking emotionlessly at her mother, Adrena asked, "Will I have to stay with her day and night? School's not out for the summer yet."

Licking her lips, Mildred said anxiously, "No. A nurse will come by every day during the week for a few hours. If Mama has to spend a few hours alone, it'll have to do. That's all. You won't have to spend the night if you don't want to either. Just give her breakfast before school. Dinner after school and any medicine they want her to have. She'll be home Friday morning. Will you be able to spend the day with her on Saturday and Sunday?"

Without a blink, Adrena said, "Sure, Mildred. Anything you say. Okay? It's a deal. Hand over the papers."

Astounded, Mildred frowned and asked, "What?"

"No papers, no deal, Mildred. You're not holding them over my head again next week. I want them. If you go get some more and try to threaten me again, I won't be responsible for what happens to you. Granny won't be the only old girl in town who needs a nursemaid."

Dr. Matthews sat dazed. She couldn't believe a word Adrena was saying. How could she volunteer to go back into that environment after making so much progress? They were just using her. They didn't give a damn about Adrena. Dr. Matthews had never heard about a grandmother before today. Where had she been for the past six years? Hell, the past sixteen years?

Dr. Matthews was sure Adrena would be a babbling idiot within a week. All to squash an idle threat. With her mother's continued addiction and Dr. Matthews' report, the court would never allow Adrena back into her household. Dr.

Matthews closed her eyes and tried to regain her composure
before speaking to Adrena again.

"Adrena, these are the facts. Mrs. Hanover has the right
to file those papers if she wants to. She won't win custody,
because I will not allow it. I'll fight her tooth and nail for
you, honey, and you know it. You've accomplished so much,
Adrena. Don't let this woman walk in and pull you back six
years. Don't let your Grandmother do it either. Let them
place her in a hospice. She'll be well taken care of, Adrena.
Better than anything you could possibly do for her. You don't
owe anyone anything."

Without another word, Mildred pulled the crumpled,
filthy papers out of her pocket and extended them toward
Adrena. Feeling helpless, Dr. Matthews watched as Adrena
steeled herself for any possible physical contact. None was
made. Adrena took a pen out of her bookbag and asked
Mildred for her grandmother's address and telephone number
and then wrote it on the back of the papers.

With their business concluded, Mildred stood and said, "If
you get there by three, you shouldn't have a problem getting
in. The nurse will show you what you have to do. I'll stop by
on Friday to make sure Mama's settled in. If you need
anything, or anything happens with Mama, my address and
telephone number is on those papers. Oh, and while you're
there, see if you can find her life insurance policies, Adrena.
I know she won't tell you where they are."

Emotionally deflated, Adrena mumbled, "Call. Don't
come, Mildred."

"Okay."

Mildred turned to the doctor and said, "Thanks for
nothing, Dr. Matthews. I guess blood runs deeper than they
told you."

"Maybe it does, Mrs. Hanover. I just wouldn't bank on it,
if I were you."

With a shrug, Mildred said, "Talk to ya' on Friday,
Adrena."

Never responding, Adrena sat slumped over and staring at
the papers. Mildred left the office. Dr. Matthews sat in her

chair and looked at Adrena. Adrena's eyes never left the papers.

Dr. Matthews finally broke the silence by asking, "How do you really feel about what you've decided to do, Adrena? Please, tell me the truth. Don't try to hide anything. I need to know, Adrena."

A tiny, high pitched squeal came from Adrena. A barely perceptible, uncontrolled tremble shook her. Thick, heavy tears splashed onto the papers. Dr. Matthews darted for the door and motioned Ward into the room.

Like an approaching siren, Adrena's squeal grew louder. In a matter of minutes, the child's screams were deafening. She thrashed her arms violently. Dr. Matthews and Ward struggled to get the restraints on her, before she was completely involved in the episode.

With Adrena all snapped up in the hideous restraints, Ward pulled the prescribed Haldol-filled hypodermic out of his bag. Adrena's wild screams continued to bounce off the walls. She could only wiggle in Doc's arms now.

Ward stood by, prepared to pop the protective covering on the needle, when Dr. Matthews said, "Not yet, Ward. It's rage. I want to see if she'll get enough of it out to come down on her own."

"You want me to call for transport, Doc?"

"No, Ward. I'll get her through without it."

"Okay, Doc. Where do you want me?"

Still holding onto Adrena's screaming, writhing body, Dr. Matthews said, "Outside will be fine. Ask Millie to bring in a cool towel for me, please."

Dr. Matthews rocked and wiped Adrena's brow with the damp towel for nearly half an hour, before Adrena's screams diminished to bone-rattling, gut-wrenching sobs. As she descended, the doctor told her over and over, "Adrena, you don't have to do this. She can't make you. Those papers don't mean a thing. We'll fight for you. Let it go."

Finally, Adrena wailed, "I can't!"

"Yes, you can."

"I can't let it go. They're everywhere, Doc. They're in my sleep. If I don't face them and fight for myself, they'll win.

You've protected me all this time. I'm old enough to fight my own battles now. I have to, Doc. I have to get them out of my head on my own. All the straitjackets, drugs, and hospitals in the world can't help me, Doc. I have to do it."
"How do you think you can do it alone, Adrena?"
Adrena responded resolutely. "I have to face them. Look them in the eyes and show them I'm not afraid of them - not because I'm hiding behind you. They can't do anything to me. Please, Doc. Let me try to free myself."
Dr. Matthews knew she could have Adrena committed right this minute. It would probably retard her growth. Possibly destroy it. A great deal of work had gone into convincing Adrena that her earlier stay had only been for observation. That her medication was only necessary to control the depression that anyone would have experienced who had been mentally and physically traumatized the way she had been. The truth was, Adrena had no chance - no chance at all for a normal existence - if she believed she was insane. A trip to the hospital, jacketed, kicking, and screaming, would permanently implant that notion . . . and Mildred Hanover would have reappeared in Adrena's life, and, without lifting a finger, destroyed her again.
On the other hand, if Adrena hurt anyone else, Dr. Matthews knew it would be considered her fault for not hospitalizing her. The child had exhibited some of society's most sinister behavior. Of course, she had not killed anyone, but she had caused harm to several. However, Adrena did not act out on others - she reacted to others. She never victimized - she retaliated. And while her behavior could not be labeled socially acceptable, it was understandable.
Poor dumb Harvey came to mind. He had provoked Adrena to do what every woman wanted to do to some idiot at one time or another. Did she dare throw Adrena's entire life away because of Harvey's stupidity? Adrena had said, ominously, "for now," but nothing else had happened to Harvey.
Dr. Matthews held Adrena close to her and made her decision. She loved Adrena as if the child were her own. She had to give her a chance to prove herself. If Adrena ever

hurt anyone except in self-defense, she would be forced to commit her immediately and withdraw from her case.

Adrena lay quiet in Dr. Matthews' arms now. She was exhausted. The doctor dabbed at her sweat-soaked brow and asked, "Adrena, can you promise me you won't hurt anyone?"

"I'm not going to hurt anyone, Doc. I have to face my family, though."

"How do I know what happened today, won't happen again?"

"I can't answer that, Doc. I just got real angry looking at those papers. That's all I am to somebody. A piece of paper. A file folder. A bunch of numbers. A contributor to the national debt."

Dr. Matthews couldn't help chuckling before she said, "A contributor to the national debt? You must think I charge a fortune."

"You should, Doc. Nobody else's doctor holds and rocks them, the way you always do with me. And I don't even like being held."

Dr. Matthews bent her head, so she could look into Adrena's face and said, "You sure are comfortable in my arms, for a girl who doesn't like being held."

Adrena sniffed and said, "Nobody else better try it."

"Not even Mrs. Stanley?"

Rolling her eyes a little, Adrena said, "She might get away with it. But don't tell her. Okay?"

"I won't tell her, if you make me two promises."

Adrena asked miserably, "What's that?"

"That you won't hurt anyone. And, that you'll call me the moment you feel the rage building. This is serious, Adrena. If it happens when I'm not around, you'll be committed before I get there. They won't understand, Adrena."

"Do you understand, Doc?"

"I understand as much as anyone can who hasn't experienced what you have. In psychiatry, we learn from our patients. They tell us what's going on. What we're finding out is there are no fixed patterns to mastering the mind. Only similarities. What works for one patient, could throw another with similar problems into a tailspin. You've been doing so well on your medication and therapy that sometimes I forget how deep your wounds are. I need reassurance from you that I'm not fooling myself."

"I won't lie to you, Doc. I'm not over the hump yet. This crap brought the rage to the surface. I was just glad I didn't let Mildred see it. I couldn't let her see how easily she can destroy me. It wouldn't matter to her anyway. She's still in the same spot she was in when it happened. The minute Bart shows up, the entire routine will start from the beginning.

"I have to overcome my fear of them, Doc. My way. Whatever that means. I'll take care of Granny. I don't hate her near as much as I hate them. Maybe I'll get stronger if I start at the bottom. I just don't want to have to run and hide behind others for the rest of my life.

"Anyhow, I promise not to hurt anyone. And, I promise to call the moment I feel the rage bubble. Can I go home now? I'm tired."

"Sure. Let me get you out of this. I'll drop you off."

Dr. Matthews released Adrena from the restraining jacket, and Adrena asked anxiously, "Am I still invited to the wedding, Doc? I'll understand if you've changed your mind."

"I have not changed my mind. We'll discuss it next week. Before you leave, I want your grandmother's address and telephone number. I may stop by to check on you."

Too tired to think anymore, Adrena nodded. She let the good doctor drop her off at home and fell asleep without dinner. Incredibly, Adrena's headache didn't return after the episode in Doc's office. It wasn't there on Thursday or Friday morning. The nightmares didn't come either. Maybe there really was something to facing your tormentor. It didn't matter. Adrena's plans for extracting nothing less than payment in full from those who had carelessly destroyed her innocence had not been altered one iota by her progress - real or imagined.

Chapter Ten

The inner turmoil Vivian was experiencing for allowing Adrena to deal with her tormentors on her own terms had followed Vivian to the Board Room. If anything happened to Adrena . . . or anyone else . . . Vivian would hold herself responsible for the rest of her life. For the first time in her career, Vivian doubted herself.

"Have you changed your mind about marrying me, Vivian? After Lula's nonsense this weekend, I can't say I would blame you."

Blinking away her mind's rambling thoughts of Adrena, Vivian asked, "What are you talking about? I haven't changed my mind about anything, Howard. Marrying you, I'm sure about. Other things I've done, I'm not."

"Like what?"

"My patient lost control today. I had to have them restrained. They had a face-to-face with someone who played a key role in creating their problems. It was their first honest release of long-suppressed rage. I expected it - they wouldn't have been human if there wasn't a reaction. Honestly, I was proud of the way they handled themselves through the entire encounter. Even without medication, it only lasted about half an hour before I was able to let them go home. Still, I know they have a track record of venting when provoked, and it worries me."

"Are they dangerous, Vivian?"

"Potentially. Medication and therapy have brought them a long way. If only I could tell you how far this patient has come, Howard, you would understand why I feel the way I do. I just don't feel hospitalization will help them, although my colleagues might not agree with me. I think institutionalization tends to confirm psychosis in the minds of borderline patients - if you believe you're crazy, you act it out."

"Lula has never been institutionalized, and she acts out every chance she gets, Vivian. Ignoring her doesn't register."

Vivian laughed and said, "I'm not ignoring my patient, Howard. I'm listening to them. Giving them enough rope to swing, or hang themselves. The only problem is, if they hang, a huge piece of me will choke with them."

"If it's going to have a negative impact on you, Vivian, you should put them away. It's better to be safe than sorry. Besides, I don't like the idea of my future wife betting her sanity on one insane patient."

"I hate telling you this, sweetheart, but your future wife bets on them every day. She's built her life on the bet. Been reasonably successful. You have to come from where I do to understand the importance of a smile."

"Where do you come from, Vivian?"

Blinking slowly and speaking softly, Vivian said, "From a mother I can't ever remember smiling."

Concerned, Howard asked, "What do you mean?"

"My mother never smiled, Howard. She suffered with an acute manic-depressive disorder my entire life. Of course, they didn't call it that back then. She was, for all intents and purposes, merely crazy. Today, I know my mother could have been helped with antidepressant drugs, exercise, and therapy. As a child, all I knew was that Mommy never smiled. Happiness eluded her every day."

"Was she ever put into a mental institution, Vivian?"

Speaking as if from a distance, Vivian said, "No, Howard. My father adored my mother. He refused to have her shut away. Even when she went for weeks without saying a word and yelled like a raving maniac when she finally did. He never gave up hoping she would bounce back to being the beautiful, smiling woman he loved and married. He did everything humanly possible to make life easier for her.

"Daddy took care of Max and me most of the time and paid a babysitter when he couldn't. My mother cleaned and cooked in undisturbed silence. She never bathed us, combed our hair, or held us. All of that and every kiss we ever received came from our father. She didn't hit or hug us. Sometimes, it seemed like she didn't know we were there.

"One day, Daddy took Maxine and me for ice cream. Afterwards, we played in the yard for about an hour until Daddy said it was time for dinner. The three of us walked into the house. My mother wasn't preparing dinner in the kitchen, and Daddy went from room to room, calling her name, for what seemed like hours. She never answered. With Max and me on his heels, Daddy went down to the basement. All Max and I saw that day was Mama's shadow. I remember wondering why Mama's feet were so still . . . in the air, on the wall. Mama had finally freed herself from the private hell that no one understood but her.

"She hung herself on a magnificent, sunny, spring day. I recall there only being one cloud in the sky when Max and I ran up and down the yard. Today, I know that one cloud was the only thing Mama saw in the sky that afternoon.

"So, now you know. Every smile I get from my patients is a personal victory. Each one is so important to me, Howard."

"Jesus, Vivian. I'm sorry."

Vivian patted the back of Howard's hand and said, "You don't have to be sorry, sweetheart. It was a long time ago. I've learned to live with it. Let's talk about something on a happier note. We're getting married in less than a month."

"We sure are. Have you made any decisions?"

"Not really. How about you?"

"Aw, c'mon, Vivian. If I don't like what you say, I'll tell you. Where? What time? Where are we going afterwards? For how long?"

"Okay. We'll have the ceremony at my house. At two in the afternoon. When we come back from wherever, we'll discuss the stripes on your walls."

"Okay. I'll give up four days. We'll spend five days in Aruba and the other five in Argentina. I hear Valle de Las Lenas is a great summer ski spot. Please don't say you don't have a passport, Vivian. I know better."

"Fine, Howard. Aruba and Argentina it is. We'll probably come home with pneumonia, but if that's the best you can do, I'll accept it. Is there snow in South America in July?"

"Sure. There's always snow in the mountains. It's plentiful and powdery. The sun beams so bright, you can ski without a jacket, sunbathe, and swim. You'll love it."

"I don't ski, Howard. I swim and sunbathe. Are you making these reservations?"

"Yes, I'll do them. I'm not trusting you with Argentina. I'll wind up in Arizona."

"If there was a decent beach in Arizona, I might like it. Hot, without the water, doesn't work for me."

"We'll put your house up for sale when we get back. I don't want to get married with the sign on the lawn."

Frowning, Vivian asked, "Can't I lease it out for a year?"

"Why?"

"I hate parting with it, Howard. It's mine."

"You can lease it if you'd like. Of course, we could live there if you'd prefer."

"No, your house is bigger. With a few renovations, I might even learn to like it. If we ever have children, your house would be best."

"Yeah. When we have children, my house would be best. I have more rooms. Since you brought up the subject, when are you getting rid of those damned birth control pills?"

"After the honeymoon."

"Before."

"No, Howard. After."

"Why, Vivian? What difference does it make? What are you holding on to them for?"

"Because I'd like to know what my body is going to do on my honeymoon."

Howard frowned and said, "I don't think I want you to explain that. Just know they go when we get back. Time is of the essence. As it is, we won't be able to retire before sixty-five."

"I hear you, sweetheart. How are things working out with Sheldon?"

A gruesome scowl covered Howard's handsome face when he said, "He's still with me. Clayton's babysitting him tonight. My house is probably filled with naked dancing girls right this minute. Those two are laid back with togas on. Fat cigars dangling from their mouths. Being finger-fed ripe, seedless grapes. Throwing the stems on the floor."

"Oh? Did you say you wouldn't be going home tonight?"

"No. I probably should. Vivian, Sheldon is the oldest teenager in the world. I'm not kidding. The last time he was thrown out of his house was for throwing a keg party while Charlene was at her mother's. Not one girl there was over twenty-two."

Laughing hysterically, Vivian asked, "How long did he stay with you that time?"

"A month. I can't take him for another month."

A sudden thought made Vivian stop laughing. She asked, "Howard, are you going to start acting like Sheldon?"

"Please, Vivian. If I do, don't leave or throw me out. Hospitalize and drug me. Don't hesitate. Sheldon is the most irresponsible grown man I know. He's actually worse than Clayton."

"What if Charlene won't let him come back, Howard?"

"She will. Charlene knows Sheldon well. She's upset because Lula rubbed her face in it."

"Let's get one thing straight, Howard. If you ever give Lula ammunition to embarrass me like that, you won't be coming back."

"Knowing my insecurities the way you do, Vivian, do you really think I would do that?"

"I've seen and heard of stranger. Just don't try it with me. I mean it. Let's eat."

Chapter Eleven

Adrena arrived at her grandmother's ancient, red brick house at three on Friday afternoon. She looked up and down the neat, tree-lined street. Adrena saw the grandchildren of her grandmother's neighbors riding their bicycles, jumping rope, and playing jacks on the sidewalk - all of the carefree activities Adrena had been denied by the woman dying in this house because her mother was a junkie.

Adrena listened to the sounds of grandparents calling to one or the other. Telling them to be careful. Not to hit each other. Threats of having to come in the house rang here and there.

Adrena stood on the green, wooden porch and breathed in the scents of pine trees, fried chicken, candied yams, and pound cakes. The Ajax and bleach they used to scrub those marble steps hung in the air permanently. Nothing much had changed.

In her mind's eye, Adrena saw her grandmother, broom in hand, standing on this very porch. She wore a crisply ironed, flowered shirtwaist dress and fluffy, powder blue slippers. Her mixed gray hair, curled tightly and protected by a hairnet. A touch of lipstick.

Adrena remembered the scowl on her grandmother's face as she watched Mildred drag the filthy, five-year-old Adrena down the street and stop at her porch stoop. The way Grandma sucked her teeth, rolled her eyes, and sighed as Mildred told some tale of woe Grandma wasn't buying. The haughty way Grandma, without ever saying one word, spun around and slammed this very door in Mildred's face, never once acknowledging Adrena's presence. Never looking into her pleading eyes. These unpleasant memories threatened to derail Adrena's mission. She abandoned them, and sixteen-year-old Adrena pressed the doorbell.

After waiting for a few moments, realizing she hadn't heard any ring, Adrena knocked. She heard footsteps making their way to the front door. The reality of the situation slammed Adrena in the chest as she listened to the approaching footfall. Adrena's fear gave her two conflicting messages. The first, "Run!" The second, "If you run, don't bother going back to school or back to the Stanleys. Forget music and stop wasting Doc's time, too. Stay put! Face the demons! Take your life back!"

A woman with a brightly flowered top and white slacks opened the door and asked, "May I help you?"

A frightened Adrena responded, "My name is Adrena Reynolds. I'm here to take care of my grandmother."

The nurse extended her hand, smiled warmly and said, "Hi, Adrena. I'm Kira McIntyre, the visiting nurse. I'll show you everything you'll need to know to take care of your grandmother."

Adrena stared at Kira's hand for a few moments. Took a deep breath, steeled herself, and shook hands. The touch of Kira's hand made Adrena shudder slightly. She swallowed hard on the involuntary reflux acid burning her throat.

Kira asked, "Are you all right, Adrena? Don't be afraid. Your grandmother's care is really simple, once you've got the hang of it. Have you seen her lately?"

Still shaken by the handshake, Adrena mumbled, "No, I haven't seen her since I was a little girl."

"Well, come on in. We'll take one step at a time. Mrs. Brown is lucky to have a granddaughter. So many of the elderly and terminally ill have no one."

Adrena followed Kira into her grandmother's living room. Every piece of furniture was exactly where it had been the last time Adrena remembered being there. Plastic-covered, golden brocade, French Provincial chairs, in mint condition, displayed to perfection on the sculptured, dark green carpeting. Marble coffee and end tables. Huge, ornate gold-and-white lampshades on tall, delicate lamps. The floor model television in its mahogany cabinet, with the radio and stereo inside, and the lighted bar on the side. The antique, gilded mirror hung over the mantle, adorned with elaborately framed pictures.

Adrena chuckled when she saw her baby picture was there. She could have eaten for a week on what Granny paid for that frame. Old Grandma was a real gem. Treasure a picture and throw away the child.

Kira interrupted Adrena's survey with, "Would you like to go up to see Mrs. Brown first, Adrena? If not, I can take you into the kitchen and go over her medications with you. I've written them all down and the times she has to take them."

Not totally recovered from mustering the courage to stay, followed by Kira's handshake, Adrena said softly, "The kitchen."

As they walked through the dining room, Kira asked, "Have you ever taken care of an elderly person before?"

"No. I've never taken care of anyone. Young or old. Can she talk?"

"No, Adrena, she doesn't talk anymore. The stroke has paralyzed her mouth and esophagus. You'll have to feed and medicate her through the tube in her stomach."

Mere fear turned to terror, and Adrena asked, "What?!"

"You'll have to do everything for Mrs. Brown. She can't do anything at all, Adrena. Feed, bathe, change diapers, roll, medicate. You name it. If you can't, she'll have to go into a hospice. Personally, I think that would be the appropriate place for her. At best, she's only got a few weeks to go. I don't know why anyone insisted on bringing her home."

"Mildred told me Grandma insisted on coming home."

Kira looked at Adrena as if she had suddenly sprouted antenna and said, "Your grandmother hasn't been able to insist on anything for quite some time, dear."

"She hasn't?! I guess Mildred's done a few too many Ludes. She probably heard Granny say a lot of stuff nobody else heard. Who gave you the key to get in?"

"Your grandmother's attorney was here when we arrived at noon. Mrs. Brown has a restraining order against someone named Mildred. She can't come within five hundred feet of this house. If she does, you're supposed to call the police immediately. The order is there on the dining room table."

"Miss McIntyre."

"Call me Kira."

"Kira, I know my questions seem stupid, but I haven't had anything to do with my family for six years. Did Mildred ever visit my grandmother at the hospital?"

"Are you listening to me, Adrena? Mildred can't come anywhere near your grandmother. According to the papers on the dining room table, Mildred and a few others haven't been very nice to Mrs. Brown. One of them broke her hip. If you want to know what I think, I'll be more than happy to tell you, Adrena."

Adrena nodded.

"Your granny has more than a few pennies in the bank. That lawyer told your mother the stipulations involved in order to get them, and I'll bet the house, farm, and tractor Mrs. Brown has documents saying nobody gets a dime if she dies anywhere other than this house. You're probably the only blood relative she doesn't have a restraining order against. There's one for Mildred, Bartholomew, Antoinette, Arnold, and Clive. Are there any other children?"

"Not that I know of. Arnold and Clive? Who are they?"

"Your cousins, I guess. Oh, before I forget, the lawyer said you are to call him when Mrs. Brown expires. No one else. If you need personal items, such as groceries or cabfare, call him. His card is with the papers."

"Is he going to bury her?"

"Probably."

"Okay. I should have known Mildred was full of it. I'm ready now, Kira. You can show me everything and take me up to meet the old lady."

Kira produced the list of things Adrena had to do, including times and step-by-step procedures. Mrs. Brown's medication was administered through her feeding tube. The capsules had to be opened, put into water and poured into the tube. The feeding tube had to be thoroughly flushed out and replaced after each feeding. Mrs. Brown's diaper was to be changed every three to four hours. To prevent bedsores, she had to be shifted from side to side or turned over every six hours. A simple sponge bath and a little lotion every day would take care of any body odors.

Adrena was caught unaware when Kira said, "You'll have to give her one-half of a Valium with every meal."

Confused, Adrena asked, "Why? If she's out of it, how can she be nervous?"

"She's addicted to them. It's too late to put her into rehab. The doctor says to just give her enough to fend off the withdrawal."

"Are you telling me Granny's a druggie too, Kira?"

"I almost hate to say yes, because this is not her fault. Some irresponsible doctor created this druggie. She's been taking Valium or Librium every day for over twenty years. Nobody should be doing that, Adrena."

"Wow, that's deep. I come from a long line of druggies. No wonder I'm such a mess!"

Just as they were about to go upstairs, there was a knock at the door, and Adrena went to see who it was. Relief flushed all the fear from Adrena, and her body refilled with a foreign, euphoric sensation when she saw Dr. Matthews through the tiny window. Adrena threw the door open and said, "Hi, Doc. Come in. We were just going up to see Granny."

Surprised by Adrena's cheerful greeting, Dr. Matthews said, "Hi, Adrena. Is everything all right?"

Still smiling, Adrena said, "Sure, Doc. This is Kira. She's the nurse. She showed me how to do Granny's stuff. Now she's going to show me Granny herself. Kira, this is Dr. Matthews. She's my friend."

While Kira and Dr. Matthews shook hands and began to discuss Mrs. Brown's condition, Adrena saw Mrs. Stanley parking her car. Tears formed in her eyes when she saw how supportive and concerned both Doc and Mrs. Stanley were being. If only the dying creature up those stairs had been half as caring, none of this would have been necessary. Adrena stood in the doorway and waited for Mrs. Stanley. Of course, she brought Adrena's dinner.

Everyone exchanged greetings with Mrs. Stanley. Kira, Adrena, and Dr. Matthews headed up the stairs; Mrs. Stanley took Adrena's dinner to the kitchen and then followed the group.

Adrena tried to remember the last time she had been up those stairs and couldn't. Maybe she had never been up them. Knowing picky, old Granny she probably wasn't allowed.

At Granny's bedroom door, Dr. Matthews said, "Let me go in first, Adrena."

In no particular hurry to see what was in that room, Adrena said, "Okay, Doc."

Soft conversation between Kira and Dr. Matthews wafted into the hall, as Mrs. Stanley came up the stairs. She stood there with Adrena. For some reason, Mrs. Stanley kept shaking her head.

Adrena asked, "What's the matter, Mrs. Stanley?"

With anger tainting every word, Mrs. Stanley said, "You shouldn't be here. This woman needs things you don't know anything about. Why should a child have the dirty duty of watching someone die? Especially someone who wasn't there for them."

"How did you know she wasn't there for me? I never told you that."

"I can add, Adrena. You're with me. If you had a grandmother who acted like a grandmother, you wouldn't be. I don't know what else happened to you either, but I know it was horrific. You're still in therapy six years later. And Dr. Matthews only makes personal appearances when she thinks something wrong is happening with you. Am I right?"

Adrena considered denying it. Making up a few lies to explain what was happening. Deciding it wasn't worth the trouble, she said, "You're absolutely right, Mrs. Stanley. I just did this to keep Mildred from bothering us. She threatened to file for custody. Even if Mildred couldn't get me, like Doc said, everyone would have to dance to her tune until the judge said stop. I get here and find out it isn't Granny who really needs me here - Mildred needs me here to make sure she can collect her inheritance."

Mrs. Stanley yelled, "What?!"

Adrena put her finger up to her lips and made a shushing sound.

Mrs. Stanley quieted and mumbled, "I don't care what you say, you're not staying here by yourself. These people make my flesh crawl, and I don't even know them. I'm gonna be right here with you."

Adrena giggled. Mrs. Stanley was serious. Nothing and nobody stood a chance of destroying Adrena, without a fight with her first.

Dr. Matthews came to the door and motioned them into the room. She watched Adrena with intensity. She saw Adrena take that deep breath to steady herself and the light film of perspiration form on her face.

Adrena walked over to the bed and looked down on the pitifully emaciated body of her grandmother. Mrs. Brown slept peacefully, curled in a fetal position, with her toothless mouth wide open. The only feature Adrena recognized was her grandmother's hairline. Her hair had gone completely gray and thinned. There were no curls or hairnet on it now. The nurses at the hospital had braided it neatly.

Kira came over, pulled the cover back, and proceeded to show Adrena how to change her grandmother's diaper and manipulate the feeding tube. She showed her all of the tricks of the trade to avoid hurting herself while caring for a completely disabled patient, the key being rolling and propping. Bathing and changing diapers or the bed could be done almost effortlessly if you knew what you were doing. Adrena stood quietly, watching everything Kira showed her.

Mrs. Brown's eyes opened just as Kira replaced her coverlets. Her gaze calmly rested on Kira for a while. Then, she saw Adrena. Mrs. Brown's body tensed immediately. Her right arm started to twitch and swing, as if out of control. She furiously struggled to communicate. The spasms in her neck and face appeared to be making her head turn backwards. She began to choke on spittle and her lifeless tongue. Kira tilted Mrs. Brown so that she wouldn't choke to death and tried to comfort her. It took a while for anyone to surmise Mrs. Brown was attempting to point at the door. She never took her horror-filled eyes off Adrena's face. Everyone in the room knew Mrs. Brown wanted her to leave.

After watching her grandmother's agonized struggle for a while, Adrena said calmly, "I'm Adrena. Not Mildred." Mrs. Brown's physical twitching stopped. She waved her good arm toward her own body. She wanted Adrena to come closer. With her fists clenched, Adrena bent forward, so her grandmother could get a better look at her. The perspiration on Adrena's face thickened. Her teeth clamped together tightly.

Dr. Matthews saw all of this. She wanted to see if Adrena could make herself touch her grandmother without repercussions.

Adrena fought valiantly with her demons for composure, and the intensity of her battle became evident when Mrs. Brown touched Adrena's face. The moment Mrs. Brown's cold, shaking hand made contact with her face, Adrena gasped loudly, closed her eyes, trembled violently for a few seconds, and then exhaled slowly. She opened her eyes sluggishly and stilled herself.

Dr. Matthews said adamantly, "Adrena, you can't do this."

Looking defiantly into her grandmother's eyes, Adrena responded, "Yes, I can, Doc. I can and I will. Please don't try to stop me."

"Why not? You don't owe this woman a thing. Is all of your progress worth gambling on this?"

"If I can't do this, Doc, I have no need for progress. I'll never be able to use it. Can't you see she's only a bar in my prison? How do I get out of the cell if I can't snap one little old bar?"

"Okay, Adrena. If you lose one night's sleep, I'm ending this. Do you understand?"

"Yes."

Mrs. Stanley injected, "Don't worry, Doc, I'll be here with her. Adrena's not staying in this house alone. I don't care what point she has to prove."

Dr. Matthews gave a deep sigh of relief and kept any other objections to herself.

Kira asked, "Would you like to do her feeding and meds while I'm here, Adrena?"

Adrena nodded slowly. Then she finally looked at Dr. Matthews and said, "Read over the papers on the dining room table, Doc. That should relieve you some."

"Why? What do they say?"

"Just read them, Doc."

Adrena saw Dr. Matthews and Mrs. Stanley look at each other briefly and they both headed for the stairs. As Adrena and Kira made their way to the kitchen, they heard Dr. Matthews say, "This is a formal notice of occupancy and deed made out to Adrena Reynolds. Technically, Adrena could throw Mrs. Brown right out the front door anytime she feels like it. This house and all of its contents have been hers for more than two years."

Mrs. Stanley responded, "I can't make head or tails of what's going on with this family. The grandmother leaves Adrena in foster care for years, without so much as a phone call; then, she asks the child to take care of her until she dies, in exchange for the home she wouldn't share with Adrena before she became infirm. Do you understand any of it, Dr. Matthews?"

"At this juncture, I'm just as confused as you are, Mrs. Stanley. Will you really be able to stay here with her? Adrena doesn't always like to acknowledge her own fragility. If anything happens to her, or to Mrs. Brown, I'm going to wish I insisted she not do this."

"At the most, she'll only have to spend an hour alone - I have to take care of my husband a little, you know. Oh, by the way, congratulations on your engagement. Maybe you'll have some babies of your own to try to figure out and run behind now."

Laughing, Dr. Matthews replied, "Not if they don't come soon, Mrs. Stanley. I'm not new."

"Depends on who you're talking to, honey. From where I'm standing, you're new."

Adrena gritted her teeth and did what she had to do. With the help of Kira, Adrena prepared her grandmother's meal and medication and poured it into her feeding tube. Adrena dropped the bowl when her grandmother's hand moved toward her face. A tremor of revulsion rattled Adrena, but she conquered it quickly.

An hour after Mrs. Brown's feeding, Dr. Matthews and Kira left. Mrs. Stanley and Adrena agreed it might not be such a good idea to leave her grandmother unattended overnight. They would spend the night, run home in the morning, pack a few things and return. Mr. Stanley could join them at Mrs. Brown's if he liked; if not, he would have to fend for himself for a little while.

The ringing telephone made Mrs. Stanley and Adrena jump. Neither one knew where the telephone was, and Mrs. Stanley saw it first. She pointed to it, and Adrena answered.

Without so much as a hello, Mildred said, "Did Mama get home all right?"

Completely devoid of emotion, Adrena said, "Yes."

"How is she?"

"Dying."

"Did you find those insurance papers?"

"No."

"Call me when you do.

"Why?"

"Because I'm gonna need that money when Bart comes home in a few weeks. We're gonna need someplace to live. I'm getting evicted from here real soon. Do you think we could come stay there without Mama knowing?"

"Git a grip, Mil, you're not coming in here."

"If you got the key and the nurse don't see us, why not? You wouldn't put your own family out on the street, would you?"

Drunk with the power Mildred had just bestowed on her, Adrena laughed hysterically. Her mind screamed, "Mom, I'm gonna give you a permanent residence soon enough . . . in hell!" When she could speak again, Adrena said slowly, "Yes, I would. In the middle of a blizzard. In a heartbeat."

"To hell with you then. Just call me the minute you find those damn papers. I'm moving in the day Mama dies anyway."

Adrena hung up the telephone and let the laughter slide up her spine and out of her mouth. If Granny hadn't given

Adrena anything else, she had given her some real good laughs at Mildred's expense.

Mrs. Stanley looked at her and asked, "Who was that? And what's so funny?"

"That was my mother. She wants me to give her Granny's insurance policies. Then she asks if I would let her stay here without anybody knowing. Not just her either. She wants to bring my stepfather over, too - after he gets out of jail! She got mad when I said no. I bet you can't even guess what she said next."

Not getting the humor in this, Mrs. Stanley said, "No, I can't guess. You tell me."

"She thinks she's moving in here the day Granny dies."

That's when Mrs. Stanley got the joke. Adrena's mother obviously didn't know the house had already been deeded to Adrena. Without custody, she couldn't come anywhere near Adrena. However, Mrs. Stanley didn't know how good it felt for Adrena to have the upper hand on Mildred, or how Mildred's emotional squirm tickled the hatred that had become such a large part of Adrena. Still, the two laughed at Mildred's foolishness together, although even to Adrena, the laughter seemed eerily out of place in her grandmother's living room, while she lay upstairs, slowly dying.

Mrs. Stanley and Adrena made themselves comfortable watching the television in the living room. They took turns running upstairs to check on Mrs. Brown. At ten, Mrs. Stanley thought they should start looking for bedding. Somehow, without a conscious memory of ever being upstairs in her grandmother's home, Adrena knew exactly where it was kept.

Mrs. Stanley and Adrena examined the middle bedroom and found it to be in very good shape. The room was clean, and the bed looked comfortable, but when Mrs. Stanley suggested Adrena sleep there, Adrena said, "Not me. This was my mother's room. I'll take the back room; if not, I'll sleep on the sofa."

After making the bed, Adrena decided she needed to take a shower before turning in. Without checking to see if everything she needed was in the bathroom, Adrena absentmindedly adjusted the temperature of the shower. She took off her clothes and viciously kicked them toward the hamper. Adrena stepped inside the stall, felt the rush of hot water against her skin and clenched her fists tightly. A tiny, uncontrolled tremor began in Adrena's ankles and slowly climbed up her calves. The squeal of rage growing in her throat threatened to choke her if she didn't allow it out into the air. She clamped down on her jaw, gripped the washcloth and pulled it tight. That squeal would surely bring Mrs. Stanley running, and Adrena could not have that happen.

Weeping silently and trembling from head to toe, Adrena scrubbed at her face and body violently. She had to get the feel of her grandmother's touch off her. She washed, wept, and shook for thirty minutes. The time she spent harnessing the rage gave Adrena a greater sense of her emotional power, but as the rage dissipated she felt physically weaker than before.

The moment Adrena turned off the tap, Mrs. Stanley knocked on the door, asking, "Are you all right, Adrena?"

"I'm fine. I'll be out as soon as I lotion myself. Would you see if my grandmother has a slip I can sleep in, please?"

"Okay. Do you need a Halcion to sleep?"

"Yes, but I didn't bring one. I'll be all right without it."

"No, you won't. I have one in my purse for you."

"You're turning into a traveling dispensary, Mrs. Stanley. Thank you."

An exhausted Adrena Reynolds examined herself in the mirror. Other than the small red welts on her face, arms, and hands, she looked normal. If she could get the pill and the slip without Mrs. Stanley seeing her, everything would be fine.

As she hoped, Mrs. Stanley passed the slip and the pill through the bathroom door without peering in at the possibly naked Adrena. Adrena slid the slip over her head and washed the pill down with water from the sink. As she headed for her room, Adrena said goodnight to Mrs. Stanley.

There was a sigh of relief when Adrena sat down on the bed. This room had belonged to her aunt, Antoinette. Adrena had no feelings about her at all - had never met her, that she could recall. Adrena only knew her aunt's name because people used to ask Mildred about her sister all the time. Adrena might be able to sleep in Antoinette's bed, without scratching every inch of her skin off. However, as it turned out, Adrena lay sleepless in her aunt's bed, devising a plan to end her grandmother's misery.

She couldn't give Granny an overdose of her own medication; Kira would catch the shortage right away. God knows, Adrena didn't want to give her any of hers. She decided she would give Granny the package she had intended for Harvey - powdered castor beans from Mr. Stanley's hothouse. It was just fine enough to pass through that tube with her regular feeding.

Before Adrena drifted off to sleep, she mentally ran through the deadly scenario for her grandmother many times. Adrena turned each act and observed it from every angle. Finally, she viewed the end result through the eyes of all involved parties - Mrs. Stanley, Kira, her grandmother's physician and lawyer, the authorities, and the most important and knowledgeable critic of them all, Dr. Vivian Matthews.

Chapter Twelve

On Tuesday morning, both Adrena and Mrs. Stanley were in the room with Mrs. Brown when she died. They tilted her and checked her mouth for obstructions, just as Kira had shown them. Mrs. Brown had not suffocated.

Kira arrived ten minutes after Mrs. Brown stopped breathing, confirmed that she was in fact dead, and automatically went to check her remaining medication. Seeing that all of the medication added up properly, Kira was satisfied. Mrs. Brown obviously was not overmedicated, and, as far as Kira could tell, the elderly woman had simply stopped breathing.

The news of Mrs. Brown's death hit Dr. Matthews like a loaded train. Three days. Kira told Dr. Matthews she probably had about three weeks. Knowing that no one could clinically call it to the minute didn't make Mrs. Brown's rapid demise any easier for the doctor to swallow.

Dr. Matthews arrived at Mrs. Brown's home forty-five minutes after Adrena called her. Adrena said she hadn't gone to school that morning because her grandmother's breathing appeared to be labored, and there had been a bout of nausea during the night. Dr. Matthews knew that heart patients often became nauseated before an impending attack.

After giving Mrs. Brown's body a cursory scanning for obvious signs of foul play, Dr. Matthews asked Mrs. Stanley, "Has Adrena been alone with her grandmother at all this weekend?"

"No, she hasn't."

"Did Adrena have any extra medication with her?"

"Well, you know that Adrena's not allowed to carry more than one pill at any given time. She's not allowed to carry any medication on school premises. I had to personally give

Adrena a sleeping pill two nights in a row. I also dispensed her other medications."

"Are you sure she took them?"

"As sure as I can be. Adrena slept through both nights, Dr. Matthews. She hasn't had an anxiety attack or any of the other strange stuff she goes through when she doesn't take her medication."

Dr. Matthews found absolutely nothing that could point to Adrena as being connected to Mrs. Brown's death. Because Mrs. Brown was terminally ill and was officially under hospice care, there would be no autopsy. Not being Mrs. Brown's physician, Dr. Matthews could not request that any tests be performed on the body without filing a police report and couldn't file a police report without giving a reason for her suspicion. In fact, she could attach her license to such a report if she mentioned Adrena since, like priests and lawyers, psychiatrists are bound by oaths of confidentiality and cannot take steps leading to the conviction of their clients.

No one of consequence questioned Mrs. Brown's passing. Mr. Lewis, her attorney, came to the house and called the coroner and funeral director Mrs. Brown had designated in her papers. The coroner pronounced Mrs. Brown dead, and the funeral director whisked her away. She was to be buried without a funeral and had requested that no one be notified until she was in the ground. Mrs. Brown's wishes were followed to the letter; she was buried unceremoniously beside her late husband on Wednesday morning.

After determining that Mrs. Stanley was Adrena's custodian, Mr. Lewis told her he would be reading Mrs. Brown's will on Friday morning in his office. He suggested that she should attend on behalf of Miss Reynolds so that there would be no contact with Mildred and other family members who would be present. Mrs. Stanley agreed and insisted that Dr. Matthews be there, too.

As the undertaker quietly removed Mrs. Brown's remains, Adrena sat alone in the living room, with a bland expression on her face. None of the details interested her. Mrs. Brown's passing only mildly relieved her; gleeful satisfaction didn't come and wasn't expected. Adrena hadn't held as much animosity toward her grandmother for abandoning her to Mildred and Bart's madness as she held for Mildred and Bart. Adrena's fists and teeth were not clenched. There was no nervous perspiration. No rage. No sadness. No tears.

On Wednesday afternoon, as she waited for Adrena's arrival in her office, Tuesday's events ran through Dr. Matthews' mind again. Millie interrupted her thoughts when she buzzed and announced Adrena was in the office. No one would ever have guessed the beautiful, smiling young lady who bounced into Dr. Matthews' office had just lost her grandmother.

Adrena's smile was genuine when she said, "Hi, Doc. When's the wedding?"

Not returning Adrena's smile, Dr. Matthews said, "Hi, Adrena. It's July thirteenth."

Adrena's smile faded slightly, and she asked, "What's the matter, Doc? Did you change your mind about me coming? Have I done something wrong?"

"Did you do anything wrong, Adrena?"

Excited and confused, Adrena asked, "When?"

"At your grandmother's house."

The light of understanding dawned on Adrena's face. She spoke matter-of-factly, saying, "If you're asking if I helped Granny out, the answer is no, Doc. Why should I? She was better than halfway gone when I got there. Remember?"

"Are you absolutely sure you didn't sprinkle anything into her feeding tube by mistake?"

"I don't make mistakes, Doc. I didn't sprinkle anything. If I had, you know I would tell you. She didn't mean anything to me."

"She didn't help you when you needed her either. Why didn't you ever mention you had a grandmother, Adrena? We never discussed how you felt about her."

"What was there to mention? She refused to feed me when Mildred begged her to? She lived in that big old, pretty, comfortable house while I slept on the floor in the corner of a cold, filthy, one-room efficiency? Other times, in a box in an alley drenched with urine, feces, and vomit? Or, that she completely overlooked me when she passed me on the street? How about the little bit about her refusing to take custody of me after the incident? What part did you think I should have brought up first, Doc?"

"Why wouldn't she help you, Adrena?"

Angrily, Adrena snapped, "How the hell am I supposed to know?! I was a fucking kid caught up in the middle of a bunch of crap I had absolutely nothing to do with! They trashed me! All of them! I was an inconvenience to everybody! My mother, grandmother, aunt! Hey, Doc, where is my father? You never heard me talk about him either. Do you think I killed him, too?"

Running her fingertips over her temples, Dr. Matthews said, "No, Adrena. I don't think you killed him. Do you know who he is? Where he is?"

"All I know about him is that he left a pregnant Mildred on Granny's step one snowy morning. I've never heard anyone call his name. For all I know, Doc, he could be the guy you're getting ready to marry."

"That's not funny, Adrena. Howard wouldn't do anything like that."

"Whatever you say, Doc. All I can tell you is, my family has a stockpile of secrets. Everybody whispering about each other. Saying don't tell so and so, such and such. I still don't know why my aunt and grandmother fell out. Why my aunt refused to take me in." Adrena dropped her head. Tears threatened to fall as she mumbled, "I don't know why nobody wanted me. I don't know anything, but the things I've learned since the incident. I don't know, Doc. I don't know."

"You know how you feel about them, Adrena. Say it."

Seething, Adrena hissed, "I hate those fuckers, Doc. I hate them all. I want them all to die slow, agonizing deaths. But I didn't do anything to Granny. She croaked all by herself."

"Would you kill any of them if you had the opportunity, Adrena?"

"I will never get the opportunity to torture them the way they tortured me. To simply kill them would never satisfy me, Doc. Not to be able to look into their eyes and know they were suffering would be a waste of time."

Knowing Adrena was justified in feeling all of the bitter anger she felt, Dr. Matthews decided to change the subject slightly by asking, "What are your plans for the house?"

Confused again, Adrena asked, "What house?"

"The one you inherited."

"How do you know I inherited it?"

"I read the papers the first evening you were there. Remember?"

The color suddenly drained from Adrena's face when she asked, "Will the state make me go live in it by myself? I don't want to live there."

"You're a minor. They can't do that. You'll probably get some flak from Mildred about it though."

Adrena startled Dr. Matthews when she threw her head back and howled hysterically with laughter. She told her the story about the telephone call from Mildred.

Dr. Matthews thought about it and said, "Adrena, she's going to come after you with a vengeance now. The only way she can get her hands on that house is if she has custody of you."

Off the cuff, Adrena said, "I'd hang myself before I lived ten minutes in her custody."

Without knowing it, Adrena had just pressed Dr. Matthews' panic button. She yelled, "Don't you ever let me hear you say that again, Adrena Reynolds! I haven't wasted my time with you for you to hang yourself! You will not do that! You will not!"

"Okay, Doc. Okay. I was just joking. But, I wouldn't stay with Mildred ten minutes."

"Am I laughing?"

"No."

"Then, it wasn't funny, young lady. Don't you ever say that again."

"You're my psychiatrist. I'm supposed to be able to say whatever is on my mind. If I wanted to hang myself, that's not how you're supposed to stop me."

Knowing Adrena was toying with her didn't lessen Dr. Matthews' anger. She said, "I don't care what I'm supposed to be doing. Don't you ever say that again."

Rolling her eyes and mumbling, like a normal teenager does with a frustrated parent, Adrena said, "I was just joking."

With tears in her eyes, Dr. Matthews said, "Don't ever use hanging yourself in a joking manner with me, Adrena. I will never find humor in it. Never. Are you absolutely sure you've never entertained the idea of suicide?"

"No! I'm sorry, Doc. I didn't mean to upset you."

Dr. Matthews took a few deep breaths and then said, "I want you to be prepared for Mildred's next move. It might be anything, now that you own that house. You may want to sell it to help with your college bills in a couple of years."

Adrena smiled and asked, "Could I sell it and buy a car?"

With that question, Dr. Matthews knew she needed a vacation. Adrena was driving her crazy. She briefly wondered if her own children would do this to her someday. Maybe she should rethink having children. Of course, Howard would be more than a little disappointed.

Adrena asked impatiently, "Well, can I, Doc?"

"Let's cross that bridge when we get there, Adrena. You don't even know how to drive yet."

"You and Mrs. Stanley can teach me, Doc. Please?. I'll be a good student. I promise."

"We'll see, Adrena."

♦ ♦ ♦

It was a dog-tired, frustrated, and tense Vivian who ran into Howard's arms at the Board Room that evening. His greeting kiss and hug helped. His news didn't.

As they sat at their favorite table, in their favorite restaurant, Howard said, "Viv, there's a little problem with our wedding plans."

Vivian's gaze came up from the glass in her hands slowly, her mind suddenly gone numb. Wordlessly, she stared at Howard's pleading face.

"Lula says she's not coming if the wedding is at your house. She thinks we should get married in a church."

Vivian's stare never wavered. She sat completely still, waiting for Howard to explain what that was supposed to mean to her. Vivian was in no mood for Lula's crap.

Howard added nervously, "I know that wasn't our plan, sweetheart, but I would like Lula to be there. She has been like a mother to me. Would it be too much to ask to move it to my house?"

Without taking her eyes off Howard's agonized face, Vivian removed her engagement ring, laid it on the table and rose to leave.

Howard asked anxiously, "What are you doing, Vivian? I just asked a question."

"You asked the wrong question, Howard. There is no way you can take care of me and hold on to Lula's apron string at the same time. Let's just forget the whole thing. I wouldn't want to upset Lula."

Vivian headed for the door. Howard snatched the ring off the table, whispered into Paul's ear and followed. Vivian saw him coming and kept going. She had all she could take for one day. Listening to real problems from nine to five and coming home to Lula's nonsense wasn't exactly what Vivian had in mind. If Howard wanted to kiss his sister's feet for the rest of his life, that was his business. Damned if Vivian was signing on to do it, too.

Vivian's car was parked, and she was in her kitchen making herself a sandwich when Howard rushed in and frantically asked, "Why did you leave like that, Vivian? What's wrong with you? I only asked a question. If you don't want to move the wedding, I understand, but you don't have to call everything off because I asked a question."

Without looking up, Vivian said, "Look, Howard, you asked me to marry you. Not Lula. If I move the wedding, I'll be changing things to suit Lula from now until the day I die. I'm not doing it."

Howard said miserably, "You won't have to do anything to suit Lula, Vivian. I only mentioned it to you because she made such a fuss about us not getting married in a church. We don't have to move it, Vivian."

"I know damn well I don't have to move it, Howard. If I move it anywhere, it will be moved off the calendar. Now, I've had a really rough day. I'm going to eat this sandwich and watch television or something. I don't want to talk about this anymore."

"Well, what are you saying about us, Vivian?"

"I've said it."

"Maybe we should think about this a little more than a month."

Truly pissed by that remark, Vivian said, "Fine. Go see when Lula says it will be all right. Get all of the other details on how it's supposed to go from her, too. Like what we should wear and the right place for our honeymoon. How long we can stay. What would be appropriate for us to do."

"You know it's not like that, Vivian."

"Oh, it's not? Why did Talia have to run away to get married, Howard?"

"That's a long story. We're not them."

"I want to hear it."

"Lula didn't like Teddy from the first moment she set eyes on him. She said he was a hoodlum. That wasn't true. He's a hardworking, nice guy. Teddy loves my little sister with all of his heart and wouldn't hurt her for anything in the world. That's all anybody can ask for. Lula had run off every other guy Talia tried to date for years, but Talia was eighteen when she met Teddy and determined to see him.

"One night, Lula started a great big argument with Teddy. She told him to get out of the house. He refused, like she thought he would, and Lula called the police.

"When the police came, Lula made a lot of noise about wanting him out of her house. Talia told the policeman she was eighteen years old, and Teddy was her guest in the house. That really pissed Lula off. She told the policeman to check Teddy's pockets. Said she knew for a fact he was selling drugs, and she didn't want that shit in her house.

"Teddy's jacket was draped over the banister in the foyer. After the officer pulled out three tiny bags of marijuana and

another with pills in it, they arrested him. He was charged
with possession with intent to sell.

"Lula planted that stuff in Teddy's pocket. She refused to
tell the authorities she did it. Teddy got off with probation,
because it was his first offense. Talia and Teddy took off a
week later and got married. They wouldn't speak to Lula or
come anywhere near her for over a year."

Vivian looked blankly at Howard and asked, "Am I
supposed to wait for Lula to plant something on me? Make
me lose my license to practice? Have my picture splattered
all over the television and newspapers? I don't think so.
Your sister is sick, Howard. She doesn't need a psychiatrist
for a sister-in-law. She needs a psychiatrist, period."

"You can't let Lula do this to us, Vivian. We've done
great for too long to even be having this conversation. Please
put the ring back on, and let's go on as planned. I'm sorry as
hell I ever mentioned Lula."

"No. You keep it until the coast is clear. You'll need both
hands to love me the way I need to be loved, Howard."

Completely frustrated, Howard spun around, cursed and
left. He didn't call Vivian that night, or the next day. When
he tried to reach her at the office on Friday, she was at Mr.
Lewis' office, listening to the reading of Mrs. Brown's will.

Chapter Thirteen

Mrs. Stanley met Vivian in the parking lot of Mr. Lewis' office building where they exchanged warm greetings and then headed for the elevators. Inside, Mrs. Stanley asked, "What do you think this is all about, Doc?"

"Mrs. Brown probably had an insurance policy and some money in the bank. They'll have to divide it, I guess. The house isn't part of her estate because she changed the deed over to Adrena two years ago."

"She can't change Adrena's living with us, can she? I mean, there's absolutely nothing they can say here that will force Adrena to have to move?"

Vivian saw how anxious the thought of losing Adrena made Mrs. Stanley and assured her, "There is absolutely nothing any of these people can do about Adrena. She belongs to you and the state."

Sighing heavily, Mrs. Stanley said, "Okay. Let's get this over with."

They stepped off the elevator and into a hallway filled with arguing people. Vivian recognized only Mildred Hanover, but guessed that the woman Mildred was arguing with was her sister - there was enough of a resemblance for family.

Mildred stopped arguing long enough to leer at Vivian and ask, "What the hell are you doing here?"

Refusing to play into Mildred's hands, Vivian smiled and said, "Good morning, Mrs. Hanover. Mr. Lewis requested the presence of Adrena's guardian at this meeting."

"You ain't her guardian. You're her damn shrink. Where's Adrena? She can think and talk for herself."

"This is her last day of school, Mrs. Hanover. She's in school."

"Don't git smart with me, you uppity bitch. I'll whip your conceited ass for you."

"No, you won't. Excuse us."

Vivian and Mrs. Stanley quietly brushed past the little hostile group, with Mrs. Stanley never taking her eyes off Mildred. Without being told, she knew that was Adrena's mother. Vivian was the least of Mildred's problems. If Mildred played her cards wrong, she would have a problem with the older woman who loved Adrena dearly. Unlike Vivian who was too intelligent and sophisticated to slug her, Mrs. Stanley would have no problem doing it.

A short, pleasant woman directed Vivian and Mrs. Stanley to a small conference room at the end of the hall. She told the two ladies Mr. Lewis would be with them in a moment. Then she asked if the others would be joining them, or staying in the hallway.

Mrs. Stanley and Vivian looked at each other and laughed. Vivian said, "I think they will be joining us, if Mr. Lewis can start before a fight begins!"

The little receptionist said, "I'll pass that information on to him right away."

Two minutes later, Mr. Lewis led the procession of angry people into his office. He shook hands with Vivian and Mrs. Stanley and asked the others to have a seat. Still grumbling, they separated into groups and sat as directed.

Mr. Lewis passed out envelopes with their names on them. He handed Mrs. Stanley one with Adrena's name on it. It was easy to see Adrena's envelope was thicker than the others. With that accomplished, Mr. Lewis took his seat and slowly read the contents of Mrs. Brown's will to a group of people who grew more astonished with every word.

Mrs. Brown left Mildred, Antoinette, and her two sons, one hundred dollars each. She wanted it thoroughly understood this was only done because the law mandated blood relatives be mentioned and bestowed at least one dollar. The extra ninety-nine dollars could be considered an act of generosity or an insult. Mrs. Brown did not care which. In conclusion, Mrs. Brown left the remainder of her estate to Adrena Reynolds, her granddaughter, to be held in trust until her twenty-first birthday. If Adrena Reynolds expired prior to her twenty-first birthday, the estate was to be willed as she wished.

Antoinette and Mildred both jumped up and asked breathlessly, "How much was left?"

Mr. Lewis smiled courteously and asked, "Would you like a complete breakdown, or the bottom line?"

Antoinette snapped, "Break it down."

Mildred growled, "Just give us the damn bottom line. She's my daughter, I've got a right to know."

"Approximately five hundred thousand dollars."

Mildred and Antoinette both screamed, "What?!"

Obviously deriving great pleasure from their reaction, Mr. Lewis smiled somewhat maliciously and said, "Give or take a few thousand, of course."

Antoinette bellowed, "I don't believe you! Where did Mama get that kind of money from?!"

"I'll tell you that your mother lived carefully. She did not squander money, and she inherited from her own parents many years ago. When your father died in the accident at work, fourteen years ago, his insurance came to over two hundred thousand dollars. Double indemnity. Your mother lived comfortably on Mr. Brown's retirement benefits.

"Ten years ago, Mrs. Brown hired the investment firm of Williams and Shaw to invest half of her money. They've obviously done a wonderful job since Mrs. Brown's portfolio with their firm is worth over three hundred thousand dollars today."

Vivian spoke for the first time when she asked, "Did you say Williams and Shaw?"

"Yes. Mrs. Brown's broker is Mr. Howard Shaw. Do you know them?"

Speaking softly, Vivian said, "Yes."

Mildred snapped, "Enough of the small talk. We don't agree with the terms of this will. What can we do to change it?"

With complete confidence, Mr. Lewis said, "Absolutely nothing."

"Adrena gits the money. What about the house?"

"The house has belonged to Miss Reynolds for two years, Mrs. Hanover."

Again, Mildred and Antoinette screamed, "What?!"

Calmly passing out sheets of paper, Mr. Lewis said, "If you all will sign these release forms, I can give you your checks."

Antoinette snapped, "I'm not signing shit! You'll hear from my attorney before the day is over! This is a bunch of bullshit, and it's not over!"

Smiling again, Mr. Lewis said, "Fine. I'll look forward to his conversation."

Antoinette stomped out of the office. Her husband and sons followed silently. Mildred quickly scribbled her name on the form and held her hand out for her check. Mr. Lewis promptly handed it to her.

Mildred glanced over the check and said, "Thanks for nothing. Oh, Doc. You can tell Adrena I'll be filing for custody this afternoon. She won't be spending all of that money by herself."

Mrs. Stanley came out of her seat in a sudden, unexpected flash. Through clenched teeth, she hissed threateningly, "You'd better leave Adrena alone."

"And who the hell are you?"

"Since you don't know, it's none of your business. You'll find out who I am if you bother Adrena. Bet on that."

Nonchalantly folding her check, Mildred said, "I don't really give a damn who you are, lady. That's my kid and I'm gittin' her back."

Heading in Mildred's direction in a menacing manner, Mrs. Stanley snarled, "Not if I break your neck first. You've done all you're doing to that child."

Vivian rose quickly and sprinted over to the two women, planting herself firmly between them. Mr. Lewis moved in their direction also. There were dangerous sparks flying.

Mildred said, "Dr. Matthews, you don't have to help me. That old lady better stay out of my face. Ain't nobody gittin' none of Adrena's money, but me."

Vivian responded calmly, "No one wants Adrena's money, except you, Mrs. Hanover. You will never get Adrena or any of her money. I suggest you abandon the thought."

"The only thing I'm abandoning is this place. My next stop is Child Protective Services."

Mildred sauntered out of that office as if she had just received a million dollars. She really thought she could get at least a half million from Adrena.

Vivian bowed her head and massaged her temples. A stress headache was beginning over her eyes. Tears formed in her eyes as she thought, "There is no way this can all turn out well. Simply blocking custody won't stop Mildred from pestering Adrena. Not for control of that kind of money. In trust or not.

"That insane, drug-driven woman will torment Adrena at every opportunity, and if Mildred dallies in Adrena's presence too long, Adrena will react violently and have to be institutionalized - perhaps, for the remainder of her life. For Adrena, that would be approximately sixty years. God couldn't possibly be that cruel to a child who has already suffered more deeply than most people will ever know. Something has to be done to keep that she-devil away from Adrena."

When Vivian broke the incredible news of the inheritance to Adrena, she responded as if she were bequeathed that kind of money every day. All Adrena wanted to know was when Doc was taking her shopping for a dress and shoes for the wedding. Not wanting to tell Adrena that the wedding had been postponed, Vivian promised they would discuss it at her appointment on Wednesday.

Adrena took the long, white envelope Mrs. Stanley had given her up to her room to read in private. Mrs. Stanley had asked Vivian to put the large manila envelope in her safe deposit box for Adrena. Before opening the envelope she held in her hand, Adrena sat on the side of her bed and thought about what she had done to old Granny.

Mr. Stanley talked all of the time about his greatly loved plants - how they were not only beautiful and rare, but were also medicinal. Of particular interest to Adrena was the castor plant which originated in Africa. It provided the world with the most hated laxative of all times, castor oil, but the beans of the plant were poisonous. Mr. Stanley would pluck them off, dry and powder them. He would sprinkle them on cookie crumbs and put them out for mice and any other varmints venturing into his precious hothouse.

When Mrs. Stanley and Adrena had rushed home on Saturday morning to pack a few things for their stay with Mrs. Brown, Adrena retrieved the little baggie of powdered castor beans from her shoe. Anything Adrena didn't want Mrs. Stanley to find during her inspections, she hid, tightly packed into the toes of her shoes in the closet. There were all kinds of drugs in Adrena's shoes. Old medications she and some of the other children at the hospital, orphanage, or in foster care had been prescribed but never taken.

Adrena hadn't felt the need to use any of her hidden medications on anyone since she had come to live with the Stanleys. She had even thought about throwing them away once but decided that wasn't a good idea. If she ever wanted to give someone a little something, it wouldn't do for it to be her personal medication. Adrena had stolen the castor for her old school chum, Harvey. She didn't want him to get sick, high, delusional, or take a nap. She wanted Harvey, the groper, to drop . . . stone-cold dead.

By Sunday, Adrena had endured all the touching of Granny she could stand without bursting into screams. That afternoon, after watching Adrena prepare Mrs. Brown's liquid concoction and medication, Mrs. Stanley turned to go upstairs to be present when Adrena poured it into the stomach tube.

Adrena soundlessly opened the kitchen drawer where she had stashed the baggie, dumped its contents into the measuring cup, and stirred it with her finger while following Mrs. Stanley up the stairs. Together, at Mrs. Brown's bedside, they watched the thick, milky substance disappear down the tube. Adrena momentarily worried about it clogging. It didn't. The residue was slightly thicker than usual, but Mrs. Stanley didn't notice it. Granny never made a sound.

Late Sunday evening, Granny became nauseated. She vomited violently. After an emergency call to Granny's physician, they did not feed Granny the food supplement anymore. They were instructed to give her Pediacare and half of a Valium until her stomach settled.

Granny held on until Tuesday morning. As Adrena and Mrs. Stanley watched, Granny breathed her last breath, and Adrena breathed her first easy breath since she walked through the front door three days earlier. No more touching, or being touched by those rough, cold, ancient fingers.

Adrena felt no connection to the woman who had left her over half a million dollars and a house. Foremost in Adrena's memory of her grandmother was the fact that Granny did not rescue Adrena from the clutches of Mildred and Bart. Right behind that, Granny refusing to take custody of Adrena after the incident.

As she opened the envelope, Adrena felt absolutely nothing. There was a small, navy blue booklet inside the crisply folded sheets. Adrena saw that her name appeared on the cover. It had Universal Savings and Loan in bold gold letters across the top. Shrugging, Adrena opened it and saw her name and social security number printed inside of the jacket. She flipped the pages until she got to the final entry. Balance: $36,543.19.

Never having stepped inside a bank once in her sixteen years, the balance in the bankbook represented nothing more significant to her than the large numbers used in hypothetical math problems at school. Adrena had hoarded seventy-six dollars of her allowance, and it was the largest sum of money she had ever personally seen. The largest sum she could imagine being real was a hundred dollars. So, not really knowing what the bankbook meant, Adrena laid it aside. She would discuss the book with Doc on Wednesday. Adrena moved on to reading the letter.

Dear Adrena:
I know you probably thought you would never hear from the grandmother who disowned you so early in your life. Know now I am not apologizing.

*Merely explaining. There can be no forgiveness for
my allowing Mildred and Bart to do what they did to
you. I do, however, feel obligated to give you the
hand up life has denied you.*

*Anyway, your mother ran away from home at
twelve, to live with a man your grandfather and I
objected to. He was over thirty years old. We knew
he was only going to use Mildred and toss her out
when he was done with her, which is exactly what he
did.*

*After all of the turmoil we went through with
Antoinette's addiction, Mildred's premature
defection was all we could take. Your grandfather
took Mildred's pregnancy badly. He wanted so
much more for his girls. Worked like a demon
possessed to give them everything they wanted. He
was a good man, Adrena, and had he lived, he
would have rescued you from your mother. I just
didn't have the strength or inclination to fight with
Mildred anymore.*

*Mildred brought you to your grandfather and me
after you were born. She came back briefly when
you were two. When you were three years old, she
went back to the streets and the man who had
abandoned her the first time. He told her the state
would pay them for keeping you, and so Mildred
came back for you. It was a year later when I found
out where the two of you were. Mildred dragged
you to my front door and begged for money every
other day for years. When it was obvious to me she
wasn't feeding you with the money, I cut off the
assistance I was giving her. I had to, Adrena. The
last time I spoke to Mildred, she promised to give
you to me if I gave her a thousand dollars. Like a
fool, or a grandmother who cared, I gave it to her.
Afterwards, she cried and said she couldn't part with
her baby.*

*Mildred didn't care about you. I knew it. I
could see it in her sick, pathetic eyes. She held you
as an insurance policy. A meal ticket. Used you to
bilk me and the system.*

*Do you remember Mrs. Townsend? She was a
church friend of mine. I asked her to look out for*

*you. I sent her clothes and things for you. She told
me how Mildred wasn't half feeding you. Never
sending you to school. That she never bathed you.
My heart ached for you, Adrena. Still, I knew that
was what Mildred was banking on.*

*The day Mrs. Townsend called to tell me what
they had done to you, I became physically ill. How
could my own daughter allow something like that to
happen? How could she sit by and watch her
husband do things like that to his own child? My
husband, God rest his soul, would have had a
hatchet planted in his skull for a lot less.*

Adrena re-read that last paragraph again. Granny must
have made a mistake. Bart was her stepfather. She shrugged
and read on.

*Mildred told the social services people I would
take you when you got out of the hospital. I told
them I would not. If I had taken you, Adrena,
Mildred and Bart would have access to you. Known
exactly where you were. I couldn't risk that.*

*Then, I heard she tried to persuade Antoinette to
take you. Antoinette could just barely take care of
her own family. She didn't want Mildred on her
doorstep every time the state sent a check for you
either. Honestly, the only person in the world your
aunt hates more than me is Mildred.*

*As hard as it is to believe, Adrena, you were
safer wherever you were. Bart would have
prostituted you the way he did your mother. He
called himself preparing her for the street, too, and
she got pregnant with you.*

Adrena sat shaking her head from side to side. Her
grandmother was telling her Bart was her real father. Adrena
had been raped by her real father - not her hateful stepfather.
A sharp pain shot through Adrena's temple, as the thought
fought to take root. Fresh anger bubbled in her soul. No
wonder she was so sick. She had been passed from the loins
of a sick man, to the womb of a sick woman. Started to grow
up with a sense of normalcy and wound up in the cold,

deformed shadow of her sick, perverted parents. They had even tormented poor old Granny until she'd been forced to circle the wagons.

Still, Adrena felt her grandmother could have stayed in touch with her. Visited her in the hospital. Somehow, let her know she was there in spirit, if not in flesh. Adrena shrugged again and continued reading.

> *The bankbook inside this letter has enough money in it to rescue you from any immediate distress you may be in. If you're satisfied with your present living conditions, hold on to it for school. Get an education and take good care of yourself, Adrena. Men who take care of their families either don't exist anymore, or they're harder to find than Camelot.*
>
> *If circumstances dictate the necessity to use your trust fund before your twenty-first birthday, discuss it with Mr. Lewis. If he's satisfied with your reasoning, he will help you get enough out of it to make it through. Learn to live on interest and residuals, Adrena. Make your money work for you, and you'll be fine financially.*
>
> *In closing, I would like to say that it was never the lack of love that stopped me from coming to you. I loved you. Since you're reading this letter, I know you granted my last wish. I would like to thank you for allowing me to die in my own home.*
>
> *May God grant you peace now, Adrena. You deserve it more than anyone else I've ever known.*
> *Loving you from an even greater distance,*
> *Your Grandmother, Hazel Brown*

Speaking to the letter, Adrena said softly, "Why did you wait until now to say you loved me, Granny? I needed your love when I was five. I needed your love when I was in that hospital, with all of those tubes shooting out of everywhere. I was scared to death, Granny.

"All I ever knew was fear. There were always strangers around me. The older I got, the more they gawked at me.

One day, a man asked Bart, 'How much for the girl?' That was all anyone had to ask, Granny."

Tears produced by painful memories began to flow down Adrena's cheeks. The night of horrors played out once again behind Adrena's tortured eyes.

Thinking Adrena was asleep on the stack of dirty clothes in the corner, Bart had said, "It's past time for that girl of yours to start earning, Mildred. She's plenty big enough, and they're asking me what I want for her."

Mildred said, "Hell, what they want with her? She ain't nothin' but a baby."

"That's what they want, Mildred. The little girls is sweetest. She's old as you and Antointette were, ain't she?"

"Damn near, just not quite. What you gonna charge for Adrena, Bart? I'm telling you, she ain't gonna act right. That girl hates to be touched now. She hit me in the face the other day for patting her shoulder. They're gonna have to whip Adrena's ass to git to them drawers."

"Shit, I can git a hundred dollars for her first pop. Yeah, it's time."

Adrena lay in the dark corner trying to imagine what they thought she could do to earn anything. She stole every morsel of food eaten around there. She also cleaned out the wallets of any trick dumb enough to take his pants off or fall asleep in the joint. Bart took her along when he robbed apartments to drop through small windows and open the doors. If they had deadbolts, Adrena passed everything out to him through the window she had climbed in. What Bart had Mildred doing all of those years was out of the question, as far as Adrena was concerned. She wasn't touching anybody, and nobody was touching her.

In the middle of the night, the unexpected ordeal began. Bart scooped Adrena's sleeping body up and threw her down on the bed. Although frightened and confused, the little girl masterfully tussled with the grown man. Adrena fought Bart with such determination that Mildred tried to help him. In an attempt to tie her, Bart twisted Adrena's arm so hard it snapped near her wrist. She let out a high-pitched howl that deafened her attackers. However, it didn't stop them, and the ferocious battle continued.

To subdue her, Bart had to put his knee down on Adrena's chest which made it hard to fight or breathe. Bart wasn't a huge man, but all of his weight concentrated on that one knee in her tiny chest was so painful that it temporarily paralyzed the little girl. He tied one end of something around her wrist, and just as Bart tightened the other end of the noose on the bedpost, he leaned forward, and there was a loud pop. The pressure of Bart's weight and the pull had broken Adrena's collarbone. A pathetic whine was all she could muster for the searing pain. Not only did Adrena feel her collarbone break, every move after made a sickening, crunching sound. Together, Mildred and Bart managed to tie the wounded child's hands to the bedpost.

With Adrena tied, Bart slammed his fist into her face. That was supposed to insure there would be no more screams. It didn't. Mildred shuffled around the nasty room and found a dirty sock. She shoved the stinking thing into Adrena's mouth, slapped her face as hard as she could and yelled, "Shut the fuck up, Adrena!" Adrena only quieted because she was gagging on the moldy sock.

Kneeling on the bed between her legs, a heavily sweating Bart quickly pulled his pants down around his thighs. Before he could touch himself, Adrena squealed, raised both of her feet, and kicked him in the chest. Bart flew off the bed backwards.

Adrena couldn't raise her head to see Bart get up and kick his pants off, but she heard his curses and was terrified.

"You nasty little bitch, you're gonna pay for that! Mildred, get her damn feet!"

Back up on the bed, Bart breathed his putrid, alcohol-saturated breath into her face and squeezed her throat. The lack of oxygen and the pain from her collarbone made Adrena's world swim in and out of focus. Bart grabbed his penis and roughly tried to work himself inside Adrena. He couldn't get in. Using his fingers, he tried to stretch her. When that didn't work, he looked around the trash-strewn room, pointed, and told Mildred, "Give me that fuckin' pop bottle over there in the corner."

Without a complaint about what he was doing or looking even once at the pop bottle, Mildred did as she was told. The bottletop was deeply chipped.

Mildred resumed her position at Adrena's feet. She clamped her bony fingers around Adrena's ankles and said, "Go on, man. Let's git this over with."

After that, Adrena drifted in and out of a nightmare filled with pain and terror. She screamed hysterically when Bart used that bottle like a battering ram into her tiny body. As he did what he started to do in the beginning, Mildred sat smoking a joint and watched nonchalantly. Adrena's tortured cries didn't evoke the slightest maternal flinch from her.

Together, they untied Adrena's wrists and attempted to turn her over. She surrendered another ear-piercing scream and gave Bart a sharp kick in his throat. He grabbed his neck, squirmed, and gasped for air. He was furious when he snatched Adrena's flailing foot and flipped her over. She continued to kick and cry as he shifted her body to penetrate her from behind. The moment he touched her hip, Adrena's efforts to escape escalated. Bart pulled hard and clamped down on Adrena's wriggling hips. Her right hip popped out of the socket. Adrena lay helpless and screaming as Bart repeated the entire scenario from the back.

Mildred sat balled up in the corner. Her eyes never left Bart's face. She worshiped that man.

When the policeman kicked the door in, Adrena thought she was dreaming and faded into unconsciousness. All she heard him say was, "Sweet Jesus. This is a baby. Call the paramedics before she bleeds to death."

With hot, miserable tears flowing down her cheeks and onto the letter she had shredded during her recall of the long-ago helpless fury, Adrena moaned miserably, "I needed your love that night, Granny."

Chapter Fourteen

All Friday afternoon, Vivian pondered calling Howard. After not hearing from him for two days, she wondered if she had gone overboard. He hadn't left any messages for her at home, and she didn't ask Millie if he had called. Millie was already upset enough by the missing ring and the lack of radiance in Vivian's face.

Lula had finally gotten what she wanted all along - to have Howard to herself. Lula's behavior was beyond the empty nest syndrome; she truly seemed to enjoy spreading misery and doled a dose or two out to all of her siblings at every opportunity.

It seemed so silly to Vivian. If Howard were in his early twenties, Vivian might have attempted to understand Lula's fears - might even have stretched her imagination to include some maternal attachment. But Howard was thirty-six, and Vivian had no sympathy, empathy, or understanding for Lula's nonsense.

Vivian was determined that Lula's name was not going to be mentioned every time she and Howard decided to do something. If she didn't stand her ground now, Lula would take the entire hill.

In the two years they had been together, Howard had only mentioned his sister when she was supposedly sick - the occasional nights that they were summoned to Lula's house so Howard could sit with her. Even then, Vivian wondered why Lula's husband wasn't enough. Where were her children? Why didn't she plague the hell out of them?

None of that mattered. Vivian knew what she would stand for and what she would not. Lula could not dictate to her where she could get married, what time the wedding would be, or anything else. She could go straight to hell . . . as long as she didn't take Howard with her.

Before leaving the office, Vivian called Howard's office, and Barb told her Howard had just left for the day. There was a question in Barb's silence, but she didn't ask it. Vivian told her she would try him at home and hung up.

The moment she set her purse down at home, Vivian dialed Howard's home number. A laughing Sheldon answered.

Vivian said, "Hello, Sheldon. You're still in the doghouse, I see."

"Oh, yeah. I may be in it for good this time."

"I'm really sorry to hear that. Is your brother in yet?"

Sounding surprised, Sheldon asked, "He's not with you? I haven't seen the old boy since he left for work Wednesday morning."

"No, he's not here. Okay, Sheldon."

"I'll tell him you called, when I see him."

"Yeah. Thanks."

Before Vivian had the chance to digest what Sheldon said, her doorbell rang. She swallowed hard on the lump in her throat, closed her eyes to stem the tears burning them, and went to answer it. God knows she wasn't in the mood for company this evening. When she opened the door, Howard stood there, drenched in sunlight.

Vivian looked up into the haggard, handsome face of the man she loved more than any other and asked, "Where have you been since Wednesday? Why didn't you use your key?"

An unsmiling Howard responded, "I don't use keys to houses I'm not sure I'm welcome in."

"Okay. That explains the key. Where have you been?"

"Thinking."

"Thinking what? Where?"

"Thinking about us. If we were doing the right thing."

"That explains what. You still haven't told me where."

"At Lula's."

Vivian stepped back and slammed the door shut in Howard's face. Her tears flowed unrestrained, as she snatched up her purse and ran up the stairs. Vivian never felt more surrounded by crazy people in her entire life. She left them at Huntingdon and the office, then came home and was confronted with Lula and Howard.

Using his key, Howard opened the front door and bounded up the stairs to find a weeping Vivian, lying across the bed. He stood next to the bed and asked, "What's the matter, Viv? I don't know what to do. I don't know what's going on."

Crying and stuttering, Vivian said, "I can't deal with your sister, Howard. I don't want to hear her name every time I ask you a question. I need you. Just you. If you're going to say her name every time I ask you a question, let's just forget it. I feel like madness is chasing me."

"Is that what this is all about? My sister?"

"Your sister and my patients. Yes. I come home to you expecting a hug, a kiss and peace of mind. Not to hear your sister's opinion of the plans we've made, Howard - that you're at her house for two nights, without calling, while I'm going crazy by myself."

Howard sat down next to Vivian and gently stroked her back. He didn't say anything for a few minutes. When he spoke, Vivian heard pure sincerity.

"Vivian, you should know by now that you're the most important person in my life. If I had known mentioning any of that to you would have upset you this much, I never would have brought it up. I guess I wanted to think I could negotiate a truce between you two. I see now, that's never going to work."

"Well, what are you going to do about it?"

"Honestly, Viv, I don't know. I can't give you up to please my sister. I love you too much for that. The best I can hope for is that the two of you can learn to live with each other somewhere down the line."

"Not if she's going to keep butting into my business, Howard. We make the decisions about our life, or we have no life together. I don't run to Max and bring her opinions back to you."

Howard fell back on the bed, so he could look into Vivian's eyes and said softly, "I promise not to bring my sister into anything involving us again."

"Are you sure, Howard?"

"I've never been more sure of anything in my life."

Vivian buried her face in Howard's chest and cried her frustrations out. They spent the remainder of the evening quietly. Ordered pizza and beer, watched television and made love. Howard didn't bring up any sensitive subjects. Vivian didn't cry or stare at him. They fell asleep in each other's arms a little after midnight.

At two in the morning, the telephone rang. Blinded by sleep, Vivian scrambled for it. Sure one of her patients was in a crisis, Vivian said quickly, "Dr. Matthews."

The voice on the other end spat sarcastically, "Dr. Matthews? Yeah. Right. Is my brother there?"

Still more than half asleep, Vivian asked, "Excuse me? Who is this?"

"Don't worry about who it is. Just put my brother on the telephone."

"If I don't know who you are, how am I supposed to know who your brother is?"

Howard asked groggily, "Vivian, who are you talking to?"

"I don't know. They don't want to say."

"Who did they ask to speak to?"

Staring at Howard through mere slits, Vivian said, "They want to speak to their brother."

Howard groaned, shook his head, and turned his back to her.

Vivian said to the caller, "I'm sorry, you must have the wrong number." She put the receiver down and curled around Howard's back. Just as she was about to doze off, the telephone rang again. This time, Howard reached over Vivian and answered.

"Yes, Lula?"

Speaking so loudly that Vivian could actually hear every word she was saying, Lula said, "Howard Shaw, don't play games with me! Why didn't you take the telephone from that quack?! You knew it was me! Who does she think she is anyway?! When I call for you, I expect to speak to you!"

"Lula, don't you ever call her anything other than Vivian again! If you don't know how to use the telephone, leave it alone! What the hell do you want?!"

"I want you to come take me to the hospital! My pressure is up, and I'm having pains in my chest!"

"Lula, where is Bruce?"

"He's downstairs somewhere! Probably drunk!"

"The drunk's going to have to take you tonight, Lula. I've already gone to bed, and I'm not coming out again."

"You don't care what happens to me, do you?! Now that you've got Dr. Matthews, you think you're better than everybody else! You don't need me anymore! You are so stupid, Howard! I've seen women like her before! You're nothing but a showpiece for her! The moment you don't do what she wants you to, you'll find out what she really thinks of you! You're setting the stage for a nightmare, Howard Shaw! Dr. Matthews is going to walk off with half of everything you own when it's over!"

"Yeah. Fine. Whatever you say, Lula. Goodnight."

Howard slammed the telephone down and started mumbling, "What is wrong with everybody? Two weeks ago, everybody was fine. Now, everybody's losing their minds. I mention your name to her, she's foaming at the mouth. I mention her name to you, you're throwing your engagement ring back at me. Sheldon's digging in and destroying my damn house. A little more of this, and I'm running away from home."

Vivian giggled and said, "You're not leaving me, Howard. You've already agreed to allow me to drive you crazy for the rest of your life."

"I'm not like you, Vivian. I can't take more than one crazy person at a time. You're screaming and crying. She's screaming and dying. Sheldon's demolition man. I can't take it."

Howard flopped down and threw a pillow over his head. Vivian laughed and snuggled up close to him. She tenderly massaged the taut muscles in Howard's back and kissed him lightly.

Not hearing Howard's familiar snore, she said, "Everything's going to be fine, sweetheart. Change is difficult for some people. Maybe that's what's wrong with your sister. You've been a bachelor for a long time, and she just feels threatened by the thought of another woman taking first place in your life."

Howard mumbled under the pillow, "If that's what's wrong with her, what's wrong with you?"

"I've had a stressful week or two at work. I thought an error I made had come back to haunt me, but it doesn't seem to be what I thought it was. I'm really sorry I upset you, Howard. Everything will be fine when we're lying on a nice, hot beach in Aruba for a few days."

"Are you sure, Vivian?"

Giving his back a contented kiss, Vivian said, "I'm sure."

Howard abandoned his pillow and wrapped his arms around Vivian. He looked into her eyes and smiled weakly.

She said, "Poor baby. I'm not going to throw any more fits before the wedding. Okay?"

"Okay. Does that mean all bets are off afterwards?"

Vivian smiled mischievously and said, "I don't know what's going to happen afterwards, Howard. I promise I'll try not to be a pain."

Howard groaned deep in his throat. They snuggled and rubbed noses for a while. Kissed and stroked each other's bodies. Made deliberately slow, very slow, love to each other and fell asleep in each other's arms again.

On Saturday morning, Howard and Vivian went shopping for things they would need for the wedding. Before they left the house, Howard slid Vivian's engagement ring on her finger for the second time and said, "If you take it off again, I'm taking it back to the store."

Vivian rolled her eyes at him.

With everyone busy getting ready for the wedding, the next three weeks flew by. Both Howard and Vivian had to make arrangements to be absent from their offices. After the stress of the past few weeks, Vivian decided she would abandon her duties for a month. Howard went with three weeks. Clayton screamed about it, but Howard didn't care.

Howard had to persuade his brother to either find a place of his own or go home before they returned from their honeymoon. Sheldon wasn't happy about it, but promised to do one or the other. Lula called Howard every day to remind him he was making a mistake and swear she wasn't coming to the wedding. Howard assured her that would be fine - somehow they would proceed without her presence. Nevertheless, he knew she would be there . . . although what she would do once she arrived, worried him.

Without mentioning it to Howard, Vivian disposed of her birth control pills. Hopefully, she wouldn't get pregnant for at least a few months - she didn't want him to think that he got his way most of the time. Vivian couldn't really envision being pregnant anyway and didn't worry about it anymore.

Vivian and Max shopped three days in a row for Vivian's wedding dress. She didn't want anything too formal or frilly, and they finally found exactly what Vivian had in mind. It only took one evening to find accessories, bathing suits, and sunglasses for the honeymoon. Vivian had no intention of skiing, so she disregarded making any purchases for that leg of the trip.

Jessica and Eunice gave Vivian a surprise bridal shower at the Board Room. They called Howard and got Talia's telephone number and were able to pull together quite a group. Of course, Millie and Barb were there. Vivian's future sisters-in-law, Charlene and Madelaine, came with Talia. Lula did not attend, and no one mentioned her.

With all that behind her, the only person left unattended to was Adrena, and Vivian promised to devote the week before the wedding to getting her ready.

Every once in a while, Vivian would experience a nagging suspicion in the back of her mind about Mrs. Brown's death, but for the most part, she proceeded under the assumption that Adrena had done nothing to hasten her death. Moreover, to Vivian's surprise, she actually enjoyed every minute of the time she spent with the troubled teen. Adrena Reynolds was truly an amazing and rare young lady.

Chapter Fifteen

Maxine sat in Vivian's waiting room on Monday afternoon talking to Millie, while Vivian busied herself with paperwork in her office. The Matthews sisters were waiting for Adrena. The threesome would be shopping for Adrena's outfit for the wedding.

The shopping excursion was designed to introduce Adrena to Maxine before the wedding in the hopes that Adrena would feel more comfortable on the day of the great event. More than anything, Vivian wanted Adrena to experience something wonderful and to perhaps be able to communicate a good feeling without discomfort. If she enjoyed the wedding and derived any of the positive meaning from it, perhaps the entire day could be considered Adrena's baptism of belonging.

Adrena bounced into the office at exactly four-thirty. Her smile was vibrant until her gaze fell on Maxine. Seeing Adrena's stunned expression, Millie attempted to introduce them, saying, "Adrena, this is . . ."

Finishing Millie's introduction for her, Adrena said in a reverent voice, "Maxine."

Max stood, smiled and extended her hand. Adrena stared at it. She stiffly took the three steps necessary to reach the hand of the woman who had singlehandedly rescued Adrena many times in the younger woman's dreams and imaginings. There was no need for a precautionary deep breath to brace herself for the physical contact. The moment Max's soft hand closed over hers, Adrena closed her eyes. There was no wave of nausea for Adrena from Max's touch. Instead, an emotional sigh of release occurred. There was an unfamiliar tightness in Adrena's chest, and a lone tear found its way out of her eye.

Vivian walked in, saw the contact and tear, and hurried to
Adrena's rescue. Smiling broadly, Vivian asked, "Are you all
right, Adrena? I see you've met Maxine."

Without relinquishing Maxine's hand, Adrena wiped at the
tear quickly. She gave an abbreviated nod in response to
Vivian's question.

Adrena's eyes were riveted to Maxine's smile. The Doc
had described her little sister perfectly. All of Doc's pet
phrases for Maxine echoed in Adrena's mind. "Cinnamon in
sunlight. An angel in repose. Attila's little sister. Einstein's
illegitimate offspring. Cartoons after school."

Comfortingly, Max wrapped her free arm around Adrena's
shoulder and said, "It's okay, honey. I have that effect on lots
of people. They cry the moment they see me."

Believing Max, Adrena asked anxiously, "Do they?"

"Naw. I'm just kidding. Most people don't even notice
me. Are you all right now?"

"I'm fine. Everybody notices you, Max. You're even
prettier than Doc."

Vivian yelled, "Hey, wait a minute! No, she's not!"

Adrena giggled and said apologetically, "I'm sorry, Doc.
I mean she's prettier - in a different way."

Maxine said sharply, "Leave her alone, Viv. The girl's got
taste - and I am prettier than you! It's about time someone
noticed. Let's go."

When Max turned to retrieve her purse, Adrena saw the
signature piece of all her dreams. Max's glossy, black braid
hung heavily down her spine and extended beyond her waist.
It was as exquisite as Doc had told Adrena it was. Doc
herself had been blessed with a handsome braid, until she cut
it after a patient grabbed it and held her hostage during her
internship at a mental institution. The two sisters had
inherited their beautiful hair from their mother.

Maxine's voice mesmerized Adrena. It was strong,
confident, melodic, and caring. Her touch had been
electrifying. No one could do anything to Adrena in Max's
presence. No one. For the first time in her life, Adrena felt
free to be herself. She couldn't label all of what she felt.
Surely, happy was at the top of the list.

They left the office with Maxine chattering away, "What colors do you like best, Adrena? I bet you look fabulous in greens. You've got natural pink highlights in your skin. Are you old enough to wear makeup? Maybe we should stop at the Fashion Fair counter, Viv. Does she have to wear a dress? Do I have to wear a dress? Wouldn't you prefer a sharp pantsuit, Adrena?"

Vivian could only shake her head. Max was in charge - not allowing anyone a word in edgewise or interested in anything they had to say. *She* would take care of Adrena. Dress her from head to toe with impeccable style. See that she was powdered and perfumed to perfection and would dare anyone to look at her funny.

For the first time in her sixteen years, Adrena felt wonderful. Here she was, the damaged child of two pathetic junkies, in the company of two beautiful and successful women who were treating her like a princess. It all felt so good, Adrena now struggled with ebbing the flow of tears. In the sea of pain that was Adrena's emotional life, this tiny island of bliss made her long for land on a permanent basis.

Adrena, Maxine, and Vivian roamed from mall to mall. They leisurely surveyed boutiques, shoe stores, lingerie salons, and makeup counters. When they were done, Adrena had three new outfits. She also had shoes, underwear, accessories, makeup and nail polish to match each one. Of course, Max gave her explicit instructions on what went with what. What time of day she could wear it and all of the personal things she should do beforehand.

Laughter was the theme of the evening. Layers of polished professionalism and unpredictable psychosis slipped away in the atmosphere of sisterly camaraderie. They shamelessly laughed with and at each other, without any negative repercussions. Everyone tried on things they knew they would never buy and screeched like wild teenagers when they saw each other. Their outfits ran the gamut from extravagant hookers to frumpish schoolteachers. Finally, in calf-lengthed, flowered, and flowing tunics, they were wealthy ladies, ready to water and prune lavishly pretentious gardens. They called each other Betsy, Mitsi, and Kipper.

In the dressing room, Adrena noticed the tiniest bruise on top of Vivian's breast. She pointed and asked, "How did you get that mark on your chest, Doc?"

Vivian looked in the mirror to see what she was pointing at. Max answered the question. "Looks like Howard strikes again, Kid."

Adrena grabbed Vivian's arm so roughly it made Vivian wince. In the bat of an eye the good humor in Adrena's eyes was replaced with stony anger. Rigidly, the teenager asked, "Are you going to marry him, and he's hitting you already?"

Vivian pleaded, "Please let my arm go, Adrena. Howard has never hit me."

Without releasing her arm, Adrena asked adamantly, "How did you get that mark then?"

Assuming her Dr. Matthews' authoritarian posture, Vivian said, "I'm not answering anything until you let my arm go."

Adrena took a deep breath and removed her hand. The pout of her mouth told Vivian she was still angry. Max didn't have a clue because she knew nothing of Adrena's past, so she watched the exchange with cautious curiosity.

Vivian sighed and said, "He kissed me, Adrena. That's how the mark got there."

Completely baffled, Adrena said incredulously, "Kisses don't make marks. Do they, Doc?"

"Sometimes they do."

"Well, why aren't your lips blue? He kisses your lips, right?"

With the earlier atmosphere of camaraderie and joviality returning, Vivian said, "Yes, Adrena. He kisses my lips. He kisses me everywhere. Sometimes, it makes a mark."

"Oh. Does it hurt?"

"What?"

"Kisses."

"No, Adrena."

Adrena turned to Max, who was balled up in a knot. She laughed hysterically in mime at Vivian and Adrena's conversation. Tears streamed down her face. Adrena asked, "What's so funny, Max? Nobody ever kissed me. I don't know. Do you have any kiss marks on you?"

Laughter bubbled beneath the thin veil of composure when Max responded, "No, Adrena. I don't have any. Nobody's kissed me in a while either."

Everything calmed down until Adrena saw a similar bruise on Vivian's thigh. Regaining control of her gaping mouth, she asked, "Did he kiss your leg, too, Doc?"

A fresh batch of laughter made the clerk peek in to see if everything was all right. Vivian inspected the spot on her leg, smiled devilishly, and said, "Yes, that looks like Howard did that, too."

"What's wrong with him, Doc? Why is he kissing your leg? That's a long way from your mouth. Are the lights out when he does that? Is that why he keeps missing your mouth?"

Unable to laugh anymore, Max whined miserably, "Stop, Adrena. You're killing me. We'll have to talk about kissing another time. I can't take any more of it tonight. I'll just tell you this much. The lights were not off."

Max held up her finger and shook her head, stopping another barrage of questions.

Adrena pouted and mumbled, "If the lights were on, then he's just blind and can't tell the difference between lips, chests and legs. Howard sounds like a real dummy to me. I wouldn't marry him."

Just as they were leaving the last mall, Max turned to Adrena and asked, "Do you have a disposable razor?"

Looking puzzled, Adrena said shyly, "No. What do I need that for?"

As if it were the most natural thing in the world, Max said, "To shave your underarms. Don't tell me Vivian hasn't taught you how to do that yet!"

Adrena looked at Vivian, shrugged her shoulders and said, "No, she hasn't."

"And why not? Vivian, you know there is nothing tackier than a woman thinking she's sharp, with giant puffs of deodorant-matted hair hanging under her arms. We can't have that. Do you have any at home, Viv?"

"You know I do, dear."

"Good. Let's get something to eat and show Adrena how to shave those pits."

The next stop for the group was a sandwich shop. They ordered take-out and headed for Vivian's house. It was after nine, when they walked through her front door. Vivian and Max headed straight for the kitchen.

Adrena had never visited Vivian's house before. She surveyed everything as she followed the noisy sisters. The size of the rooms. The furniture, drapes, paintings, flowers, knick-knacks and carpeting. Adrena was quietly admiring all of the appliances in the gleaming black and white kitchen, when she smelled an unfamiliar, tangy fragrance. It was an interesting aroma. Still, Adrena couldn't imagine where it was coming from. Something brushed her bare ankle and made a tiny noise. Adrena jumped and screamed in terror.

Spinning around, Adrena stood face-to-face with the six-foot, muscular, dark brown, smooth-skinned and smiling, Howard Shaw. He wore a white tank tee shirt, navy blue dress pants, socks and no shoes. Even though he was smiling, his long-lashed eyes slanted down and gave the impression of deep sadness. Adrena couldn't tell if Howard's eyes were open or closed.

Vivian pointed toward the floor and said, "Adrena, that's Snow." She pointed up and said, "Adrena, that's Howard. Howard, this is Adrena Reynolds."

Howard extended his hand and said, "Hello, Adrena. I'm pleased to meet you."

Adrena stared at Howard's hand mutely. Vivian took Howard's hand and gave him a kiss, but he never took his eyes off the attractive, young lady who had just refused to touch his hand.

Maxine came over, gave Howard a kiss and hug, and said, "How are you this evening, Mr. Shaw?"

Still watching Adrena, Howard said automatically, "I'm fine, and you, Dr. Matthews?"

"I'm fine. Are you all ready for the wedding?"

"I think so, Max. Vivian, did you say her name was Adrena Reynolds?"

"Yes, Howard. Did you eat anything?"

Locked in a staring match with Adrena, Howard answered, "No, I was waiting for you. I've got a new client named Adrena Reynolds. Is that you?"

With an eyebrow arched, Adrena said softly, "I don't know."

Vivian answered. "Yes, Howard. That's her. You handled her grandmother's account. Mrs. Hazel Brown. Adrena inherited the bulk of her estate."

Maxine steered the staring Adrena toward the counter, and shoved her sandwich and soda in front of her. Adrena refused to take her eyes off Howard.

Maxine finally said, "Adrena, Howard doesn't bite anyone he doesn't love. You can stop looking at him now."

Adrena whispered, "Are you sure?"

"I'm sure. Now eat your sandwich."

Occasionally stealing glances at Howard, Adrena ate as instructed. Howard was sharing Doc's sandwich, touching her face with his finger, whispering and kissing her lightly on the mouth. Adrena watched to see if her lips would turn blue.

Finishing their sandwiches, Max cleared the mess and asked, "Are you ready for that lesson, Adrena?"

Smiling again, Adrena said, "Yes."

"Where's the razor, Viv?"

Howard snapped, "Razor! What are you going to do with a razor?"

Max said, "I've got a patient who needs your liver, Howard. Didn't I mention it?"

"Very funny, Dr. Matthews."

Vivian said, "Quit it, you two. They're in the shower cabinet, Max. Be careful."

"I'm a surgeon, Vivian. I had to master hair removal before they let me into the operating room."

Laughing at her sister's remark, Vivian eased over and whispered in Adrena's ear, "Did you take your medication this evening?"

Adrena shook her head slowly. It was plain to see she was tired. Fatigue and famine are triggers for the emotionally challenged.

"Do you have it with you?"

Adrena nodded.

Stroking Adrena's hair, like a concerned parent, Vivian said, "Take it when you get upstairs. Don't forget, Adrena. I'll tell Max to drop you off at home as soon as she's done."

"Okay, Doc. I've had a great time. He's not so bad. Kind of cute, in a man kind of way. Looks like he should be able to find your mouth though. He sure found it enough times while we were here."

Stepping away from Adrena, Vivian waved her hand in hilarious frustration and said, "That's it. Max, take her away."

Not hearing the exchange between Vivian and Adrena, Maxine asked, "What did you say, Adrena? Come on. You can tell me when we get upstairs. I bet that was a doozy."

The moment he heard Maxine and Adrena on the stairs, Howard asked, "Vivian, what's wrong with her? She looked at my hand like urine was dripping off it."

"Oh, Howard, that's disgusting. She's fine. Just tired from a long day."

"There's more to it than that, and you know it. Just tell me what it is. I don't want to do anything to upset her. That little girl will be worth better than a half million in stocks and securities, by the time she's twenty-one. If I do the wrong thing, your ring might have to go back to the store."

"You'd better sell that car first. No ring. No Jag."

"I don't know if I can do that. Just tell me."

"I can't tell you anything about her problems, Howard. I will tell you to just relax and let her approach you. If she doesn't, just talk to her the way you do anyone else. Don't touch her, but, don't make it obvious you're not touching her."

"What'll happen if I touch her?"

"Believe me, you don't want to know that."

"What do you mean? Is she dangerous, Vivian?"

"I can't answer that kind of question, Howard. All I can say is, Adrena has come a long way. Be nice to her. Please, be nice to her."

"Oh, I've got to be nice to her, sweetheart. She's paying for your ring and my Jag."

Chapter Sixteen

The hectic morning of the big day came, and God seemed to be cooperating. Saturday, July thirteenth, was a gorgeous day. The gardener had made Vivian's lawn look like expensive, plush carpeting. The housekeeping service had made the house gleam. Now, if all of the other pieces fell into place, Vivian and Howard would have a perfect wedding day.

Max picked up Adrena, and the two of them met Vivian at nine that morning at the beauty salon where Vivian and Adrena had appointments. Adrena was getting her hair done. Vivian was getting the works - hair, facial, manicure, and pedicure. Of course, Max sat and observed. No one ever touched her hair, and Max preferred it that way.

Vivian's hair was to be swept up into a sleek, glossy french roll, with two wavy wisps of hair dangling down her back from the nape of her neck. Her veil would flow down over her face from the ring of flowers surrounding her head. Vivian thought that the combination of her hair and the veil swinging would distract her; with her hair up, there would be less to worry about.

In the excitement of the wedding and all the preparations, Adrena had given no thought to being primped by strangers. She had never been to a professional beautician in her life. Mrs. Stanley washed Adrena's hair, pressed, and curled it every Saturday night. As Adrena watched the beautician run her fingers through Vivian's hair, she was completely unprepared for anyone attempting to do the same to her.

The technician stood holding the plastic protective cape and motioned Adrena toward the vacant chair. Not knowing what was expected of her, Adrena stared at the young woman vacantly.

Seeing Adrena's reaction, Maxine asked, "Is something wrong, Adrena?"

"No."

"Are you going to let the nice lady perm your hair?"

Without moving, Adrena answered, "Yes."

Walking over to Adrena, Maxine placed her hands on Adrena's shoulders and gave her rigid body a gentle push toward the shampoo chair. The thought of the strange woman touching her made Adrena's heart pound so loudly, all other sound disappeared momentarily. As she had done many times in her dreams, Adrena focused on Maxine's face and the touch of her hands. The escalating paranoia slowed. The tremor and the urge to scream diminished and disappeared.

Adrena heard Maxine's voice say soothingly, "It's okay, sweetheart. They're going to do a really good job with your hair. You know I wouldn't let them touch you if I didn't believe that myself, Adrena. Sit back and relax. It's a wonderful experience. I'll be right here with you, and Vivian's right next to you."

Taking a deep breath to still her remaining fears, Adrena did as instructed. She stiffly moved toward the chair, sat down and allowed the technician to prepare her for the application of the perm. An occasional bout of trembling, however, plagued Adrena throughout the morning. Maxine protectively hovered over Adrena, giving her an occasional, reassuring pat on her arm. Adrena relaxed enough to absorb every detail of the manipulations to which she and Vivian were subjected.

On Maxine's insistence, Adrena's hair was cut short on top, curled to cap her face, and tapered flat at the temples. The back flowed freely into a smooth page boy that kissed her shoulders. Adrena's eyes gaped in disbelief when she saw herself in the mirror.

Closely inspecting the younger woman's eyebrows, Maxine had the technician wax Adrena's naturally arched eyebrows to perfection. Both times, Adrena yelped her unexpected pain and stared at Max angrily. However, when they were done, Adrena was impressed. Before leaving the salon, Max caught a glimpse of Adrena's soft pink nail polish and asked the manicurist to paint a dainty flower on her little fingers. Fascinated by this intricate process, Adrena kept butting heads with the manicurist, as she tried to see.

In a daze, Adrena asked, "Why do I need flowers on my nails, Max?"

"You're not wearing any rings. It gives your hand an air of intrigue. Don't ever do that when you start wearing jewelry, Adrena. It's too much."

"Okay. Do you have any flowers?"

"No. I have a ring on."

If Max had told Adrena being run over by trains took unwanted inches off of your waist, she would have been somewhere stretched out on the tracks, patiently waiting for the Metroliner.

The three women left the beauty salon and arrived at Vivian's house at noon. The florist's truck was waiting at the curb. Before Max closed the door, the caterer and his crew arrived. Paul assured Dr. Matthews' sister he knew what had to be done and went about doing it. With Vivian and Maxine busy upstairs, Paul greeted the photographer and musicians. The house buzzed with the transformation team in place.

Vivian and Maxine helped Adrena dress first. Maxine brushed color onto her face, carefully outlined and painted her lips. Vivian snapped tiny, dangling, jade earrings onto her earlobes and draped a gold chain with a jade medallion around her neck. To complete the accessories, Vivian clasped a shiny gold bangle onto Adrena's wrist.

Finally, Adrena stepped into the short-sleeved, hunter green coatdress with gold buttons and slipped on her matching low pumps, with golden toes and heels. Vivian touched up her hair. Maxine sprayed a large cloud of Bijan perfume and said, "Walk into it and spin around, Adrena."

Pressing Adrena's shoulders, Vivian steered her to the floor-length mirror. Adrena couldn't believe her own eyes. No one treated her the way Doc did, and absolutely no one made her feel the way Maxine did. Tears piled up in Adrena's eyes and dangled from her lashes.

Maxine saw them first and said, "Adrena, don't you dare cry before Vivian comes down that aisle."

Adrena swallowed hard and blinked the tears back quickly.

Vivian said, "You look beautiful, Adrena. How do you feel?"

Fighting tears, Adrena smiled weakly. She didn't trust her voice. If she said one word, she knew she would cry. Adrena's answer to Vivian was a meek nod of her head.

Everything stopped when two little girls, in gaily flowered pinafore dresses, burst into the room and jumped into the arms of Vivian and Maxine, identical, ribboned ponytails swinging. These had to be their younger sisters. They didn't look exactly like the older Matthews girls, but they were awfully pretty in their own right.

A tall, well-built, handsome, cinnamon-colored man in a black suit and tie and white shirt walked into the room. He looked like Maxine and slightly resembled Vivian. There was someone else behind him. The moment the figure came into Adrena's line of sight, she saw a younger, mirror image of the man. Everyone kissed, hugged, and laughed easily.

Adrena thought, "Now, this is a family. Everyone looks like everyone else, and they're all glad as hell to see each other."

Vivian turned around and said, "Everyone, this is my friend, Adrena. Adrena, this is my father, Vance Matthews. My sisters, Patricia and Melanie. My brother, Junior."

All of the children waved and said, "Hi."

Vance walked over with a generous smile, closed his hand over Adrena's, and said, "Hello, Adrena. I'm pleased to meet you."

Before Vivian could intervene, Adrena smiled back warmly and said, "Hello, Mr. Matthews. I'm pleased to meet you, too."

There was no fear of Vance Matthews for Adrena. She remembered the way Doc spoke of her father. There was so much more to it than just what she said. Adrena saw genuine adoration of a parent in Doc's eyes when she mentioned "Daddy." Vance Matthews had been both mother and father to Vivian and Maxine. He had given them all of the consistent love and security they ever needed. They had flourished into beautiful, brilliant, successful, and loving women in his care. In Adrena's estimation, he was wonderful.

Patricia asked, "Where's my basket, Vivian?"

"It's in my bedroom, sweetheart. I'll give it to you when the wedding starts. I don't want you to spill your petals before the service."

Pouting, Patricia said, "Okay. Max, can you fix my lips? Mommy won't do it."

"I sure will. Can't have my sister running around with inappropriate lips."

Melanie squealed, "Me too, Max!"

"Okay. Then I have to get dressed. I have to help Vivian get ready, too."

After Max painted their lips and did the perfume routine with them, they all happily piled down the stairs. Adrena stayed with Max and Vivian. She was the official run-and-fetch girl and proud to be it, too.

Adrena got to look into Vivian's closets. Inside, she saw Howard's clothes and shoes and smelled his cologne. Packed luggage lined the wall near the window in Vivian's elegantly furnished bedroom. Everything was so neat, Adrena wondered how they did it. Her room turned into a disaster area if she just changed her shoes.

The photographer came up and started snapping pictures while Vivian dressed. He even took one of Adrena sliding Vivian's silky, white heels on for her. Adrena had never felt so much a part of anything in her entire life. The excitement absorbed her. She didn't even mind Patricia and Melanie tapping her every time they wanted something. Snow still irritated Adrena, though, and eventually Maxine locked her in the guestroom.

At exactly two, music started playing. Adrena wanted to run down the stairs to see where it was coming from. She didn't. She waited until Vivian was perfect. Then Maxine told her to run, fetch the girls and Mr. Matthews.

Seeing all of the people in Vivian's living room made Adrena slightly nervous. She took a deep breath and stilled herself. Mr. Matthews was talking to a man who looked like Howard. Later, she would be told that was Sheldon Shaw.

Approaching the two men, Adrena said, "Excuse me, Mr.
Matthews. They're ready for you and the girls upstairs."
"Thank you, sweetheart. I'll try to find them."
"They're in the dining room. I'll get them for you."
Adrena took each of the girls by the hand and led them to
their father. Then, she looked for a seat in the sea of
strangers. Millie stood and waved her over. Adrena sighed
with relief and gladly took the seat next to Vivian's secretary.
Millie introduced her to Howard's secretary, Barb. Adrena
smiled nervously and waved. Barb did likewise. They all
waited with growing anticipation for the wedding to begin.

At two-fifteen, Howard, his best man Clayton, and the
minister walked down the aisle that Paul and his crew had
created. Adrena was impressed with Howard's style of dress.
He wore a pale, olive-green suit, with a cream shirt. The
collar was thin and brocaded. The brocade pattern ran down
the center of his shirt, giving it a tie effect. His shoes
matched his suit perfectly.

As Adrena sat inspecting Howard, she decided he really
was cute, in a man kind of way. He'd better not do anything
to hurt the Doc, though. If he did, he would be checking the
prices of stock on the big board in the sky.

The bridal march began to play. Everyone wrenched their
necks to see the bride come down the stairs. Adrena followed
suit.

Dressed elegantly in pink, grey, and pearls, Maxine came
down first. Melanie and Patricia followed. Adrena wondered
where they all got those pretty flowered halos. She hadn't
seen them before.

After clearing the stairs, the girls daintily dropped pink
rose petals on the floor. Finally, arm in arm, Vivian and Mr.
Matthews began their slow, careful descent.

Adrena watched Vivian. Even with her face covered by
the veil, Vivian looked beautiful. Her crepe dress, cream-
colored and soft, was exquisite. The delicate spaghetti straps
and plunging neckline accentuated her breasts. Tiny pearls
and rhinestones glittered in the draped front. As they passed,
Adrena was mesmerized by the sparkling, jeweled accents

around the outline of the back of the dress which barely swept the floor.

When Adrena saw how Howard looked at Vivian, she conceded he might not be too bad. His eyes glistened with adoration. None of the angry lust Adrena knew so well. As Vivian approached, he glowed. Hating to admit it, even to herself, Adrena was impressed with Howard all the way around.

Adrena leaned close to Millie's ear and whispered, "Who is the other guy?"

"That's Clayton Williams. He's Howard's partner."

Mr. Matthews and Vivian finally reached Howard. They all faced the minister. He spoke glowingly about love, marriage, God and glory for a few minutes. Then he asked, "Who gives this bride?"

Smiling proudly, Mr. Matthews said, "I do." He stepped back and sat down next to his wife.

Howard, Vivian, Maxine, and Clayton stood close together, facing the minister. That was the first time Adrena noticed Clayton was wearing a grey suit and pink shirt to match Max's outfit.

The minister proceeded. He said, "Before sanctioning this union, I must ask if anyone knows of a lawful reason these two cannot be joined. Speak now, or forever hold your peace."

A tall, heavy lady seated in the back, dressed from head to toe in black, stood and said, "I know of one. She's not good enough for him. Nowhere near good enough."

Clayton and Maxine spun around immediately. They glared in the direction of the lady. Howard and Vivian ducked their heads, as if someone had hurled something over them. People came up out of their seats. When Vivian turned around and looked at the woman, she was furious. Howard bowed his head and covered his face with his hand.

The room erupted in moans, groans and gasps. Folks were saying, "No, she didn't say that!" "I can't believe she said that." "Who the hell is she?" "Is she crazy?" "This is exactly why no one has weddings in our family!"

Adrena could only frown in confusion. She didn't know anyone was supposed to actually answer any questions, except the bride and groom. And, what did she mean? "She's not good enough for him?" Who?

Maxine, Vivian, and Clayton stomped off in the woman's direction, but Maxine got there first and asked the question Adrena wanted answered.

"What the hell do you mean, she's not good enough for him?"

Clayton said, "I thought you weren't coming. Why can't you ever go anyplace without making a damn scene?"

Vivian snapped, "Get out of my house, Lula! Get out!"

Lula said, "I don't have to get out. My brother's getting married in this dump today, and I've got something to say about it."

"I don't give a shit what you have to say, Lula! You're getting out of my house right now!"

"And if I don't, what are you going to do?!"

Max passed her bouquet to a stunned Talia and said, "Don't answer that, Vivian. I'll show you what's going to happen, Lula."

After that, everybody moved at once. Lula balled up her fist to defend herself. Max threw the first punch, hitting Lula in the face. Clayton shoved an already-swaying Lula and grabbed Max before she could do any more damage. Reaching over Maxine, Vivian snatched at Lula's head and came back with her black hat in her hand. Howard and Mr. Matthews dashed down the aisle. They both grabbed Vivian at the same time.

Adrena eased out of her seat, darted to the back of the room and pushed Lula toward the door so hard, she fell. Horrified, Talia shrieked. Sheldon, Gary, and Teddy were convulsed in laughter - they couldn't help or hinder anyone.

Adrena yelled, "Get up and get out, lady! Doc says you're not welcome! You're messing up her wedding!"

From the floor, Lula asked indignantly, "Who the hell are you? The bastard baby Vivian's been keeping in the closet?"

Adrena growled, "No, lady. I'm the friend who's going to kick your teeth in, if you don't hit the bricks right now."

Getting up, Lula moved too slowly for Adrena. Adrena shoved Lula toward the door before she was all the way up, and again, Lula stumbled and fell.

Attempting to come to his wife's rescue, Bruce said, "You don't have to do that - she's leaving!"

Fearlessly, Adrena turned around and hissed, "Have you got a problem with the way I'm handling this, Mister? Maybe I should give you a few swift kicks, too. I'd just as soon kick two asses as one."

Bruce frowned and decided not to press the issue. He took Lula's arm, helped her get to her feet, and led her out the door. The room breathed a collective sigh of relief.

The minister cleared his throat loudly and said, "If we could take our places, perhaps we can proceed. After all, I asked for a lawful reason; her answer was irrelevant. Before commencing this time, we'll take time out to pray for the disturbed soul of our sister."

Mr. Matthews said angrily, "Well, Reverend, I suggest you throw that question out altogether from now on."

"You may have a point, Brother Matthews."

A weeping Talia gave Max her flowers back, and the bridal party returned to the front of the room. The guests took their seats, and Adrena stood guard at the door. If that crazy woman came back, Adrena would bang her and her husband's heads together before they set foot in Doc's house again. The photographer snapped continuously through it all.

Adrena watched the rest of the ceremony with rapt interest. The kiss was of special interest to her. To her surprise, it was the most beautiful thing that happened during the entire wedding. Howard and Vivian embraced and kissed each other for a long time. It was a kiss filled with tenderness, passion, and genuine love. Howard kissed Doc like he loved her more than anything in the world. Adrena had nothing to compare it to; still, it held top honors in her eyes. Everyone grinned and applauded happily, and Adrena joined them.

As the glow returned to the festivities, all the guests congratulated Howard and Vivian. No one mentioned Lula, or the incident. There were plenty of hugs and kisses for the bride and groom. Max and Adrena, however, still fumed with anger. They would have loved for Lula to come back. Now that the ceremony was over, they could have set her straight the way they wanted.

Not wanting to upset Vivian any more than she already was, Vivian's best friends, Eunice and Jessica, had only one question for Maxine when their turn came. "Who is that girl?"

Max smiled proudly and said, "Adrena. She's a friend of Vivian's. The girl's hell on wheels. I love her!"

Jessica said, "Well, she certainly wasn't going to let Lula upset Vivian any more than she already had. That's for sure. She would have stomped that old fool until she became a permanent pattern in the carpet. Did you see the way she looked at her, Max? I've never seen an expression to beat it."

Max said quietly, "She got her point across, didn't she?"

The remainder of the day went exactly as Vivian had planned. Laughing, eating, drinking, accepting gifts, and socializing. Smiling, as they cut the cake, threw the garter and bouquet. Romantically kissing each other during their first dance as husband and wife. Vivian and Howard beamed on the surface. Beneath it all, they seethed.

Max introduced Adrena to Clayton, and Adrena decided immediately she didn't like the way Clayton looked at her. Max laughed hysterically when Adrena refused to shake his hand.

Other than her too obvious rejection of Clayton's attention, Adrena managed the crowd well. She spoke when spoken to and kept an eye on the two adorable little girls, but Adrena's most important accomplishment of the day was holding an entire conversation with Junior.

During their conversation, without being asked, Junior brought Adrena cake and punch, handed it to her, sat down, and started talking again. He never breached the forbidden, formidable, private space of Adrena Reynolds. He didn't pull any stupid teenage stunts to embarrass her. Adrena was so impressed with Junior, she gave him her telephone number when he asked for it.

At the conclusion of the festivities, Adrena had two gifts for the Doc. In an elegantly wrapped box lay the first, an exquisite Mikasa crystal picture frame. Etched into it at the top was, "Mr. and Mrs. Howard Shaw." At the bottom, it said, "Our Journey Together Begins." Of course, that was for their wedding photo.

Before Adrena and Max packed and left, Adrena approached Vivian and Howard. She smiled at Vivian and said, "Everything was beautiful, Doc. I really enjoyed myself. Thank you for inviting me. You already know I wish you the best of everything." Adrena then bestowed her second gift of the day by embracing Vivian and kissing her on the cheek.

Adrena turned to Howard and said, "I don't care what you do with my money, Howard. It's just money. If you lose it, I won't miss it, because I never had any. You just take really good care of Doc. I wish you the best of everything, too."

Without breathing to brace herself, gagging or flinching, Adrena wrapped her arms around Howard and kissed his cheek. She even allowed him to return the gesture.

Vivian and Max exchanged strange glances and shrugged. Adrena was either growing, or playing a game with which Vivian was unfamiliar.

Chapter Seventeen

The moment Maxine, Adrena, and Clayton closed Vivian's front door, Vivian and Howard collapsed onto the sofa. Vivian plopped her stockinged feet into Howard's lap, and he skillfully massaged every inch of them. They looked at each other through eyes filled with pitiful, pleading exhaustion. It was after midnight.

Howard asked, "Did you know weddings took this much out of you, Vivian?"

"No, Howard, I didn't. If this is what happened with just our families and a few friends, can you imagine what it would have been like if we had gone all out?"

Howard groaned miserably and closed his eyes.

Vivian said matter-of-factly, "I'm killing your sister the very next time I see her, Howard."

"I should have let you kill her today. I will go to my grave not believing my own sister did that. Is she menopausal or something, Vivian? What the hell is wrong with Lula?"

"You may not be able to grasp this right now, Howard, but I don't care what's wrong with her. If we had gone to a church and she did that in front of all of our friends, I would have been humiliated just enough to kill. As it is, I'm sure everyone will know what happened before we get back from the honeymoon."

Lazily running his finger up Vivian's leg, Howard said, "I am so sorry she ruined your day, Vivian. How she came up with 'you're not good enough for me,' beats the hell out of me."

"She believes it. That's how."

"No, she doesn't."

"Yes, she does. Why else would she come into my home, on my wedding day, wearing black, on a sizzling July day?

Stand up and boldly proclaim me not good enough for you. Nowhere near good enough."

"She's confused, Viv. I thought you, of all people, would understand what Lula's problem is and excuse her."

Vivian sat up straight and stared at Howard with one perfectly arched eyebrow raised. She didn't say anything for a few moments. Finally, Vivian asked, "What the hell makes you think I know what's wrong with your sister?"

"You're a psychiatrist, sweetheart."

"Does that mean I have a key to every mind, or just the really sick ones, Howard? When are you going to realize I don't have a crystal ball or a Ouija board lodged in my brain? I don't understand what motivates a person to stand up and embarrass her own brother that way - not one she claims to love as much as she claims to love you. I know I haven't done a thing to provoke her. So, who does she hate, Howard? You, or me?"

"Why would she hate me?"

"I don't know! Why would she hate me?! You're the one with the history with her! She doesn't know me! Never so much as held a conversation with me! So, you think about that for a while! Who the hell is the crazy woman mad at?!"

"I don't know what you mean by that. Lula definitely loves me. I know that as well as my own name."

"Does she, Howard? Loving means allowing to grow and letting go. Loving means wanting the very best for, and more happiness than a heart can hold. There's no weakness in loving. It's filled with trust. If Lula loved you the way she was supposed to all of these years, she would know her place is guaranteed in your heart. Expecting to keep you as you were as a child, in her life forever, is either sick or stupid. Tonight, I say stupid."

Howard took a deep breath, as if he were about to respond. There was an obvious change of heart because he fell silent.

Snatching up her shoes, Vivian stormed up the stairs muttering, "Crazy people. They're everywhere. What did I do to her? Not a damn thing. I'm not good enough. That old bat is going to be sorry she said that about me! Max should have knocked her teeth down her throat! That's not insanity anyway. It's ignorance. She's stupid as hell! That's what's wrong with her."

Howard followed, asking, "What are you saying, Vivian? Are you still calling my sister stupid? She's not stupid. She's strange. You're a doctor. You're supposed to understand people like Lula."

Vivian struggled with the zipper on her dress and mumbled, "I'm supposed to understand people like Lula? Like hell I am. I don't know Lula from a can of paint. To me, she's stupid."

Trying to help Vivian with her zipper, Howard said, "She's not stupid, Vivian. Stop saying that. When you have a chance to think about it, you're going to be sorry you said that."

Slapping Howard's hands away from her, Vivian yelled, "Don't bank on it! I'm never going to be sorry I said it! I'll say it again tomorrow and the next day! She's stupid!"

Tired of watching Vivian squirming, he pushed her hands out of the way and unzipped her dress. Also tired of arguing about his sister, stupid or crazy, Howard ran his finger along Vivian's neckline and slid the top of her dress down. He bent down and kissed her bare shoulder.

Vivian rolled her eyes, clutched her falling dress, and moved away. She said coolly, "You can keep your fingers and kisses to yourself. Maybe Lula needs them. She's probably in the emergency room right now. Pretending to die. Anything to keep her precious brother from going on a honeymoon with the worthless hussy he married."

Moaning, Howard said, "Come on, Viv. Let's not argue about Lula for the rest of the night. If she dies, they'll have to bury her without me. We got married today. That should prove how much you mean to me, sweetheart. You're my wife."

Still steaming, yet knowing Howard was right, she asked, "Is there anything at all left downstairs to drink?"

Pretending to inspect his shoe, Howard said nonchalantly, "I don't know, Vivian. If you promise to be nicer to me when I come back, I'll go look for you."

"If not, I have to go myself?"

Never looking up, Howard said, "I think so."

Vivian relented and said, "Okay, Howard. I promise to be nicer to you when you come back."

"Can I get one kiss before I go?"

Rolling her eyes, Vivian said sullenly, "Okay."

Howard smiled happily and pried Vivian's fingers away from her dress. It slid to the floor, revealing an elaborate, cream, satin bustier with garters. Howard's eyes stretched wide, as they roamed the length of Vivian's body. Lingered a few extra moments on her partially exposed, perfectly propped, full breasts. His mouth fell open soundlessly for a few seconds. Then, he gave a low, long whistle.

Vivian asked, "Well, are you going to kiss me, or not?"

Slowly licking his lips, Howard said in a barely audible voice, "Maybe I should get that drink for you first. Don't move while I'm gone, Viv. I'll be right back. Don't move."

"Can I wash my face while you're gone?"

Without taking his eyes off of the stimulating lingerie, Howard asked, "You won't have to take anything off to do it?"

"No, Howard. I won't take anything off."

Dashing out of the bedroom door, Howard said, "Okay."

Before Vivian emerged makeup-free from the bathroom, Howard had returned with the last bottle of champagne and two glasses. He set them down on Vivian's night stand, along with a snack tray Paul had prepared as his personal gift to the couple.

Howard picked up Vivian's dress and laid it over the chair. Then, he started to undress. The water stopped. Howard stopped and stared at the bathroom door. Vivian appeared in the doorway, still wearing stockings and the bustier.

She asked, "Were you planning on getting undressed without me, dear?"

Shaking his head, Howard said, "No."

"Good. You know I don't like missing the floor show."

Vivian pranced over to the radio and turned it on. Soft jazz floated through the room. From there, she glided over to the champagne. After filling both glasses, she spun around and said happily, "Proceed."

Never taking his eyes off Vivian, Howard undressed. He watched her sit down on the bed and cross her long, silk-stockinged legs. Loved the way she sipped champagne ever so sensuously from the glass. He stopped momentarily when she lay back on the bed.

Howard sat down on the bed to take his socks off, Vivian sat up and watched. Just as she knew he would, he rolled them and put them into his left shoe. Smiling, Vivian lay back and enjoyed the sight of him.

Not only was Howard intelligent, warm, and loving, he was the best-looking man Vivian had ever seen. She thought fleetingly, "To hell with Lula. That man could have married anyone he wanted. Thank God he chose me."

In his black briefs, Howard crawled up the bed. Gently parting her legs, he slid up Vivian's body and buried his face in her breasts. The combination of the sight and smell of her, the feel of her bare skin, satin and silk, completely aroused him. He groaned deep in his throat.

She closed her eyes and felt the tiny stirrings in the base of her stomach. Cradling Howard's head in her hands, Vivian whispered, "Am I ever going to get that kiss?"

Completely intoxicated by the smell and feel of Vivian's breasts, Howard mumbled, "You most certainly are, Mrs. Shaw."

Howard's warm face slid up to Vivian's. His perfectly sculpted, slightly-parted lips were so inviting, Vivian immediately closed her eyes and opened her mouth to receive them. Howard's hot tongue did a slow dance inside her mouth. He delighted in the champagne chill of her mouth. She, in the complete warmth of his. Their synchronous sway began automatically.

As Howard's attention wandered down Vivian's body, without losing lip contact with it, he mumbled, "How do I get this thing off?"

"Pull the string, Howard."

After massaging her satin-encased breasts a few more times, Howard pulled the string to free them. Vivian breathed her first unencumbered breath and gasped when Howard's mouth closed over her nipple. She stroked his neck and the hard, thick ripples of his back. Switching his attention to her other breast, Howard kept the abandoned one warm with his hand.

Howard relunctantly relinquished Vivian's breasts and devoted his full attention to getting all of her out of the bustier and stockings that had given him so much pleasure earlier. The rustle of the silky material in his heightened state of arousal made him all the more impatient. Giving Vivian no opportunity to participate, he slipped out of his briefs.

She protested, "Howard, I wanted to do that."

Kissing her pouting lips passionately, he said, "Next time, sweetheart. I promise. Come here."

Kneeling in front of Vivian, Howard leaned back on his heels. He guided her to his lap. Planted tiny, passionate kisses down the valley between her breasts and stopped. With no help from Vivian, Howard lifted and lowered her onto him. She hissed loudly, dug her nails into his shoulders and met his thrusts enthusiastically. As Howard took Vivian to familiar heights, he breathed heavily and asked questions. She panted, gasped, and answered.

"Do you love me, Vivian?"

"Yes."

"Are you sorry you married me?"

"No."

"Are you sure?"

"I'm sure."

"Are you happy, sweetheart?"

"Yes."

"What's your name?"

"Vivian."

"What's the rest of it?"

"Matthews."

Stopping momentarily to look into Vivian's eyes, Howard tilted his head, as if to ask, "Who's the dummy now?"

Finally, catching his meaning, she said, "Um, Vivian Shaw."

Picking up where he left off, Howard asked, "Do you still love me?"

"Oh, yes."

"Are you sure?"

"Ah, yes, Howard."

"Are you going to have my babies?"

"Yes, Howard. Yes."

"When?"

"Oh, God. Whenever you're ready."

"Jesus. I'm ready, Vivian. I'm ready!"

That scene played out, with major and minor variations, every day and night for the next ten days. In the sunshine, heat, and balmy breezes of Aruba. In the frigid, fresh air of Argentina. They sunbathed, swam, ate, and drank. Howard went skiing under the watchful eye of his wife. The women smiled at him a little too enthusiastically and made remarks in languages every woman understands. They took a few short hikes with other couples they met, laughed a lot, and forgot the responsibilities of work. One or the other was always snapping pictures.

Most of all, they spent lots of time together. Laughing, loving, and relaxing. At least once a day, for the first three days, Vivian started up again by saying, "That damn Lula." They bickered vigorously about her for a few minutes and let it go. Overall, their honeymoon was a smashing success. And, no matter what that damn Lula said, they were in fact, Mr. and Mrs. Howard Shaw.

Chapter Eighteen

An exhausted and happy Adrena Reynolds paraded into the Stanley home after the wedding. Not only did she feel proud of herself for functioning reasonably well in a house filled with strangers, but she had hugged and kissed the bride and groom. She shook hands with several people, with no repercussions. Let those two little girls touch her, without slapping either one. Adrena had held a very pleasant conversation with the cutest boy she had ever seen. She ate with him, gave him her telephone number, and came away not wanting to kill him.

If it hadn't been for Snow and Lula, the day would have been a complete success. Adrena could have disposed of those two without remorse. Maybe she would have felt a little sorry for the poor dumb cat - it only did what came naturally to it. On the other hand, that Lula had devised and executed her charade, knowing how damaging it would be. Adrena made herself a promise concerning Lula. If she ever spent more than fifteen minutes in her company again, Adrena would show her how a prank should play out.

As Adrena passed the kitchen, she noticed the light was on. Sticking her head through the door, Adrena was surprised to see Mrs. Stanley sitting at the table alone. The elderly woman was so mesmerized by thought that she didn't hear Adrena speaking to her.

Adrena walked into the kitchen, touched her shoulder, and said, "Hi, Mrs. Stanley. What are you doing up this time of night?"

Mrs. Stanley jerked back to reality and said, "Oh, hi, Adrena. Don't you look pretty? You cut your hair. It really suits you. Did everything go all right?"

Beaming, Adrena said, "Everything was so beautiful, Mrs. Stanley. Doc looked gorgeous. So did Howard. I met Doc's father, brother, two little sisters, and her stepmother. Howard's family was there, too. You'll never guess what his sister did."

Mrs. Stanley waited for Adrena to tell her what his sister had done. Adrena waited for her to take a guess. Finally, Mrs. Stanley said, "She objected when the minister said, 'Speak now, or forever hold your peace.'"

Looking perplexed, Adrena asked, "How did you know that?"

"No, she didn't, Adrena!"

"Yes, she did. She said Doc wasn't good enough for him."

"She wasn't good enough for him? Who would be then? I think the Queen of England is spoken for. Doc should have ripped her tongue out of her ignorant mouth. What happened?"

"Max slugged her, and I knocked her down. Then I put her and her husband out."

"Good for you, Adrena. Did Doc get very upset? Poor girl. That had to be extremely embarrassing for her."

Flopping down into a chair, Adrena said, "Only because she couldn't get a clear shot at her."

"Did Doc and her new husband like your gift?"

"Of course they did."

Mrs. Stanley smiled weakly and said, "Something came today from the Social Service people."

A cloud fell over Adrena's face when she asked, "What?"

Sighing heavily, Mrs. Stanley said, "Your mother has filed for custody. We have to go to a screening on Thursday."

"I'm not going."

"We have to go, baby. If we don't, they'll snatch you out of here so fast, neither one of us will know what happened."

"But Doc won't be back by then, Mrs. Stanley."

"I know. We'll have to do whatever we can to hold them off until she returns, Adrena. Mr. Stanley went over to your mother's address that was on the papers. He wanted to try to talk her out of it - to tell her how well you were doing here with us."

Shocked that Mr. Stanley had gone to that much trouble on her behalf, Adrena asked, "What happened?"

"There was no one home. He can't believe they'll make you leave here to live in that kind of squalor. Mr. Stanley said he could smell the filth through the door. He asked a neighbor what they knew about her. All anyone knew was she's a doper. A garbage head - whatever that is. You know he's not a violent man, Adrena, but he was so upset, he wanted to punch somebody when he came home."

"A garbage head is a person who gets high on anything, Mrs. Stanley. No real preference. Did you tell him she thinks she's taking me to my grandmother's house?"

"Yes, I did. Then he rode over there. Came back and said that place would be a shambles inside of a month with that woman in it. She'd sell everything - including the kitchen sink."

Adrena mumbled, "Everything, me and the kitchen sink."

Frowning, Mrs. Stanley asked, "What did you say?"

"Nothing. She has to be stopped."

"Yeah. We'll pray on it and do whatever we can. She won't get you without a fight, Adrena. I'll do anything I can to stop her."

The two sat at the table in silence for a few minutes. Then, Adrena got up slowly and said goodnight. Mildred had come in the mail to ruin the best day of her life. Adrena's thoughts flowed as she carefully put away her outfit and headed for the shower.

As the hot water struck her body, the final touches of a plan Adrena had dreamed became crystal clear. Mildred only wanted one thing. To get high. Well, Adrena had the means to make that happen for her.

On Sunday, Adrena rose early and ate breakfast with the Stanleys. She rambled on happily about the wedding. Thrilled to death to see her joy, Mr. and Mrs. Stanley asked all kinds of questions. Adrena described the cake, caterers, flowers, rings, the house and garden. She even mentioned Snow.

After breakfast, Adrena told them she wanted to go check on her grandmother's house. When Mr. Stanley said he had been there the day before and it looked fine to him, Adrena told him that without the key she knew he hadn't gone inside and that thieves have a way of getting in without making it obvious.

Adrena turned down his offer to take her and caught the bus over to the house, walked up the porch steps, and opened the door with her very own key. The mailbox was overflowing with bills, fliers and magazines which she collected. Once inside, Adrena whispered to herself, "My house. This is my house."

After surveying the place and satisfying herself no one had been in it, she walked to the telephone, but before she could pick it up and dial, there was a knock at the door. Hoping desperately it wasn't the Stanleys, Adrena went to see who it was.

Adrena didn't recognize the elderly woman standing on the porch, and she asked through the door, "May I help you?"

Almost screaming, the lady said, "I'm Catherine Hunter. I live next door. There's something I think you should know."

With her shoulder jammed against the door, Adrena opened it just enough for the lady to see her face. She asked, "What do you think I should know, Mrs. Hunter?"

A little put off by Adrena's precautions, Mrs. Hunter said, "Your mother's been dawdling around this house. You know your grandmother didn't want her in there."

"Do you know who I am?"

"I knew who you were before you did, Adrena. I used to babysit you for your grandmother. Everything was fine, until that twisted Mama of yours showed up and took you off."

Adrena opened the door all the way and asked, "If I gave you my telephone number, would you call me if you see Mildred over here? I don't want my grandmother's things stolen and sold for drug money."

"I sure will. What are you going to do with this place anyway? You're not old enough to live here alone."

"I don't know yet. I do know Mildred won't be living here."

Rolling her eyes up into her head, Mrs. Hunter said, "Thank God for that. One junkie can do more damage to a block than a shipload of termites."

Adrena walked into the dining room, wrote her name and number on a piece of paper. She turned to find Mrs. Hunter standing in the living room looking the place over thoroughly. While this invasion of space irritated Adrena, she stifled the automatic scream and strike impulse. After all, she wanted something from this neighbor.

Smiling casually, Adrena handed her the piece of paper and said, "Thank you, Mrs. Hunter. I'm sure I'll be seeing you from time to time. I'll be checking on the house often."

Not knowing anything else to say, Mrs. Hunter stuffed the paper into the pocket of her housedress and left. She shook her head as she walked up the street. Adrena knew she wanted to pry into her grandmother's business, so she could spread it around the neighborhood. People loved nothing more than gossiping about dead folks' business; no matter what was said, they couldn't come back and slap the tar out of you for it.

Back at the telephone, Adrena dialed Mildred's number. It rang six times before she managed to answer. Adrena could tell by the sound of her voice, she was hung over. Flatly, Adrena said, "Mildred, this is Adrena."

In a stupor, Mildred said, "Yeah? What do you want?"

"That's what I want to know from you. What do you want? Since we both know it's not me."

"I want my damn share of that money you got. I'm going out in the street next week, and you got a half million bucks. That ain't happening, Adrena. Now, if you want me to back off, you're gonna have to ante up, sweetheart."

When Mildred called Adrena "sweetheart," it didn't sound anything like it did when Mr. Matthews said it. Mildred's version made Adrena want to puke. There was no time for that though. Adrena had to get rid of Mildred permanently.

"How much and when, Mildred? I can't get too much at one time. I'll have to ask Mr. Lewis for it."

"Damn, that's right. Mama put it all in trust. Bart's coming home on Wednesday. I'm meeting him at the bus depot at three. Do you think he'll give you a grand by then?"

Adrena's excitement level shot through the roof with the thought of being able to get both Mildred and Bart at one

time. It was coming together as if fated. To contain the thrill
of it all, Adrena squeezed herself tight. There was no need to
tip Mildred off.

"I don't know if I can get that much, but I'll see what I can
do. I've got some stash I want to get rid of, too. You want
it?"

More excited by the thought of the drugs than the money
now, Mildred asked, "Sure, what you got?"

"A little of this and that. You know, I spent a lot of time
in the hospital and the wacky farm. I've got something for
anything that ails you."

Adrena's mind's eye could see Mildred perking up and
licking her lips. Heard the thrill of anticipation in her voice
when she asked, "Where are you now, Adrena?"

"At home. Why?"

"When are you going to Mama's house? I can pick that
stuff up from you over there. I don't want that newsy cow
you live with in my business."

"I'll get there on Wednesday. I'll put a package together
for you and leave it in the mailbox. You and Bart can have a
blowout welcome home party. I think I even have some of
his favorite. Weed and coke."

"Aw, shit. Can't I get it today, Adrena? I'll save it for
him."

"No. Wednesday will have to do. I don't want you
cheating dear old Dad. By the way, why didn't you ever tell
me Bart was my real father?"

"It wasn't none of your damn business. Still ain't."

"Hey, if you're gonna act like that, Mildred, I'll see you in
court on Thursday."

"No. Hold your damn panties in place. If I had ever said
Bart was your father, Mama would have had him locked up
for statutory rape. I was only twelve when I got pregnant.
Bart was a lot older."

"Why is my last name Reynolds? Nobody else's is."

"What's with all of these questions?"

"I want to know."

"Damn. I told Mama your father's name was Gregory
Reynolds."

"Why? Who was he?"

"Some fool the cops killed when I was three months pregnant with you. I needed a name, and he couldn't object," Mildred said with a laugh.

Unimpressed with Mildred's creativity, Adrena continued, "Just for general information, why did you two do that to me?"

"Jesus, Adrena. You know why we did it - for money. They would pay a nice piece of change for a young girl like you. Don't take that shit personal. Some man is gonna use you sooner or later. Bart would have taught you good. You would have known what you were worth when you went out on your own. You wouldn't be giving it away, the way you probably are right now."

Dismissing Mildred's crude remarks, Adrena said, "I would have died, if the police hadn't come, Mildred. That bottle was broken. As it was, I stayed in the hospital for months."

"It was? Damn. I didn't know that. But, you wasn't gonna die, Adrena. Don't no woman die from that. If they did, there'd be bodies everywhere."

"I wasn't a woman, Mildred. I was a little girl."

"So was I when he did it to me the first time. I didn't die."

"Did he use a broken bottle on you?"

"No. But I didn't fight like you did either. All you had to do was shut up and go with the flow. Bart is good at what he does. You would have seen that if you'd cooperated."

The venomous smile on Adrena's face grew more lethal with every word Mildred spoke. After all this time, there was still no remorse for what they did. No talk of family, love, or forgiveness. Just more threats. Demands.

"He was my father, Mildred."

"So what. Don't go acting like your father is the first one to ever do that."

"Did your father do that to you?"

"Hell, no! Daddy loved me and Antoinette too much for that. He used to give us anything we wanted. Money. Clothes. Trips. Shows. Drove Mama crazy. They argued like cats and dogs about us. She said he was spoiling us and he'd regret it one day. He told her to mind her own business; she didn't lack for nothing. We were his girls. I think she knew he loved us more than her."

Abruptly changing the subject, Mildred said, "Never mind about all that. Just pack that stuff up and leave it in the box. I'll get it. Don't put it in there before the mailman comes either."

Adrena sighed and said, "I won't. Goodbye, Mildred."

That afternoon, Adrena helped Mr. Stanley in his hothouse. They watered, pruned, and talked to the colorful plants. They even said a few things to each other. Preoccupied with his thriving, fragrant darlings, Mr. Stanley did not see Adrena scoop arsenic into a baggie and slide it into her pocket.

Two of the Stanleys' former foster children joined them for dinner that night. They ate a wonderful dinner, laughed, and talked until late. Adrena wondered how people like the Stanleys could have so much love for the children of other people - people who couldn't be bothered with loving - sick people, like Mildred and Bart.

That night, as the Stanleys slept, Adrena retrieved her pill collection from the toes of her shoes. Ritalin, Prozac, Lithium, Percocet, Darvon, Haldol, Librium, Thorazine and Seconal. Adrena separated the tablets from the capsules. There was an impressive array of colors displayed on the carpet next to Adrena's bed. White and beige, green and yellow, red and grey, green and white, clear and orange. Then there were the large orange capsules Bart really loved.

No matter which ones they took, Adrena wanted to make sure they would do the job. Wearing disposable rubber gloves from Mr. Stanley's hothouse, Adrena crushed all of the tablets. It seemed to take forever, because she had to do it quietly. With that done, she added the arsenic. Then, very carefully, she opened each capsule and emptied their contents into the mix. She refilled the capsules with her personal concoction, put them back together, wiped the excess dust from them individually, and dropped them into a baggie. Just to be safe, Adrena wiped down the baggie before putting it into the brown paper bag which she then hid inside her new makeup kit.

After cleaning up all of the mess, she walked down to the bathroom and poured the excess powder into the sink. She wrapped the gloves and baggie tightly in a wad of toilet paper and threw them into the toilet. She flushed the toilet, ran the water in the sink, and watched the final remnants of white, yellow, and pink powders disappear down the drain.

On her way back to her room, Mrs. Stanley came to the door and asked, "Are you all right, Adrena? You're not having nightmares again, are you? Do you need to take something to help you sleep?"

"No, I'm fine. Just had to go to the bathroom."

"Okay. Call me if you need me."

"I will. Goodnight."

On Monday, Adrena called a girl with whom she had been in foster care. She knew Kelly could get the weed and cocaine she wanted - Kelly had been smoking the stuff since she was six. She used to try to get Adrena to join her, but after living with Mildred and Bart, Adrena didn't want anything to do with drugs. Even the medication she needed to protect her sanity was not willingly taken.

The two girls met in the schoolyard - that way they wouldn't be close to either foster home. Adrena gave Kelly the money for the cocaine and a dime bag of marijuana, as well as twenty-five dollars for her trouble. Kelly disappeared and reappeared so quickly, Adrena knew she must have had had the stuff on her all the time. It didn't matter. She threw in the Top paper for free. Kelly thanked Adrena for the business, and the two girls headed in opposite directions.

Back at the house, Adrena wiped the plastic bags down and placed them into the brown paper bag with the pills. She made sure there was enough room for the fifth of Jack Daniels from Granny's liquor cabinet. She put her last twenty dollars in there, too. Adrena thought, "What a waste of good allowance money. Oh well, it's for a good cause - 'cause I want them to pay for what they did." She laughed out loud at the thought.

Adrena waited for Wednesday. She filled the time replaying Mildred and Bart's death scene out in her head. She could see the glee on their faces, when they saw what all they had in their goody bag.

Bart would say, "Hell, baby. We done died and gone to heaven."

Mildred would say, "All for you, baby. Welcome home!"

They would roll a few joints. Snort up any particles of cocaine left on the table, sit back, and smoke leisurely. Bart would pour a few drinks. That would give them their wake-up buzz. The higher they got, the higher they'd want to get. They'd sift through the little stack of pills and choose a few. Throw them down their throats and wash them down with another drink.

Adrena wondered if the idiots actually knew the effects of the pills. Or, if they chose by color - the way she did with M&M's.

Glasses in hand, Mildred and Bart would head for the bed, and, there, they'd attempt to do hideous things to each other. Feel strange. Start flinching, jumping, and scratching. Coughing to clear their throats. Wanting to wash the itch away, they'll take a few more sips of Jack Daniels. Water would never cross their minds.

Mildred would puke. She always did. Instead of taking the hint, they'd go back to square one. Smoke a little and pop a few more pills. Then, they'd start arguing for no sane reason, screaming like banshees. Bart would slap Mildred down on the floor. She'd lie there and whine. Get up, pop a few more pills and take another drink. Maybe try to smoke another joint.

Because his system was cleaner than hers, he'd pass out first. If her fried pea-brain was still functioning, Mildred would curl up next to her big old lover boy. They'd be stinking up the neighborhood before the weekend.

That was Adrena's bedtime story for the next two nights, and she slept like a baby. Mrs. Stanley, however, wasn't getting much sleep at all, and it showed. She would be worrying herself to death until this custody mess was over.

Adrena hated Mildred and Bart even more for upsetting that nice lady.

A smile crept across Adrena's face when she thought, "Even if they miraculously escape dying, neither one of them will make it to the screening on Thursday."

On Wednesday afternoon, Adrena caught the bus to her grandmother's house. She saw the overflowing mailbox and purposely left it filled. She walked into the dining room, took the bottle of Jack Daniels out of the cabinet, wiped it down and placed it into the bag. After a quick, casual inspection of the house, Adrena headed out.

Carrying the brown paper bag close to her body, in case Mrs. Hunter was watching, Adrena took the mail out of the box and placed the bag inside. She flipped through the letters as she walked toward the bus stop, then stuffed them into her purse and boarded the bus five minutes later.

The wait for Mildred and Bart's death knell would be hard on Adrena. It was, after all, what she had survived for - to kill the two of them.

Chapter Nineteen

Adrena had been excused from her Wednesday appointments until Doc returned. Somebody named Harper was filling in for her in case of emergencies. Doc knew Adrena would say little to another psychiatrist, and a male psychiatrist would get nothing but hostile stares. Adrena called Millie and talked to fill that time.

Adrena really missed seeing Doc and hoped she was having a good time. Adrena also hoped Howard wouldn't put too many kiss marks on her before she got back.

After making the delivery at her grandmother's house and talking to Millie on Wednesday, Adrena called and left a message for Max. It didn't seem to be too soon to call her. With nothing else to do, Adrena played the piano for an hour and then ate dinner.

Calling it a night, Adrena was on her way up to her room when Mrs. Stanley called her to the telephone. Assuming it was Max, Adrena ran down and answered cheerfully. To her surprise, a young male voice responded.

"Hi, Adrena."

Frowning, she asked, "Who's this?"

"Junior."

With Mrs. Stanley looking on, Adrena smiled shyly and said, "Oh, hi, Junior. I thought you were Max. I just left a message for her."

Speaking hesitantly, Junior said, "Oh . . . if you're expecting another call, I can call you some other time."

"You don't have to do that. I can talk to you for a while. How's your summer break going?"

"It's going okay. I work at the gas station every day during the week. My dad makes me cut the grass and take my sisters to the pool on Saturdays. Then I can do anything I want. What about you?"

"I'm always trying to catch up, Junior. I kind of got a late start in school. Doc enrolled me for some summer courses, but they don't start until next week."

"Why did Max enroll you in summer school?"

Adrena giggled and said, "Not Max. Vivian. She's been my guardian angel for a long time."

"Really? I barely know either one of them. They were already in college when I was born. Sometimes I wish I knew them better."

"They don't visit you and your sisters?"

"Not too often. My mom thinks they remind Dad of his first wife too much. He always seems sad after they leave. I know he's as proud of them as he can be though. If I don't become a doctor, lawyer, or a prince, he's going to disown me."

They both laughed before Junior asked, "Do you have any brothers and sisters, Adrena?"

"No."

"Wow, that must be great. Having the house to yourself. No tiny creatures playing in your stuff. Drawing pictures on your homework. Crying and changing the station on the television."

"I wish I did have someone to do that stuff. Being alone is no fun, Junior. Especially when you have two warped parents, like mine."

"They don't let you do anything, huh?"

"I don't live with them anymore. I'm in foster-care. That's why your sister is my doctor. I'd be lost, or dead, without Doc. Get to know them, Junior. You've got two really great sisters."

"When Viv comes home, would you ask her if you can go to the movies with me, Adrena? I mean, if you want to."

Shocked, Adrena asked, "Who, me?"

"Yes, you. We're both sixteen. Why not?"

"I just can't believe you want to go to a movie with me, Junior. You're playing some kind of prank on me. Right? Just tell me what it is, so we can both laugh together."

"Why would I be doing that? Are you saying you've never been to a movie with a boy?"

"No. Mostly, they tease me. Have you ever gone to a movie with a girl?"

"Dad wouldn't let me go with one alone. He said I could this year though. I've got my permit. He's teaching me how to drive, and I'll be able to take the car out alone for my prom next spring."

"Really? Doc won't even discuss driving with me yet. If you came over and talked to her, I bet she would, Junior."

"I'll do it, if you'll go to the movies with me."

"Okay."

"Good. Maybe I should let you wait for your call from Max now. I'll call you on Saturday."

"Okay. Goodbye, Junior."

"Goodbye, Adrena."

The minute Adrena hung up the telephone, Mrs. Stanley asked, "And who was that, young lady?"

Answering innocently, Adrena said, "Junior. He's Doc's brother. He asked me to go to the movies with him when she gets back."

"Really? That's nice. Do you like him?"

Shrugging her shoulders, Adrena said, "He's all right. He's really cute . . . for a boy. Looks like Max. His hair is different though."

"Really? How old is he?"

"Sixteen. He's a year ahead of me in school though. Do you think it'll be all right for me to go to a movie with him, Mrs. Stanley?"

"Well, you are sixteen, Adrena. My only concern is, you don't mix with others very often - you might not know exactly how a date goes. I don't want you to be upset if he tries to hold your hand or puts his arm around your shoulders in the movie. Boys do that, you know."

A crease of concern appeared on Adrena's pretty forehead. She hadn't thought about anything like that. Touching was one of her least favorite things. She would have to take some time to decide if she liked Junior enough for that. It wouldn't look too good for her to jump all over him for doing something he didn't know about, and Doc might get upset with her for slapping her brother, too. Maybe Max would give her some advice about it.

Looking Mrs. Stanley in the eyes, Adrena said, "We'll take one day at a time. Won't build any unnecessary bridges."

Musing, with her finger resting on her chin, Mrs. Stanley asked, "Now, where have I heard that before?"

They laughed together. The telephone rang again. Thinking it was really Max this time, Adrena answered. She was surprised for the second time. It was Mrs. Hunter.

"Adrena, your mother and that man are over there on your grandmother's porch right this minute."

Sounding casual, Adrena asked, "What are they doing, Mrs. Hunter?"

"He's looking through the windows. She's standing at the door. I think she's ringing the bell. Look at Mildred - she's a nasty-looking mess. Good thing her daddy's dead. I can't believe a man would walk down the street with a woman looking like that."

Adrena said nothing.

Finally, Mrs. Hunter said, "They're leaving."

"Did they do anything?"

"No. They're headed toward the corner now."

"Okay. Call me if they come back. Thank you, Mrs. Hunter."

Adrena hung up the telephone before the older woman could say another word. The last thing she wanted was a conversation about Mildred and Bart - not with that newsy lady anyway. At least she hadn't seen Mildred taking the bag out of the mailbox. That might have caused a problem.

Mrs. Stanley asked, "Now, who was that? You've turned into a regular chatterbox since that wedding, Miss."

"That was Mrs. Hunter. She called to tell me Mildred and Bart were on my porch."

Puffing up, Mrs. Stanley said, "Let's get Mr. Stanley and go over there right this minute. Did you tell her to call the police if they make a move to get in?"

"They've left already. She said she would call again if they came back. Believe me, Mrs. Stanley, they won't get in without Mrs. Hunter seeing them. I won't have to tell her to call the police. She'll call them on her own."

"To be on the safe side, maybe we should go over and spend the night. I owe your mother a good slapping. Breaking and entering ought to give me the right to slap and kick her."

Adrena laughed, and shedding her anger, Mrs. Stanley joined in. They sat together in the kitchen for a while talking. Then, satisfied that Mrs. Hunter wasn't going to call right back, they joined Mr. Stanley in the living room, and the three watched television together.

Mrs. Stanley looked over at Adrena from time to time. She still worried about their meeting scheduled for the next day, but not wanting to upset Adrena, she didn't discuss it. Tomorrow would come soon enough.

Anticipation robbed Adrena of the ability to concentrate on the television program. Daydreaming about Mildred and Bart boozing and cruising off the planet excited her. Thinking about Junior's telephone call worried her.

Without any protests from the Stanleys, Adrena excused herself after half an hour and went to her room. Knowing she would never fall asleep on her own, Adrena took the one sleeping pill she was allowed to keep, and after showering, sleep came easily.

Mrs. Stanley shaking her awake was the next thing Adrena was conscious of. Through the fog, Adrena heard her say something about the telephone.

Mumbling and half asleep, Adrena said, "I'll talk to Max tomorrow. I'm too tired now."

"It's not Max, Adrena. It's Mrs. Hunter."

Sitting up, Adrena asked, "What does she want? Did they come back?"

"No, Adrena. She's calling to tell you something else."

Still trying to shake off a drugged sleep, Adrena stumbled down to the telephone. Mr. Stanley stood next to it. Adrena couldn't begin to guess what time it was. All she knew was that everyone was dressed for bed.

With her eyes still rolling lazily around in her head, Adrena said, "Hello."

An excited Mrs. Hunter said, "Adrena, the police were just at your grandmother's house. I went over to see what was going on. They said there was a fire blazing at Mildred's apartment."

Truly shocked, Adrena asked, "A fire? Where's Mildred and Bart?"

"I think they're in the apartment. You better get over there, Adrena."

"Why? What can I do?"

"That's your mother, child. Go see what's going on."

Sighing, Adrena said, "Okay. Fire, or no fire, they're not getting into my house. Goodbye, Mrs. Hunter."

Still holding the telephone, Adrena turned to the Stanleys and said, "There's a fire at Mildred's. Mrs. Hunter thinks they're inside."

With genuine concern, Mr. Stanley said, "Okay, Adrena. You just stay calm. We'll all get dressed and go over. They're probably sitting on the curb, sweetheart. Don't you worry yourself."

Unable to shake the drugged haze, Adrena simply shrugged her shoulders and hung up the telephone. The three filed up the stairs. Twenty minutes later, they were sitting in the Stanleys' car. It was a real wonder Mr. Stanley didn't hit something because he kept looking anxiously at Adrena in the rearview mirror.

Adrena went back to sleep about three blocks into the ride, and when Mr. Stanley shook Adrena, they were already parked on the block where Mildred lived. Flashing red, yellow, and blue lights flooded the night. Men's voices yelling commands shattered the stillness. Old smoke and an unfamiliar stench, intermingled, filled the air. Pools of water glistened on the asphalt.

The moment Adrena got out of the car, she saw two fire trucks, three ambulances, four police cars, and a coroner's station wagon. Still honestly unable to process what was going on, Adrena asked, "What do we do now?"

Mr. Stanley said, "I'll go ask the police if they know where they are. You two stay here."

As he walked away, Mrs. Stanley asked, "Why are you so groggy? Did you take a sleeping pill, Adrena?"

Scratching her hair, Adrena nodded.

"I knew all of that talking was going to upset you. Maybe you should slow down a little. You can't just go from not talking to anybody, to talking to a bunch of folks overnight."

Not up to arguing, Adrena responded, "You're probably right. Anytime Mildred's mentioned, I can't sleep. And don't forget, we were supposed to meet with her tomorrow."

"Jesus, I knew you were upset about that. Why didn't you call me? No wonder you're so drowsy. What did you take?"

"Just something to help me sleep. It was the emergency Ativan you put in my jewelry case. I'm all right."

They watched Mr. Stanley talk to the officers. He pointed in their direction once. One officer walked him over to the coroner's vehicle and unzipped a thick, grey plastic bag. Mr. Stanley's head jerked and dropped. The two of them walked toward Adrena and Mrs. Stanley, who wrapped her arm protectively around Adrena's shoulders.

The officer addressed Adrena right away, saying, "Miss Reynolds, I'm sorry to have to tell you, we think your mother and stepfather are two of the three bodies found in the building."

Tilting her head, Adrena asked, "Who was the third?"

"I don't know, but from the looks of the third body, they didn't die in the fire."

"What do you mean?"

"The body has been in there for weeks, Miss Reynolds. Maybe even months. Two people said they saw your parents enter the building earlier this evening."

"Can I see them?"

Looking uncomfortable, the officer said, "There's nothing there you should see. Nothing to identify."

With mounting excitement, Adrena asked, "Well, how do we know it's them? Who's the other person? Why would they live in a building with a corpse?"

"According to the neighbor two doors down, your mother was the only one living in the building. Your stepfather came in with her today. There was a lot of yelling. They think they were arguing. You do know your mother had a drug problem, don't you?"

"Yes, sir. I know."

"Of course, I'm just guessing, but I think they got high and fell asleep smoking. That other person probably overdosed a long time ago - nobody reported it because they would have to answer questions. We find them like this all the time. I'm sorry. I'll just take your name, address, and telephone number. When the coroner finishes with them, he'll contact you."

Never having thought anyone would expect her to do anything with the bodies, unexpected terror crept up on Adrena. In an obviously agitated state, she asked, "What am I supposed to do then?! I don't know what to do with dead people! Can't they just keep them?!"

Mr. Stanley said, "Adrena, calm down. We'll see what has to be done after the coroner calls. Maybe your grandmother's lawyer will know what to do. Either way, we'll take care of it for you. Don't worry yourself. Please?"

He turned to the officer and said, "Thank you for your help. I'll give you that information and take the child home."

As Mr. Stanley walked and talked with the officer, Adrena stared at the building. It was entirely black and gutted. Wanting to remember the smell of Mildred and Bart's demise, Adrena took in deep breaths of the rancid smoke. She never wanted to forget what sweet revenge and freedom smelled like.

However, Adrena was disappointed to hear she couldn't look into their charred, empty eye sockets. See their fire-tortured flesh. She wondered how long it took them to die. If they knew they were dying. What their final thoughts were. Adrena hoped with all her heart that Mildred and Bart knew she was responsible.

She saw them close the coroner's doors. Knowing she was being closely observed by the Stanleys, Adrena was careful not to express the joy that permeated her entire being. She thought cheerfully, "Goodbye, Mom and Dad. I hope hell is all they say it is . . . and so much more!"

Chapter Twenty

Twelve days later, Mr. and Mrs. Howard Shaw returned from Argentina, relaxed and rejuvenated. Just as Vivian had predicted, they both had colds. Howard laughed every time he sneezed; Vivian scowled and mumbled at him every time she did. "Skiing in July. I've married an idiot, and I'm traipsing right behind him."

Clayton picked them up from the airport. He assured Howard there had been no major catastrophes at the office during his absence. He reported that Sheldon had vacated the premises. Charlene wasn't too happy having him back at home, but she was dealing with it. And Lula had been having blood pressure problems since the wedding. Knowing how concerned Howard would be about it, Clayton went to see Lula and thought she looked fine.

Rolling her eyes, Vivian said, "Surprise. Surprise."

Howard said, "Don't start, Vivian. She might really be sick, you know. Lula's not a young woman anymore."

With a sudden flash of anger in her eyes, Vivian said, "Well, you can just drop me off at home and run right over, Howard. That's all she wants anyway. If you think I'm going to try to stop you, you're wrong."

Turning quickly to look at Vivian in the back seat, Howard yelled, "Did I say I was going anywhere, Vivian?!"

Blinking slowly, Vivian stared at him. They hadn't been back ten minutes, and Lula was driving a wedge between them already. Vivian refused to fight with a man's sister for him - there was something a little too bizarre about that for her. If he truly loved her, Howard would make the correct choices on his own.

Frowning, Clayton said, "Jesus, I'm sorry I said anything about her."

Howard said, "Not as sorry as I am, Clayton. Vivian's still upset about the wedding."

"I can't blame her for that, Buddy. Lula was definitely out of order on that one."

"So, what can I do about it? It's done."

Looking at Vivian's angry scowl through the rearview mirror, Clayton said, "Don't ask me. I failed Relationships 101 and 102. Remember?"

They rode in silence after that exchange. Fifteen minutes later, Clayton pulled up in front of Howard's house; Clayton and Howard unloaded the luggage and took it in. Vivian didn't budge; she sat steaming in the backseat.

Howard came out and asked, "Why are you sitting there, Vivian?"

Vivian rolled her eyes and shook her head. She was trying to collect herself, but failing. The last thing she wanted was to argue with Howard their very first day at home, but she could see there wasn't going to be a way to avoid it. If he didn't confront Lula about what she did, Vivian would never let him hear the end of it. He didn't have to do it today, but he'd better convince her he planned to do it soon.

She took a deep breath, let it out, and got out of the car. Howard put his arms around her and said, "Don't get upset about that today, Vivian. I'll take care of it. I promise. Don't you trust me?"

Laying her head on his chest, Vivian said, "Not when it comes to Lula, Howard. You're afraid. You think you'll alienate her. I know that's the last thing you want."

Howard lifted Vivian's face with his finger. He looked into her eyes and kissed her. As always, there was more than passion in his kiss. There was love and devotion, and Vivian felt it with every ounce of her being.

He whispered, "The only person I worry about alienating is you. The only person I truly need is you. If we're all right, everything is all right. Are we?"

Laying her head on his chest again, Vivian stroked Howard's back and said, "Yes. We're all right."

Holding on to each other, they walked up to the front door. Howard stopped at the door and scooped Vivian up in his arms. She laughed. Howard said, "Welcome home, Mrs. Shaw."

He carried her over the threshold into the living room and plopped her down on the sofa. Vivian looked around the extremely masculine room and said, "These stripes have to go, Mr. Shaw."

"Do whatever you like, sweetheart. All I ask is that you stay away from my office. Try not to put too many flowers in the den either. I entertain men in there. You can't seriously shoot pool and lift weights if everything is light, airy, and coordinated."

Smiling again, Clayton asked, "Did he say you're planning on putting flowers in the weight room?"

Before Vivian could say a word, Howard responded, "I'm telling you now, Clayton, she will. I'll be up to my eyeballs in powder blue, pink, vases, bric-a-brac, daisies, and lilies if I don't put my foot down now."

"Well, put it down, Buddy. Put both of them down, if you have to. Here, borrow one of mine, if you need a third."

Vivian crossed her arms and said, "Very funny. I'll deal with this place later. Can you entertain Howard for a few minutes, Clayton? I want to call my office before Millie leaves."

"Sure."

"May I use the telephone in your office, dear?"

"Sure."

Vivian pranced off to Howard's office, as both men watched her leave. Howard hit at Clayton for staring.

After telling Millie the honeymoon was great, except for the colds they came back with, Vivian inquired about her patients. There was an unusual, uncomfortable pause from Millie.

Vivian asked, "What happened, Millie? Who did Harper incarcerate?"

"He considered sending Mrs. Baker. I told him you wouldn't like that. She kept calling. I think she's got a crush on him."

"Okay. If everyone escaped the bin, what's up?"

Millie took a deep breath and said, "Adrena's parents died in a fire."

Vivian yelled, "What?! How is she, Millie?! Adrena wasn't anywhere near them, was she?!"

"She's fine, Vivian. And, I don't think she was anywhere near them."

"Okay, what happened?"

"All I've heard is they had a party, took too many drugs, fell asleep, and set the apartment on fire. If you want any more details, you'll have to speak to Mrs. Stanley."

"Jesus, Millie. I hope Adrena didn't have anything to do with it."

"I really don't think she did, Vivian. Adrena's been doing so well. She handled the wedding easily enough. Others may have found her behavior a little strange, but I was proud of the way she went to bat for you. She didn't really hurt anyone, and we both know she was capable - she's torn your office up enough times over the years."

"I know, Millie. Adrena even gave Howard and me a kiss. God knows she's come a long way. I'll talk to Mrs. Stanley. Anything else?"

"Not a thing. You forgot to refill Mr. Burton's prescription. Dr. Harper took care of it. There's been no noise from Huntingdon."

Vivian sat and collected her thoughts for a few minutes, before calling the Stanley home. She knew she would have to know all the facts surrounding Mildred's and Bart's deaths. If Adrena was implicated in any way, she would commit her and turn her case over to Harper. It would throw Adrena back a few years - possibly permanently - but Vivian could not act as an accomplice to murder . . . not even for her beloved Adrena.

Mr. Stanley answered. When Vivian identified herself, he said, "Well, congratulations, Doc. I hope the honeymoon was good."

Smiling, Vivian said, "Thank you. It was wonderful, Mr. Stanley. My secretary told me about Mr. and Mrs. Hanover. Is Adrena handling it all right?"

"She's been pretty good, Doc. Hasn't had to take anything special. Been sleeping without help. Reading books. Playing the piano. Talking on the telephone. Everything she's been doing. I don't think Adrena was very connected to those people. She didn't cry or get upset, until she thought she had to bury them."

"Good. Did she have to bury them?"

"No. The state cremated what was left of them."

"Please don't take my next question the wrong way, Mr. Stanley. Had Adrena been in touch with her mother before the fire?"

"No, not really. Her mother had filed for custody. We were scheduled for a screening at Social Services the next day. The notice came the day of your wedding. But Adrena never spoke to anyone other than my wife about it. You know my wife watches her like a hawk. Monitors every telephone call."

"Exactly what did the Hanovers die from, Mr. Stanley?"

"A better question would be, what didn't the Hanovers die from, Doc. Those people had a laundry list of drugs and alcohol in their systems. They also had smoke in their lungs. The coroner said they were going, fire or no fire. Did you know that woman was living in that apartment building with a corpse, Doc?"

"With a corpse?!"

"Yes, ma'am. There was a third body pulled out of the fire. He'd been dead for weeks. No one even knows who he was. That was the stench I smelled when I went over there that day."

"You went over there?"

"Yes. The day of the wedding. I wanted to try to talk her mother out of dragging the child through that custody mess. I'm sorry those folks died, Doc, but I'm not sorry they can't get their hands on Adrena."

"I understand, Mr. Stanley. Did the coroner list the drugs they took on the death certificate?"

"No, Ma'am. I asked him though. He gave me a copy of the sheet he listed them on. Do you want me to get it and read them off to you?"

"Yes."

Mr. Stanley left the telephone for a few minutes. Vivian nervously searched Howard's desk for a pen and pad, with fear quaking her soul at the prospect of what she would hear. Mr. Stanley returned and muddled through the long list of technical names. "Alcohol, arsenic, aspirin, caffeine, chlordiazepoxide, chlorpromazine, cocaine, codeine, fluoxetine, formaldehyde, lithium, marijuana, methylphenidate, oxycodone, propoxyphene, and secobarbital. She had a lot of heroin in her system, too. He didn't."

"What?! They were dead before they hit the ground. Where on earth would anyone get all that from, Mr. Stanley?"

"The street, Doc. They can get anything you can. I asked the coroner if all of this was unusual. He assured me he had seen worse. The levels of this stuff were low. The combinations were lethal. He figures they called themselves mixing up some kind of unique trip. They must not have had any sense of what's too much, or what shouldn't be taken with what. By the way, there's nothing on that list Adrena takes."

Nervously, Vivian asked, "How do you know that? Did anyone ask?"

"No. Mrs. Stanley crosschecked it and mentioned it in passing."

"Adrena didn't have any extra medicine, did she? Something she may have taken before and stopped?"

"No, ma'am. Mrs. Stanley checks her room at least twice a week. Don't tell Adrena, but she even checks her pockets, purses, and bedding when she's not at home. We've had children with problems before, Doc. We pretty much know how far they'll go. Believe me, Adrena's been good."

Letting out a deep sigh of relief, Vivian said, "I'm so glad, Mr. Stanley. I hate being suspicious of Adrena. I just know how she felt about her parents."

"Well, I think you can rest assured, Adrena had nothing to do with their deaths. They'll never bother her again either. Maybe she'll be able to make that final step now. Thanks to you, she's so close."

"You and your wife have been a big help, Mr. Stanley. You gave her that secure environment she needed so badly.

I think you've been able to begin the remolding of her impression of men."

"Who, me? I'm just being myself."

"Well, just being yourself, you've shone a light in the darkness for a devastated little girl. I assume she's not there."

"No, Ma'am. She and Mrs. Stanley went over to check her grandmother's house."

"Okay. You can tell her to call me when she comes in. For my own peace of mind, I'd like to hear her voice."

Vivian gave Mr. Stanley Howard's telephone number and hung up. She would talk to Adrena. See how she sounded. If she needed to be seen, Vivian would go over and talk to her.

In the meantime, with loud protests from her new husband, Vivian excused herself and promised to return shortly. Millie was surprised to see her walk into the office.

Vivian went straight to the files and pulled out Adrena's. It was thick, but all of her past and present medications were listed together. Comparing the list Mr. Stanley gave her to her own, Vivian found two matches, but they had been administered more than four years ago, in the hospital. If Adrena had somehow smuggled them out, it was very unlikely that they'd still be around after all the moves she had made. And besides, Adrena was much too smart to risk keeping them around that long. As far as what Adrena had access to currently, there were absolutely no matches.

Sitting at her desk for over an hour, Vivian pondered any possibilities that would tie Adrena to her parents' deaths. From what she'd heard and the facts in front of her, Vivian kept coming up blank. However, she also knew that if Adrena did have anything to do with it, it would be difficult to make the connection. That was the way she worked. There was only one way to find out for sure; Vivian would have to ask her. Adrena had always confessed in the past, even without being asked.

Vivian was glad to know the Stanleys were on the case, too. She hated feeling that she was the only one with any suspicion. Knowing Mrs. Stanley thoroughly searched

Adrena's room made Vivian feel a lot less suspicious of her beloved demon child.

Maybe Mildred and Bart really did fry their own brains, and then their own bodies. There was nothing Vivian wanted more than to know it was divine justice. For what they had done to Adrena, they didn't deserve much more. And they wouldn't be trying it with any other unfortunate ten-year-old.

Forcing thoughts of Adrena to the back of her mind, Vivian left her office and rejoined her husband and his friend. Howard wanted to know if she needed to go home before they went shopping since there was nothing in the house to eat. She told him no.

Then, he asked, "By the way, what are you making for dinner?"

Vivian looked around and asked, "Who, me?"

"Yes, you. You did look through that cookbook I gave you. Didn't you, Vivian?"

She whined, "Yes, but I can't cook anything in it."

Clayton said, "You can't cook, Vivian? I knew there was something wrong with you. Now, I know what it is."

"Shut up, Clayton. Howard knew I couldn't cook before he married me."

Howard said, "Well, your first lesson begins tonight, sweetheart. I'll help you."

"If you can cook, why do I have to learn?"

Howard's head dropped before he asked, "Are you thinking I'm going to be the sole cook, Vivian?"

Smiling, she said, "You could be, Howard. There's nothing wrong with it. I'm the one who'll have to have the babies. You can't do that."

Waving her off, Howard said, "Yeah, well you have a few first. Then, we'll discuss this again. Until then, we'll share the cooking."

Vivian rolled her eyes at Howard.

Cheering his best friend on, Clayton said, "That's right, Buddy. Put those feet down."

Vivian snapped, "Shut up, Clayton."

Chapter Twenty-One

At eight that evening, the telephone rang. Howard dried his hands and answered. The fact of it now being her telephone too had not sunk in for Vivian; she continued washing dishes and clearing the counter.

After a brief conversation with the caller, Howard handed Vivian the receiver and said, "It's for you, Vivian."

Taking the telephone from Howard, Vivian answered. An excited Adrena said, "Hi, Doc. Did you have a good time? Do you have lots of blue marks? I know he kissed you non-stop."

Smiling, Vivian said, "I've got my share, Adrena. The honeymoon was wonderful. I heard about Mildred and Bart. How are you?"

"I'm fine, Doc. You didn't think I would lose any sleep over them, did you?"

"Not really. I didn't know how you would react. Sometimes, regardless of extenuating circumstances, children feel a sense of loss. Death has a way of forcing good memories to surface."

"There are no good memories, Doc. I never had one good time with them. All they ever taught me was to be invisible. Never to speak to anyone. Lie, if forced to speak. And steal, if no one was looking. Should I mourn those things?"

"No, Adrena. Don't you remember a hug or a kiss? A sunny day and a walk? A conversation you can keep?"

"Not really, Doc. They weren't big on hugs and kisses. Seldom walked during the day. Sunny, or otherwise. If they weren't directing me to steal, they were demanding I be quiet. Honestly, Doc, I'm fine. Mildred and Bart's departure gives me a great sense of relief. That's all."

"Had you spoken with her lately?"

"Not one word since she called Granny's to see if I could sneak her in. We didn't exactly have much to talk about, Doc. The thought of her gave me nightmares."

"Have you had any since the fire?"

"Not one. No headaches either."

"Are you sure you never visited your mother, Adrena?"

"Who, me?! Are you nuts?! Why would I visit her?!"

"Calm down, Adrena. I'm only asking questions."

"You're asking because you think I might have done something to them, too. Well, take a nap, Doc. I didn't do anything. I haven't seen or spoken to Mildred. The first time I saw where she lived, it was already burned and gutted."

"I'm sorry if I've made you angry, Adrena. Sometimes you forget that I'm your doctor first."

"If I have, it's because you made me forget. Told me you were my friend. That you loved me. Now, you're accusing me of killing everybody who dies. You did it with Granny, too. You should know me better than that by now. If I had done anything to them, I would have told you and not batted an eye. I hated them all, just that much. Never tiptoed over the issue. So, if I'm not acting appropriately, please forgive me."

Fully understanding Adrena's venom, Vivian said, "I know, Adrena. I have to be very careful where you're concerned, because you are my friend . . . and I do love you. Will you ever forgive me for trying to wear two hats?"

Warming up again, Adrena said devilishly, "If you teach me how to drive, I might."

"Oh, I don't know about that."

"Your Dad's teaching Junior. We're the same age."

"Oh, is he now? Well, Daddy's got more nerve than I do. Let's see how you do in school. If all goes well, I'll look into driving lessons."

The levity returned to Adrena's voice when she said, "Great! I can't wait to tell Junior. He thinks he's going to have to help me persuade you."

Alarm made Vivian's voice shake when she asked, "Have you been talking to Junior while I was away?"

"Yes. I talked to him three times while you were gone. I only talked to Max twice, and I talked to Millie on both Wednesdays you were gone. I missed you, Doc."

Still unable to process a possible budding relationship between Adrena and Junior, Vivian spoke stiffly when she asked, "Did you?"

"Sure did. You're the only person in the world I can tell everything to. Good or bad."

"Have you done anything good or bad I should know about?"

"I didn't tell you about the book Granny left me in her letter. Is that bad?"

"What kind of book, Adrena?"

"I think it's a bankbook. At least that's what it has printed on the front. I've never had one. So, I'm not really sure. In her letter, Granny said it had enough money in it for emergencies - if I don't like where I'm living, or something."

Interested, Vivian asked, "How much emergency money is in the book, Adrena?"

"I can't recall exactly, Doc. It's more than thirty-six thousand though."

"Dollars?! Are you sure?!"

"That's what it says, Doc. I'll bring it to the office. Did I do something wrong?"

Stunned beyond belief, Vivian said, "No, Adrena, but you shouldn't leave anything like that lying around. Does Mrs. Stanley know you have it?"

"No. Should she?"

"I think so, sweetheart. You don't want it to fall into the wrong hands."

"Will she take it away from me? I'd like to keep it, if it's mine."

"I'm sure she'll let you keep it. I just think she should know you have it."

"Is it enough to buy a car with, Doc?"

Without hesitation, Vivian said, "You are not buying a car, Adrena Reynolds. You're not old enough. When you finish school and get ready for college, we'll talk about it again."

Disappointed, Adrena said, "Okay, Doc. When am I going to see you?"

"I'll be back in the office in two more weeks. But, Howard and I are having a few friends and family members over when we get our pictures developed. Perhaps you can come then. Unless you feel you really need to see me sooner."

Sounding exactly like a child whose mother has just remarried and begun the process of abandoning her, Adrena said, "No, I guess I can wait. You're probably busy being Howard's wife now."

Hearing the disappointment in Adrena's voice, Vivian relented by saying, "He's going back to work next week. I'll come get you, and we'll have lunch together. How's that?"

Beaming again, Adrena exclaimed, "Fantastic!"

When Vivian hung up, she was a ball of conflicting emotions. Everything and everyone pointed to Adrena not having anything at all to do with those deaths, and Adrena had denied having anything to do with them. She had told Vivian all of her secrets in the past, and she had been open enough with her feelings about them; but this was an entirely different thing - would Adrena tell Vivian she had killed people? For her own peace of mind, Vivian decided she should look into the drugs. If that turned out to be negative, she would accept Adrena's innocence. If not, she had no idea what she would do.

Then, there was Junior. Vivian had no problem with Adrena being friends with Max. She was confident in Max's ability to handle Adrena. Her little brother was another story. If he did something to upset or alarm Adrena, he could get hurt. Or, worse. Junior was at the age where boys wanted nothing more than to touch girls. She would have to talk to both of them. Alone and together.

As much as Vivian loved her brother, she was still happy for the apparent progression in Adrena. The young woman in her was blossoming. She had referred to a young male without hostility. She sounded as if Junior were a real friend of hers. Vivian was impressed with Adrena and Junior. She was also afraid for Adrena and Junior.

To make matters even worse, Adrena had money. Lots of accessible money. The only security Vivian had in it was Adrena's complete lack of knowledge - she wasn't even sure she had a bankbook. A more streetwise child would be missing by now. God knows anything could happen with two teenagers and thirty-six thousand dollars.

Howard came up behind Vivian, slid his arms around her waist and kissed her neck. She moaned in pleasure at his touch.

Speaking into her hair, Howard asked, "Would you like to tell me about the blue marks I've been putting on you?"

Vivian laughed and said, "You already know about them."

"No, I don't."

"You should know. Every time you kiss my body parts passionately, you leave a mark."

"Oh, is that what those are?"

"What did you think they were?"

"I thought you might be a hemophiliac, or something."

"Very funny."

"What did little Miss Reynolds have to report?"

"She's been talking to my brother on the telephone, and her grandmother left her thirty-six thousand dollars no one knows anything about."

"Wow! Mrs. Brown was a smart woman, Vivian. That's money Adrena won't have to pay inheritance taxes on. Mrs. Brown was the only older client I had who would call to ask if I knew there had been an earthquake or flood in some remote corner of the world."

With a hint of a smirk on her face, Vivian asked, "What's that got to do with anything?"

"They grew some crop that directly affected the price of her stock. I'm going to miss her - now, I'll have to catch more of these things on my own. So . . . is there anything wrong with Junior and Adrena talking on the telephone? I can see why Junior's calling. She's a very pretty girl, Vivian."

"I know that. She's a very pretty girl who has had some devastating problems. Anyone trying to deal with her will have to be patient. I don't know any patient sixteen-year-old boys. Do you?"

"I don't know any patient forty-year-old men, sweetheart. They'll be fine. He might get slapped a few times, tops. Who hasn't?"

"Oh, yeah? Who slapped you, Howard Shaw?"

"I forget."

Chapter Twenty-Two

During the week following the honeymoon, the Matthews-Shaw households underwent major changes. Howard and Vivian argued more than they ever had. From the time they woke in the morning, until they lay in bed at night, there was one disagreement after another.

Vivian felt her toiletries could simply join Howard's in the bathroom. Not wanting to have to scavenge through a mountain of female products, Howard thought they should have a second vanity installed. Because they both had more clothes than they knew what to do with, Vivian wanted Howard to move some of his things from the master bedroom closet - turn one of the other bedrooms into a storage room, and rotate seasonally. Howard couldn't imagine any of his clothes being in another room.

After breakfast, Howard wanted to wash the dishes right away. Vivian thought they could wait until the end of the day. Howard wanted to know why.

"First of all, we have other things to do. Second, those dishes aren't going anywhere. There's only a couple plates, saucers, glasses and cups. Third, you have a dishwasher you have never used. We can stack them in there, push the button at the end of the day, and go to bed."

Unconvinced, Howard said, "Since there are so few, we could just wash them."

Still irritated about the vanity, Vivian snapped, "Why do you have a dishwasher, Howard?"

"In case I have company. Alone, it would take an entire week to collect enough dishes to run a dishwasher."

"The key word here is alone. You're not alone anymore. I'm stacking the dishes in the dishwasher. After dinner and snacks, I'll turn it on."

"Okay, Vivian. I don't like it, but okay. What's washing a few dishes?"

"Let's go, Howard."

After stacking the dishes in the dishwasher, under Howard's disapproving glare, Vivian led her husband out to her car. There, he gave her a different glare and asked, "What's wrong with *my* car?"

"I want to bring some things from home, Howard. Your car hasn't got enough trunk space for a decent set of silverware. But, if you'd like to take it, you can. I'm driving my own car."

Howard relented and insisted he drive. Vivian didn't really care who drove, as long as she got where she wanted to go and did what she wanted to do.

At Vivian's house, Howard vetoed every piece of furniture she wanted moved to his house. Vivian rolled her eyes at him and held her peace.

When he said they didn't need her paintings, Vivian yelled, "Yes, we do! *I* do! Why are you acting like this, Howard? We have to incorporate. You can't have all of your things, while I abandon mine. You can't have all of your routine, while I abandon mine. You can't have all of the closet space, while I dress in the garage. Now, either you give a little, or I can just stay right here."

"Why are you yelling, Vivian? We're supposed to discuss these things rationally."

"You're not discussing, Howard. You're saying I can't do this, and I can't have that."

"No, I'm not. You just haven't said anything I agree with yet. You can take anything you want. I don't have to like it."

Puzzled, Vivian asked, "Why would I want to do things you don't like? I'm trying to pull us together here."

"It's very simple, sweetheart. Don't ask, or tell me anything. Just do it. I'm a creature of habit. I don't want anything moved or changed. I just want you."

"You are a confused man. Why didn't I see that before?"

"You weren't trying to move into my house."

"Shut up, Howard. Get those tags off my desk and start tagging the things I tell you to tag. The movers will be here on Thursday. I'd like to do a couple of rooms before we leave here today. We have to pick up Snow from my father's house before it gets too late."

"What are you going to do with the things you're not taking, Viv?"

"I'll have to store them or sell them."

"What if I knew someone who would like to lease the house as it is?"

Frowning, Vivian asked, "Who?"

"Clayton and I hired a new broker from Swedesboro. He's married with one child. No pets. They're not interested in buying right now."

"I thought you said it would be better if I sold the house, Howard."

"I thought you said you wanted to lease the house, Vivian. I was just trying to help."

Smiling, Vivian said, "That would be nice. If they don't seem like people who'll tear it down, it would save me the trouble of having to figure out what to do with all of this stuff."

Smiling too, Howard said, "You won't have to bring any of it over to my house either. They're willing to live with it."

"No matter what, there will be things coming over to *our* house, Howard. Beginning with those paintings. There are personal items I wouldn't want anyone to use."

"Such as?"

"Towels, bedding, dishes, pots and pans, for openers."

"We don't need any more towels, dishes, pots and pans. Your sheets don't fit my bed. They would look ridiculous in my bedroom anyway. Lilac and green? Come on, Viv."

"Our bedroom will be changing."

"Not that much."

"You're giving me a headache, Howard. I'll do this by myself. Let's go upstairs. I want to pack up my clothes and toiletries."

Howard mumbled, "There's no room for it. How much of that stuff does one person need anyway? All bunched in with mine."

Vivian yelled, "I'm not leaving a sock, or an eyeshadow brush! So, you may as well stop mumbling, Howard Shaw!

Your house is twice the size of mine. Nothing's going to be bunched. I never knew you were so selfish."

"Just what we need. More eyeshadow brushes."

As they climbed the stairs, Vivian hit Howard in the back to hurry him along. She never thought there would be this much fuss about what to do with what. Of course, he was irritating her on purpose most of the time. Howard loved torturing Vivian. Actually, she knew she could do anything her little heart desired.

The telephone rang, and Howard answered it. Obviously, it was for him; he didn't call Vivian to the telephone. Peeking into the room at him, Vivian could tell by the expression on his face she wouldn't like something. She kept packing up the bathroom.

After hanging up, Howard said, "That was Talia. Lula's not feeling any better, and she's refusing to go to the hospital. She thinks I should go over."

Vivian didn't say one word. She just thought, "Lula, Lula, Lula."

Howard stood in the bathroom doorway and silently watched his wife pack up her belongings. Sheepishly, he asked, "What do you think I should do, Vivian?"

Without looking up, Vivian said blankly, "I can't tell you what to do for your sister, Howard."

Pulling her up, so he could look into her eyes, Howard said softly, "I know how you feel about Lula, sweetheart. But, if anything happens to her and I don't do whatever I can, I could be sorry for the rest of my life."

"Go do what you have to do, Howard."

"Are you going to be upset with me for it?"

"Yes."

"Why, Vivian? If you know I have to do it, why don't you understand?"

"I do understand. Lula's feigning another illness to send you on a guilt trip. She's going to prove she's top dog in your life if she has to die doing it. You run along - I have things to do here."

"I'll just run over there, see how she's doing and come right back."

"Oh, she's much too ill for you to be able to do that. If you don't come back to get me, I'll just shack out here. Maybe I'll just stay here. You're fighting me over furniture and closet space. She's fighting me over you. There's too much fighting going on, all of a sudden. I know you probably never noticed that Lula hasn't had a headache for the last year, but the day she found out we were getting married, her health took a turn for the worse. She was strong enough to come to our wedding, stand up and say I wasn't good enough for you. Run along, Howard."

Giving Vivian a soft peck on the forehead, Howard whispered, "I'll be right back, Vivian."

The moment she heard the front door close, tears began to stream down Vivian's face. She sat down on the commode and wondered how this could be happening. Howard loved her and she knew it. Why was Lula refusing to leave them alone? Why didn't she call her own children? Why wasn't her husband enough for her?

Knowing there were no immediate answers to those questions, Vivian wiped her face, blew her nose, and resumed her packing. Lula wasn't ruining her life with Howard before it got started. While Vivian did not like the idea of fighting, she definitely intended to stand her ground. Lula was safe, as long as she didn't step into Vivian's face or space.

Two hours later, the bathroom and most of the bedroom was packed. Vivian heard Howard slam the front door and bound up the stairs. Astounded his mission was completed so quickly, she smiled weakly. Howard slid his arms around her waist and tenderly kissed her forehead. Vivian raised her face to receive the kiss she fully expected and received. They exchanged quite a few kisses before the task at hand was remembered.

Happily, Howard asked, "What do you want me to do, Viv?"

There was a small wall of shoe boxes at the foot of the bed. Five wide, three deep and five high. Howard asked, "Why are you taking all of these shoes today?"

"Those are my summer shoes. You can start loading them into the trunk. I prefer transporting my clothes inside the car. I don't want any oil or dirt to get on them."

"Vivian, there is no way we can get all of these into the trunk today. If this is what you call your summer shoes, how many pairs of shoes do you actually have?"

"I don't know. My winter shoes and boots are in the spare room."

"There is no way you're going to fit these into my closet. You'll bunch up my things."

Speaking softly, Vivian said, "Howard. Howard. Take the shoes down and load them into the car."

As Howard carried boxes down the stairs, he mumbled, "She's not dressing in the garage. Before it's all over, I probably will be. Bunching all of this stuff into my closet. Clothes can't breathe. Can't find anything."

Ignoring his complaints, Vivian continued to carefully pack boxes. It would take a week to get her clothes out. She didn't want the movers taking them over. If Howard's new employee leased the house, Vivian could probably cancel them anyway, and she would get Howard and Clayton to bring the things she absolutely refused to leave behind.

An hour later, Howard and Vivian sat side by side in the car. "How was your sister?" she asked.

Unemotionally, Howard said, "She'll live. I think Lula's delusional though."

"Why?"

"She actually thinks you've hypnotized me."

"Why?"

"I never mentioned marriage before. Seemed perfectly happy living alone. She says you'll probably have babies, divorce me, and take me to the bank - that good-looking, educated women play that game on men smarter than me every day."

"The very next time you talk to your sister, there's a few things I want you to tell her for me. If I have babies, I'm not taking you to the bank. I'm sending you to day care, the pediatrician, and the playground. You don't have enough money to convince me to take care of the little darlings all by myself."

"I'll tell her that for you, sweetheart. Now, are we going to my house or your dad's first?"

"We're not going anywhere, until you stop calling it your house, Howard."

"I'm sorry. Our house or your dad's?"

Rolling her eyes, Vivian said, "Dad's."

◆　　◆　　◆

Junior answered the door at the Matthews home. When Howard and Vivian walked into the living room, they found Vance reclined in a lounge chair, with Snow sleeping comfortably on his lap. The beautiful, white cat looked up at them lazily and cuddled up again.

Vance looked up at the newlyweds and said, "Well, hello, Mr. and Mrs. Shaw. I hope the honeymoon went well."

Giving her father a kiss on top of his head, Vivian said, "It was wonderful, Dad. Where are the girls?"

"Out with their mother. Have a seat."

"Howard, have a seat with Dad. I want to talk to my brother for a few minutes."

"Okay, sweetheart."

Vance laughed and said, "Howard, you said that like a real married man. Just keep saying, 'Okay, sweetheart,' and you'll have a wife forever."

Over her shoulder, Vivian said, "Believe me, that's the first time he's cooperated today, Dad."

Vivian found Junior in the yard, changing the tire on his bike. He looked up at her, smiled, and said, "Hey, big sister. What's happening?"

"I thought I'd ask you that."

"There's nothing much happening with me. You know Dad."

Laughing at the memory, Vivian said, "He can't still be that bad. Besides, you're a boy. We were girls. There's no way he could sustain the grip on you that he had on Max and me."

"Don't bet on it, Viv."

"Junior, have you been talking to Adrena on the telephone?"

"Yeah, why?"

"Nothing really. I just want you to be careful with her, that's all. She's not as mature as you."

"We're the same age, Vivian. Girls mature faster than boys. Or, so I've heard."

"Under normal circumstances, they do. Adrena hasn't exactly grown up under normal circumstances."

"I know. She told me you were her doctor."

"Did she tell you why?"

"No. Are you going to tell me?"

Smiling, Vivian said, "I can't do that, Junior, but just in case you two spend any time in each other's company, I feel I have to tell you she's very sensitive to physical contact."

"Are you telling me not to touch her, Vivian?"

"Yes and no. I'm telling you I know where you are on the male touch scale. If you want to be friends with Adrena, you'll have to restrain yourself. Let her touch you first. If she doesn't, let it go. If she protests or becomes agitated in any way, apologize and let it go."

"Is she crazy, Viv?"

"Not crazy, Junior. Adrena has demons. She's troubled. I don't want you to do anything to make her transition any more difficult. If you really like her, you'll be her friend, and let her grow. Can I trust you to control yourself?"

"What do you think I am? A animal? Of course, I can control myself. She sure is pretty though. It would be nice to touch her."

"Have you ever touched a girl before, Junior?"

"Sort of. Once. Dad won't give me enough free time to persuade anybody to let me touch them."

Vivian laughed and said, "Your dad's a very smart man."

"I didn't say Dad wasn't smart. He's just hard to live with sometimes."

Vivian and Howard only stayed a few minutes after her talk with Junior. She collected the litter box, Howard collected Snow, and they headed home to fight over dinner and closet space.

Chapter Twenty-Three

Adrena sat on the porch of the Stanley home waiting for Maxine to pick her up for the honeymoon photo get-together. Everyone was expecting Adrena to attend, as if she had always been involved in their lives. Adrena felt she had a family and friends for the first time in her life.

With Mildred and Bart gone, Adrena promised herself there would be nothing to interfere with her happiness ever again. They could never hurt or haunt Adrena. Now that there were no more ghosts, she could actually hope to have everything good that everyone else seemed to have. If she could persuade Doc to take her off her medication, she might actually feel like a normal human being.

Almost everyone who attended the wedding came to see the honeymoon pictures. Howard, Max, and Adrena did most of the cooking. Vivian helped as much as she could. Everyone ate, drank, talked, and laughed with no mention of the Lula fiasco. One at a time, Max took Adrena and Junior to Howard's office and gave them a sex education class. Adrena was emphatic about not needing the information, because she had no intentions of doing anything like what Max was talking about with Junior, or any other boy.

Max's response was, "I didn't ask you what you intended to do, Adrena. Most people don't plan to do it. It just happens, and you're not leaving this room until you show me you know how to use a condom."

Vivian talked to Adrena about boys when they had lunch together. They discussed them occasionally in their weekly sessions - generally, when a young man had done something Adrena didn't understand. During their luncheon talk, Vivian gave Adrena a more in-depth description of how boys act and how Adrena should react, interested or not interested.

In Vivian's living room, Adrena and Junior sat side by side, looking at the pictures of Howard and Vivian on the beach. Adrena smiled happily, sitting close to Junior. His easy wit always put her at ease. He returned her smiles and kept the conversation flowing, talking about his friends at home and school. Since Adrena didn't have any friends to speak of, he monopolized that subject.

The facet of Junior's personality that won Adrena over was that he never made fun of her. His teasing never included personal criticism. When Adrena didn't know or understand something, Junior would try to explain it to her. Moreover, Junior never made an unannounced move.

Junior gave a low whistle at a photo of Vivian in a midriff top and shorts. His whistle pitch rose at the sight of Vivian in a bikini.

Confused by Junior's reaction, Adrena asked, "Why are you whistling?"

"My sister is lethal in that bathing suit. I never knew she looked like that. Howard got a good deal, even if she can't cook."

Adrena flipped back to see Vivian in the bathing suit again. Of course she was gorgeous. Vivian was gorgeous to Adrena, no matter what she wore. The concept of Vivian's sexuality escaped Adrena. Howard and Vivian both looked great in bathing suits, but Adrena didn't feel the urge to whistle at the sight of Howard. Not getting it, Adrena moved on.

Every now and then, Junior's hand would brush Adrena's. Her initial response was to snatch her hand away. Then Adrena realized Junior's occasional touch didn't offend her at all, and she relaxed a little. She even purposely brushed his hand a few times. She checked her internal reactions carefully, thought it rather pleasant, and by the evening's end, Adrena was able to casually touch Junior and laugh.

That night, Adrena dreamed about Junior's touch. The warmth of it. The sense of security it transmitted. Adrena could never envision Junior forcing her to do anything she didn't want to do. No clutching, groping, and clawing. Junior never had that familiar, drooling, lusty look in his eyes when he looked at Adrena. He always smiled and spoke so nicely to her. If he was playing a game, she liked it better than the others.

Adrena and Junior spoke on the telephone more often after the get-together at Vivian and Howard's house. The two teenagers shared everything Max and Vivian had told them individually. When Junior asked Adrena if she had ever had sex, she didn't know how to answer. To avoid it, Adrena told Junior that Mrs. Stanley was calling her, hung up and dialed Vivian's home number immediately.

Adrena asked in a worried rush, "Have I ever had sex, Doc?"

Caught completely unprepared, Vivian asked, "What?"

"Have I ever had sex? I don't know if what Bart did was what Junior meant."

Peeved, Vivian said sharply, "First of all, Junior has no business asking questions like that, Adrena."

Adrena was stunned by her response and asked, "He doesn't?"

"No, he doesn't - but that's what all young people want to know."

Profoundly puzzled by that statement, Adrena said, "Not me, Doc. I never gave it a thought. Does that mean there's something wrong with me?"

"No, Adrena. Everyone gets to it at different times. You would have sooner or later, too. Believe me."

Satisfied with the sound of that, she asked, "Okay. What about me? Have I?"

There was a long pause. Adrena heard Vivian ask Howard to hang up the telephone when she picked up the extension. After picking up the receiver in the kitchen, Vivian said, "You haven't had sex in the sense that Junior's talking about. You were sexually violated, Adrena. There was no desire, excitement, or romance involved. What happened to you is nowhere near the way it's supposed to go. What Bart did is called deviant. Unnatural."

"So, you're saying it's never going to be that way again?"

Sounding like she was sending up a heartfelt prayer, Vivian said, "I hope not, sweetheart. One day, when you're ready, sex is going to be one of the most anticipated, thrilling, and natural activities of your life."

"How will I know when I'm ready, Doc? It could take forever for me. I haven't even thought about it, and Junior's already talking about it."

In a rush, common for parents, Vivian said, "You just don't worry about what Junior's talking about. You run on Adrena's clock."

Reacting to Vivian's parental tone, Adrena said, "Okay, Doc. I'll run on my own clock. Now, how will I know what my clock's saying?"

Snapping back, Vivian explained, "When two people are attracted to each other, sex is part of the natural progression. It's a mutual decision. When it's right, it's one of the most wonderful things you'll experience in life. The fantasy aspect of it leads people to think that attraction is love. Honestly, it's biological. The brain produces chemicals that stimulate the loins. It's a powerful feature God gave us to insure our stay here.

"You'll know you're ready when you've found someone you can communicate with. Someone you share a mutual respect with. Someone you can agree to disagree with. No strain. No pain."

Completely soothed by the way Doc described sex, Adrena asked, "Is it wonderful for you and Howard?"

"It is. I love Howard, and he loves me."

"Even when he puts blue marks on you?"

"Even when he puts blue marks on me. It's part of our passion for each other. Not every woman likes it though. There will be parts of the mating act you won't like either, Adrena. You tell your partner you don't like it right away. If he can't handle it, that's his problem. There is nothing more stressful than having to do something you hate repetitively."

"Have you ever had to tell Howard you didn't like something he did?"

"No. I've had to tell others though."

Shocked by her open admission of having sex with other men, Adrena asked, "How many men have you had sex with, Doc?"

"If you're asking if Howard was the first, the answer is no. There were a few before him. That's how I know I love the man I have. I've experienced pure physical attraction and a couple cases of infatuation. I enjoyed each for a time, but then, I realized something was missing . . . love.

"There are lots of people who disagree with me. They think you should marry first. All I can say is, if I had married any of the men I knew before, I wouldn't be the doctor, I would be the patient."

"Why did Mildred have sex with all of those men, Doc? If she loved Bart as much as she claimed to, why wasn't he enough?"

"Drugs, Adrena. Drugs wreak havoc on the thinking process. They strip a person's pride away from them."

"Why didn't Bart have sex with women for drugs?"

Unable to stifle her laugh, Vivian said, "There's not a big market for men. Women have better control of their sex drive than men. If we're paying, we're truly pressed to it, Adrena. After all the years of drug abuse, Bart probably didn't have much to offer anyway."

Having heard Mildred and Bart's names more than she cared to, Adrena said, "Okay. So I can say I've never had sex before. Right?"

"You most certainly can, and it will be the truth."

Adrena passed that information on to Junior. She never mentioned Mildred and Bart to him though. That was history. Except for an occasional inquiry into their behavior, because she had no other reference point, Adrena stopped talking about them altogether.

Max picked up Junior and Adrena and dropped them off at the movies twice during the summer. They held hands, as they happily walked into the movie complex. The first time they went to the movies, that was all they did.

During the second movie outing, Junior drummed up enough nerve to kiss Adrena's forehead. When she didn't object, he kissed her on the lips. Not used to having anyone that close to her, Adrena squirmed in her seat.

Junior asked, "What's the matter, Adrena? Am I bothering you?"

Adrena didn't want to drive him away, so she said quickly, "No. I've never been kissed before, Junior. It feels a little strange. That's all."

With his arm casually draped over her shoulder, Junior kissed Adrena again. This time, he slipped his tongue into her mouth. She bit it.

Checking for blood, Junior said angrily, "You're not supposed to bite, Adrena. That hurt."

"Well, you should have told me that before you put your tongue in my mouth. I told you I didn't know anything about this. Try it again. I won't bite you. Go ahead."

A little apprehensive after the bite, and with Adrena addressing the issue as if it were a science project, Junior approached her carefully. If her teeth touched his tongue, he pulled away from her. Adrena found Junior's fear funny. She shrugged her shoulders and laughed.

Max and Doc had told Adrena boys liked nothing better than touching women's breasts. Junior never touched Adrena's. Not knowing if she should feel bad about it, Adrena dismissed it - but if Junior didn't do it the next time, she would ask him why he hadn't.

Other than Doc, Adrena had never voluntarily tolerated the company of another human being for more than an hour. Adrena learned to endure Junior's closeness for long periods of time. After all, he occupied Adrena's every waking thought. In her dreams, Junior talked, smiled, and kissed her through the night. By the end of the summer it was safe to say, Adrena loved him. Of course, Adrena referred to it as liking Junior. Nothing had happened to make her take the leap to owning or expressing love.

Chapter Twenty-Four

Vivian brought in an interior decorator. They sketched out preliminary plans for the living room, dining room, master bedroom, bathroom, and a closet. Howard was most impressed with what they had come up with for converting one of his four bedrooms into a spacious, orderly his-and-her dressing room. There would be more than enough closet space for Howard's clothes to breathe.

Vivian loved the way the decorator combined their styles. Howard could keep a softer version of his stripes; Vivian could have her flowers and paintings. Everything would meet Howard's rigid, sophisticated standards and comply with Vivian's light, airy, relaxed nature.

Most evenings, they cooked together. Vivian set off the smoke alarms when Howard left her alone in the kitchen. For the life of her, Vivian couldn't tell when things were done, so she either cooked the meat until it was as tough as leather, or it bled. When dinner was a complete disaster, they ordered out. Howard thanked God Wednesday had remained their official night out. Actually, he considered recommending more than one evening a week.

Howard hit the ceiling many evenings about his beloved Snow. She indiscriminately scratched expensive tables, knocked over rare statues, shredded drapes and sofas. The night Howard noticed a tear in the leather sofa in the den, Vivian thought Snow was out for sure. Instead, Howard gave Snow a serious talking to, as if she understood what he was saying. He told Vivian and the housekeeper to make sure Snow wasn't in the den when they left the room, and to close the door. The very next day he called the veterinarian and scheduled a declawing.

The one habit Snow had that absolutely drove Howard nuts was walking the kitchen counters. After all, she was a pet, and he prepared and ate his meals on those counters; the two should never mix. To make matters worse, Snow ate half of Howard's breakfast one morning. That permanently frayed Snow's residential expectancy in the Shaw household.

Still, Howard and Vivian loved coming home to each other every evening. Howard found out how much Vivian treasured her alone time in the bathtub. Her head was always buried in a folder or a book. She collected tons of literature on new and updated mental disorders and medications which she brought home and didn't want to throw away. That's when Howard knew she needed an office at home, too; the storage room would be the very next renovation.

Vivian found out how much Howard really worked. She couldn't get his attention at all if he was scanning the screen of his computer. Some days he did this for hours on end, and occasionally left their bed in the middle of the night to return to it. Of course, these scannings had a beneficial aspect. Vivian loved telling Lula, "Howard's busy." She never gave Lula an opportunity to leave a message; she simply hung up.

Every Saturday morning, Clayton arrived around nine. He and Howard went to the weight room for three hours and then scanned the computer screen together. They brainstormed about fluctuating stock prices and the stability of the market, deciding what to buy, keep, or dump for which clients. Vivian was only invited to eat lunch with them.

Shut-down time in the Shaw household, they agreed, would be at ten every night. From that point on, they belonged to each other. They lay in their huge bed and discussed schedules for the next day. What he needed her to do for him. What she needed him to do for her. They both loved sharing the burdens of everyday life with each other - knowing no matter what happened, at the end of the day, there would be someone who loved them more than life itself - to hold, kiss, and caress through the night.

By September, the renovations were well underway. The mess made Howard crankier than usual, but he gritted his teeth and kept his mouth shut as much as possible. He kept it shut a little too tight for Vivian, and she embarked on a drive to cheer him up. Every evening of the week, she found some activity that kept them away from the house. They went to concerts, movies, plays, exhibition basketball games, and pre-season football games. They visited family and friends. While Howard enjoyed the whirlwind activities immensely, it interfered with his work, and that gave him something else to grumble about.

Having to sleep in the guest room was less than enchanting for him, too. It was a blessing that the new dressing room was completed, before moving out of their bedroom became necessary. Howard spent more time in the dressing room than he did in the bedroom with Vivian. He loved it.

For Vivian, it was no secret that she loved Howard's kisses and caresses. She usually cuddled up to him so close at night he woke with imprints from her hair and body on his. But suddenly, in October, feigning fatigue, Vivian began to occasionally reject his attentions. Sometimes during the night, she retreated to her side of the bed. Howard was too hot, too heavy, or his touch had become unusually rough. Vivian wasn't sure which of those was true.

As the renovations were wrapping up in November, a climate change fell on Vivian. She started feeling as if someone had poured cold water through her veins. Vivian was less and less inclined to cater to her husband's miseries. As a matter of fact, Howard's whining made Vivian want to slap his face. Attempts to humor him slacked off and eventually stopped. They stayed home, in silence, more and more.

During November, she started going to bed early every night. If Howard tried to touch her, Vivian complained of headaches and balled up tightly. Howard's attempts to talk were brushed aside. His stares ignored. The only time Vivian remotely felt like Vivian was when they cooked together - burning food still entertained her.

Howard was so wrapped up in his inconveniences that it took him until the end of November to notice Vivian had somehow changed. She never pretended to be nice to Lula on the telephone anymore, hanging up the moment she recognized Lula's voice. Vivian refused to eat lunch with

Howard and Clayton on Saturday afternoons, and, more than once, yelled at Clayton for just inviting her.

Vivian listlessly accompanied Max and Adrena on a Christmas shopping trip. With genuine concern, Max told Vivian, "You look like you need to take some vitamins. Maybe you should consider another vacation. Marriage and renovations must be putting more pressure on you than you realize, Vivian. Your color's not right. You're pale."

Vivian snapped, "Mind your own business, Max!"

"You are my business, Vivian!"

Vivian ignored her sister and walked on as if nothing had been said.

In conversation with Howard, Vivian seldom mentioned work anymore. Her patients had always been the most important people in her life - she was always worried about one or the other . . . and especially Adrena. While Vivian didn't push Adrena away, anyone could see Vivian wasn't as attentive as she usually was. She started speaking in clinical terms to Adrena all of the time. On more than one occasion, the lack of warmth caused a reflection of pain in Adrena's eyes. While Vivian saw this, her normal maternal instincts didn't move her to attempt to soothe the young woman.

Vivian's father, the original love of her life, only got one-word answers from Vivian on any subject. When he asked what was wrong, she simply told him she was tired. Vance was so concerned that he stopped by the Shaw house often and tried to get Vivian to talk to him. He called Vivian every day. She heard her father beg Howard to keep an eye on his daughter. Vivian thought they were all making more out of her little emotional slump than necessary.

◆   ◆   ◆

Before leaving for Max's Thanksgiving dinner, Howard asked a distant Vivian, "Sweetheart, what's wrong? Please don't say nothing. You don't talk to me, or anyone else I know of. You don't want me to touch you at all. If you're having second thoughts about being married because I acted silly about the renovations, just tell me."

Vivian dropped down on the bed, cupped her face, and began to cry.

Howard was completely surprised by Vivian's reaction and said, "Come on, sweetheart. I'm sorry if I've upset you. I just wanted to know what was going on. Just forget I asked."

A weeping Vivian said, "I can't answer your question, Howard. I really don't know what's wrong with me. I feel so cold inside. I know it's depression, but where did it come from? I don't have one legitimate reason to be unhappy. It's probably some kind of a hormonal change, but I shouldn't be experiencing any of that yet. I'm too young."

Sitting next to his wife, Howard lovingly stroked Vivian's back and said, "Maybe you should have a physical, sweetheart. Max told you your color was blotching weeks ago."

Frustrated, Vivian snapped, "I don't feel physically ill, Howard! I feel cold. I feel like curling up in a corner and crying all of the time. Absolutely nothing hurts physically."

"Maybe you should talk to one of your colleagues. If something emotional is happening to you, Vivian, you might not be able to diagnose yourself objectively."

In a whisper, Vivian said, "I know that. I'll take the physical route first though. Vitamins might make a difference, and maybe I'll make an appointment."

Vivian stopped and a fresh flood of tears began to flow when she said, "Please don't think I don't love you, Howard. I love you as much as I ever have. I just don't know what's happening to me right now."

Tightening his hold on her, Howard kissed the top of Vivian's head and said, "Don't worry about what I think, Viv. I love you. I'm not going anywhere without you. We'll find out what's going on. You just keep your chin up."

A week later, Vivian had not gone to see a doctor. Her mood and behavior became more and more erratic. It swung from one end of the spectrum to the other, without provocation. One night, in the middle of lovemaking, she said, "Stop, Howard."

He asked, "Stop what?"

"Stop what you're doing!"

Confused, for more reasons than one, Howard asked, "Now?"

"Now! Get off of me!"

In complete frustration, Howard got up and went to the guest room. During the night, Vivian came in and cuddled up next to him. Howard let her hold him but kept his hands to himself.

Two nights later, Howard came in to find Vivian slamming pots and pans. She screamed as loud as she could and kicked Snow so hard, the poor cat ricocheted off the wall and bounced back.

After checking Snow, Howard looked at his wild-looking bride and asked, "What's the matter now, Viv?"

"That cat's got to stop sneaking up on me, Howard. I have never liked it. Right now, her life's in jeopardy when she does it."

"Just lock her in my office when you're feeling like that, sweetheart. Don't hurt her. You'll be sorry you did, once you snap out of whatever's going on. Did you ever make an appointment to see the doctor?"

"No."

"Why not?"

"I haven't had time."

"Make time, Vivian. We can't keep going like this forever. Not without knowing what we're dealing with."

Sighing, Vivian said without concern, "I'll take care of it tomorrow."

"Good. I went to the cleaners today. Did you remember to pick my shirts up from the laundry?"

"Yes, they're upstairs."

Turning to leave, Howard asked, "Are you going to be okay while I change?"

Taking a deep breath, Vivian said, "I'm fine."

Intent on putting together dinner, Vivian didn't notice Howard's return. His voice startled her when he asked innocently, "Why didn't you hang my shirts, Viv? They'll probably all have creases in them now."

What started in a low rumble, sounded like a siren at its end. Vivian growled, "Bitch, bitch, bitch. Don't you know how to do anything besides bitch? I can't do anything to satisfy you. Why the hell didn't you just leave me in my own house? That way I wouldn't be touching your precious things! I wouldn't have to listen to you whine about dust, when the walls are coming down! Or making mascara stains on your bathroom counter! Oh, let's not forget how I frivolously waste water and power by running the dishwasher every other night! Had to run the washing machine twice, because I forgot there were clothes in it overnight, too! Exactly what did you marry me for?! So far, I'm more of an inconvenience than anything else!"

Extending his hand to soothe Vivian, Howard said, "Stop that, Vivian. You knew how I was before you married me. Said it didn't matter. Now, you're upset about everything I say. Come here and stop this."

Vivian swatted Howard's hand down as she passed him and ran up the stairs. She slammed the bedroom door so hard, the china in the breakfront shook dangerously. Howard ran up behind her. He could hear her talking and throwing things around. He called Vivian's name over and over. Pleaded with her to open the door. She never answered, never stopped ranting and throwing things.

Not getting a rational response from his wife, Howard rushed downstairs and called her family. He didn't have to explain anything to Vance. The moment Vance heard the panic in his son-in-law's voice, he came running. Maxine returned Howard's call immediately. Vivian's rampage stopped suddenly, and Howard dropped the telephone.

Dashing up the stairs, Howard was relieved to see Vivian standing in the hall. She held two suitcases in her hands. Howard asked, "Where are you going, Vivian?"

"Home."

"Do you mean your house, honey?"

"That's my home, isn't it?"

"Yes. But, you know the Bufords live there now."

"They'll have to leave. I'm going home."

"Shouldn't we talk about this, before you go over there and throw them into the street, Viv?"

"I'll let you talk for a little while, but I'm going home, Howard. Maybe it's this house that's driving me nuts."

"Would it make you feel better if we moved into your house, Vivian?"

"No. It would make me feel better to move back into my house, and you stay in yours. The way it was before the madness."

There was a knock at the front door. Howard reluctantly backed down the stairs to open the front door. Vance and Maxine nearly ran Howard over looking for Vivian. She stood calmly, bags in hand, at the top of the stairs.

Vance smiled up at Vivian and said, "Hi, honey. Are you having a bad day?"

Vivian put the luggage down, covered her face, and started to cry. Vance flew up the stairs to comfort his daughter. There was no doubt in his mind now that what Vivian was going through, her mother had gone through and hadn't survived. As Vance cradled Vivian in his arms, he saw their bedroom over her shoulder. The devastation made bitter tears sting his eyes.

Max said, "Daddy, bring her down. We're taking her to the hospital right now."

"I don't want to go to the hospital," Vivian whined. "Daddy, please make Max leave me alone."

Vance reassured her. "You have to go, sweetheart. I'll be right there with you. So will Max and Howard. We won't leave you alone for a minute."

With the most heart-wrenching expression on her face Vance had ever seen, Vivian said, "Howard thinks I'm crazy, Daddy. Tell him I'm not crazy. He thinks I don't love him. That's not it at all. Tell him."

Rocking his daughter, Vance said, "Howard knows you love him, Vivian. He doesn't think you're crazy either. But if it'll make you feel better, I'll tell him. Now, let's go find out what's really happening."

Vivian held onto her father's arm and descended the stairs, the same way she had the day she married Howard. She sat quietly between Howard and Vance during the ride to the hospital. She gripped Howard's hand like a petrified child, every time someone mentioned her name. Still holding on, she fell asleep. It seemed to take an eternity for any answers to come. They drew blood twice. Max wanted every test known to man run on Vivian and their results immediately. Max made tentative preparations for a CAT scan and had already decided that if there were no answers there, she would wake the entire MRI department before the night was over.

At three in the morning, Max and another female doctor came into Vivian's cubicle. Vance and Howard popped to attention immediately, both searching the doctors' eyes for bad news. The sleeping Vivian held onto Howard's hand and never stirred.

Max spoke first. "Dad, Howard, Vivian's physically rundown. The girl has practically no iron in her system at all. Her white cells have seen better days, too. If she so much as catches a cold, it will turn into pneumonia. We also found an extremely low estrogen level. Our best guess is that's the major cause of those awful mood swings."

Unable to wait for Max's complete chemical rundown, Vance asked irritably, "Just tell me if there's anything that can be done for her, Maxine."

"For now, Dad, all we can offer her is vitamins and rest. If her estrogen continues to fall, we'll have to think about trying to bring it up. Other than that, all we can do is wait for the next six months to pass, deliver the baby and see if she bounces back."

Frowning, Vance asked, "She's pregnant? That's what this is all about? Are you sure, Max? Will it reverse after the baby's born . . . or get worse like your mother?"

Max looked up at the ceiling before saying, "This is probably what happened to Mom, Daddy. We'll just thank God we know what the problem is now and have a relatively simple solution for it. Because Vivian and I were conceived so close together, Mom didn't have a chance to recoup. What they diagnosed as acute depression was actually a young woman experiencing something similar to acute premature menopausal symptoms."

Turning to the other doctor, Maxine asked, "Is there anything you'd like to add, Dr. Fleur?"

Smiling, Dr. Fleur said, "Not really, Dr. Matthews. For a surgeon, you did a fine job explaining. I'd like to give my new patient a pelvic exam before she leaves though."

That's when Max noticed Howard's stunned expression. He sat stone still, with his mouth hanging open. Max walked over and touched her brother-in-law's shoulder. He jumped.

Laughing, Max said, "You can wake her up and tell her now. We'll wait outside. Tell her the doctor needs to do a pelvic exam too, Howard."

The glassy stare never left Howard's face. Max asked sternly, "Are you listening to me, Howard Shaw?"

Dumbly, he said, "Uh . . . yeah, Max. I'll tell her."

Everyone, except Howard, left the cubicle. Howard stood and looked down at his beautiful, sleeping wife. He searched her face and body for signs he should have noticed before this. Then, it dawned on him. Vivian hadn't let him look at her, in peace, for weeks. Seldom let him touch her.

Howard stopped his musings and shook Vivian's shoulder. She struggled to focus and sat up. Howard sat down on the bed next to her, and Vivian looked around the room with large panic-filled eyes. She asked, "Where's Daddy, Howard?"

"He's just outside the door, sweetheart. Are you feeling any better?"

Shrugging, Vivian asked, "Better than what?"

"Never mind. Max just came down and told us what's wrong with you."

Looking directly into Howard's eyes, Vivian asked, "Well, what's wrong with me?"

"You're pregnant."

"I knew that, Howard. What else is wrong with me?"

Angrily, Howard asked, "If you knew that, when were you going to tell me? In the delivery room?"

"It was supposed to be your Christmas present. Merry Christmas, Howard. What else did she say?"

"You're rundown, anemic, and have low estrogen levels."

"That's why my mood swings have been so rough. Did she say they could do anything about it?"

"They want to monitor it for a while first."

"They don't want to do anything until I'm in my last trimester. Everything affects the baby now. That's what I thought they would say. So, I get to be nuts until the baby's born. Wonderful."

"Since you know more than me, I'll go get the doctor and wait in the hall, while she does the pelvic exam."

"No, you won't. You'll come right back in here. You wanted this baby. Talked about it every chance you got. Well, it's showtime, Howard Shaw, and I'm not letting you skip out on one act. If I'm going to go nuts, you get to watch."

With his face twisted in agony, Howard asked, "Even the pelvic exams, Vivian?"

"Even the pelvic exams. They won't be doing a thing you haven't done yourself."

Chapter Twenty-Five

Vivian rested peacefully the following morning. After spending the majority of the night before in the emergency room, her day had been officially cancelled. The gynecologist ordered total bedrest, and Howard intended to see that Vivian followed those instructions. If Vivian continued to use all of her physical resources, she wouldn't be strong enough to carry the baby full-term, and neither one of them wanted anything to happen to their unborn child.

The telephone rang at seven. Disoriented by fatigue, Howard answered. The tone in the caller's voice startled Howard. Without hesitation, he shook Vivian and handed the receiver to her. Too tired to sit up, Vivian mumbled, "Dr. Shaw speaking."

It was Mrs. Stanley who spoke urgently. "Doc, something's wrong with Adrena. She was screaming. She was fighting us. We had to give her a shot. Please come!"

Vivian struggled to a sitting position and responded, "Calm down, Mrs. Stanley. Where is Adrena? Is she still conscious?"

Choking on tears, Mrs. Stanley answered, "No, she's out now, Doc. She's upstairs in her bedroom."

"Okay. Tell me exactly what happened."

"About half an hour ago, we were all asleep. My husband and I were rattled out of a good night's sleep by a strange-sounding squeal. It scared us so bad we were clutching each other, Doc. When we came to our senses, we realized that hideous sound was coming from Adrena's room.

"We jumped up and ran down the hall. I opened the door, and what I saw frightened me even more than that God-awful sound, Doc. Adrena had ripped her sheet to shreds. She was holding rags in her fists and sitting in the middle of the jumbled mess, trembling and shrieking like a wild animal. "I don't think she even knew we were in the room with her until Mr. Stanley moved toward the bed. She hissed something at him I couldn't understand. I do know she mentioned Mildred and Bart, Doc. I think she thought that's who we were.

"Before Mr. Stanley could say a word to her, Adrena leaped at him, screeching, scratching, kicking, and completely out of control. The desperation and fierceness of her battle amazed both of us, Doc. When she gets like that, her strength is limitless. She knocked Mr. Stanley down twice. She bit a chunk out of his shoulder and kicked him in more places than we thought possible.

"I called her name to divert her attention before she killed my poor husband. Sweet Jesus, then she growled and pounced in my direction. Mr. Stanley quickly bear-hugged her from behind. I hustled to the closet and retrieved that Haldol hypo you gave me when we were at her grandmother's house. I tried to administer the shot in Adrena's thigh, Doc, but with her carrying on like that, it was impossible. The child kicked like a rabid mule. In desperation, I stuck her in the shoulder right through her nightgown.

"She quieted quick enough after the shot, Doc. Mr. Stanley was really in agony. He slid down the wall to the floor with the child still in his grip. That's where I left them, Doc. I've got to get back up there to see how my husband is. You've got to come make sure Adrena's all right. If she wakes up like that again, we won't be able to stop her, Doc!"

Moving as if she planned to dress quickly and dash out, Vivian asked, "Do you have any idea what might have triggered this episode, Mrs. Stanley?"

"I don't think Adrena's been taking her antidepressants on schedule for the past few days, Doc. I saw how jittery she was and tried to get her to take a sleeping pill the last two nights, but she refused."

"Okay, Mrs. Stanley. You go check on your husband and make sure Adrena is asleep. I'll be there in about half an hour." Vivian hung up the telephone and moved toward the bathroom.

Seeing the panic in his wife's eyes, Howard said, "You can't go to Adrena today, Vivian. Call your relief physician and send him over there."

Without looking at Howard, Vivian said, "You don't understand. I can't send anyone else. Adrena won't let them touch her. She won't understand my not being there, Howard. I have to go."

"What about our baby, Vivian? You dash out to save Adrena and lose our baby. How about that? I know you love her, Vivian, but you're not the only psychiatrist in the world. Today, Adrena has to accept one of the others."

"She needs me, Howard. I know how to handle Adrena. Others won't understand. They'll see her condition and hospitalize her without asking one question. She could languish in a mental facility for weeks before anyone attempts to interview her. I won't let that happen to Adrena."

"Is Adrena out of control, Vivian?"

"Not now, Howard."

"You can't go. I can't have you wrestling with an out-of-control mental patient. You can't go."

After arguing for fifteen minutes with a husband who wasn't budging on the subject, Vivian called Maxine and asked if she could go over. Of course she did.

Fifteen minutes after Vivian's call, Max walked into the Stanley home. Adrena was still out from the Haldol, and Max forced Adrena's medication down the sleeping girl's throat. After taking Adrena's blood pressure and making sure her breathing was normal, Max told the Stanleys she would stop by at suppertime. Maxine also looked at Mr. Stanley's wounds and found that Mrs. Stanley had done a very good job cleaning and dressing them. Just in case there was an infection, Maxine gave him a prescription for an antibiotic. Before leaving, Maxine called Vivian and assured her Adrena was fine. Knowing Vivian had stressed the importance of coming off the antidepressants slowly, Maxine reserved her anger for Adrena.

The minute Howard left for work that morning, Vivian got dressed and drove to the Stanleys' house. She sat in the kitchen having coffee and danish with Mrs. Stanley, while waiting for Adrena to wake up. The two women chatted pleasantly about husbands and having babies. Vivian told Mrs. Stanley about the problems she was having keeping her own head on straight.

To relieve Vivian's troubled mind, Mrs. Stanley said, "All women go batty to some extent when they're pregnant, Doc. If you find one woman who says she didn't, the poor girl's in denial. When I was pregnant with our first child, I acted so badly, Mr. Stanley threatened to leave more than once. He actually did leave for a week with our second. He threw his hands in the air and constantly shook his head through the third."

Vivian laughed hilariously at Mrs. Stanley's pregnancy recollections. Mrs. Stanley talked about intimate details of her life as if it were the most natural thing in the world. As the kids were fond of saying, "There was no shame in her game."

Vivian wished her mother had been able to do that with her. Vivian and Max had grown up without an adult female to explain the intricate mechanics of their bodies and minds. Their grandmother popped their lips if they asked about what she called "women problems." She swore they didn't need to know about anything that didn't concern them.

Maxine and Vivian had to learn everything through experience and textbooks. Mostly books. Somehow, when a book says mood swings, it doesn't translate. The well mind sees happy and sad. That's not it at all. There was no happy - at least, not in the sense Vivian was accustomed to. As close as Vivian could ascertain, she had fallen into a hole filled with different shades of black.

What Vivian was experiencing certainly felt like insanity. She would definitely commiserate with her patients more genuinely if this ever came to an end. She would know more about what they meant when they said something without a name ached in their souls. Vivian had a glimpse of the pit they so often referred to. Like anything else you haven't seen or experienced, it's difficult to imagine.

Adrena's stumbling footfalls in the upstairs hallway told Mrs. Stanley and Vivian that she was awake. Mrs. Stanley insisted Vivian let her go up first to assess Adrena's condition. If there was any fight left in her, a pregnant woman shouldn't have to handle it. Vivian agreed to wait on the stairs in case there was a problem.

Mrs. Stanley found a bleary-eyed and bedraggled Adrena holding onto the wall and asked her, "Where are you trying to get to, Adrena?"

In a wobbly whisper, Adrena said, "The bathroom."

"Let me help you. Doc's here to see you."

Tears pooled in Adrena's eyes when she asked, "I really made a mess, didn't I?"

"You made a mess, Adrena. Not an insurmountable mess though. Keep that in mind."

"I'm sorry, Mrs. Stanley."

"I know, baby. Come on. Let's get you cleaned up for your company."

Adrena was presentable when Vivian entered Adrena's bedroom. Adrena sat on her bed with her head hung low. Knowing she was in trouble, Adrena had very little to say.

Vivian asked, "When did you stop taking your medication, Adrena?"

In a barely audible whisper, Adrena said, "Three days ago."

"Jesus, that's a long time. Tell me the truth, Adrena, did you hurt anyone while you were off of it?"

"No."

"Did you want to?"

"Yes."

"That's normal during withdrawal. You want to tell me why you did it? There has to be more to it than driving lessons."

Tears splashed onto Adrena's clenched hands as she said, "I'm tired of being a legal junky, Doc. I want to laugh, dance, and look forward to the future like everybody else. I can't see me in ten years, Doc. I can't see me next year."

Vivian sat down next to Adrena and wrapped her arm around the shoulders of the weeping teenager. Adrena had come a long way and still had no idea where she was going. Vivian wished with all her heart that she could give her an answer, but that would be irresponsible - not getting there could do Adrena irreparable harm.

Vivian told her, "None of us knows, for a fact, where we're going, Adrena. We make plans and head out. Sometimes, we get sidetracked. Sometimes, we get back on track. You have your entire life in front of you. You've got more than enough time to make plans and begin the traveling process.

"I know how you feel about having to take the drugs, Adrena, but it was the only way I could keep you stable long enough to know that there were tracks. Now that you know, we can slowly set you on them. Please don't try to take yourself off the medication too quickly, Adrena. Life will wait for you."

"Will it, Doc? Can I look forward to a career, a husband and a family, like you?"

Without realizing the danger of what she was saying, Vivian said, "Of course, you can look forward to a career and husband. You can even adopt children, if you'd like."

Looking puzzled, Adrena asked, "Why would I have to adopt children? Have the pills I've been taking done something to me?"

"No, Adrena. You remember the surgery you had, don't you?"

"Yes."

"Well, they had to remove your uterus. That's where babies are carried. That's why you haven't gotten your period. You did know that, didn't you?"

Adrena's shoulders slumped in defeat, and a fresh batch of painful tears fell. Vivian stroked her back and let her cry. She honestly thought Adrena understood more of what they had done to her body. Everyone was letting this poor child down. Mildred and Bart, the medical and educational community . . . and even Vivian.

Vivian asked, "What are you feeling, Adrena? Talk to me."

In the most vulnerable voice Vivian had ever heard Adrena use, she said, "No matter what I do, I'll never be able to put Mildred and Bart behind me."

"You can still have a rich life, Adrena. You can still pursue any career you choose. Find a great guy, fall in love and get married. Adoption may not be the road you would have wanted to choose originally, but it's an option to emptiness. You've got time to sort all of that out, sweetheart. It's not as bleak as you're thinking right now."

"I'll never be a complete anything, Doc. I can lay all of the tracks I want. I'll always be running from a past I can't escape. Mildred was right - Bart really was good at what he did. I know exactly what I'm worth. Nothing."

Adrena gave a defeated smirk and said she was hungry. Vivian knew there was no talking her out of the space she was in. A meal, some rest, and her medication would offer her more solace than anything she could say.

This episode further assured Vivian of Adrena's tenacious desire to live and to do it normally. That determination was necessary to keep the door of hope ajar. However, Adrena was emulating Vivian's life choices - using Vivian as her personal yardstick. Vivian's pregnancy would certainly heighten Adrena's perception that her inability to have children was a permanent, irreversible shortcoming.

Soon, the pit of despair would become Adrena's new residence, everything ringing hollow in her ears as she freefell into the emotional darkness. It was this Adrena that Harvey would have the misfortune of pestering again.

Chapter Twenty-Six

As Vivian returned home from seeing Adrena a little before noon, Howard was frantically dialing the telephone on the kitchen wall. The moment he heard the front door close, he slammed the receiver down and started yelling her name.

"Vivian! Vivian! Is that you? Where on earth have you been?"

"Yes, it's me, Howard. Who else were you expecting?"

"Where have you been?"

"I wanted to check on Adrena, Howard. She's my patient. She had a rough night. Calm down. I'm home in one piece."

Leaning on the back of a chair in the living room, glaring at his wife's calm demeanor in the face of his anger, Howard demanded, "You think this is some kind of a joke, Vivian? I walk out of the door to go to work at eight-thirty. I call back at nine, and you're gone. The doctor said you had to rest. I cannot work and worry, Vivian."

"Stop worrying, Howard. I'll be fine. I had to check on her. That's my job."

"Your job is to have our baby, without losing your own mind!"

Vivian pleaded, "Please stop yelling, Howard, you're giving me a headache. If it'll make you feel better, I won't go out again."

"Make me feel better? What do you care about me feeling better? As long as Vivian can run all over town worrying about everybody. Hell, you don't care if you go crazy and take me with you. Our kid's going to have a nursery at Huntingdon - to be close to both of his parents."

Giggling, Vivian said, "That's not funny, Howard. This is one of the reasons why I never mentioned being pregnant to you. I knew you would be a pain in the butt."

"Who are you calling a pain in the butt?! You're the one who can't follow instructions from your own doctor! I'm trying to do everything I can to see that you're comfortable, happy and well cared for. What do I get for it? Called a pain in the butt. Well, this pain in the butt is going back to work. You just run behind your patients all you want. I'll scrape you off the ceiling when I get home."

Waving Vivian off, Howard headed toward the front door. To her genuine surprise, he walked right past her. Vivian followed on his heels. Just as his hand touched the doorknob, Vivian slid her arms around his waist and laid her head on his back.

Howard sighed and said, "I've got to go, Vivian."

"I know. I'm sorry for worrying you, Howard. I'll try to do better."

"I certainly hope so. We've got a long way to go. You pull that stunt one more time, and I'm disabling your car."

"You don't have to do that. I've already promised to behave. Can't you forgive me?"

"I forgive you."

"Enough to kiss me goodbye?"

Vivian truly felt sorry for her handsome husband. His head had to be swimming with her constant contradictions. Touch me. Don't touch me. Kiss me. Don't kiss me. She knew he had gritted his teeth for sanity's sake and started a mental countdown. Six more months, and this will all be over.

Looking at Vivian over his shoulder, Howard sighed in resignation and shook his head. He turned around and wrapped his long, strong arms around her. She nuzzled the front of his shirt with her nose; he closed his eyes and kissed the top of her head. Finally, she lifted her face to receive the kiss she'd asked for. It stirred that familiar tickle of desire at the base of her stomach. The harmonious rock of two people undeniably attracted to each other began.

Howard groaned, "Not now, Vivian. I have to go."

Nibbling his chin, Vivian said, "Now, Howard. You're the boss. You can be a few minutes late."

After a strenuous hour of making love, Howard showered, dressed and started his workday over again. He left a contented Vivian, curled up like a kitten and fast asleep. The ringing telephone woke Vivian from her nap at four. Lula's angry voice bellowed from the receiver, before Vivian offered a greeting.

"Talia told me you were pregnant, you slut! Howard didn't have the decency to tell me himself! He knew what I was going to say about it! I told him you were going to do this, and you're not wasting a damn minute, are you?! Redecorating his damn house to suit yourself, using his last name now, too, I hear - and probably his last dime as well! You think you're going to lock Howard in and strip him! Well, I've got news for you, Miss Hot Shit, it's not going to work!"

Undisturbed by Lula's tirade, Vivian said, "I've done all of that and a few things you know absolutely nothing about, Lula. I'm sure Howard told you I was good at anything I do. That's why your brother loves me. You have a nice afternoon, and I'll chat with you some other time. Howard will be home soon and we're going to change his will, so I have to get my rest. Goodbye."

As Vivian smiled and hung up the telephone, she heard Lula's spastic screams. Vivian hadn't been called names like that since she was in junior high school. Turning over to resume her nap, Vivian mumbled, "Throw a fit over that for a while, Miss Lula. That's just my thank you for your attendance at my wedding."

Later that week, when Vivian told Adrena about her pregnancy, it was received with mixed emotions. Adrena openly shared her feelings on the subject with Vivian, telling her she had already noticed the change in the Doc's behavior toward her. The way Adrena saw it, now that Doc would have her own child, she would be relegated to the back seat. Of course, Vivian denied feeling that way, but Adrena knew that people felt differently about their own flesh and blood children. Foster care had taught her well.

As her pregnancy progressed, Vivian would see more and more distance in Adrena's eyes. This was a crucial part of life

that Adrena would never experience. Her inability to have
children placed a permanent, last-act stamp on the lives of
Adrena, Mildred and Bart. Beyond herself, there was no hope
of redemption for the past sins of the family.

If Junior had not been playing a major role in Adrena's
life, her reaction to the baby might have been even more
profound. Maxine's presence helped a great deal, too. Adrena
was seeing Junior at least three times a week, and they were
often accompanied by Max who took them to concerts, the
aquarium, the zoo, and the state fair. The days she didn't see
Junior, they talked together on the phone. Adrena was always
amazed that Junior didn't wait for her to call; he called her.
It was inconceivable to Adrena that he was as preoccupied
with her as she was with him.

◆   ◆   ◆

The holiday season came and went without much fanfare.
Howard and Vivian hosted Christmas dinner. By then,
Vivian was only setting off the smoke detectors two or three
times a week. She could actually help Maxine, Adrena, and
Howard prepare the meats and vegetables. Of course, they
kept telling her to go take a nap.

An exhausted and sad Adrena gently stroked Vivian's
slightly swelling stomach in passing. Adrena was unprepared
for Vivian's touch of consolation. She jumped and asked
hurriedly, "Oh, did I hurt you, Doc? I'm sorry. I'm so sorry."

Vivian assured her over and over that she hadn't hurt her.

While Adrena now sometimes seemed to be emotionally
above water, there were long periods of melancholy that
troubled Vivian.   Adrena had been so quiet during her
sessions, Vivian was becoming concerned about her stability.

As Adrena and Vivian sat alone at the dining room table,
Adrena asked, "Does it hurt, Doc?"

"No, it doesn't. Looks like it should though, doesn't it?"

"Yeah. Can you sleep on it?"

"So far, I can. That'll end soon though."

"Howard's real happy about the baby, isn't he? He gets all
in a huff if you do anything."

"Well, I have some problems that worry my poor husband."

Looking alert and concerned, Adrena asked, "What problems? Nothing's going to happen to you, is it, Doc?"

"I'm fine, sweetheart. My estrogen levels go out of whack every now and then. I experience wild mood swings. One minute, I'm fine. The next, I'm angry. The next, I'm depressed. I'm driving Howard crazy."

"He's still being nice to you though. Right?"

"So far, Adrena. If I didn't know he loved me before, I know it now."

With great interest, Adrena asked, "How?"

"He's putting up with a lot from me. If he gets three good nights' sleep a week, he's doing good. It's pretty frustrating living with a person who cooks dinner and says they don't want what they cooked."

Confused, Adrena asked, "Well, why'd you cook it, if you didn't want it?"

"I don't know."

Smiling for the first time that day, Adrena said, "Sounds like you're in the same boat I'm in, Doc. Want one of my oars?"

They both laughed at Adrena's joke. Then, Adrena said sadly, "Junior's looking forward to the day he has a home and family of his own, too."

Now Vivian knew why finding out she couldn't have children had such an adverse effect on Adrena. She asked, "Did you tell Junior you couldn't have children, Adrena?"

Looking down at her hands, Adrena said, "Yes."

"What did he say?"

"He says by the time we're ready to have children, they'll have found a way to fix whatever's wrong with me. They're growing babies in test tubes now anyway. Junior's silly sometimes, Doc."

"No, Adrena, he's optimistic. He cares a great deal for you, and he's letting you know there are alternatives. He doesn't want you to worry about it."

"I'll never be able to do what you're doing, Doc. I'm not going to allow myself to indulge in hopeless optimism.

Junior's going to find someone who can give him what you and Howard have. No one wants a freak for life."

"Don't you ever let me hear you call yourself a freak again, young lady. You've had some bad breaks. You've had some good ones too, Adrena. Your life can be every bit as rich as mine. Perhaps richer. If you give yourself a chance, you'd see it for yourself."

"You have to admit, you had more to work with than me, Doc. You had your Dad and Max to love you all of your life. I've only had you for seven years."

"Have those seven years been good, Adrena?"

"Most of them."

"I don't have to tell you about the children who grow to adults, without one good year and make wonderful lives for themselves, do I? You've seen them with your own eyes."

With tears in her eyes, Adrena said, "I'm trying, Doc. I can see that my life has possibilities, but nothing like you have. I'm confused again. Mildred and Bart are back in my dreams. They're taunting me from the grave. I thought I would be free of them if they died."

Vivian noted Adrena said, "if they died," instead of "when they died." Was that a slip of the tongue . . . or an unconscious confession of guilt? She made a mental note to bring the subject up during session again and then asked, "So, you haven't been sleeping? Have you been taking the Ativan?"

"No."

"Look at me, Adrena. I want you to promise me you won't go without sleep for more than one night. Promise me now."

Softly, she said, "I promise."

Junior walked over when he saw the tears in Adrena's eyes. He wanted to know what was wrong. Vivian told him they were talking and that Adrena was fine. Adrena looked up at Junior, and Vivian saw the tug of war going on in her beautiful eyes. Adrena desperately wanted to love Junior but was afraid. The two teenagers went off to the den to talk.

In the months since Junior and Adrena began their relationship, Vivian had grown to accept it. All of her fears had not evaporated, but she was proud of the way Adrena reached out to Junior. It was a major step in her recovery. Vivian was ecstatic with her brother's mature manner of dealing with Adrena. Junior couldn't have been better for Adrena if they had been raised together. If he noticed there were any peculiarities in her behavior, he never shone a light on them.

Beyond Adrena and Junior, Vivian couldn't help noticing the drastic change in Maxine. She was suddenly happier than she had been in years. When Vivian questioned her after dinner, Maxine's response was simply, "Clayton."

Stunned, Vivian asked, "What about him?"

"He'll do in bad weather."

"Just bad weather?"

With a facial twist that told Vivian that Maxine hated admitting this, she said, "Honestly, he's much better than that. I just can't let him know I know that now. Clayton thinks he's God's gift, you know, Viv."

Vivian looked at her sister and waited for the rest of the story. Realizing it wasn't forthcoming, Vivian asked, "Well, is he, Max?"

"Just using the kiss as a meter, I'd say he was. I couldn't see a thing for five minutes after that kiss, Viv."

"Don't tell Howard that, Max, he'll be very upset. I was only blinded for three minutes after his first kiss!"

Clayton didn't give Maxine any space after Chrismas dinner. He wanted to know her schedule every day. If she was free for dinner, he met her at home and took her out. Having suffered a minor bite from Clayton when he stood her up previously, Maxine continued to hold Clayton on a short leash. Two weeks later, she gave in and went home with Clayton after dinner. He must have been God's gift to Maxine because the following weekend they flew to Vegas together. Howard and Vivian didn't know what was going on until they came back.

After the holidays, Vivian's estrogen levels had been stable long enough for her to go to the office twice a week. She was never happier to escape from the house in her life. Vivian had worked at something since she was fourteen.

Staying home bored her to death, and a housekeeper coming in twice a week left her nothing to do. As far as Vivian was concerned, her quality of life had diminished drastically when the highlight of her day was cooking dinner.

There were still occasional wild moments Vivian couldn't control. For her safety, Snow resided with Vance full time. Vivian cried at the drop of a pin. She consumed more food than she thought humanly possible and was still hungry. She craved peanut butter and strawberries in the middle of the night. She kept Howard up to ungodly hours talking about nothing, and if he fell asleep she would be furious. Vivian carried on so badly one night, Howard left her in their room alone. He slept in the guestroom. When he woke up, Vivian was in the bed with him. The first time Vivian felt the baby move, she woke Howard at four in the morning. He waited two hours for it to do it again. An hour later, Howard had to get ready for work. Vivian slept like a baby, while her bone-weary husband went to the office.

As Vivian grew larger and declared she looked like a bloated warthog, Howard assured her she was evolving into a magnificent specimen of pregnant womanhood. Vivian didn't want Howard to see her without anything on, and if he came into the bathroom while Vivian was in the bathtub, she screamed and threw water at him.

As time progressed, Howard could tell when Vivian's levels were falling. She always complained about being cold first. On those nights, he would build a fire in the bedroom fireplace for her. Vivian would stack pillows and blankets on the floor in front of it and insist they sleep down there. During the night, Vivian would warm up and want to make love, which was Howard's bonus for sleeping on the floor - he wasn't exactly the floor type.

Millie was extremely happy to have Vivian back, even if it was only part-time. Millie didn't like working for Harper alone. He was as stiff as cinderblock and had the personality of a long-dead fish. He wasn't even creative enough to eat a different lunch occasionally - sardines and crackers every day. The smell alone made Millie retch. Millie knew without asking that he bored his wife to tears. All she wanted to know was whose couch was Mrs. Harper on, and had anyone actually ever seen her?

All of Vivian's patients were glad to see her. They brought her all kinds of things to make her comfortable. Footstools, pillows, portable armrests, stuffed animals, and herbal teas. Adrena massaged Vivian's shoulders and back the entire time they talked. She dropped down on her knees and carefully inspected Vivian's stomach every chance she got. She would touch it and marvel at the baby's kick.

Howard worried about Vivian being in the office, but had to admit she was happier. To make this pregnancy easier for Vivian, he was determined to do whatever was necessary. Vivian often questioned the strange look Howard donned quite frequently, as she moved from one tantrum to another, but Howard never explained the look to her.

Chapter Twenty-Seven

Sweat-drenching nightmares of Mildred and Bart, followed by blinding headaches and insomnia continued to plague Adrena. Taking the Ativan afforded Adrena her only respite, but after taking the tiny pill, sleep was one long black event, giving her no sense of rest - instead, it was just a brief trip to nowhere.

Adrena's deepening despondency left Vivian with no alternative but to increase her antidepressant medication. The new daily dosage provided Adrena with the hollow, flatline sensation of many zombies before her. There were no emotional ups or downs. If anyone penetrated the stillness of her mind, they were disappointed with her lifeless responses.

There was no more talk of driving lessons. No enthusiasm in her piano playing or her school lessons. She didn't even seem to care if she talked to Junior. His invitation to take her to his senior prom failed to excite her, and only Max's intervention persuaded Adrena to accept.

Adrena had functioned mechanically for weeks after she took it upon herself to stop taking the antidepressants. She now knew that while the medication didn't make her euphoric, it provided the base that stabilized her existence. The fact that she couldn't have children continued to weigh her down - not because Adrena wanted them, but because Junior wanted children, and Adrena wanted him. In Adrena's depression-distorted mind, Doc had slammed the brakes on any success at normalcy with that information.

In spite of her distress, Adrena struggled against the odds to maintain her academic achievement; education had been designated as her ticket out - out of what she wasn't sure, but she focused all of her energies on to that avenue. Unfortunately, this drained her of the energy needed to battle any other external demons, and it was this moment in time that her perverted schoolmate, Harvey, chose to make his presence intolerable.

The touching had stopped for a long time after the acid incident. Harvey knew Adrena poured that acid on purpose, and so he avoided provoking her physically. Still, he couldn't resist tormenting her. Whistles, catcalls, flicking tongues, undulating fingers, and crotch-grabbing were Harvey's basic tools.

In her new space with Junior, Adrena had easily ignored Harvey. She had been so satisfied with her new life that harming Harvey had fallen away from her daily thoughts. Now that Adrena's focus was wavering once again, those disturbed thoughts returned. As long as Harvey kept his hands to himself, Adrena lacked the passion necessary to formulate a serious plan; but Harvey changed that one day in February, by tiptoeing behind Adrena in the hallway and groping her breasts.

Realizing the danger of repeating any performance, Adrena ran through many scenarios. Walking up behind Harvey in an abandoned hallway, palming the back of his head, forcing it forward, and silently slitting his throat from ear-to-ear with a razor. Watching his body drop to its knees, groping the gaping hole in his neck, the same way he had mauled her breasts. She would slowly walk away, while the final remnants of his despicable life escaped his grasp. Adrena dismissed that scenario because it required touching Harvey. The mere thought caused a tremor of revulsion in her.

There were no more effective drugs at Adrena's disposal, her stash having been spent on Mildred and Bart - not that she couldn't buy them on any street corner, but someone might remember her and run their mouth. The light of an idea worth researching blinked when Adrena went to check on her grandmother's house. All of Granny's medication still sat in the kitchen cabinet. One of the ways Doc had helped Adrena with her reading skills was by going over the side effects of her medications in the *Physicians' Desk Reference*. She always asked Adrena lots of questions to make sure she fully understood what she was taking. Adrena wrote the names of

Granny's medications down on a piece of paper to research them in the library.

By the end of her school day, Adrena knew exactly how she would deal with Harvey. Now, all she needed to do was stay prepared and maintain enough patience to wait for an opportunity. Hating Harvey the way she did made the latter more difficult than Adrena ever imagined.

Harvey always socialized in the cafeteria and often walked away from his lunch. Adrena rehearsed walking by and dropping things into Harvey's cup. She only missed once. If anyone ever saw her doing it, they never came forward. Not even the day she tripped Harvey on a Ritalin she'd found jammed into the toe of one of her seldom worn shoes. Harvey never knew what hit him. The fool couldn't make himself sit still, and he was suspended before the school day ended.

One day, a classmate, Felicia Mays, approached Adrena and asked her if she would like to volunteer for the junior class dance refreshment committee. Usually, this activity would not have been given serious consideration by Adrena. She hated the sophmore, junior, and senior class equally, and generally, they all kept their distance from her, too. However, Felicia must have noticed the change in Adrena's attitude after summer break and decided she might want to join in the festivities now.

Mustering a fake smile, Adrena said, "Sure, Felicia. What will I have to do?"

"Help decide what refreshments we'll have and take a turn serving. That way everybody will get a chance to dance and have a good time."

"I'm not really a dancer, but I'll give it a shot."

Amazed, Felicia said, "I can't believe a person who plays the piano as well as you can't dance."

"Truthfully, I've never tried, Felicia."

"If you're not doing anything after school some afternoons, you can come over my house. I'll teach you the little I know."

In shock, Adrena asked, "Are you kidding? You would take time to teach me how to dance?"

"Sure. You're a little strange at times, but you don't look like you have fleas. You can be pretty snappy sometimes, but you don't look like a mass murderer either. If you can stand my company, I can stand yours."

This time, Adrena gave Felicia a genuine smile and said, "Okay. I think I'd like that. Maybe we can do it tomorrow afternoon."

"It's a date."

The offer of dance lessons intrigued Adrena because she was going to the prom with Junior in the Spring. Felicia earned Adrena's respect because she had fearlessly scaled her protective wall and offered an olive branch. By doing so, she singlehandedly rescued Adrena from the black hole of despair by giving her something to look forward to - dancing and talking with someone who was almost as naive on the issues of life and boys as Adrena. The two girls laughed and talked about boys and their bodies every afternoon except Wednesday. That's when Adrena saw Doc and crossreferenced what she and Felicia had been pondering.

The afternoon of the dance, Adrena and Felicia worked the refreshment stand together. They made soft ice cream cups and milk shakes in vanilla, chocolate, and strawberry. Everyone who passed through their line smiled and made idle chit-chat with Adrena, as if she had been one of the in-crowd forever. While this newfound acceptance fascinated Adrena, it did not distract her from her mission.

In her smock pocket, lay a tiny pill envelope. Inside, finely crushed digoxin tablets. The only way Harvey wouldn't ingest the contents of her envelope would be if he didn't ask Adrena for any refreshments. Knowing Harvey the way she did, Adrena knew he wouldn't be able to resist the opportunity to harass her.

An hour into the activities, Harvey and his gang appeared in the gym. They came late to make an entrance that impressed no one. Harvey wore his red-and-white track jacket proudly. As far as anyone knew, running was the only thing Harvey was good at. He certainly was a lousy student and a nuisance.

The moment Harvey spotted Adrena, he casually cupped his crotch, leaned, and swaggered over. Felicia nudged her friend, to let her know he was coming. Adrena nodded and continued making fancy ice cream cups for those in line.

Without standing in line, Harvey walked up to Adrena and asked, "Hey, hot stuff, wanna make me a thick chocolate shake?"

People in line started grumbling. Harvey asked, "Is there a problem?"

One girl said angrily, "Yes. Can't you see there's a line?"

Giving her one of his nasty smirks, Harvey said, "Yeah, I see it. So what?"

"Git your ugly ass in it, Harvey."

"Who are you talking to? You picky-headed, bony-ass bitch? I'll slap you down for breathing in a minute."

Someone went to get a chaperone. When they returned, a real ruckus played out. With everyone watching the event, Adrena had her opportunity to make Harvey's milkshake. She pushed the cup against the ice cream dispenser and half-filled it. With a barely noticeable flick of the wrist, Adrena shook the contents of the tiny envelope into the cup. The green powder made a sharp contrast to the chocolate ice cream. Adrena shrugged her shoulders, finished filling the cup, and placed it on the blender. Letting the blender run the entire time they argued, Adrena removed it, snapped on a lid, and jammed one of the thick straws into it. Adrena handed the milkshake to Harvey as he was being escorted from the gym. He took it and grinned rakishly over his shoulder at her. Adrena grinned back and blew him a kiss.

Felicia said, "I can't stand that boy. He's a troublemaker - always grabbing at people. If he couldn't run fast, they would have thrown him out of here a long time ago."

Adrena said matter-of-factly, "Someone will break him of that filthy habit one day, Felicia. Don't worry about it."

The two girls went back to serving ice cream. Adrena dropped the envelope between two cups and threw them into the trash. She carefully cleaned the blender before making the next shake.

When their duty was up, Adrena and Felicia joined the crowd on the gymnasium floor. Adrena was surprised to see how many of the young men came over and asked her to dance. With lots of prodding from Felicia, Adrena shyly accepted. No matter what, she only fast-danced; being touched by them was still more than she could handle.

After the dance, Adrena and Felicia walked home together. Two guys offered to walk with them, but Adrena said no. Since they couldn't walk with them, the boys stayed behind the two girls, and there was a great deal of good-natured teasing back and forth. Adrena and Felicia said goodnight at Adrena's walkway; neither girl gave Harvey another thought.

Adrena ate dinner, took her medication and talked to Junior on the phone before going to bed. Mrs. Stanley was very glad to see that Adrena had had a nice time and appeared to be in better spirits. She had honestly worried about Adrena's ability to rebound after tampering with her medication, and the smile Adrena gave them before retiring granted both Mr. and Mrs. Stanley their first relieved breath in weeks.

At school the next morning, silence met Felicia and Adrena when they walked into the hallway. Felicia asked Jeffrey Stone, "What's the matter with everybody?"

Looking dumbstruck, Jeffrey said, "Harvey went home after he ran laps yesterday and dropped dead on his front steps."

Felicia screamed hysterically, "What?!"

Turning to Adrena, Felicia asked excitedly, "Did you hear what he said, Adrena?"

Adrena nodded slowly.

Felicia asked, "Isn't that horrible?!"

Realizing Felicia wanted a reaction Adrena didn't own, she said numbly, "Yes, that's horrible, Felicia."

Not wanting Felicia to know how much she hated Harvey, Adrena had never discussed him with her - after all, when he dropped dead she didn't want anyone looking in her direction. There would be an easy leap from what Adrena assumed was Harvey's last meal and the milkshake she served him. The

Physicians' Desk Reference said digoxin was a regulator for the malfunctioning heart, but the arrhythmia it caused in normal hearts could cause death. Adrena liked the fact that all humans naturally manufactured the chemical. That meant that if they found it in Harvey, they would more than likely dismiss its presence.

Because Harvey was the despicable creature he was, there was no openly hysterical reaction to his death by the student body. The principal called an emergency assembly and announced Harvey's death. He also made it known there would be counselors available for any student experiencing problems handling his announcement. The students who stopped by for counseling only wanted to discuss the possibility of dropping dead themselves; of course, they felt badly for Harvey, but the truth was they preferred it happening to him than anyone else.

They talked about Harvey on the news that evening, and the newscaster reported that he died from natural causes. He made reference to other high school and college jocks who met the same fate. A doctor came on and explained why the arrhythmia leading to heart attacks was often undetectable in the young before it turned fatal. There was no mention of drugs being found in Harvey's system.

Adrena sat in front of the screen and thought, "They wouldn't have detected Harvey's arrhythmia in a million years."

As the newscaster was giving his version of a heartfelt report on the sudden lost life of a local high school athlete named Harvey Jacobsen, Vivian was delivering a loud diatribe on Howard's callousness that completely drowned him out. If Vivian hadn't been pestering Howard that night, she would have made the connection between Harvey and Adrena, but Howard had gone to the store and come back with the wrong kind of mustard. Vivian wanted the spicy mustard to dip her cheese in. The last time she had the spicy mustard, she kept Howard up all night complaining about indigestion. For that reason, he had bought the wrong kind on purpose.

Chapter Twenty-Eight

No matter what Vivian's physician said, three-day work weeks were as far as Howard allowed Vivian to go. That doctor had no idea how contrary and argumentative Vivian was at the end of a work day. And the larger Vivian grew, the more disconcerting her behavior toward Howard became. There were actually times when she couldn't stand to be in the same room with him, and he knew it; but, the moment he left the room she would throw temper tantrums. A compliment from him on the way she looked drove her up the wall. Howard literally said and did nothing without invitation.

In March, Vivian and Maxine launched the drive to get Adrena ready for Junior's prom in May. Vivian and Maxine were ecstatic with the way Adrena had come around since the December fiasco. Vivian's happiness with Adrena's making a new friend was evident, and she insisted Felicia join them on their shopping trips. Of course, Vivian and Maxine did a magnificent job of turning Adrena into a princess for the evening.

As a matter of fact, the two sisters shopped the entire week because Howard and Clayton were at a brokers convention in Salt Lake City. Clayton was disappointed about not being able to take Maxine with him, but she was Vivian's official babysitter in Howard's absence.

Vivian and Howard had a rough time figuring out how Clayton and Maxine's relationship held together. They were both so headstrong. A fresh argument broke out between them every fifteen minutes. They wore Howard out, just listening to them.

Maxine told Vivian everything about Clayton. Clayton told Howard and Sheldon nothing about Maxine, which meant he was more enamored of his partner's fiesty sister-in-law than he was comfortable with. Caring for a woman wasn't what Clayton was best known for. From the looks of things, it was beginning to seem that Maxine was the hydrant of Clayton's dreams.

At the end of April, barely able to walk anymore, Vivian was spending her final week in the office. Giving birth to this baby wasn't happening fast enough for her. Every time Vivian moved, she felt like she had to hoist a city block. Not wanting her to drive any longer, Howard dropped her off three days a week and picked her up after work.

That Monday started on an upbeat. Vivian saw her patients, jotted reminders, and dictated notes between appointments as usual. Everyone wished her well and hoped to see her back soon. During lunch, Vivian always leafed through the mail while she ate. That day, Millie hesitated in bringing it in. Vivian buzzed her and asked for it.

Millie always opened all of the mail and sorted it. She only bothered Vivian with bills when they seemed exorbitant and never gave Vivian patient payments from insurance companies. Most of the time, she handed Vivian a stack of sample medications, patient request letters, or invitations from the medical community to this affair or that.

Today, Millie had found something in the mail she wasn't sure she should give to Vivian. Millie didn't know exactly what to do with it. She wanted to call Howard and warn him, but if the contents of the envelope were legitimate, he didn't deserve to be warned. Millie bowed her head, gave God a call and took the mail in to Vivian. Of course, she put the large manila envelope on the bottom.

Vivian smiled and thanked Millie for it, flipped through the envelopes and then noticed Millie still standing and staring at her. Frowning, Vivian asked, "What's the matter with you?"

Wringing her hands, Millie said, "Please don't get upset, Vivian. I just didn't know what else to do."

"You didn't know what else to do about what?"

Millie closed her eyes momentarily, winced and pointed at the envelope. Vivian picked it up and peered inside. Millie flinched and covered her face when Vivian yelled, "What the hell is this?!"

She reached into the envelope and pulled out ten, eight-by-ten, color photographs of Howard and Lydia. They were lounging around a swimming pool, in an obviously well-appointed hotel, wearing bathing suits and sunglasses. Vivian's mouth fell open a little wider each time she flipped to a new photograph.

Howard and Lydia gazing into each other's eyes longingly. Howard leisurely applying suntan lotion to Lydia's back and long, shapely legs. Howard and Lydia holding hands as the sun set. Howard and Lydia locked in an intimate embrace. And finally, Howard and Lydia indulging in what certainly appeared to be an extremely passionate kiss.

If Vivian had been struck by lightning, she couldn't have been any hotter. The only time Howard had been away without Vivian since they got married was for that convention in Salt Lake City. He had not gone out of town without her once while they were dating, so the convention had to be when these photographs were taken.

Vivian sat looking at the photographs over and over. Unable to come to grips with Howard's betrayal, she grew angrier and angrier. The baby must have felt the temperature rise, because it jumped around like it had a hot foot. Howard was as close to being murdered at that moment as he ever would be, without breathing his final breath.

Picking up the telephone, Vivian yelled, "Millie, cancel the rest of my appointments for the day!" She dialed Howard's office. The moment she heard his voice on the line, she growled, "Come get me now."

A little alarmed by his wife's tone of voice, Howard asked, "What's the matter, Vivian? Are you feeling all right?"

"I'm fine! You just come get me right now, Howard Shaw!"

Thinking Vivian was in the throes of one of her hormonal tantrums, Howard said, "Okay, sweetheart. Calm down. I'll be there in fifteen minutes."

Without a word to the panic-stricken Millie, Vivian heaved herself out of her chair and began to pack her things. She viciously threw things into her bag. She slammed her briefcase lid so hard, the air swooshed out. Then, without notice, Vivian began to slam her desk drawer over and over again. Bitter tears flowed unchecked down her face.

Millie walked over, put her arms around Vivian, and lulled, "Vivian, please stop. There's got to be an explanation."

Pushing Millie away roughly, Vivian said through her tears, "You want an explanation? Look at me."

"What am I supposed to see when I look at you, Vivian?"

"A big, fat, unattractive pregnant woman, with a foul temper her husband's tired of ! That's what!"

"I don't believe you're saying that. If I had looked half as good as you do when I was nine-months pregnant, I would have made pregnancy my career choice. You're beautiful. Vivian, I can't believe you're torturing yourself, or Howard, with that kind of nonsense."

"You don't know how particular my husband is about looks, Millie. He can't possibly find me attractive, when he's got someone who looks like her hanging around. Look at her, for God's sake."

"Yes, he can find you attractive. You're carrying his baby - you know? Has Howard ever said you looked bad?"

"Howard's stiff, not crazy, Millie."

Millie smiled and said, "He hasn't said it, because it's not true. Calm down and talk to him before you kill him."

"I'm not making any promises."

Vivian waddled to the bathroom and splashed cold water on her face, before collecting her things and catching the elevator down to the lobby. Millie went with her. They stood inside in silence until Howard's gleaming Jaguar pulled up.

Millie whispered, "Give him a chance, Vivian. Please?"

Vivian rolled her eyes at Millie and waddled out to the curb. Without asking any questions, Howard took the things Millie carried and put them into the car. He walked around the car and opened the door for Vivian. When he attempted to help her get in, she slapped his hand so hard passersby stopped and gaped. Howard's head dropped back. With his gaze on the sky, he sighed and said, "Please?"

It took Vivian quite a while to get into the car on her own. She cursed the fact that the dumb thing was so close to the ground. She huffed, puffed, and squeezed her way in.

While he waited, Howard silently mouthed to Millie over the car, "What happened?"

Millie shook her head slowly and mouthed, "Good luck!"

A completely miserable Howard Shaw closed the door once his wife was settled in. Not wanting to fight while the car was moving, Howard drove home without asking any questions. The second act of the drama began when he tried to help Vivian out of the car.

She screamed, "Don't touch me! I hate you, Howard!"

Throwing his hands in the air, Howard collected Vivian's things and carried them into the house. It took his wife twice as long to get out of the car as it had taken to get in. While he wanted desperately to help her, Howard knew how ugly Vivian could get when she was in this mood. He stood quietly, until Vivian slammed his car door so hard, Howard thought the window would break.

"Hey! Watch that door, Vivian! I don't know what's wrong with you now, but don't take it out on my car!"

"You and your car can go straight to hell, Howard Shaw! Take that slut you went to Salt Lake City with you, too!"

Looking around, as if there might be another Howard Shaw she was talking to, he asked, "What are you talking about?"

Reaching into her bag, Vivian retrieved and slammed the envelope into Howard's chest before going into the house. She needed to sit down. Getting out of the car had taken quite a toll on her. The moment she got her wind back, Vivian fully intended to go into the kitchen and get a nice big frying pan to slap Howard with.

Through the opened door, Vivian heard Howard talking to himself. "What the shit? Where did these come from?"

He stormed into the living room and said, "These are not from Salt Lake City, Vivian. I don't even remember where it was."

"Yeah, I bet. I'm pregnant, not stupid. That's the weakest excuse for infidelity I've ever heard."

"It's not an excuse, it's the truth. Where did you get these pictures from?"

"They came in my office mail, and you'd better come up with a better explanation for them than you don't remember. You're dangerously close to getting the birth announcement of your own kid in the mail."

"You can't do that, Vivian. I really don't remember when or where these pictures were taken. I haven't been anywhere near Lydia since Talia's cookout, and you were there with me."

Snatching the pictures from Howard's hand, Vivian looked at the dates on the back. They were over four years old. Confused, she snapped, "Why would Lydia send these to me now? Does she want you back that bad?"

Looking like the dog died, Howard said, "Lydia didn't send those to you, Vivian."

"Well, who did?"

Before Howard could answer, Vivian said, "Lula. Why does she hate us, Howard? That's the most hateful thing I've ever had done to me. She could have hurt me and the baby."

"I honestly think that was her intention, Vivian. She really thinks you're going to use the baby against me. Lula's been going on and on about it for months. I thought she was just talking. I would have bet my life on her not doing anything to hurt the baby, but I guess my sister is sicker than I could have ever imagined."

"Well, sick or not, I'm slapping the dogshit out of her after the baby's born. That's a promise I intend to keep. She got away with the wedding thing. I owe her big time now. Sorry as hell I can't do it today."

Howard didn't respond to Vivian's threat. However, that afternoon, Lula had her hands full with Howard's anger. Never having disrespected Lula in his life, he felt she left him no choice. He yelled, cursed and threatened his oldest sister, broke several smaller pieces of furniture to make his point, and punched Bruce in the mouth for getting into something he knew nothing about.

Afterwards, Howard refused to take any calls from Lula or Bruce. Bruce came to his office wanting to know what was going on. Fresh anger filled Howard's eyes at the sight of the man, so Clayton had to tell him. Bruce moved out of the home he shared with Lula and two weeks later filed for a divorce. In disgust, Talia, Sheldon, and Gary cut their ties with Lula, too.

Lula was alone now. There was no Howard at her every beck and call. He even tore up letters she wrote to him without reading them. No Howard appeared at her hospital bedside when she feigned illness.

One week later, Vivian returned the photographs to Lula with a note that read:

Dear Lula,

Enclosed you will find your photographs. While I found them entertaining, I don't think I'm the one who needs them. I'm not interested in the woman in them, and I have the man. We have a lovely wedding album of photographs. Also enclosed you will find a psychiatric reference card. Please use it. You need more help than Howard, or I, could ever give you.

Dr. Vivian Matthews-Shaw

Chapter Twenty-Nine

Without Harvey's oppressive presence, school took on a more pleasant air for Adrena. Her heart felt lighter. The sun shone brighter. Colors she never noticed before seeped into her consciousness. The bounce in her step reflected a more genuine chord in her soul, and she was a straight A student again.

The prom would be Adrena and Junior's first official date. Adrena looked forward to it as she had nothing else. She loved the fuss Doc and Maxine made over everything from the color of her lipstick, to the texture of her stockings . . . the hours she and Felicia spent playing with each other's hair and discussing what they thought would happen on prom night.

Finally the great day came, and after two hours of primping and patting, Maxine and a very pregnant Vivian stepped back and surveyed their handiwork. The almost identical heads nodded.

Turning to each other, Vivian said, "Good job, Dr. Matthews."

Maxine said, "A very good job, Dr. Matthews-Shaw."

Adrena was truly a vision in the palest green shimmering gown, shoes, and purse. The jeweled collar wrapped snugly around her neck and flowed into a sleeveless, fitted bodice in front with a bare back. The entire dress lovingly cradled Adrena's shapely body and flared from the knees to her ankles. Her high, firm breasts, small waist and perfectly rounded hips would definitely give Junior's male classmates something to talk about at the prom.

With her hair done similarly to the way it was for Vivian's wedding, emerald green earrings, and smelling like heaven, Adrena was ready to go. All she needed was Junior. He drove up in his father's shining, black Cadillac fifteen minutes later. With cameras in hand, Vivian, Maxine, Mrs. Stanley, and Felicia dashed down the stairs to take pictures.

Mr. Stanley opened the door for Junior. The room filled with the gasps of the women - Junior was indeed a handsome, well-dressed date. Howard had gone with him to choose the black tuxedo he wore, and it showed. There was a pale green, brocaded vest under Junior's jacket. The gleaming, white shirt didn't have a traditional collar or a tie. Instead, the silk trim of the abbreviated collar traveled down the front of the shirt.

Junior came in carrying a stunning, white orchid corsage for Adrena. To Vivian and Maxine, he looked like Vance had when they were little girls. Vivian started to cry. Maxine frowned and shook her head at her older sister. They all told Junior how handsome he looked while Maxine went to call Adrena.

The expression on Junior's face when he saw Adrena on the stairs was priceless. His mouth literally fell open. He knew Adrena was pretty, but the woman descending the stairs was a breathtaking beauty. Junior's hands shook as he tried to slip the corsage onto Adrena's wrist. Adrena's did likewise, as she attempted pinning his boutonnière to his lapel.

Flashes exploded wildly, as Junior and Adrena made their way to the car. Junior had promised his father they would stop at home before leaving for the prom, because his mother wanted to see Adrena. Vivian and Maxine followed the young couple in Max's car.

Vivian asked, "Do you remember your prom, Max?"

"Oh, boy, do I. If Daddy knew half of what went on that night, he would have had a stroke."

Laughing, Vivian said, "Yeah. I'm a little worried about Adrena having that much fun."

Frowning, Maxine asked, "Why?"

"Adrena's had some problems that might make her hurt Junior if he makes a wrong move."

"Did you see the way she looked at him, Vivian? He couldn't make a wrong move in those eyes."

"Those eyes are hiding a mountain of devastation, Max."

"No, they're not. I've seen some things from time to time. Someone raped Adrena, didn't they, Vivian? Who was it? A friend of the family? An uncle?"

Looking miserable, Vivian said softly, "Her father. Her mother watched."

Maxine pulled the car out of traffic and stopped. She turned to Vivian and asked, "What did you say?"

"You know I'm not supposed to be telling you this, but it was her father. She was ten years old."

"Sweet Jesus. No wonder she looks so lost. You have worked wonders with her, Vivian. By rights, she should be a babbling idiot. I don't want the details, but are the scars on her body a result of what he did?"

"Yes."

"He's dead, right?"

"Yes."

"Good. Should have died when Adrena was nine. Nasty, heartless bastard."

Vivian said no more. Maxine had as much as she could handle, without anyone to vent on. She closed her eyes to compose herself and proceeded to their father's house. They stayed until the glowing couple was happily on their way, with Vance's endless list of instructions. Vivian and Max knew Vance had been saying those things to Junior for over a year by then. He wouldn't be Vance, if he hadn't. Max took an exhausted Vivian home afterwards.

In the car together, Adrena and Junior breathed a sigh of relief. Still nervous with each other being all dressed up, they said very little. Adrena asked if he had the tickets. He'd told her to ask him that the week before. He patted his pocket and nodded. Adrena remarked on how well he drove. Junior whispered his thanks.

After driving for twenty minutes, Junior said, "You look beautiful, Adrena."

With a twisted frown, she said, "No, I don't. I look like a fraud. A poor little girl from the wrong side of town all dressed up."

"Don't say that. It's not true. You have no idea how beautiful you are. I do. So don't contradict me. Just say thank you."

Smiling at the way he defended her against herself, Adrena said, "Thank you, Junior. You look awful good yourself."

"Are you sure? Howard didn't overdo it with the vest?"

"No, I like it. Howard really knows how to dress. He's all gussied up every day."

"Yeah, I know. He can keep his clothes, but I'd kill for that car."

"No, you wouldn't."

"Maybe not actually, but I'd give it a thought."

They pulled into the parking lot of the Manchester Hotel. A valet collected the keys and handed Junior a ticket. He walked around and opened the door for Adrena. Junior held her hand until she was steady in the glittering, green, high-heeled shoes and then politely took her arm for the walk in.

All of Junior's classmates stared at Adrena in stunned silence. Pure jealousy provoked the girls to roll their eyes. Undiluted lust and envy made the guys drool. Junior and Adrena walked through the room arm in arm. He stopped and introduced her to his friends. Girls and guys. They all smiled and said hello.

Everyone stood in line for photos. They wanted them taken before any accidents. The last thing anyone needed was to have to tell their parents they couldn't take a picture because something happened to the duds they spent all of that money for. Adrena and Junior took their places in line, too. It took half an hour to get it done, but at least it was behind them.

Junior and Adrena picked at the tasteless dinner they were served. All of the kids made jokes about it, and some of the guys started throwing chicken parts around the table. Not wanting to have to slug anybody for hitting her with flying meat, Junior asked Adrena if she wanted to dance.

They danced fast for what seemed like hours. Finally, a slow song was played. Junior slid his arms around Adrena, and she timidly slid hers around him. Junior took the first step, and she followed him nervously. By the end of the song, Adrena's head rested on Junior's chest, and she followed him effortlessly.

Slow dancing with Junior gave Adrena a sense of floating on a cloud. Feeling so safe and cared for, she could have fallen asleep in Junior's arms right there on the dance floor. It wasn't anything like the way she felt when Doc or Max held her. The only way she could explain it was that all the particles of Adrena had come to rest.

The prom ended much too soon for Adrena, but she didn't know Junior was taking her to another party. They actually went to two parties after the prom. At four in the morning, Junior pulled off the highway and drove into the park, stopping the car on a low, flat cliff from which they could see the entire city. Street lights glittered in the darkness below. Stars glittered in the darkness above.

After drinking in the sight for a few moments, Adrena asked, "Why are we stopping here, Junior? Are your friends coming up, too?"

"No, they're not coming up. I thought you might like to spend a little of the night with me. Alone."

Smiling, Adrena said, "Sure. Why not? You're pretty good company."

"Thanks. You want to slide over here and give me a kiss for it?"

"Sure. Why not? You're a pretty good kisser, too."

Adrena slid close to Junior. He casually draped one arm over the back of the soft, leather seat, placed his other hand on her waist and lowered his lips onto hers. Adrena closed her eyes and glided into the warm, secure feelings she experienced whenever Junior kissed her. When Junior's hand left her waist and found her breast, Adrena wasn't alarmed. She expected it. Since their third movie date, he always did that when they were alone in the dark.

As Junior's tongue explored Adrena's warm, wet mouth, one hand massaged her breast, and the other began to stroke her bare back. While he had never touched her skin before, Adrena really liked the feel of Junior's hand; so when his hand slid across her back and released the buttons on her collar, she wasn't shocked. That didn't set in until the front of her dress moved enough for the cool air to touch more of her exposed skin.

Adrena clutched the front of her dress, pulled away from Junior, and asked, "What do you think you're doing?"

Still trying to nuzzle her hair, Junior said, "I'm touching my girlfriend. What does it look like I'm doing? Are you afraid?"

Unsure how she felt, Adrena said, "No. It's just not a good idea to do things to me without notice. Have you forgotten the tongue bite?"

Junior replied in a whining tone, "You're beyond biting, aren't you, Adrena? I just want to touch you. Not your dress or your underwear. You."

"Are you saying you intend to touch my bare breast?"

Nodding dumbly, Junior said, "Yeah. I was hoping I would get to touch more than that, but it's a start."

"A start in getting to where?"

"Do I have to tell you that, too?"

Adrena nodded.

Junior sighed, let his head drop back and unbuttoned his shirt collar. He said, "Adrena, I know Max and Vivian talked to you about sex. They talked to me about it."

"Yeah, so what? I don't do everything I talk about. Do you?"

"I'm sorry. I thought you liked me. I know you never did it before, and neither have I. I was hoping we could do it together the first time."

Getting excited, Adrena yelled, "You mean now?!"

"Yes. When would you like the first time to be?"

Lying, Adrena said, "I don't know. I never thought about it."

"Well, we're alone. We've got until the sun comes up to get to Vivian's for breakfast. The way I see it, we could do it and have time to spare, if you'd cooperate."

"But, I don't know what I'm supposed to do."

"According to Max and Vivian, it should come to you naturally."

Remembering Doc saying that, Adrena relaxed, let the top of her dress fall and said, "Okay. If it's supposed to come naturally, we'll see."

Junior's eyes lit up when he said excitedly, "Really? Okay!"

They moved to the back seat, and everything flowed smoothly. Junior took off his shirt and draped it over the front seat. Adrena took off her dress and draped it over the front seat. Junior undid the clasps on Adrena's strapless bra and gasped at the sight of her bare breasts. Completely fixated, Junior touched both of them at one time.

Adrena closed her eyes and waited to see what came next naturally. The warmth of Junior's hands on her breasts stirred something inside and relaxed her at the same time. She lay back on the seat. Still massaging Adrena's breasts, Junior lay on top of her and kissed her lips passionately. Adrena was honestly enjoying it all. When Junior's hot, wet, mouth closed over her nipple, she was flooded by the most pleasantly intoxicating sensations she had ever experienced.

Suddenly, Junior's hand slid down her hip. It didn't elicit the same silky-smooth feelings. As if a switch had been thrown, Adrena experienced fear, loathing, and disgust. Junior's unknowing, excited fingers were pushing buttons in Adrena's psyche.

Adrena fought to stay focused on what she was doing. She was losing. All of her attention followed Junior's hand, as he stroked her hip and thigh. A desperate struggle brewed inside her. More than anything in the world, she wanted to please Junior, but as his hand moved toward the inside of her thigh, Adrena wanted to scream.

Without recognizing her own voice, Adrena said softly, "Don't do that."

So engrossed in what he was doing, Junior either didn't hear Adrena or chose to ignore her. His hand kept moving. Junior didn't notice Adrena's body tensing up, or hear the change to loud, raspy, rapid, and shallow breathing.

Pictures flashed in Adrena's mind as Junior's hands touched, rubbed, and explored. Those were Bart's hands clutching at her hips, groping the inside of her thighs, and painfully jamming between her legs. Adrena couldn't move. Her hands were tied and cold, clammy fingers clutched her ankles. It was so vivid, Adrena couldn't even smell Junior's clean body or his smooth, spicy cologne. Adrena smelled the rancid stench of Bart. The moment Junior's hand touched her pubic hair, Adrena's body flexed violently. Her foot crashed into the window. Without using her hands, she flicked Junior to the floor and screeched wildly. In Adrena's mind, there was a sock in her mouth.

Not having a clue what was happening, Junior got to his knees and asked, "Adrena, what's wrong? Did I hurt you, or something? Stop screaming and talk to me. Please."

The tense, shrieking Adrena never heard a word he said. Junior was frightened. He had never seen anyone act the way Adrena was acting. Still, he knew he had to stay calm and somehow persuade her to do the same. Junior firmly wrapped his arms around the rigid, nearly-naked body of his girlfriend and spoke directly into her ear.

"Adrena. Adrena. It's all right. You don't have to do anything you don't want to. Talk to me. Adrena."

A miserable, tormented child responded to Junior's pleas. "You didn't hurt me. He did."

Still wound up, a confused Junior asked, "Who? How?"

With tears streaming down her face, Adrena responded miserably, "You don't want to know."

"Yes, I do. Who hurt you?"

"Bart."

Thinking there must have been another guy in Adrena's life she had neglected to tell him about, Junior said in a defeated tone, "Okay. Who's Bart?"

"My father."

For the first time, Junior looked at Adrena as if she might not have all of her screws set just right. Something inside told him not to press the issue any further. While Adrena appreciated Junior's not pursuing the details, she knew she would have to tell him what happened to her one day. This just wasn't the right time.

Adrena saw Junior's strange expression and said sadly, "I guess I'm the wrong girl for you after all."

Still a little frightened and frustrated, Junior asked, "Why are you saying that?"

Angry with herself for not being able to contain her demons in Junior's presence, Adrena said in defeat, "Because I can't even cooperate, without screaming like a damn nut case."

"How do you know that's not what comes naturally to other people, too?"

"I don't think so, Junior."

"Okay. Maybe not, but I should have talked to you about it before now. Given you time to come to grips with your decision. Don't worry about it, Adrena. Maybe it'll work out better next time."

Adrena lightly stroked Junior's cheek and asked pitifully, "Are you sure there's going to be a next time, Junior?"

"As far as I'm concerned, there will be. I can't speak for you."

Smiling, Adrena said, "Thanks."

"You're welcome. Now, would it be all right if I just lie next to you for a while? I'll probably kill us both if I don't calm down before we hit the road again."

"I'm so sorry for ruining your prom night, Junior."

"You didn't ruin anything, Adrena."

She quieted and tried to believe him. He lay down on the seat next to her. Junior cradled Adrena in his arms and looked into her sad eyes for a long time. He kissed the tip of her nose. Glad he still wanted to kiss her, Adrena kissed his nose. Junior kissed Adrena's lips. Twenty minutes later, they were back where they started.

This time, Adrena never closed her eyes. If Bart was behind her lids, she wouldn't see him. She kept her eyes on Junior. As he explored the parts of her body that evoked frightening responses, she clung to Junior. Sweat flowed down her face, breasts, and stomach from the effort.

Adrena felt like she had really accomplished something, as she watched Junior slip into his condom. She knew she had, when she didn't push him through the roof of the car, when he entered her. It hurt. But, nothing like before. Just like Doc said.

Feeling much more confident, Junior actually did it a second time. Adrena didn't enjoy the act as much as Junior, and fear of losing control again stripped her of the ability to know how she felt about it. At best, she felt a sense of accomplishment. Her reward was being close to Junior, not having him reject her after screaming and throwing him on the floor . . . and the satisfied expression on his face after he had finished. She thought, "Someday. I'll learn to like it. Someday."

Sunlight woke Junior about an hour later. His heart almost stopped beating when he noticed the sunlight was shattered. Adrena had broken his father's car window with her bare foot.

Junior shook her and said excitedly, "Adrena, get dressed. We've got a problem."

In a stupor, Adrena asked, "Like what?"

"Look at the window."

Looking at it through eyes filled with sleep, Adrena exclaimed, "Jesus! Did I do that?!"

"Don't worry about it. Just get dressed. Max'll help us get it fixed before Dad sees it."

Bumping into each other, they both attempted to dress in a hurry. When Adrena slid her underwear over her foot, she winced and kept moving. Putting stockings on the foot made her cry out. The shoe was impossible. Her foot was so swollen it would never fit in that shoe.

With tears flowing, Adrena said, "Junior, I think my foot is broken, too."

Ready to cry himself now, Junior asked, "Are you sure?"

"I've never had a broken foot before, but I have had other things. I think it's broken. We're really in trouble now."

Holding his hand up, Junior said, "Just hold on, Adrena. If Max will help us fix the car window, we can say you broke your foot on something else. She'll know that if Dad makes the connection between your broken foot and his broken window, he'll break my neck, my back *and* my face! She's gotta help. We just have to stay calm until we get to Max."

"How do we get around Doc finding out?"

"Don't ask me any more questions, Adrena. I don't know."

At Vivian's, Junior rang the bell and thanked God when Maxine came to the door. Everyone else in the house was still asleep. She and Clayton had spent the night since Maxine had promised to prepare breakfast for the promgoers, and Vivian wanted to participate also. A terror-stricken Junior told Maxine what happened.

After making sure Adrena only had a broken foot, Maxine laughed like a crazy woman and said, "I thought I came up with some good stuff. I think you guys have started a brand new category. Adrena, how did you get that stocking back over that foot? It had to hurt like hell."

Grimacing at the memory, Adrena said, "I slid it on and cried."

Shaking her head, Max said, "Okay. I want all of the real details after we straighten this mess out. Now, this is how we have to do it - there won't be time for dawdling.

"Vivian usually wakes up around ten. It's seven-fifteen. Junior, you take the car over to Art's Body Shop. I'll call and tell him you're coming. He'll have the window fixed in less than an hour. You come right back here afterwards. Don't ring the bell unless you see my car.

"I'll take Little Miss Window Breaker to the hospital, get some x-rays and cast that foot. We should all be back here before nine-thirty. The broken foot story is you two were goofing off, and Adrena jumped down from the wall at the hotel. Junior, you took her to the hospital. Everybody got it?"

A relieved Junior said, "Got it, Max."

Adrena shrugged and said, "Got it."

When Vivian came down at ten-thirty, Maxine, Junior, and Adrena were eating breakfast. Howard and Clayton were in the weight room. Adrena's crutches leaned against the counter. Junior told Vivian the story Max made up about Adrena's foot. Vivian scowled at them and fretted over Adrena, but then sat down, ate breakfast, and asked questions about the prom.

After breakfast, Junior drove Adrena home and helped her into the house. He told Mrs. Stanley the same story he'd told Vivian.

She grumbled, "Kids. Always playing around. You'd think you all would at least try to act like adults when you're all dressed up like that." Then she fussed and fretted over Adrena.

After driving home, Junior carefully parked the car in the driveway and inspected it inside and out before going in the house. Vance sat in the living room, watching television with the girls. Junior told him Max's version of what happened to Adrena, and Vance expressed disappointment in Junior's inability to take the young lady out and bring her back in one piece. When Vance asked how the prom had gone otherwise, Junior told him it was great and waited for his father to ask about his car. Vance never mentioned it. Everyone was at home and asleep by two.

Chapter Thirty

Howard Devon Shaw II, called Devon so as not to be confused with his father, came kicking and screaming into the world on Tuesday, May twenty-third. Vivian appreciated the fact that her son was in a hurry to get out, once the labor ball began to roll. Only one hour elapsed between her first contraction and his entrance. The senior Howard Devon Shaw only caught the tailend of his birth.

Vivian called Howard after the second contraction forced her to her knees. The doctor after the third. The ambulance and Howard again, after the fourth. That's how hard and fast they came. The housekeeper held Vivian's hand and breathed with her, until the ambulance arrived. Barely in the delivery room, the baby's head appeared.

A green-robed Howard arrived just as his son's body made its way out. The first words from Howard's mouth were, "Why didn't you wait until I got here, Vivian?"

She screamed, "Don't ask me! Ask him!"

Tripping over electrical lines while trying to see the baby, Howard said, "Calm down, sweetheart. I forgive you this time."

In utter exhaustion, Vivian sighed and rolled her eyes at him. She closed them until the nurse laid her brand-new baby boy in her arms. Tears formed in Vivian's eyes when she realized what she had done - she had given birth to a real, live baby! It had all happened so fast that the reality of it had escaped her.

At first glance, Vivian saw that he had Howard's eyes and mouth. He didn't have very much color and was covered with thick, black hair. Unwrapping him, Vivian checked his limbs and fingers. She thought he was the most precious thing she had ever seen. Not cute though.

Howard wanted to hold him first, but he managed to contain himself until Vivian got a brief look at him. As he stared at the squirming little bundle in Vivian's arm, Howard asked, "Why does he have so much hair?"

The nurse looked at Howard, as if he were demented. She asked, "How can you ask a question like that, when your wife has a braid as thick as my arm halfway down her back?"

"He's a boy though. He shouldn't have that much hair."

Before the nurse could say another word, Vivian interjected, "If it'll make you feel better, you can take him to a barber the minute we get him home, Howard."

"If his hair grows like yours, I probably will have to, Vivian. May I hold him now?"

"Go ahead. Watch those wires. I didn't go through all of this for you to drop him in the delivery room."

Not believing his wife had made such a statement, Howard said, "*You* didn't go through? Vivian, please be quiet."

Vivian, knowing Howard was referring to the nine months of torture she had subjected him to, didn't respond. Instead, she looked down at her stomach and realized it hadn't gone down very much. The doctor was still working down there when Vivian asked, "How long will my stomach stay like this?"

"It might take a few weeks, but I'm sure you'll see a difference soon. You're breast-feeding, right?"

"Yes."

"You'll see it a little sooner than most, then. As a matter of fact, you'll feel it pulling the very first time you feed the little fella."

After all was said and done, Vivian had thirty-five pounds to lose. Without the baby to blame it on, Vivian felt more vulnerable to Howard's possible rejection than ever. She couldn't even think about dieting until the baby was weaned. Light exercise would be her limit. If Lula sent those pictures to her again, Vivian would slit her wrists.

Still, the good news was that Vivian now only experienced sporadic temper tantrums and crying spells. She didn't eat all day and night anymore, and she lacked the

stamina to hold long, rambling conversations with Howard
until all hours of the night. Vivian actually smiled more
frequently and found her husband's touch tolerable. It only
took three weeks for her to get the old charge out of watching
Howard undress again.

Howard brought Vivian and the baby home on Thursday
at noon, and by six, the house was filled. Vivian and the baby
slept until six-thirty. Tired of waiting, Maxine woke Devon
by picking him up, and his tiny complaint woke his mother.
Maxine wanted to take him down to his company, but Vivian
insisted on feeding and changing him first.

Max sat on the foot of the bed and watched her sister with
great interest. Tears fell into Max's lap. The pipping sound
made Vivian look up and ask, "What's the matter, Max?"

Sobbing unashamed, Max said, "Nothing. That's just the
most beautiful thing I've ever seen. He's a gorgeous little
hairball, Vivian."

"If you and Howard don't stop calling my baby a hairball,
I'm going to slap both of you."

"Don't be so sensitive. I said he was gorgeous, didn't I?"

"Yes, you did. I can't wait to see what yours is going to
look like."

"You'll only have to wait five more months."

Sitting straight up, Vivian asked, "What did you say?"

"You'll only have to wait five more months."

Vivian asked, "Does Clayton know that?"

"No."

"Why?"

"Because he's a pain in my behind, and I don't need it."

"Does Daddy know?"

"No."

"Max, he's going to have kittens. You're not married.
Hell, you're not even talking to Clayton."

"I don't intend to talk to him either. Let him talk to the
woman who's been answering his telephone for the last week
or so."

"What woman?"

"The drowsy one who told me Clayton wasn't up yet."

"That's funny, Howard hasn't mentioned a woman. If there was one, I think he would have told me, Max. Clayton's been a little distant with everybody, since you two stopped seeing each other."

"It doesn't matter. I'm having a baby. It'll be mine. No problem. Don't you say a word, Vivian."

"Not me. Was this a planned pregnancy, Max?"

"It most certainly was."

"Without Clayton knowing?"

"He knew, but he didn't really need to know. I wanted a baby. If I never have a husband, life will go on. I can't control that. If I never have a child, that's my fault. I control that."

"I understand that, Max. I just thought you might want to at least be in love with your baby's father."

"I do love him. He's a jerk though, which is a stumbling block I can't move. Do you know Clayton looks at women so hard when we're together that he turns completely around? I've popped him in the back of his head more times than I care to mention. If I go to the ladies' room, he strikes up conversations with them. I'm not dealing with a gutter rat as my husband for the rest of my life. I bet Howard doesn't do any of that."

"Well, no, Max, but Howard is naturally a lot stiffer than Clayton. He's too busy worrying about somebody looking at me. That's not always a walk in the park, either."

"I'd rather have that, than someone who will probably kill me in a car wreck, looking at women on the sidewalk."

"You can call Clayton what you will, but he's not a sneak, Maxine. He does what he does out in the open, where you have a fighting chance."

"I don't feel like fighting, and I'm tired of talking about it. Just keep your mouth shut."

"I will."

"Good. Hurry up. I want to take my nephew downstairs."

"Is Clayton down there?"

"He wasn't when I came up."

With Devon fed and changed, Maxine carried him down to the waiting crowd. Vance demanded to see him first.

After all, this was his first grandchild. The poor little thing was passed from arm to arm for three hours. Even Patricia and Melanie held him. They thought he was the most adorable baby they had ever seen. Loved his hair. Adding to Vivian's irritation, everyone else had something different to say about Devon's hair.

Adrena was the last to hold Devon. At first apprehensive about holding him, she wouldn't give him up once she got the hang of it. Adrena bonded with Devon, as she never had with anyone else. He was brand-new. She could love and protect him, the way his mother had done her, but when he started to cry, she gingerly carried him back to Vivian.

The next day, Vivian asked Max if she had told Clayton about the baby. A resounding, "No!" was her response.

Vivian and Howard didn't have much time to worry about Maxine and Clayton. They had a tiny baby who had a mind of his own. Devon slept whenever he felt like sleeping. He demanded to be fed, held, and talked to the remainder of the time. Vivian tried to amuse Devon at night, so Howard could get some sleep, but she was failing horribly. She was bone-weary most of the time. Having a baby took more out of her than she wanted to admit. There was very little time left for Howard, after taking care of Devon.

Six weeks later, Devon took more of Vivian's time than he had when he was first born. He seemed to be hungry and fussy all of the time. Vivian complained, "Howard, I think Devon thinks I'm a pacifier. He's not eating. He's holding my nipple in his mouth and pretending to be asleep."

Howard's response to that was, "I don't blame him. I wish I could do that myself."

"You're a big help!"

The first time they tried to make love with the baby in his cradle next to their bed, Howard's constant talking woke him. If Vivian made the slightest sound, Devon's head popped up. Their first real Devon argument was over him sleeping in his own room. Vivian thought he was too little to leave alone, with or without a monitor.

Howard asked miserably, "Why can't he sleep in his own room, with a monitor? Other babies do it."

"Will that monitor tell you if he stops breathing, Howard? Will it tell you his head is under the cover?"

Hating to admit she was right, Howard said, "No."

"Have you noticed how he scoots down in the bed? He scooted down so far in the bed with us last week, we couldn't find him. I'll take him into his room soon, Howard. We'll just have to be quiet for a while longer."

Howard mumbled, "I don't like being quiet. Can't even touch my wife the way I want. Milk's squirting everywhere. Baby's crying. Feels like I've waited forever for you to stop screaming. Jesus, when does it end?"

"Do you want me to stop breast-feeding the baby, Howard?"

"No. I want to be able to touch you, without you or him screaming."

"Max has been begging to babysit one evening a week, so we can go out to dinner. Would you like me to take her up on it?"

"Will you be upset if we don't go out to dinner?"

"No, Howard. I know you don't believe this, but I've missed you, too."

"You're right. I don't believe you. Scooter's got all of your attention now."

"Excuse me? You're the one who wanted Scooter more than anything in the world. Talked about him for a year before he was conceived."

"I didn't know he was going to come along and knock me off the map."

Stroking Howard's back, Vivian said, "He hasn't knocked you off the map, sweetheart. He's a baby. They require a lot of attention. If I didn't give it to him, you would want to know why not. I love my little Scooter, but there's a few things he can't do for me."

Still pouting, Howard asked, "Like what?"

"If I have to answer that, you're in worse shape than I imagined!"

Maxine and Clayton became the Wednesday evening babysitters. Devon, now permanently nicknamed Scooter, could only stay with them for four hours because Vivian had to feed him. He didn't take breast milk from a bottle very well either. Every Wednesday night, after spending those few precious hours alone, Howard and Vivian picked up a screaming Scooter.

Maxine was six months along in her pregnancy before Clayton noticed. She never told him and only begrudgingly admitted it when he asked. Clayton wanted to marry her, but Max wouldn't hear of it. After making Clayton's sleepy female visitor show legal proof that she was really his sister, Maxine agreed to allow Clayton the opportunity to establish a stronger track record.

Vance didn't hear about Maxine's pregnancy until she was seven months along. As expected, he was livid. When Max told him she had no plans to marry Clayton, Vance preached, stomped, and hollered like a Southern Baptist minister for hours. He didn't move Maxine though. The best she could do for Clayton, or her father, was give the baby Clayton's last name. If they upset her before it was born, Vivian knew Max wouldn't do that either. Vance knew it, too. Maxine Matthews was just like her father. You couldn't tell either one of them anything. They knew it all.

Chapter Thirty-One

Every day after the prom and through the summer drew Adrena and Junior closer. They called each other constantly. Reporting every minute, asinine movement they made. Questioning every empty space between them large enough for a breeze to blow through.

Vance gave Junior permission to visit Adrena every Tuesday, Thursday, Saturday and Sunday. If Junior wasn't home by midnight, he could forget seeing Adrena for a week. The fact that Junior was graduating from high school and headed for college meant absolutely nothing to Vance. As far as he was concerned, the boy had more than enough rope to hang himself.

Adrena and Junior worked within the set parameters. During the week they went roller-skating, bowling, or watched television at the Stanleys' with Felicia. On the weekends, Junior insisted they spend time alone together. If Vance let him use the car, they packed a picnic lunch and spent the day in the park, or they might visit a museum. Junior's favorite date place remained the movies. Public places weren't always what Junior had in mind, but when you're seventeen you take what's available.

As Junior and Adrena were going out one Saturday in June, Mrs. Stanley asked, "When was the last time you checked on the house, Adrena?"

"I haven't been there for a couple of weeks."

"Since Junior's driving, why don't you do it today? Mail is probably all over the porch by now. You can open those windows for a few minutes, too."

"Okay."

In the car, Junior asked, "What house is she talking about?"

"Mine."

Laughing, Junior said, "You have a house? Yeah, right. Where is it?"

"It's on Bleigh Street."

"Where'd you get a house, Adrena?"

"From my grandmother. You want to go there first?"

"Sure. Why not?"

Junior pulled up in front of the house with a strange look on his face. Adrena asked, "What's the matter with you?"

"If you have a house, why do you live with the Stanleys?"

"I'm a minor, Junior. I can't move in here until I'm eighteen."

Junior followed Adrena onto the porch and helped her collect all of the mail. He followed her through the house and opened the windows as she directed him. After checking the entire first floor, Adrena headed upstairs with Junior on her heels.

She walked through all three bedrooms opening windows and turned to go back downstairs just as Junior asked, "Why can't we spend the day here, Adrena?"

Shocked, Adrena asked, "Here?"

"Yeah. It's your house. You can spend the day here, if you want to. Can't you?"

After thinking about it for a few seconds, Adrena said, "Yes. I can spend the day here, if I want to. What will we do here all day though, Junior?"

"We'll think of something. Do you have a television?"

"There's a big one in the living room and a little one in the kitchen."

"I can bring the little one from the kitchen up here. We can kick back, relax, eat lunch, and watch television."

"I thought you wanted to go to the park."

"I have two choices here, Adrena. I can go to the park and maybe run into my friends, probably be forced to play ball with them, or spend the day playing with you. Let me see." Junior tapped his cheek as if in thought and said, "I choose you."

Laughing, Adrena said, "You are silly."

"What do you say?"

"Okay, Junior."

Grinning from ear to ear, Junior dashed down to the car and retrieved the lunch basket. Adrena stood in the doorway looking at him. The simplest things excited Junior, as far as Adrena was concerned. By the end of the day, she would understand why Junior was so excited.

Junior put the contents of the basket into the empty refrigerator. He unplugged the television and carried it upstairs. Adrena was already up there. She wanted to change the sheets on the bed. They hadn't been changed since her grandmother died.

Walking through the upstairs hallway, Junior looked into the first two bedrooms and didn't see Adrena. He found her in the smaller room in back. Confused by her choice, he asked, "Why are we in this room? The front room is much bigger."

Adrena looked down at her feet and said, "I can't stay in there. That's my grandmother's room. She died in there."

"Are you afraid of ghosts, or something?"

With a defiant look in her eyes, Adrena said, "I'm not afraid of anything, Junior."

"Well, then, let's go to the other room."

"Okay."

Intermittently taking deep breaths to calm herself, Adrena made the bed in the larger room. Each time, the smell of her grandmother filled her nostrils. When Adrena was finished with the bed, she sat near the open window and breathed deeply of the fresh air. Not understanding Adrena's reluctance to stay in this room, Junior watched her carefully. He said, "If this room is going to make you sick, Adrena, we can go to the back room."

Looking at him with a straight face, Adrena said, "No, I'm fine. I just have to get used to the smell again."

After taking a while to find an outlet to plug in the television, Junior turned it on and found an afternoon movie, walked over to the window and reached for Adrena's hand. Momentarily startled by his movement, she took it and stood.

Junior wrapped his arms around her protectively. Adrena easily slid in close and automatically felt better, breathing deeply and filling her nostrils with Junior's clean, spicy scent. His kiss wiped all thoughts of Granny's odor out of her mind.

They stood in each other's arms, lost in their passionate kiss, Junior pulling Adrena closer and closer. She, enjoying feeling the entire length of his body pressed against hers. His lips left hers and wandered down her neck. Adrena closed her eyes and allowed the titillating sensations to sweep her away.

He slowly backed Adrena toward the bed. The moment she touched it, Adrena jumped. Junior asked again if she would prefer going to the other room. Refusing his offer for the second time, Adrena took a deep breath and sat down on her own. Junior sat next to her and wrapped his arms around her again. He gently pushed a rigid Adrena back onto the bed and kissed her. A few minutes into it, she relaxed and returned Junior's embrace and warmth.

As they lay on the bed, his hands roamed freely. Familiar with his touch now, Adrena didn't flinch. Junior was accustomed to Adrena nervously clearing her throat the moment he touched her hips and wasn't distracted by it at all. He avoided them, whenever possible. His hand found its way inside her blouse and massaged her breasts. Her hands stroked his neck and back.

Finally, without any resistance, Junior slipped Adrena's blouse over her head. He slid her shorts down and pulled them over her sandaled feet. She kicked the sandals off on her own. Standing over Adrena, absorbing every inch of her scantily-clad beauty, Junior removed his shirt, jeans, and sneakers. Junior noticed the scars on Adrena's body, but he didn't comment on them. He would let Adrena explain them whenever she wanted.

In his underwear, Junior lay down next to Adrena again. Searching for the clasp on her bra, he kissed her forehead and nose. Finding it, he freed Adrena's young, supple breasts. Unlike prom night, Junior didn't touch them right away. Instead, he leisurely studied them in the daylight for a while. Adrena smiled at his obvious curiosity about them. Without touching either one, Junior lowered his mouth to one of the inviting nipples. The warm, slick sensation made Adrena moan out loud and grip the back of his head.

Sliding his other hand down Adrena's stomach, he found the elastic of her panties. He slipped inside and touched her. Adrena didn't tighten up or move away. Shifting his weight a little, Junior moved his attention to the other nipple. Adrena's head hung limply, her breathing heavy and ragged.

After as much stimulation as he could bear, Junior asked, "Can I, Adrena?"

Irritated by the sound of Junior's voice, in the midst of the daze of passion he had created, Adrena snapped, "Can you what?"

"Touch you?"

"You are touching me, Junior."

"I mean really touch you."

Wanting to slap him, Adrena said, "Please stop talking and do whatever, Junior."

Junior retrieved his condom from his wallet and was preparing to put it on when Adrena popped up and asked, "Can I do that, Junior? Please? Max showed me how."

Looking as if he wasn't so sure he trusted her, Junior said timidly, "Okay."

After examining Junior's penis with the same curiosity with which he had studied her breasts, she put the condom on. Having seen her share of male body parts, none compared to Junior's in Adrena's mind. Thoughts of ugly, nasty, and cruel never contaminated her thoughts of Junior. Adrena's smile told Junior she was quite proud of her accomplishment. He breathed a sigh of relief and pulled her up to her feet. Junior slid Adrena's panties down and studied her completely nude body with great interest. Adrena kicked her panties away.

Unable to take any more suspense, Junior pulled Adrena down onto the bed. He kneeled in front of her and entered her, without touching her hips. Adrena closed her eyes and gasped, as the initial pain of his entrance registered. Junior's movements made Adrena alternately moan and hiss. With more room to work in, his aggression was enhanced. There was more to the act than Adrena remembered - it even lasted longer.

It wasn't until Junior's soaking wet body collapsed on top of her that Adrena realized she hadn't opened her eyes once. There was no Bart behind her lids. Just heat, passion, and Junior. Smiling to herself, Adrena kissed and nibbled Junior's salty collarbone.

Junior's voice didn't bother her at all when he asked, "Are you biting again, Adrena?"

Rubbing her nose in his sweat, Adrena said, "Nope. You want me to?"

"Nope. Was that as good for you as it was for me?"

"I don't know."

"What do you mean, you don't know?"

"I mean, I don't know how you're judging it. Did you like it better than playing volleyball with your friends?"

"Volleyball?!"

Giving Adrena's question no other response, Junior jumped up and went to the bathroom down the hall. The air in the room seemed cold to Adrena, without Junior. She crawled under the sheet and laid her head on the pillow. It only took Junior a few minutes to return. He crawled under the sheet with Adrena and wrapped his arms around her.

Looking into her eyes, Junior asked again, "How was it for you, Adrena? Really."

Unable to truly express how it felt for her, Adrena said, "It was fine, Junior. It didn't hurt as much this time."

Kissing her forehead, Junior said, "Good - did I frighten you?"

"No."

"Good. You want to tell me why you were so afraid when I touched your hips the last time?"

"Now?"

"Yes. I want to know. We've got the rest of the day."

Hating every minute of it, Adrena told Junior about her mother and Bart. She shared some of the smaller acts of cruelty first, then worked her way up to Bart gripping her hips so tight one of them snapped out of the joint under the pressure. Adrena's greatest fear in sharing this with Junior was the possibility of him somehow blaming her for what happened or backing away from her. Maybe seeing her as being dirty. Adrena couldn't imagine going back to life without Junior. Everything about him meant so much to her.

There was fury in Junior's eyes when Adrena finished her tale. He didn't comment on anything she said. He tried to imagine his father doing something like that to one of his sisters, and the thought wouldn't take hold. Fathers don't do things like that; they would kill anyone else for doing it. Junior did not understand.

Junior stroked Adrena's shoulder and looked into her eyes. There was no self-pity. No tears. Just a reflection of the love she felt for him.

Adrena didn't relax until Junior said, "They're dead, Adrena. Let it go. No one's going to hurt you anymore. You've got people all around you who love you now. Vivian, Maxine, Mr. and Mrs. Stanley, and me."

"You love me?"

"I sure do."

"Why? Because I had sex with you?"

"No, that's not it. I loved you before that."

"How do you know?"

"I just do, Adrena. It's inside me. I think about you all the time. Look forward to seeing you. Can't wait to talk to you. Would die if you left me for another guy."

"You wouldn't die, Junior."

"Maybe I wouldn't. But I sure would feel like it! Don't know what I'm going to do without you, when I go to school in August."

"Let's not think about that right now. I don't know what I'm going to do without you either."

Liking the sound of that, Junior snuggled closer to Adrena and fell asleep. Adrena studied his handsome, sleeping face for an hour. He hadn't rejected her or thought she was damaged goods. In the silence and the afternoon sunlight, Adrena said something Junior never heard. "I love you too, Vance Matthews, Junior."

From that day on, whenever Junior was free, they spent every Saturday and Sunday at Adrena's house, occasionally stealing away to go there during the week. Adrena never experienced an orgasm with Junior, but it didn't matter. She had no idea what it was anyway. He never mentioned Adrena's sexual reticence. Her inability to move with him, was another remnant of what Bart had done. The moment her hip physically snapped, Adrena unconsciously disconnected from it and only acknowledged the existence of her hips when touched. Junior seldom touched Adrena's hips, and she appreciated that.

It was the summer of memories for Adrena and Junior. They had the entire future to look forward to, and they were so much in love with each other. Letters, cards, and telephone calls would have to sustain them while Junior was away at school. They promised to tell each other everything - both afraid the other would feel abandoned and find someone to replace them.

Their last night together at the house was difficult. Saying goodbye to the only man she could ever remotely imagine loving tore Adrena in half. She actually felt like he was going away forever. Junior's promise to be home for Christmas did not relieve Adrena's grief. For weeks after Junior left, Adrena didn't know whether she was coming or going. Felicia was a great friend, but she wasn't Junior.

Adrena was living in a time in which there was no one she despised, for the first time in her memoried life. The Stanleys and the Matthews were her family. They did nothing without her. She had been one of the first-called when Devon was born and automatically picked up by Max the day Vivian brought him home from the hospital. Without fear or reservation, Adrena had been invited to hold the most precious member of the family. They even left her alone with him. Adrena felt loved and trusted.

When Junior came home for Christmas, Adrena had been carefully weaned from her medication, under the watchful eye of Vivian. Glad to be free of the burden, Adrena absolutely glowed. The doctor and patient had long discussions about honesty and the need to report any unusual changes in sleeping or eating patterns. Adrena was only given medication for her occasional anxiety attacks and inability to sleep.

Adrena and Junior spent Christmas Eve together at the house and made love like two people who missed each other desperately. She had bought and decorated a tiny tree just for them. They exchanged gifts in the nude, ate a dinner Adrena prepared all by herself, and were at home before twelve to meet Vance's still-imposed curfew.

Junior came home again in May, just in time to take Adrena to her senior prom. They double-dated with Felicia and her date. The foursome went to several after-parties; then Junior and Adrena dropped Felicia and her date off at three and spent the remainder of the night at the house. They were at Vivian's for breakfast, bright and early that Saturday morning. The only one up was Scooter.

Chapter Thirty-Two

After Junior left for college and after Vivian started working again, Adrena never resumed her psychiatric office appointments. Vivian spent more time with her in a personal setting. For all intents and purposes, it was understood that Vivian was still Adrena's physician. Weaning Adrena from her daily medications worked this time without incident. She was finally able to take professional driving lessons. She wanted her license before she left for college in August.

Vivian and Adrena had long talks about her relationship with Junior. Without ever mentioning love, Adrena told Vivian all about her sexual relationship with Junior - the whens, wheres, and how she felt about it. When Vivian questioned Adrena about the lack of orgasm, Adrena said, "Doc, I know there are going to be lots of things I'm never going to experience. An orgasm, the way you describe it, is probably one of those things. I'm satisfied with my life the way it is. As long as I can share whatever with Junior, I'm satisfied."

"Are you saying you love Junior, Adrena?"

"No, Doc. I'm saying I'm satisfied with my life with Junior in it."

"That makes you and Junior a couple, Adrena. Are you afraid of losing your identity with Junior? That maybe somewhere down the line he'll be abusive?"

"Who, Junior? Abusive? Doc, please. He wouldn't ever hit anyone who didn't hit him first, and girls would be out of the question. As far as my identity goes, Junior doesn't want it, so it's safe with me."

"What would you do to Junior if he hit you, Adrena?"

"Honestly?"

"Honestly."

"I won't bother saying I wouldn't hit him back, because you wouldn't believe that for one minute. Unfortunately, there would be a real fight, Doc. But, there would only be one fight. I'm out of the story after that."

"Would you die to protect Junior, Adrena?"

Smiling, Adrena responded, "More than once, if I could, Doc."

While Vivian wished Adrena and Junior had waited for sex until they were a little older, she didn't condemn or criticize Adrena. During their talks, Vivian noticed that Adrena was always very careful not to divulge any of Max's involvement in anything. Vivian knew Max encouraged them to some extent, because her fingerprints were all over the relationship. That cast on Adrena's foot the night of the prom was one. The hospital couldn't have done that without the consent of her parent or guardian. The personal condom lessons were another Maxine Matthews touch.

Vivian was extremely pleased with Adrena's progress. Her ability to form a physical relationship with Junior spoke volumes about how far she had come. Honestly, Vivian had never thought Adrena would cross that bridge so soon. The occasional flashbacks were expected; in one form or another, they would stay with Adrena for the rest of her life, but Vivian thought Adrena was handling them well.

Her friendship with Felicia showed a new receptiveness and trust for outsiders. There was no fantasy connection between them, the way there was with Max. Together, Adrena and Felicia socialized with other girls their age. That signified hope for other future friendships. As long as no one made aggressive overtures toward Adrena, she was fine. Vivian realized unwanted touching by outsiders would always be a problem for Adrena.

For the first time, Vivian wasn't worried about Adrena's impending departure for college. On medication and still acting out, Vivian would have had to object to her going out of state. As it was, Adrena had full intentions of joining Junior, and he couldn't wait for her to get there. That pleased Vivian and frightened her. If Junior ever tried to pull away from Adrena, the repercussions could be catastrophic.

However, there were no signs of that happening anytime soon, so Vivian thanked God and accepted the inevitable.

Maxine had given birth to Aria Matthews-Williams in October. As promised, Maxine gave the baby Clayton's last name. Although Maxine had no hormonal problems like Vivian, she did suffer through a long and tortuous delivery. Maxine threw Clayton out of the labor room five times in those twelve hours. Never giving up completely, Clayton kept going back.

With two new babies in the family, there was always something going on. Schedules changed constantly. Arguments over who was doing what. Maxine had gone back to work when Aria was three months old, and Clayton didn't like it one bit. He thought she should do everything just as Vivian had done. Vivian didn't return to work until Scooter was seven months old. Maxine vehemently reminded Clayton her name was Maxine, not Vivian, and ignored his complaints.

Adrena and Felicia had been a big help to the two families. They were there to babysit on Wednesday nights and most of all, they could be depended on in an emergency. Adrena loved those two babies as if they were her own. In her eyes Scooter and Aria did no wrong, and they had their way at all times with Adrena. Their parents' only complaint was that Adrena spoiled the children.

Life for Vivian settled into an emotionally fulfilling adventure. She had everything she ever wanted - the career of choice, a husband and son she loved with all her heart, and a big comfortable home. Life didn't get much better than that.

Just before Vivian and Howard were to celebrate their second anniversary, Howard came home from work with a long face, and Vivian knew something was terribly wrong. Howard didn't even take notice of the fast-toddling Scooter who followed him around. Normally, Howard looked for Scooter the moment he walked in the door.

After a silent dinner, Vivian asked, "Are you going to tell me what's going on, Howard?"

With a blank expression, Howard asked, "What's going on where?"

"With you. You've been home long enough to eat dinner, and you still haven't picked your son up. You haven't even acknowledged his presence."

Dropping his head and rubbing his temple, Howard said, "It's Lula."

Calmly, Vivian asked, "What about her? Is she sick?"

"I got a letter from her psychiatrist today. He wants us to begin family therapy with her. Naturally, they want to see me first."

Smiling, Vivian said, "That's good news, honey. Why the long face?"

Raising his voice a little, Howard asked, "Have you forgotten Lula, Vivian?"

"No. I remember her very well. She's your sister, and she's trying to mend some fences."

Jumping up from the table and yelling, Howard said, "She's the one who tore the fences up! Why should the rest of us have to go to a shrink to help her mend them?! I like my life without Lula in it!"

"Granted, it has been rather serene without her, Howard. But, wouldn't you prefer sharing your life with all of your siblings? She's never seen Scooter."

Pacing, with his hands in his pockets, Howard snapped, "Not with the one who stood up at my wedding and embarrassed the shit out of me. Or the one who sent my very pregnant, half-crazy wife pictures of me and some other woman. I fall for this ploy, and Lula positions herself to do some more damage. Do you know Sheldon hasn't been sent packing from his own home once since Lula's been out of our lives? Talia and Teddy have never been happier either. No phone calls at all hours of the night for no good reason."

"I understand that, honey, but you're not answering my question. Wouldn't you prefer sharing your life with all of your siblings?"

Without answering, Howard walked over to the sink and wet a washcloth. He came back, wiped down Scooter's food-smeared face and took him out of his high chair. Then he walked out of the kitchen, leaving Vivian sitting there, still waiting for an answer to her question.

After loading the dishwasher and cleaning the kitchen, Vivian found her husband and son, playing in the den. The sight filled her heart with so much joy that she decided not to bring up Lula anymore that evening. As usual, Howard played with Scooter until about eight o'clock, after which he turned him over to his mother and disappeared into his office until ten.

Vivian bathed her precious little demon and put him to bed. Scooter was a good baby. He'd lie down immediately if Vivian stayed in the room with him. If not, he could be difficult. They took turns sitting with him many nights. Howard insisted Scooter sleep in his own bed though. That was the only time he had Vivian to himself.

At nine-thirty, Vivian sank into a hot tub, with a thick blanket of bubbles floating on top. She lay back, closed her eyes and cleared her mind. Losing track of time, Howard's movements in the bedroom startled her. Vivian bathed quickly and joined him.

Howard was already in bed when she came in. He stared at the television screen and still wasn't talking. After a year of dieting and exercise, Vivian was back at her original weight and in better shape. Whenever Howard ignored her, she questioned the accomplishment all over again.

Lying down next to him, Vivian asked, "Did you kiss Scooter goodnight?"

"Yes."

"Are you going to pout all night, Howard?"

"I'm not pouting. You just don't understand."

"I'm all ears. Make me understand."

"What would you do if Maxine stole your credit card and ran the bill up two thousand dollars?"

"I'd steal her checkbook and pay the bill."

"You're joking, and I'm serious, Vivian. That's the kind of thing Lula does to cause problems between her siblings and their mates. She pulled that little prank on Talia. Teddy wanted to press charges against Lula, after a week of believing Talia did it. Of course, Talia came to Lula's defense. She couldn't send her own sister to jail."

"Did Lula pay the bill, Howard?"

"Eventually. One of Lula's sick manipulations sent Gary to jail for spousal abuse. Did he do it? No. Does it count? Yes!"

"She sent Sheldon perfume-scented "Thinking Of You" cards for months. Lula knew Charlene would never give them to him, but she also knew that when the fat hit the fan, those cards would be thrown into Sheldon's face. Sheldon hasn't done half the things Charlene thinks he's done. Every one of their sexual problems is directly related to Lula's crap.

"Lula called Child Protective Services and reported sexual abuse by Sheldon, Gary and Teddy. They had no idea what was going on when those people came into their homes, demanding to examine and question their children. I could go on and on, Vivian."

"How old was Lula when your parents died, Howard?"

"Nineteen."

"Did she take care of all of you?"

"Pretty much. Sheldon was only sixteen at the time. Lula was determined to keep us together. They wanted to ship us out to different relatives."

"That was very courageous of her. In the meantime, she ran a tab. Lula put you all first in her life. Now, she feels she should be first in your lives. You owe Lula. Is she like that with her own children?"

"No. That's what I don't get. She never bothers them."

"In Lula's mind, they were her obligation. She had them. You all were hoisted onto her shoulders. Without her, you would have been thrown to the wind, winding up, God knows where. You owe her."

"I don't owe Lula, Vivian. I've been there for her longer than anybody."

"Did Lula put you through college, Howard?"

"She helped a great deal, but I went on a scholarship."

"Did she help any of the others through college?"

"No. They wanted to get away from her so bad, nobody went to college right after high school. Sheldon and Gary both joined the Air Force to get their educations. Talia never went to college. She married Teddy."

"She's upset with them, but she's really disappointed with you. You were supposed to be the one who stayed. She did more for you than the others. Your reluctance to marry early reinforced that thought for her. Lula honestly thought you were rejecting others because you loved her more."

"Vivian, please. If that's what Lula thinks, then she's in trouble. The family doesn't owe her any more than we've already given. We've put up with her tricks for more years than we should have."

"Well, she's trying to get it together now. Are you going to help her?"

"I don't know."

Changing the subject to their impending anniversary vacation, Howard asked, "Did you ask your father if he would take care of Scooter while we're gone?"

"Yes. You know he wants him, Howard. The girls want him even more. He'll be so spoiled by the time we get back, we won't get any sleep for weeks."

"Do you really think I should go, Vivian?"

"If you're referring to Lula's family therapy, yes. It will give you all an opportunity to cut some old ties and establish new, healthier ones."

"Are you still upset with her?"

"Of course, I am. She's not my sister!"

Howard laughed for the first time that night. He wrapped his arms around Vivian and showed real appreciation for all of the work she'd done on her body.

Chapter Thirty-Three

Life for Adrena Reynolds could only be compared to the budding of a rare flower. Closed, the colors dark and brooding. Nourished by rain and sunlight, every new day revealed more vibrant shades of color, with a staggering array of patterns . . . standing tall, reaching for the sky, and impressing every passerby with its unique beauty.

There were no more barriers in Adrena's path. Only an open road, lined with well-wishers. With all of that and the love of a man she loved back, the sky was the limit for her.

Graduation day for Adrena was a whirlwind of congratulations, gifts, and parties. Vivian, Maxine, and Mrs. Stanley flipped a coin to see whose home would host Adrena's surprise graduation party. Vivian won. They prepared everything the night before and attended the graduation ceremony.

A smiling Adrena Reynolds received five awards, the most precious being a four-year college scholarship. It was her guarantee of being close to Junior. Vivian didn't cry until they announced the highest academic achievement award and called Adrena Reynolds' name. The child who had not attended school one day before she was eleven, had indeed deserved that award. She had battled to achieve a twelve-year education in seven years, and not only won, but did it with ease and excellence. Adrena's academic accomplishments were a personal victory for Vivian, too; she truly felt like a proud mother that morning.

Afterward, Vance, Howard, Clayton, Mr. Stanley and Junior presented Adrena with gigantic bouquets of flowers and balloons. She couldn't even hold them all at one time. There were kisses and hugs from Vivian, Maxine, Mrs. Stanley and Millie. Adrena's most special hugs and kisses came from Scooter. He had no idea why he was doing it. Scooter just loved hugging and kissing Adrena.

When Felicia found Adrena in the crowd, the two girls embraced, squealed, and jumped . . . the sheer joy of accomplishment and friendship making them giddy. Looking on, Vivian cried again. Felicia's parents congratulated Adrena and, after introductions, shook hands with her guests.

Junior was the official chauffeur for the girls, and Felicia's boyfriend, Tommy, joined them. There were luncheons and parties they had to attend. People to say goodbye to. Vivian gave them her car and watched the four happy teenagers disappear into the crowd, only stopping to take pictures along the way. Vivian cried again. Adrena's obviously genuine joy was all Vivian could take. Knowing that a little extra attention and a large dose of love had fostered that joy made Vivian want to wrap Adrena in a bone-crushing embrace and cover her with kisses.

At seven that evening, Junior brought Adrena, Felicia and her friend to Vivian's house. He used the ruse of having to check in. They noisily followed Junior up the walkway to the darkened front door. Junior rang the bell and said, "Be quiet. Scooter and Aria may be asleep."

They giggled their response.

An unsmiling Howard appeared at the door, and Adrena's smile immediately disappeared. She had never known Howard not to smile when he greeted people. Thinking they had done something wrong, Adrena silently followed Junior into the foyer. Once inside, everyone yelled, "*Surprise!*"

In terror, Adrena screeched and gripped Junior's shirt so roughly, it tore. She wouldn't let go until the lights came on, and she could see everyone. There were balloons, streamers, and a bold red-and-white banner saying, "Congratulations On Your Graduation Adrena."

Embarrassed and shaken, Adrena buried her face in Junior's chest and wept. Vivian and Max ran to help Adrena get herself together. Adrena kept saying, "I feel so stupid. No one's ever given me a party before."

Max told her, "Well, you've earned this one, and you've got it. Now, straighten up and act like a scholarship-winning, college-bound black woman."

Sniffing and wiping at her face, Adrena said, "Okay. Thanks, Doc. Max. Thanks."

The party was a great success. The babies enjoyed it as much as the adults, and both were passed from arm to arm. Scooter tried to keep up with Patricia and Melanie, but with the big crowd, the little fellow couldn't get enough speed in his step. Aria hustled around on her knees trying to keep her eyes on Scooter. Everyone ate, danced, and talked about Adrena's accomplishments.

Adrena opened all of her gifts. Howard and Vivian gave her a computer, with every accessory known to man. Maxine and Clayton gave her a very expensive calculator, tape recorder, dictionary, and thesaurus. Mr. and Mrs. Stanley couldn't bring their gift over - it was a new set of encyclopedias. Millie and Barb gave her a desktop stereo. Knowing college students needed all kinds of things, others gave her money and gift certificates.

As the midnight hour approached, Mr. and Mrs. Stanley asked Adrena if she was going to ride home with them. She told them she wanted to stay out with Felicia and Junior for a while. Telling her to be careful, they left. Now that Adrena was officially over eighteen and had graduated from high school, she was not considered a ward of the state anymore. The Stanleys, however, were leaving their home open to Adrena, as they had all of their other foster children. Adrena greatly appreciated their generosity because she had never felt at home anywhere, except with them.

Just as the graduates and their dates approached the front door, Vivian asked, "Where are you guys going?"

Adrena, Felicia, and Tommy's eyes turned to Junior. He was the big college guy who was supposed to have all of the answers. Junior's eyes turned to Maxine.

Maxine shook her head. "It's graduation night, Vivian. There's always something jumping off on graduation night. You do remember that much, don't you?"

With Vance paying close attention to the conversation, Vivian said, "Sure. Junior, you drive carefully."

Vance said, "You'd better be home when the sun comes up, Junior. Don't make me come looking for you."

Looking at his father respectfully, Junior said, "Yes, sir. When do I have to bring the car back, Viv?"

"Sometime this weekend would be nice. I don't have any plans for tomorrow. Besides, I can always use Howard's car."

They left and went directly to Adrena's house. Felicia's friend, Tommy, had never seen it before, and he was impressed. Adrena had cleaned and done some shopping. Junior had been home for a week before graduation, and they spent as much time there as they could.

While Junior offered Tommy refreshments, Adrena took Felicia upstairs and showed her the guestroom. Of course, Felicia didn't have to use it, if she didn't want to. Since Tommy was a relatively new conquest for Felicia, they might just stay in the living room and watch television, or listen to the radio. Adrena and Junior, however, retired to their room. There, they made love and plans for the coming school year.

Since Adrena had won a scholarship, she thought she should be able to use some of her college money to rent an off-campus apartment. Junior would be responsible for food and utilities. Adrena planned to buy a car with the money she had in the bank. Hopefully, with Max's help, they would be able to convince Vivian it would be all right. Of course, Vance couldn't be told any of it.

They were extremely successful in achieving their goals. Mr. Lewis guaranteed payment of rent, car note, insurance, school supplies and a wardrobe allowance for the entire four years. Because of the scholarship, there would even be change, if Adrena needed anything else.

While Vivian hated pulling the wool over Vance's eyes, she gave Adrena and Junior her blessings. Howard and Clayton helped them find a beautiful, cherry red Mustang that ran like a car should. Turning both babies over to their grandfather, Vivian, Maxine, Howard, and Clayton rented a truck and took Adrena and Junior back to school in August.

They all stayed for three days, sleeping on the floor of Junior and Adrena's tiny, one-bedroom apartment.

The first morning they spent in registration lines. Howard checked and double-checked Junior's class assignments. He hadn't chosen his major, but Howard wanted to be sure they weren't giving him a bunch of classes which were simply not worthwhile. Howard forced Junior to change two of them.

While Vivian and Maxine fussed over Adrena's scheduling, Clayton stared at the girls. He whispered to Howard, "The girls didn't look like this when we were in college. I know. I'd still be there, if they did."

Howard said, "They look exactly the same, Clayton. They just didn't dress like this. While you're drooling, you'd better remember Aria will be one of them one day."

Shaking his head, Clayton said, "No, she won't. She's going to a nice, all-girl Catholic college in the mountains."

After lunch, they browsed through thrift stores where Adrena bought a beautiful bedroom set, as well as furniture for the living room. Vivian insisted their mattresses be new. Junior and Adrena had bought a little dinette set at home and brought it with them. Vivian and Max took Adrena to every sale they could find. Adrena had more than enough sheets, towels, pots, pans and dishes.

On the second day they found Sears. There, Adrena bought bedding, a hamper, a complete bathroom set, and an apartment-sized washer and dryer. At the telephone company, they made arrangements for a telephone to be installed.

Howard wanted to find some art to put on the walls. At least some posters. Vivian told him they could pick those things up at their leisure. They took them grocery shopping instead.

For two nights, they had a giant sleepover. Maxine and Vivian had brought pillows and sheets from home. They ate pizza, sandwiches, chips, and drank soda. Howard and Clayton found the spirit shop. They bought wine, cheese, and crackers. They all kicked back every evening, listened to oldies and reminisced about their college days. The elders made Junior and Adrena promise they would never do the dumb things they had done. Maxine assured them Adrena and Junior could come up with their very own dumb things.

On the third day, they piled into Clayton's burgundy BMW and headed home, leaving Junior and Adrena to their own devices. Just before pulling off, Max said, "Junior, if the telephone rings after seven, make sure you answer it."

"Why?"

"You want to have to explain to Dad what Adrena's doing in your dorm after seven?"

"No."

"If there's a problem, call me, or Vivian first. Keep the noise down and you should be all right."

"Okay, Max."

Adrena and Junior's first semester was pitted in places. Adrena constantly turned Junior's music down. She told his friends they had to pick up behind themselves and leave by nine. When she produced a portable keyboard and played Beethoven and Mozart, Junior asked if she knew any music from this century.

One real argument they had was over Junior's wardrobe. He had an awful habit of taking shirts out of the dirty clothes hamper and wearing them. That drove Adrena crazy. He had two shirts he absolutely loved. One said, "If we're so smart, why are we in so much trouble?" The other said, "You don't have to be afraid of me, I'm just as stupid as you."

Trying to humor him, Adrena washed the shirts the moment he took them off. Junior would ask, "Why are you doing that?"

"Because you're going to put it right back on."

"You're going to wash all of the colors out of it. Look, the words are disappearing."

"Junior, the shirt is dirty after you've worn it."

"No, it's not. Leave it alone."

Adrena wouldn't wash them after that. For three weeks, she left them on top of the hamper. Junior asked, "Why haven't you washed my shirts, Adrena?"

"You told me not to touch them. Remember? When the appropriate time elapses for washing, you do it."

"You know I don't know how to wash clothes."

"You don't know how to clean up after yourself at all, Vance Matthews. Wearing dirty shirts. Throwing socks under the bed, instead of in the hamper. I found candy wrappers and a soda can under the bed yesterday. Have you ever heard of washing out a tub? And why can't you pee inside the toilet?"

Frowning miserably, Junior said, "I wash dishes."

"That's it, too. You spend the rest of the time playing with your friends."

"I study and work, too, Adrena. I even help you study."

"Please, Junior. Putting books on a shelf in the library is not work. You need to learn how to make a bed, dust, mop, load the washer. If you can't do any of those things, refrain from being a nuisance."

"Who are you calling a nuisance? I don't play Beethoven and have a trust fund, so now I'm a nuisance. If you want me to leave, just tell me."

"I told you what I had to tell you, Junior. If you want to leave, the door is over there."

Junior left and returned at four in the morning. Adrena sat up in bed and asked, "Do you feel better now?"

Sarcastically, Junior said, "I feel fine. If you're going to start catcalling again, I'm going back where I came from."

"You do that, Junior. Do whatever you feel like doing."

"I will, Adrena."

They didn't speak to each other for three days. Junior stayed out late. Adrena came in, ate, played her piano, and studied. She called Felicia at State University. She talked to Vivian and Maxine on the telephone, too. She went to bed, as usual. She refused to clean anything, and washed only her clothes. Adrena also rejected Junior's advances in bed.

At the end of the week, Junior asked, "What's going on around here, Adrena? This place is a mess. You won't even let me touch you."

"I'm doing what you're doing. Nothing. You don't think about me until you get into bed. I'm not a sex object, Junior."

"Do you want me to leave?"

"Is that a question, or a threat?"

"It's a question. All you've been doing is complaining about me lately. I thought you needed some space. If you're tired of me, I'll move into a dorm."

"You do what you want, Junior. That's what men do. Right?"

"What are you talking about?"

"You don't have to do anything unless you want to. I'm adopting your attitude. That's all. If you leave, I'll clean up and live by myself. If you stay, you'll help clean up. That's the deal. We said fifty-fifty. I don't like cleaning, either."

"Why didn't you just say clean up, Junior? Why do you have to list all of the things I don't do?"

Completely lost, Adrena said, "Clean up, Junior."

"Show me where the stuff is, Adrena."

Adrena showed Junior where things were. She only had to make him do something over once or twice. Adrena assumed Vance ran a chauvinistic household. Of course, she was wrong. Junior never did any household chores. Vance and his mother did everything. Melanie and Patricia didn't know how to do anything either. It really would have thrown Adrena for a loop if she found out that Maxine and Vivian had never done those things either.

Junior did anything Adrena wanted, except giving up those two shirts. He spent less time with his friends, too. They did more things together. They found the theater and a roller-skating rink, and even went to a couple parties a month.

There were no new impediments in their lives until some idiot came up behind Adrena in the hallway at school, grabbed her by the hips, and ground his pelvis against her. Making matters worse, he wreaked of alcohol, and Adrena smelled it.

Sounding exactly like the disgusting men her mother had dealt with, he said, "Vance ain't the only one around here you can take care of, little girl. Ever done a senior?"

Adrena's hand slipped into her purse, and came out with a sharpened pencil. She spun around and viciously punctured everything she came in contact with - his chest, shoulder, arm, and both hands. Backing away from her, he tripped and fell to the floor. Adrena kicked him in the ribs, face, and head.

In Adrena's mind, she was attacking Bart, Harvey, and every one of her mother's disgusting tricks. It took two passing professors to stop her.

Adrena was expelled until further notice. Junior couldn't console her, and Adrena wept wildly, as if her life had ended. To her, it felt just that way. Losing control was Adrena's greatest fear, and that's what she'd done. It was the first time it had happened since Vivian weaned Adrena off the antidepressants. An occasional headache or nightmare was the extent of her repercussions from the past. Adrena suffered those ailments without taking medication; to do otherwise would have meant she was not living a normal life. Now, in one brash moment, normal had slipped through her tight grasp.

Vivian and Max arrived the very next day. After giving Adrena a mother's quick physical exam with her eyes and hands, Vivian cradled, rocked, and talked to Adrena for hours. She wanted to know if the young man had physically injured Adrena in any way. Adrena's fear of being put back on medication was at the front of her mind, and Vivian assured her that wouldn't happen. Only if Adrena experienced depression or anxiety for a long period of time, would Vivian have to resort to medication again.

Maxine was furious. With Vivian in tow, she stormed into the dean's office and demanded to know why Adrena was expelled. When the dean read off the young man's list of injuries, Maxine asked, "What was she supposed to do? Let him rape her? What would you have done to him if that happened?"

The dean said, "We would have handled it, Dr. Matthews. All Adrena had to do was come to us. We cannot tolerate any assault."

Max yelled, "Come to you?! How was she supposed to come to you, if he was holding her?! Those days are over! Women are taking matters into their own hands! Calling you to pick up what's left! Men, young and old, have got to learn to keep their hands to themselves. You put her back in class now, or my next stop will be the police station and the newspaper. Expelling a girl for protecting herself from sexual assault in the corridor of the university. You should be ashamed of yourself. Does he play ball here?"

Nervously, the dean answered, "Yes. He plays basketball."

"That's what I thought. Get her back into class."

Without waiting for a response, Maxine was up and out of his office. Vivian asked calmly, "When can I tell Adrena to return to class?"

"Of course, the young lady can come back, Dr. Shaw. I just thought you should know the extent of the young man's injuries. I think she was trying to kill him."

"Do you understand that every time a man violates a woman, he kills a part of her? She was fighting for her life. If more women reacted the way Adrena did, I would be counseling fewer of them."

Speaking to Vivian in a stuffy, pompous tone, the dean said, "While I sympathize with Miss Reynolds' position, she would have been able to get over his childish, aggressive act. Groping doesn't require a death sentence. He may be a while getting over what she's done."

Truly angry that a supposedly intelligent man had made such a stupid remark, Vivian snapped, "That's where you're wrong. Women never get over any of those childish, aggressive acts. They learn to live with the pain and humiliation, every day of their lives. So, please excuse them if they're not responding with appropriate feminine gentility anymore. Until you're sexually groped by someone bigger and stronger than you, don't attempt to gauge the proper punishment."

"I thought you would be more concerned for the young man's well-being, Dr. Shaw."

"I am concerned. So is my sister. It's just that we know how the system gets all excited when a woman inflicts pain on a man. How often does groping happen on this campus? I bet you have no idea. What would you have done, if Adrena had come to you? Slapped his hand and sent him on his merry way? Well, you don't have to do that now. And, if Adrena's reaction didn't break him of the disgusting habit, nothing ever will."

"Dr. Shaw, I'll reinstate Miss Reynolds this afternoon. While understanding your position, I still think you should speak to her. We cannot tolerate this kind of activity on campus. She won't be able to avoid permanent expulsion if it happens again."

"I'll speak to Adrena. You speak to your students about invading other people's space. I know groping is particularly offensive to Adrena. There are probably some other young women who would follow her lead."

"Shall I attach the young man's medical bills to Miss Reynolds' account?"

"No, you shall not. Do I have to remind you again that the young man was intoxicated and sexually assaulting women on campus? I have personally spoken to five students who are willing to come forward and testify to that."

There were no more problems after that. Every young man on campus knew what to expect if he touched Adrena Reynolds. She became something of a legend.

Junior looked at Adrena in a different light, too. He stopped teasing her when they were studying. Adrena and pencils made him nervous. He saved it for later.

Chapter Thirty-Four

Vivian resumed scheduled weekly contact with Adrena by telephone after the episode at school. Adrena shared feelings of failure, disappointment, and the continuous string of nightmares that plagued her. Concentration eluded Adrena in patches, and her grades suffered. To Vivian's surprise, Adrena openly wept when she spoke of Junior's attention irritating her.

Vivian's constant reassurances she had done nothing wrong helped Adrena make it through her first semester. Still, the entire episode haunted Adrena. She regretted her reaction to the young man's assault. It had been spontaneous and drawn unwanted attention. Students now stared at her as she walked between classes, calling her crazy and making bad jokes about the incident behind her back. Junior's excellent reputation at the university was also jeopardized whenever he confronted anyone who made a negative remark about Adrena.

When Adrena and Junior came home for the holidays, she seemed to find some peace. Scooter's constant company lightened Adrena's mood immensely. He looked for "Drena" from the moment he woke in the morning. That's who took him to the park and let him run, climb, jump and scream, for hours. Daddy didn't stay out there as long as Scooter's "Drena" did.

During the Christmas holidays, Junior spent most of his time at home because Adrena seemed to need the space. Adrena split her days between the Stanleys' and Vivian's. She checked on her own house twice, collected mail, aired the place out, and moved on. The house didn't hold any fascination for her at all without Junior.

Max brought Aria over to spend the days with Adrena and Scooter. They had a ball. Junior only came when Adrena indicated she wanted him to. Vivian could see that Junior felt lost without Adrena, but she kept her distance, to let the two young people work things out for themselves.

Vivian hosted a small Christmas dinner which her immediate family and Adrena attended. Vivian actually prepared the food alone, and she didn't set the alarms off once. With dinner and dessert consumed, everyone retired to the den. As they sat around having drinks, watching Scooter and Aria destroy the perfectly-arranged gifts under the tree, Vivian decided to take the moment to make an announcement.

Tapping a glass of fruit juice, Vivian stood and said, "I have a holiday surprise for everyone. Howard and I are expecting another baby."

There was a variety of reactions. Adrena and Junior thought that was great. Maxine and Vance stared at each other with fear in their eyes. Clayton groaned, dropped his head and covered his face. In shocked anger, Howard impulsively shouted, "What?!"

Vivian smiled and said, "We're having another baby, sweetheart. Aren't you happy? Scooter won't be an only child anymore. He'll have someone to play and grow up with."

"I don't want another baby, Vivian. I can't go through another pregnancy with you."

On the verge of tears, Vivian asked, "Oh, you can't? Well, when will you be leaving?"

"Vivian, you didn't discuss this with me."

"And I won't discuss it with you now, either."

In tears, Vivian left them there. Following her, Max said, "Howard, you shouldn't have said that."

Howard yelled, "It's how I feel! Vivian almost drove me nuts the last time! I'm not ready to go through that again! She should have asked me about it!"

Max stopped in her tracks and yelled back, "Don't holler at me, Howard Shaw! You made a baby with your own wife, and you stand in front of everybody and say you don't want it?! You've just made the biggest mistake of your life! I would shut up now, if I were you!"

"This is my house, Maxine! I don't have to shut up!"

Unable to stay neutral, Vance said, "You shouldn't have said that, Howard. Not in front of everybody. Not in private either. Vivian didn't make the baby by herself."

"I know that, Vance, but Vivian should have told me what I was participating in. This is not fair. They can decide to have babies, and we're just supposed to be quiet and go crazy while they're doing it."

"You don't know that for a fact, Howard. Has Vivian been acting strange lately?"

"No. If she were, I would have noticed it."

"So why are you getting all wound up? And please, don't say I don't know what it's like. Don't say it, Howard."

"Look Vance, you and I are two different men. I don't know how you stood it. I cannot run a business and come home to a batty-as-hell wife every night, for another however many months it's going to take. Do you have any idea what Vivian's tantrums are going to do to Scooter?"

"You said for better or worse. In sickness and health. And Vivian was Scooter in another time and place - she survived. I'm leaving now, Howard. You're making me sick to my stomach. All I have to say is, don't make me come back here tonight."

Vance collected all of his family, except Junior, and left. Adrena had joined Max and Vivian upstairs. Howard's yelling had pushed a few of Adrena's buttons, and she decided to put some distance between them, before something bad happened. Junior, Howard, and Clayton sat in the den with the children. No one said anything. Howard and Clayton refreshed their drinks.

Upstairs, Vivian lay on the bed, crying a torrent of angry tears. She could not comprehend Howard's callous behavior. He was the one who wanted children. Wasn't she giving him what he said he wanted?

Maxine wanted to go downstairs and bust Howard in the head with something. There were times when men really made her sick, and this was one of them. For hurting Doc, Adrena could have slit Howard's throat from ear to ear and

wiped the knife on his pristine white shirt. If his sorry life
didn't mean so much to Doc and Scooter, she would.

Neither Maxine or Adrena could communicate with
Vivian. She broke out in a fresh batch of tears every time
anyone said her name. Eventually, Vivian said, "Go on home.
I'll be all right. This is my mess, and I'll handle it."

Adamantly, Max said, "I'm not going anywhere, until you
swear you won't do anything stupid."

Vivian laughed and asked, "What could I possibly do?
I've already done the stupid thing. Go on, Max."

"I'll take Scooter home with me, then. He'll never go to
sleep, with you acting like this. Adrena, can you pack a bag
for him?"

Moving like a zombie, Adrena responded, "Sure."

Vivian held her head in her hands and said, "Thanks,
Max. I'll come get him in the morning."

Everyone left. No one said goodnight. Without knowing
what was going on, Scooter happily went home with his
cousin.

Howard appeared at the bedroom doorway a few minutes
later, and, without fanfare, asked, "Why didn't you tell me
before you announced it to the world, Vivian?"

There was a searing pain in her head. Vivian said, "Don't
worry about it, Howard. You won't have to be bothered with
the crazy, pregnant woman. She'll be more than happy to
pack her bags and go somewhere else."

"That's not necessary, Vivian. I just want to know why
you didn't talk to me about it first."

"It doesn't matter now, Howard."

"Yes, it does. It matters to me. Knowing what a hard
time you had the first time, why didn't you tell me?"

"After Scooter turned a year old, I went back to the
doctor. She said my estrogen levels were good. She told me
I had a fifty-fifty chance of not experiencing the same thing
I went through before. So, knowing my husband wanted
more than one child, I decided to give it another try.

"She's been testing me for the past two months. My levels
haven't dropped off the way they did the first time. I was

stupid enough to think you would be happy about it, Howard.
You didn't even give me a chance to tell you about the tests."
    "I'm sorry if I upset you, Vivian. After Scooter was born,
I made a decision not to have any more children. That was
the most difficult period of time I've ever experienced. Doing
it again frightens me."
    "You decided? When were you going to discuss your
decision with me?"
    "When you brought up the subject of another child. I
thought you would mention it first."
    "Well, I guess we were both wrong, Howard."
    "What are we going to do, Vivian?"
    "About what?"
    "The baby."
    "What would you suggest we do?"
    Howard lay down on the bed and covered his face. He
never answered Vivian's question. Without the word being
said, it hung in the air. Vivian smelled and tasted it. This
was the most disappointing moment in her entire life. Her
depression wasn't hormonal this time.
    Vivian collected some things from her drawer and left the
room. She showered in the foyer bathroom and lay down in
the guestroom. Her mind was numb. Only tears came when
a thought popped into her head. What to do couldn't get
through if it wanted to.
    The weight of Howard's leg thrown across her woke
Vivian in the middle of the night. Looking at his sleeping
face in the darkness, Vivian knew he regretted saying what
he'd said. Still, he had said it. He did not want this baby. For
the very first time since Vivian fell in love with Howard, she
felt differently about him. She still loved him; however, he
had put a horrible nick in her respect for him.
    Vivian carried her baby in silence. If she had an ache,
pain, or a craving, she took care of it herself. Vivian went to
all of her pre-natal examinations alone, and she never shared
any information with Howard. Her estrogen levels held out
through her sixth month, but as spring approached, they
began to spike and fall.

Hoping to be left alone, Vivian never returned to their bedroom. Scooter didn't understand the move. He looked for his mother in her old bedroom all of the time. Every morning he went there first and found no one. Refusing to be completely shut out, Howard slept wherever Vivian slept. There were no conversations between them. As Vivian cut down on her workload, Howard's increased. He spent more time at the office. Vivian said nothing.

Maxine and Clayton hated watching Vivian and Howard move farther and farther apart. They visited them often and tried to get them to talk to each other. It never worked. The only thing that made them look at each other was Scooter. When Scooter accidentally fell from the monkey bars in the park, Howard and Vivian didn't talk, they screamed at each other.

At the hospital, Vivian accused Howard of not watching Scooter. Howard said Vivian never watched him at all. If Clayton hadn't showed up, the two might have come to blows. Scooter came home with a huge purple lump on his forehead and a cast on his arm. That's when Howard stopped sleeping with Vivian in the guestroom. She couldn't have cared less. They bumped into each other occasionally as they checked on Scooter.

One afternoon in March, Millie called Howard's office to tell him Vivian had gone into premature labor, and the ambulance had taken her to the hospital. Howard nearly killed himself getting there. He scratched his beloved Jaguar and didn't stop to take a look at it. Vivian's doctor told him they had stopped the contractions with medication, but she needed bedrest for the remainder of the pregnancy.

Three days later, Howard brought Vivian home and put her to bed in their bedroom. Vivian's complaints went ignored. Scooter was lost again when he looked for his mother in the guestroom. He took his afternoon naps in bed with Vivian, trying to hold onto her with his casted arm. Vivian played in his huge, black curls until he fell asleep, wrapping the soft, thick locks of hair around her finger over and over.

Vivian longed for the silly arguments with Howard over Scooter's hair. If it were up to his father, Scooter would not have one curl in his hair because Howard insisted they made him look like a girl. Vivian knew Howard was attending therapy sessions with Lula, but she only knew what Talia told her about them. Vivian wanted desperately to know how Howard was dealing with the therapeutic transformations. Simply said, Vivian missed her marriage.

The charade Vivian and Howard were playing out would have to end one way or the other, after the baby was born. Vivian completely understood his frustration at the prospect of her experiencing mood swings. She even expected him to be upset about it. Vivian would never forgive him for saying he didn't want the baby though.

At night, Howard massaged Vivian's back. Instead of relaxing her, Howard's touch seemed to make her more tense. Before leaving the house every day, he made sure Vivian had everything she normally craved. She refused to call him at the office to ask for anything. Instead, Vivian called Max. Max called Clayton. Clayton paged Howard and told him what Vivian wanted. This pregnancy was worse than the first one, for entirely different reasons.

A month later, Howard came in from work at nine o'clock at night. Scooter was already asleep. Howard went down to his room, kissed his sleeping son goodnight and returned to their bedroom. Vivian did not return his greeting. She sat on the chaise braiding her hair. Howard shrugged and started to undress.

Out of the corner of Vivian's eye, she saw him fold and put his socks into his shoe. She slowly walked over and stared down at Howard's shoes. Trying to see what interested her, he did likewise. Vivian's voice caught him off guard.

"Where were you tonight, Howard?"

Still thinking his shoes didn't match, Howard answered absently, "At work. Why?"

"At work with whom?"

Giving a nervous little laugh, Howard said, "I was at work alone. Clayton didn't stay tonight."

"Where's your shirt?"

"It's on the chair. What are you looking for, Vivian?"

Vivian took the shirt into the bathroom, where the lighting was better, to examine it. She went over every inch of that shirt with her eyes, hands, and nose. Howard watched her from the doorway. God only knew what tree his wife was barking up this time.

Vivian brushed past him and put the shirt back. She picked up his jacket. Smelled it and went through the pockets. All she found were his keys. Vivian returned to the shoes. Bending, she picked up the one with socks in it and turned to Howard. "You want to tell me why you put these socks in this shoe?"

"I always put my socks in my shoes. You know that."

"I know you always put them in your left shoe. This is the right shoe, Howard."

Dumbfounded, Howard looked at the shoe in Vivian's hand and said, "Yes, that is the right shoe. So what?"

Yelling, Vivian said, "You have never put these fucking socks in this fucking shoe, Howard Shaw! Never! Why tonight?!"

"Calm down, Vivian. You're going to wake the baby."

"I'm going to wake him taking him out of here, if you don't tell me why you put these damned socks in the wrong shoe!"

"Vivian, please. I have no idea why I put the socks in the wrong shoe. I have no idea what's going on around here anymore. You haven't had a civil word to say to me in months. No matter what I say, you're going to be upset. I've apologized a million times for Christmas. I've done everything I can to let you know it's all right with me and hoped you would get over it. What do you want from me? You want me to say I've been seeing another woman? Is that what you're looking for?"

"Is that what's going on, Howard?"

Shaking his head, Howard said softly, "No, Vivian. That's not what's going on. All you hear is our marriage falling apart."

Vivian closed her eyes and fought with tears that refused to be held back. Howard was right. She just didn't want to ever hear it said out loud. Dropping the shoe, Vivian moved toward the bedroom door. Howard wouldn't let her pass. He put his arms around her and kissed the top of her head.

Between sobs, Vivian said, "It wasn't supposed to be like this, Howard. You were supposed to love me, no matter how many babies I had. No matter how crazy I went doing it."

"I do love you, Vivian. I've never not loved you."

"You just don't want me to have any more children. It might put a strain on you. Inconvenience you."

"That's not it. I didn't want either one of us to lose our minds having a baby, Vivian. I didn't want to run the risk of you pushing yourself over the edge and not coming back. I'm not Vance, sweetheart. I don't know what I would do without you. I don't know if I could pick up the pieces and start over. If you suddenly fell apart, where would that leave me? I don't have to tell you how much I'd blame myself, do I, sweetheart?

"We're not your parents, Vivian. We know what caused the problem. If Vance knew what I knew, do you honestly believe Maxine would be here today? To have your mother right now, he'd send Maxine back. I can tell by the way he looks at you, Vivian. You remind him of your mother, and it hurts him, every time he looks at you. His wife and Junior see it, too."

Knowing Howard was right, all Vivian could say was, "Daddy wouldn't send Max back, Howard, but he might not have made her though. You still haven't told me why you put the socks in the wrong shoe."

"The way things are going around here, I'm lucky I'm not putting them in my pockets, Vivian. Now, can we go to bed?"

Howard walked Vivian over to the bed and tucked her in. He picked up the shoes and put the socks into the left shoe. Howard closed his eyes and sent up a silent prayer, "Please?"

They lay in bed, looking into each other's eyes for a long time. After Howard assured Vivian he wanted the baby fifteen times, she relaxed in his arms, returned his kisses and let him make love to her ever so gently. Vivian enjoyed every minute of it, too.

Chapter Thirty-Five

Adrena and Junior returned to school together after the Christmas holidays. She was much more relaxed and a little more talkative. She even joked with Junior during the ride, saying, "Howard better stop upsetting Doc. I'd hate to have to shut him up."

Junior laughed at Adrena's remark and said, "You might have to arm wrestle my father for the opportunity."

"He'd beat me arm wrestling, Junior. I'll flip him for it."

The talk at school about the pencil attack died down after the holiday break. Adrena's concentration was greatly improved, and her grades followed suit. Junior pulled his share of the weight around the apartment, but he still wore shirts out of the hamper. Thinking he might like them all in there, Adrena put the clean ones in there, too. Junior smirked, took them out and went on his way. Adrena shook her head and smiled at him. That was just who Junior was, and she learned to live with it.

Passion returned to Adrena and Junior's life with the dawning of spring, too. They spent hours in bed together. Studying, eating, talking and making love. On the weekends, they drove to the beach and made love in the car. Once, they did it in the ocean. That was Junior's idea. While Adrena loved Junior's attention, she continued to be perplexed by his constant romantic attraction to her and his stamina.

Before they left school for the Christmas holidays, Junior had stopped trying to get Adrena's sexual attention. He wanted all of Adrena's attention - the way he had it before. Not having her eyes light up when he entered the room bothered Junior more than anything he ever experienced. The day the light returned, was the happiest Junior could imagine.

The only hitch came when Junior attempted to make love, without putting a condom on first. Adrena backed away from him as if he had a sizzling, hot poker. She asked, "Where's your condom, Junior?"

He moaned, "Aw c'mon, Adrena. We don't need it."

"Didn't Max tell you we weren't supposed to do anything without it?"

"That was a long time ago. She didn't know we would be sleeping exclusively with each other."

Looking into Junior's eyes, Adrena asked, "Are we?"

With guilty discomfort, Junior responded, "What do you mean, are we? Have you been with someone else?"

"No. You have, though."

Junior's voice rose in pitch, saying, "I have not!"

Adrena reached over Junior and opened the night table drawer. She retrieved and handed him a letter. A classmate who dated one of Junior's friends had given it to Adrena two days after they started school in the fall. Adrena waited for the girl referred to in the letter to show up. When she didn't, Adrena waited for Junior to mention her. He never did.

Adrena watched Junior's face as he read the letter. It told her all she needed to know. It was the truth. Doc told Adrena that young men often seek out numerous female conquests. They feel like they're missing something if they don't. If they're discreet, they care most for the primary female. If not, they'll probably be rolling stones for years to come - like Clayton.

Adrena didn't want Junior to miss out on anything. If this was part of his growing up, she would have to deal with it. After all, it wasn't really his fault. It was in his genetic programming. In case he decided against her, Adrena braced herself for his farewell "I've found someone I like better" speech.

Looking at Adrena and sounding more than a little desperate, Junior said, "This is not completely true, Adrena. I did go out with her a few times last year, and I did have sex with her twice. But she was never my girlfriend."

"Isn't that who you ran to when we weren't talking last semester?"

With guilt written in big letters across his forehead, and sweat forming on his nose, Junior said, "Yes. But, we only talked, Adrena. I swear I didn't touch her."

"Well, why is she saying she's going to have your baby?"

Near hysterics, Junior yelped, "She's saying what?!"

"You heard me, Vance Matthews, Jr."

"That's a lie, Adrena. Nobody's having anything of mine."

"Are you so sure, Junior? Maybe you talked her into doing it without a condom. The way you're trying to do me right now."

"I have never touched a living soul without a condom. I definitely wouldn't have done it with anyone other than you."

"What makes me so special, Junior? You got the exact same thing from her."

"No, I did not. It wasn't the same, Adrena. I swear it wasn't."

Honestly wanting to know what was different about it, Adrena asked, "Why not? She's a girl."

"Sure, she's a girl. That's where the similarities stop. You're different from her in lots of ways. You have never thrown yourself at me, the way she did . . . and I know you've never been with anyone but me."

"How do you know? If I hadn't been given that letter, I never would have known you had been with someone else."

"I know you, Adrena. You can only love sparingly. I'm fortunate you ever looked in my direction. Don't you know I know Vivian was my in with you? If she weren't my sister, you wouldn't have said two words to me."

Laughing, Adrena said, "Yeah, you're right about that. I figured you could only be so much of a beast, with her in your family. But I've never said I loved you either, Junior. Sparingly, or otherwise."

"You don't have to say it, Adrena. I know you do. Just like I know I love you."

"If you say so, Junior."

Looking uncomfortable again, Junior said, "There are more than a few lies flying around campus. Please don't let them destroy what we have, Adrena. Everyone hates the fact that we have our own place, a car, and each other. I'm surprised that's the first time you've heard anything."

Bluntly, Adrena said, "It's not, Junior. I've heard plenty. Doc told me people work overtime trying to destroy things they can't achieve themselves - not to believe anything I hear, and to only half-believe what I think I see. You're lucky I never saw anything, Junior. I don't know if I could only half-believe it."

"You don't believe she's pregnant by me, do you?"

"She's not pregnant by anyone, Junior."

"How do you know that?"

"Let's just say I know and leave it at that."

"Are you angry with me?"

"Sure, but everyone makes mistakes. Especially guys. If you lied about it, I'd know it wasn't a mistake. You would be deliberately trying to make a fool of me. I wouldn't like that at all. When you apologize and promise not to do it again, we can go on our merry way. If I find out you did it a second time, you'll go on your merry way without me."

Blowing a tremendous sigh of relief, Junior apologized profusely and swore he'd never do it again. Junior resumed his whining about wearing the condom. Tired of hearing him, Adrena relented. Adrena thought Junior was an enthusiastic lover with a condom. She was totally unprepared for what she got without it. To make matters worse, Junior never tired of doing it. Adrena thought to herself, "If Junior's father is anything like him, no wonder Doc and Max were born so close together."

Nightmares continued to bother Adrena from time to time. She would wake shaking, sweating, and whining. Junior always got up and held her until she fell asleep again. Sometimes, Adrena suffered with blinding headaches after a night of nightmares. These were the times Adrena thought she heard Mildred and Bart arguing. Of course, they couldn't be. They were dead.

After Vivian's premature labor fright, Adrena stopped sharing her problems with her, feeling that Howard and Vivian had more than enough of their own problems. It would be too much for Vivian to start worrying about her again. Besides, Junior took care of her. He was the second best thing to come into Adrena's life. If she could have had babies, she would consider marrying Junior. As it was, Adrena had every intention of giving Junior his freedom after college. She loved him that much.

The school year progressed well. Junior came out at the top of his class. He made the Dean's list every semester. Adrena fell a little short, but had done remarkably well, considering her setback. She was on the Dean's list, for the final semester only. Vivian and Max assured Adrena that was a great accomplishment.

On May twenty-first, Adrena and Junior covered the furniture and headed home for summer vacation. They would return in the fall and resume their lives together. In the meantime, they would have to play Vance's game by stealing away to spend time together at Adrena's house.

Chapter Thirty-Six

Junior incurred Vance's wrath twice during his first week at home. Vance expected Junior to resume his Saturday morning ritual of entertaining his sisters. Junior cut the grass, bagged it, and disappeared. When Vance reminded him that Melanie and Patricia were looking forward to going to some new theme restaurant, Junior asked, "Why do I have to take them?"

Hoping Junior was having a temporary lapse of memory, Vance told him, "You know they've missed you, Junior. They're still little girls who have to be taken where they want to go."

"Yeah, but, why do I have to take them?"

Realizing Junior was challenging his authority, Vance said angrily, "You have to take them, because I say so. Got a problem with that?"

Junior whined, "I'm too old to hang out with two little girls, Dad."

Coming out of his chair, Vance asked, "Would you like to get any older, Junior?"

Knowing he was no match for an angry Vance Matthews, Junior responded quickly, "Yes, sir."

"Good. You will take Melanie and Patricia to whatever it is they want you to take them to. First thing tomorrow."

Junior's next faux pas was not beating his two a.m. curfew. He had become accustomed to sleeping with Adrena all night. One night, Junior slept comfortably and didn't wake up until five o'clock the following morning. Vance met Junior at the front door, at six. He asked, "Is that sunlight out there, Junior?"

"Yes, sir. I fell asleep. I'm sorry."

"You're sorry? You're not sorry, Junior. You're losing your mind. First, you don't want to take your sisters out. Now, you're coming into my house at six o'clock in the morning.

This will never work. Get your act together. You're going to make me break your neck. Where were you anyway?"

"With Adrena."

"Until this time in the morning? I know you're crazy now. What are the Stanleys saying about that? I can't believe they let you stay there that long."

Lying, Junior said, "They were asleep, Dad. We fell asleep watching television."

"Mr. Stanley should have put his foot in your behind, on your way out. Don't ever do that again, Junior. You won't see Adrena anymore this summer, if you do."

"Yes, sir."

Knowing he was dangerously close to being grounded for the remainder of the summer, Junior started setting the alarm clock whenever they were at Adrena's house. If Vance ever found out Junior and Adrena lived together at school, he would beat Junior to within an inch of his life - probably give himself a heart attack doing it, too.

Junior wasn't a child anymore - he and Vance stood eye to eye now. Still, Vance, Senior was the bulkier of the two. Having been a hard-working man all of his life, there was still enough power in his punch to set Junior straight. When Junior had pissed Vance off the summer before, his father punched him in the chest so hard, it sent Junior crashing into the wall. A picture fell and smacked Junior in the head for good measure. Disrespect never crossed Junior's mind again.

Junior and Adrena spent every evening together, somewhere, but Junior's curfew was always met. Adrena spent more time at her own house, alone. She rummaged through old picture albums and letters. Her grandmother must have kept everything. Some of the pictures were so old, the people blended into the landscape.

She saw Mildred and Antoinette as little girls. They were extremely well-dressed, sitting or standing, smiling or laughing. Always with their father nearby. His adoration of them was etched on his long, lean face. Adrena assumed her grandmother was taking the pictures. Adrena wondered how that well-dressed, greatly loved, little girl could have ever treated her own child the way she did. What happened? There had to be more to it than Bart.

Adrena thought about the way she felt about Junior. Imagined him asking her to do the intimate things they did with someone else - wondered if she would do it. Deciding that she couldn't and that Junior wanted too much of her to share, Adrena simply dismissed the thought. Still, there had to be more to Mildred's demise than Bart.

Reading her grandparents' letters, Adrena found out her grandfather had been a soldier who had fought in World War II. Her grandmother was the daughter of a well-regarded seamstress and a mill owner. Both of Granny's parents ran businesses in town. Grandpop was the son of southern sharecroppers, so he worked hard to impress Granny's folks. They kept her under lock and key until he got a job and worked it for two years.

Their letters were full of how much they missed and loved each other. Adrena felt their longing, saw their dreams from conception, knew their troubles, and wished she'd known them under better circumstances.

In the bottom of the drawer lay a faded, pink-and-white, flowered book. Thinking it another of her grandmother's many financial journals, Adrena flipped the cover back. It was the diary of Mildred Marie Brown. The very first entry guaranteed Adrena's interest.

I spent the day with Bart, while Antoinette was in school. I pretended to be sick. If anybody knew, I'd be in hot water. They hate him. The only reason they let him live here is because Antoinette got pregnant and had to marry him. Bart's almost as old as Daddy. He used to work with Daddy.

Antoinette and Bart's son, Arnold, is six months old and a pain. He cries from sunup to sunset. Daddy only puts up with any of it because he wants to make sure Antoinette finishes school. None of that matters, because Bart says he loves me better than her. He's going to marry me one day.

Talking to herself, Adrena asked, "Bart was Antoinette's husband? He lived here?" She read on.

Bart bought me a real pretty sweater today. If Antoinette knew, I would have to kill her. He's always bringing me things. He never gives her anything. She cries about it all of the time. I think she's lucky. She gets to sleep with him every night. He said he doesn't hold her when they sleep, but I saw him doing it once. I've seen those two do more than they know.

Bart's going to show me what husbands and wives really do for my twelfth birthday. That's only a month from now. I can't wait. He only kisses me now. Touches all the right places. He says I'm still too little for everything. He's even going to get some weed for the party. We'll smoke a little and do a little. I'm going to do everything Bart wants me to do. Antoinette won't be good enough when I'm done. I know I'm better than her.

She thinks she's the cat's meow. Daddy put her up so high, all of her life. Didn't take her down when he found out she was smoking dope and sleeping with his friend either. If Mama had anything to say about it, Bart and Antoinette would be eating dust for dinner. Says neither one of them are decent people.

Adrena read the diary from cover to cover. Mildred documented every sick detail of her relationship with Bart. Antoinette and Mildred were pregnant at the same time. Granny got mad and threw Bart and Antoinette out. She had her suspicions about who Mildred was pregnant by, but Mildred refused to confirm them.

Before Bart was done, both girls were pill-popping, dope-smoking, sex slaves for him. He eventually had them both under his own roof. They walked the street in shifts. Whoever was home, took care of Bart. To hell with the babies.

Everything was fine until Antoinette caught Bart and Mildred in a compromising position. She actually heard him telling Mildred he loved her more. How much prettier she was than Antoinette. That she was better in bed than Antoinette could think about being. How he had to dope Antoinette up to get her to do anything worthwhile.

That's why Antoinette and Mildred hated each other so much. They were both in love with the same sick bastard. The way Adrena saw it, she didn't stand a chance. She simply fell out of a twisted tree. It had to die, sooner or later.

With more of the past revealed so explicitly, Adrena's dreams took on slightly different twists and turns. More depth, colors, and sounds. They always ended the same way though. With Adrena bound, gagged, and screeching.

Two weeks after Junior's confrontation with Vance, Adrena insisted he take her to the Stanleys' before going home. Granny's house was no good for her alone. It had more ghosts than Adrena originally imagined.

Every morning, Adrena dressed and waited for Junior to come by and take her to Vivian's. Taking care of Scooter and Aria pleasantly occupied her mind. Adrena never shared the contents of the diary with Vivian. Doc looked tired all of the time, and she didn't smile very much at all. Carrying this baby appeared to be a greater burden than Scooter.

In truth, this baby was causing Vivian more problems. She was already fifteen pounds heavier than she was when Scooter was born. The bed rest didn't allow her any exercise. If Vivian went downstairs more than twice in a day, the contractions started. Knowing Adrena was there with Vivian, Howard worked late at the office more often. Max didn't come by as often either. Clayton only came in with Howard to pick up his daughter.

Vivian bit Howard's head off for simple things. He bought Hellmann's mayonnaise, instead of Kraft. He let Scooter fall asleep anywhere and then put him to bed; Scooter was supposed to fall asleep in bed. One morning, Scooter came running into his mother's bedroom in his underwear. Howard had not put his pajamas on the night before.

Adrena missed most of Vivian's tirades. Junior always wanted to leave the moment Howard cleared the doorway - after all, Junior had to be home by two. To help out, Adrena always made dinner for the Shaws, and Howard never missed an opportunity to thank her for it.

In actuality, Adrena's presence saved Howard a lot of grief. He knew it only too well. Knowing raised voices agitated Adrena, Vivian never yelled in her presence. She also gave some of what she wanted to yell about a little more thought, and occasionally she dropped it completely.

God knows no one could take better care of Scooter. Adrena's eyes never left his happy little face. If he was falling, she was there to catch him before he hit the ground. The dog up the street barked at Scooter one day, making him fall and skin his knee. A furious Adrena kicked the dog so hard its ribs broke. Howard and Vivian got the vet bill for that.

Vivian's only complaints were that Adrena allowed Scooter to do anything he wanted, and when she brought him in from outside, he looked like he'd fallen out of a dustbowl. Adrena happily bathed the dirty devil and let him run amuck again. Vivian's final complaint was Adrena carried Scooter everywhere. There would be another baby soon, and Scooter would have to understand no one was going to carry him. The only time Adrena ever ignored Vivian was when it came to Scooter. She carried him whenever she felt like it.

After dropping Adrena off at Vivian's, Junior did what he had to do around the house and ran errands for his mother. He took his sisters to camp and picked them up. Most of the time, he played basketball with his friends, and they helped him wash the car twice a week.

Vance couldn't understand why Adrena insisted Junior keep the car. She drove just as well as he did. In Vance's eyes, Adrena was spoiling Junior and Scooter. If anyone had ever asked Adrena why, she would have simply said, "The women in my family will either spoil a man to death, or kill him."

Then there was the late June day that nothing fell into place. Junior overslept. He was a half-hour late getting Adrena to Vivian's. That meant Howard was over an hour late leaving for work. Scooter was his usual, noisy self. Aria was as cute and inquisitive as ever. Vivian's mood was borderline psychotic, and Adrena heard her talking to herself off and on all morning. The baby wasn't due for another month, and Adrena was beginning to doubt that Vivian's mind would hold out that long.

To keep the peace, Adrena kept the kids outside most of the day and only brought them in to check on Vivian. The second time they came in, Vivian was asleep. After lunch, Adrena put Scooter and Aria down for a nap and started dinner. The housekeeper dropped something in the den, and the Shaw household exploded.

Vivian screamed from the top of the stairs, "What's going on down there?!"

Scooter and Aria woke and screamed, "Drena!"

The housekeeper tried to assure Vivian everything was fine. She'd only knocked over a statue, and it didn't break. Although Vivian was supposed to stay in bed, she wanted to go down and see for herself. Howard would be very upset if there were the slightest nick in one of his precious statues.

While Adrena calmed the babies, and the housekeeper went back to her work, Vivian came downstairs. They thought they would have to call an ambulance ten minutes later, but Vivian felt better once she was propped up on the living room sofa. Scooter and Aria refused to sleep after that. For the remainder of the afternoon, Adrena ran from the kitchen, preparing dinner, to the den, where the children played, to the living room, where Vivian lay. By five, Adrena had a horrendous headache.

At six, neither Howard nor Junior had shown up. Adrena fed Vivian and the children their dinner. Knowing Scooter and Aria were tired, she put them to bed, and mercifully, they fell asleep the moment their heads hit the pillows. Adrena's headache was growing by leaps and bounds.

Howard came in at seven-thirty. He walked over to Vivian, kissed her head and asked, "What are you doing down here, Mrs. Shaw?"

"I'm taking a break from the bedroom. Where is Clayton?"

"He's coming. Where are the kids?"

"They're taking a nap."

"It's a little late for naps, isn't it?"

"Yes, but they didn't take one this afternoon."

Flipping through the mail, Howard asked, "Why not? I know Adrena took them out and let them play until they were tired. She always does."

"I woke them with my yelling. Mrs. Steward knocked over your statue, and I wanted to know what fell."

Never looking up, Howard asked, "Didn't you know they were sleeping?"

Nastily, Vivian snapped, "Yes. I knew they were sleeping. I just didn't know what was falling."

Seeing Vivian's mood change before his eyes, Howard said, "Okay, Viv. Where are Adrena and Junior?"

"Junior's not here yet. Adrena's in the kitchen."

Howard left Vivian rolling her eyes at him. He found Adrena with her head down on the kitchen counter. Howard called Adrena's name several times. She didn't look up or acknowledge his presence. Concerned, he walked over to Adrena and rubbed her neck. Before he could ask if she was all right, Adrena slapped his hand away.

Nervously, Howard asked, "Are you all right, Adrena? I didn't mean to frighten you."

Recognizing Howard, Adrena said, "I'm sorry, Howard. I fell asleep. My head hurts."

"Did you take anything for it, Adrena?"

"No. I'm all right. Did you eat dinner?"

"No, but don't worry about it. I'll make it myself. Why don't you lie down and rest until Junior gets here?"

"He's not here yet? What time is it?"

"Almost eight now."

Rubbing her head, Adrena said, "He's somewhere chasing a basketball."

Smiling, Howard said, "You're probably right."

"You go wash your hands. I'll make your dinner now. Junior will come babbling through the door any minute now."

On his way out, Howard asked, "Does Vivian know you have a headache?"

"No. Don't tell her, either, Howard. She came flying down the stairs today, and those contractions started again. She's been talking to herself, too. Leave her alone."

"Yes, ma'am."

Adrena gave a weak smile at Howard's humor. Standing almost blinded her, but she managed to get to the stove.

Adrena hoped Junior would get there soon; she wanted to lie down and take a nap.

Howard looked at Adrena again and silently wished Vivian could come to rational conclusions like that. That was more than he could hope for these days. He sincerely hoped Adrena wasn't coming down with anything. She looked like she was in a lot of pain.

When Howard came back down, Vivian wasn't on the sofa. He looked around for her. After what Adrena said, he should have made her go upstairs. There was no telling what she was doing now. He found Vivian in the kitchen, with Adrena trying to gently persuade her to sit down. Vivian wouldn't hear it. She could see that Adrena wasn't feeling well.

Howard intervened with, "Excuse me, ladies, but I can make my own dinner. Why don't both of you go lie down?"

Vivian said, "I don't want to. I think Adrena should, though. Something's hurting her, and she won't tell me what it is."

Forgetting his promise to Adrena, Howard said, "It's just a headache, Viv. She'll be all right."

Adrena snapped, "Didn't I tell you not to tell her that? Now she's going to worry about me."

"I'm sorry, sweetheart. I forgot. I'll get the aspirin for you and you can go lie down. As a matter of fact, you can take Vivian with you."

Vivian snapped, "Don't tell me what to do, Howard. Just get the aspirin for the child. You should have brought them the first time if you knew she had a headache."

Biting his tongue, Howard said, "You're right."

Howard ran up the stairs, two at a time, snatched the aspirin bottle out of the medicine cabinet and dashed back down the stairs. He walked into the kitchen to find Vivian pulling dishes out of the cabinet and Adrena pleading with her to stop.

Raising his voice for the first time, Howard said, "Okay. Everybody stop."

Vivian and Adrena looked at him.

Pointing at Adrena, he said, "You take these aspirin and go lie down."

Pointing at Vivian, he said, "You put the plate down, and let's get back upstairs. I can make my own dinner."

With her hand on her hip, Vivian said, "I'm making your dinner. I haven't done a damn thing for over a month. If I don't have enough strength to put food on a plate, I'm pretty damned useless."

Reaching for the plate, Howard said, "You are not useless. Just pregnant. Now, give me the plate and go sit down."

Getting angrier by the moment, Vivian flung the plate in Howard's direction. It crashed on the cabinet and slid to the floor.

Howard yelled, "That's it, Vivian, upstairs! Now!"

"You can't make me go upstairs! I've been upstairs for months! You don't even come up there with me! You come home later and later every night! I guess I'm not supposed to notice it!"

"At this point, I don't care what you notice, Vivian! Get up those stairs!"

Howard and Vivian stood less than a foot apart and they screamed. No one cared about the sleeping babies. No one cared that Adrena clutched her head in excruciating pain. No one heard Adrena say, "Mildred and Bart! Shut up!" As a matter of fact, no one noticed anything, until Adrena drove a nine-inch butcher knife through Howard's hand, pinning it to the counter.

Howard's shocked gaze fell on the knife in his hand. Vivian was so wound up that she didn't realize Howard wasn't arguing with her anymore. She kept right on yelling about not going upstairs.

Howard heard Adrena yell, "Now! I bet you'll shut the fuck up now, Mr. Hanover!"

With sweat forming on his face, Howard muttered, "My hand . . . Vivian, my hand!"

Still fussing, Vivian's eyes scanned Howard's hand on the counter. The knife in it took a little time to register. Vivian's mouth fell open, as she searched for Adrena with frightened eyes.

Adrena stood behind Howard, raising another knife over her head. Vivian yelled, "Adrena, put it down! Adrena!"

Adrena snapped, "Shut up, Mildred! Bart's gonna shut up once and for all today! I'm sick to death of hearing his voice!"

Vivian shuffled in between Howard's back and Adrena. Howard struggled with the knife in his hand. Adrena had embedded it in the counter so deeply, he couldn't get enough leverage to pull it out. Every attempt sent a blinding, hot pain through his hand and up his arm.

Speaking as calmly as she could, Vivian said, "Adrena, it's me. Doc, Adrena. I'm not Mildred. This is Howard, Adrena. Not Bart. Please, don't hurt him."

Adrena mocked Vivian's tone, saying, "Talk, talk, talk. When are you gonna learn you can't talk to a man? They're so stupid, we should be circumcising their tongues at birth, instead of their dicks. They never say one damn thing worth hearing. Now, move out of the way, Mildred. I'll get him, if I have to go through you to do it. He bitches so much, I hear that bastard in my sleep."

In tears now, Vivian said, "I'm not Mildred, Adrena. It's me. Vivian. Dr. Matthews. Look at me, Adrena."

Adrena grabbed Vivian by the arm and flung her out of the way. Vivian's body banged against the sink, and an incredible pain shot down her legs. Just as Adrena plunged the knife toward Howard's back, Vivian lunged and clutched Adrena's arm. They both fell to the floor. Adrena still had the knife. Vivian held onto Adrena's arm, with every ounce of strength she possessed.

As they struggled on the floor, Vivian kept saying, "Adrena, it's me. Dr. Matthews. Please listen, Adrena. You don't want to do this. Please stop."

Further damaging his hand, Howard finally pulled the knife free of the counter. He had to help Vivian. Adrena kept ranting about Mildred and Bart. With his good hand, Howard wrestled the knife out of Adrena's hand and threw it across the room. Adrena appeared to relax a little, but the moment Howard moved toward Vivian, Adrena attacked him viciously. Digging her nails into his eyes. Every time he tried to hold her hands, she bit his arms. When Howard finally managed to grip Adrena from behind, she stomped his feet and kicked his shins.

Unable to get up, Vivian pushed until she sat with her back against the cabinet. Breathlessly, she pleaded with Adrena. For a brief moment, it seemed as if Adrena actually understood Vivian. A tear fell from Adrena's eye.

Suddenly, recognition vanished. Adrena delivered a sharp elbow to Howard's stomach. Then, another. His hold slackened enough for her to free herself. She scampered over to the knife and walked back to Howard slowly.

Vivian was crying and pleading, "Don't do it, Adrena. It's not Bart. It's not Bart."

Adrena looked at Vivian's crumpled, weeping body on the floor. Blood soaked her clothing. Then, she looked at Howard. He clutched his side. There was blood all over him. She looked down at herself and at the knife in her hand. Adrena closed her eyes slowly.

Behind her eyelids stood a filthy, sneering, and half- naked Bartholomew Hanover. He was charred black and groping greedily at Adrena. Adrena flinched when Bart lifted his foot as if to kick her, the way he had when she was a little girl. When Adrena opened her eyes again, she saw Vivian and Howard. Then again, Mildred and Bart. Adrena threw her head back viciously and opened her mouth to let out a tormented sound no one heard immediately.

The tiny squeal of excruciating rage grew in Adrena's throat, reminding Vivian of the rage that bubbled the day of Mildred's visit. As it grew, it was deafening. Vivian knew Adrena had finally realized what she had done. Vivian prayed Adrena wouldn't turn on herself. With the knife in her hand, Adrena ran howling from the kitchen.

Struggling desperately, Howard followed Adrena. He had to make sure she didn't move toward the stairs - the babies were up there. When he saw that the front door was wide open, he knew he didn't need to move in that direction anymore.

Howard painfully inched back toward Vivian. She shook her head and said in a whisper, "The telephone, Howard. We need help."

Barely able to speak, Howard asked, "Will she come back, Vivian?"

Crying hysterically, Vivian panted, "No, Howard. We need help. Adrena needs help, too. Tell them to look for her. She's sick, Howard. Tell them not to hurt her. Please, tell them not to hurt her."

Adrena ran along the dark, tree-lined, expansively lawned streets until she was too tired to take another step. She had no idea where she was when she sat on the curb. The pounding pain in her head banished all thought. The police lights and sirens only made it worse. As they pulled up to where she sat, Adrena held her head with one hand and the knife loosely in the other.

Never hearing anything they said, Adrena struggled to her feet. Her only intention was to ask them to turn off the lights and stop the noise. She took one step toward the lights, and the world disappeared.

Chapter Thirty-Seven

After a long, confusing trip to the supermarket, Clayton pulled up in front of Howard's house. Maxine sent him shopping for the damnedest things. For the life of him, Clayton could not believe he was still doing almost everything that tyrant told him to do. Other than giving him the prettiest, smartest, and happiest little girl in the world, and the fact that he loved Maxine, none of it computed for Clayton.

These were the thoughts of Clayton Williams, as he walked up the pathway of Howard and Vivian Shaw, less than five minutes after Adrena Reynolds ran through it. Walking in, Clayton saw nothing out of place, with the exception of the front door being left open. However, that didn't alarm him. If someone came in with their arms loaded, they might have neglected to close the door. He knew someone was here. Both cars were parked outside. The only truly odd thing was the house was completely quiet. Aria and Scooter usually ran screaming through the place at this time of evening. They raced for whomever came through the door.

Clayton called Howard. The only response was a closing cabinet door in the kitchen. Clayton bounced along to it. He said, "Hey, Howard, where are the kids? Adrena didn't take them any place, did she? Max will not be pleased, if I don't get Aria home and in bed by ten."

At the kitchen door, the light was bright, but there was no one there. A worried frown creased Clayton's face. Someone had definitely closed a cabinet door when he was in the living room. Clayton smelled blood before he actually saw any. There was a puddle of it on the counter - smears of the thick, red, unmistakable substance here and there on the walls.

Feeling panic creeping up on him, Clayton yelled, "Howard! Vivian!"

Vivian gave a faint, "Over here."

Clayton was not prepared for what he found on the other side of the counter. Howard and Vivian were both sitting on the floor, in a widening pool of blood. Just then, the police and paramedics burst through the front door in a rush, hollering. Clayton ran to the living room and directed them to the kitchen.

As they feverishly ran intravenous lines into Vivian and Howard, Clayton mumbled in a panic, "The children. Aria. Scooter."

Just as the paramedic pulled the oxygen mask over her face, Vivian muttered, "Upstairs."

Clayton darted out of the kitchen and up the stairs. He found Scooter and Aria playing in the crib. Not satisfied with a mere sight check, Clayton ran his hands over them. Checking for wounds. Blood. There were none. He snatched the pair out of the crib and hurried back downstairs.

The paramedics had already taken Vivian out. They carried Howard out on a stretcher, passing Clayton at the bottom of the stairs. The police converged on Clayton and fired a barrage of questions, for which he had no answers. He only had one certain answer for them. "My name is Clayton Williams." In truth, they knew more than Clayton.

Too nervous to drive with the two children, Clayton asked frantically, "Can I get a ride to the hospital with someone?"

One of the officers said, "Sure, Mr. Williams. Are these their children? Are they injured?"

"No, they're fine. The boy is theirs. The girl is mine. Vivian's pregnant. Is she going to be all right? What happened to Howard? Who did this? Does anybody know what happened?"

The officer said, "All we know is someone named Adrena Reynolds had some kind of nervous breakdown. This is where she broke down. You just thank God she didn't hurt the children."

In a state of shock, Clayton asked, "Are you saying Adrena did all of this? Are you sure Adrena did this? I don't believe you. She wouldn't hurt Vivian and Howard. Where is Adrena?"

"We don't know that either, Sir. Come on, if you still want that ride."

Clinging to Scooter and Aria, Clayton followed the officer. Junior pulled up as they all piled into the police car. Without ever turning his car off, Junior followed the police car carrying Clayton and the children. Junior knew something had happened, and he assumed Vivian had gone into labor. Adrena and Howard probably went in the ambulance with her, and Clayton was going over with the police, because he couldn't handle Scooter and Aria and drive.

Junior ran up on a frantically-pacing Clayton, in the emergency room. Without hesitation, Junior asked, "Is Vivian all right?"

Clayton snapped, "No! She's not. Neither is Howard!"

Frowning his confusion, Junior asked, "What's the matter with Howard?"

"From the looks of it, Junior, she stabbed him!"

"Who?! Vivian?"

"No! Adrena!"

With a nervous smile, Junior said hesitantly, "Wait a minute, Clayton. Are you saying Adrena did something to Howard and Vivian?"

"That's what I'm saying, Junior. Do you know where she is?"

Dumbfounded, Junior said, "No, I don't know where she is. I thought she was here with Vivian. You're wrong, Clayton. Adrena wouldn't hurt Vivian for anything in the world."

"That's easy enough for you to say. You didn't see the pool of blood she left them in."

"Pool of blood?! Stop saying that! Adrena didn't do it! I don't know what happened, but Adrena didn't do it! Who told you that?!"

Clayton pointed to the officer at the nurses' station. Junior went to ask the officer some questions of his own. Suddenly, the doors of the emergency room made a loud clanging noise, and red lights flashed on the white tile. They ran in, wheeling someone on a stretcher. Just seeing her hair, Junior knew instantly it was Adrena.

In tears, Junior followed the stretcher down the hall, wailing wildly, "Adrena! What happened?! What's going on?!"

Forgetting the two toddlers playing on the floor, Clayton ran behind Junior. Scooter got to his feet and tried to follow his uncles and the stretcher down the hall. Hearing Junior call her name, Scooter joined in calling, "Drena!"

The officer collected Scooter and Aria. The three went in the direction of the stretcher, too. They all heard the page go out for Dr. Matthews to report to the OR, stat.

Junior stared numbly through the cubicle window as they worked on Adrena. Unrestrained tears flowed down his pain-stricken, handsome face. A passing nurse noticed how distraught Junior was and closed the curtains.

Junior and Clayton drifted off to the waiting room. They both wanted answers, but no one came to tell them anything. Not knowing what happened ripped at them for hours.

Three hours into the ordeal, Clayton told Junior to call his father, and he called Howard's sister, Talia. She would pass the word along. In what seemed like minutes, the waiting room filled with familiar, concerned faces. Everyone taking turns holding the children.

When Lula walked in, there was only silence. She already knew as much as anyone else. Knowing Lula had never seen Scooter, Talia handed him to her. Lula looked into his eyes, so like Howard's and started to cry.

Having no idea who this woman was, Scooter said, "Don't cry, lady."

Vance held on to his son, watching him emotionally disintegrate before his eyes. He kept telling Junior to hold on. Everything would be known soon. Deeply despondent, Junior never said another word.

A doctor finally came into the waiting room and asked, "Is this the family of Howard and Vivian Shaw?"

Everyone said, "Yes."

Like a mechanic saying, "Your cars are ready," the doctor said, "They're both in recovery. The baby is in the intensive care nursery." Without another word, he turned to walk away.

Sheldon grabbed his arm violently and said, "I know you've got more to say than that. What happened to them? How are they?"

Looking up into Sheldon's angry face, the doctor said, "I'm sorry. I thought you knew what happened. Mr. Shaw was stabbed through the hand. There were broken bones, and a lot of nerve and tissue damage. We were lucky to find a hand specialist at this time of night, but we did. He thinks the hand will require more surgery down the line, but, it looks good for now.

"Mr. Shaw also received several sharp blows to the abdomen and chest. Two of his ribs were broken, and his spleen was ruptured. We removed it. There doesn't appear to be any more internal bleeding. He's been listed as critical but stable."

Clayton asked, "Are you trying to tell me one little girl did all of that to Howard?"

Blinking slowly, the doctor replied, "From what I'm gleaning from police reports, the young lady is psychologically damaged, and your loved ones are extremely fortunate to still be alive."

Shaking his head, as if trying to clear it, Clayton asked, "What about Vivian?"

"Mrs. Shaw has some bad bruising down her lower back. We won't know what the ramifications of that will be until we get her up. We do know there is no paralysis. The ordeal sent her into labor, and she delivered a five-pound, three-ounce baby girl an hour ago. Of course, Mrs. Shaw lost a lot of blood, but she seems to be fine. The baby is a few weeks premature and fine, too. They're watching her closely, in the Pediatric ICU."

Speaking for Junior, Vance asked, "What about Adrena Reynolds?"

"I think she's still in surgery. Dr. Matthews has been working on her for about four hours now. One bullet did extensive damage to her heart. The other is lodged in her spine." Seeing the devastation on Junior's face, the doctor avoided saying, "It doesn't look very promising."

Truly alarmed now, Vance asked, "Where did bullets come from?"

The doctor said, "I think Miss Reynolds was wounded during apprehension. That's all I know. You'll have to get more from the officers."

Sheldon asked, "When can we see Howard and Vivian?"

"I would say tomorrow morning, but I don't think you'll want to hear that. Give them another hour. Mr. and Mrs. Shaw should both be in their rooms by then. You'll probably have better luck seeing the baby, for now."

Everyone, except Junior and Vance, moved toward the elevators in unison. Leaning back against the wall, Junior said miserably, "It's my fault, Dad. I should have been there. I took the car to be serviced. They took longer than I expected. I should have called her. Adrena was probably tired and stressed out from the kids. I let her down."

Vance tried to console him. "We still don't know exactly what happened, Junior. There's a lot of pieces missing."

Sobbing uncontrollably, Junior agonized, "The missing piece was me, Dad. I just can't imagine how afraid Adrena must have been . . . for them to shoot her! They shot her, Dad! They didn't have to shoot her."

"I know, Junior. She's such a little thing. I don't understand that myself."

With the surgery completed, a tired and distraught Maxine went in search of her sister. She found Vivian in a private room on the ob/gyn ward. Still a little drowsy, Vivian recognized Maxine immediately and struggled to focus. The moment she saw Maxine's face, she knew something was terribly wrong.

Visibly shaking, Vivian asked softly, "Has something happened to Howard, Max?"

Unable to meet her sister's gaze, Max said, "No, it's not Howard, Viv."

"Is it the baby? Did something happen to the baby?"

"No, Vivian. She's fine."

"Well, what is it? Did they find Adrena? Is she all right, Max?"

A tear escaped Maxine's eye and made an agonizingly slow descent down her cheek. Without Max saying another word, Vivian knew something bad had happened to Adrena.

Finally, Maxine managed to say, "I did everything I could, Vivian. There was just too much damage to the heart. I don't know why she's still alive. But, she is. She can't last much longer - there's too much damage, Vivian. We didn't even bother the bullet in her spine; she would have died right there on the operating table."

Screaming hysterically, Vivian asked, "What bullets, Max?! There was no gun in the house!"

"The police found Adrena sitting on a curb. They thought she was going to attack one of them with the knife she had in her hand. Two shots were fired. Both hit her in the chest. One nicked the aorta and ripped out a plug of Adrena's heart. There was even a missing valve. Every time we repaired one thing, another leak appeared.

"Her left lung was filled with blood by the time they got her here. Anybody else would have died within minutes, Vivian. She's going to drown in her own blood. We tried everything possible. I resuscitated her twice myself. Not even a spare heart would have helped."

Vivian moaned pitifully, "When we called for the police, I told them she was having a psychotic episode. I told them not to try to approach her without a psychiatrist and a sedative. I told them." Vivian's voice rose, trembling in anguish. "They didn't have to shoot her, Max . . . they didn't have to shoot her! She's just a baby!"

Max shrugged her defeat, as more tears fell. Then, she said, "Adrena's asking for you and Junior. I sent someone for him. Are you up to the trip?"

"I've got to go. Help me, Max!"

Junior was already there with Adrena when Vivian and Max arrived. Vance stood at the door. All Junior could do was cry and beg Adrena not to leave him. Driven to insanity with guilt and grief, he never gave Adrena a chance to say anything.

Max rolled Vivian to the opposite side of the bed. Vivian didn't cry. She looked directly into Adrena's beautiful, tired eyes and said, "Hi, Adrena."

Clearly struggling to breathe, Adrena swallowed hard and said, "Hi, Doc. You all right?"

Stroking Adrena's hair, Vivian said, "I'm fine, sweetheart. The baby's fine, too. It's a girl."

Adrena's eyes closed slowly. Vivian panicked and called her name loudly. Adrena's eyes opened just as slowly. She said, "I'm so sorry, Doc. You did a real good job with me. I had it all for a while. Hope. A family. A future. Friends . . . and Junior. I couldn't leave without thanking you."

"You don't have to thank me for anything. It was my great pleasure."

"I should have died ten years ago, Doc. Hate kept me alive then. Something different is doing it this time. Max told me what I did to Howard. Tell him I'm really sorry. I thought he was someone else."

"I'll tell him, Adrena. He knows you thought he was someone else."

"Good. Can you do me one more favor, Doc?"

"Anything, Adrena. What is that?"

"Take care of Junior . . . don't let him blame himself, or sit around crying over me. You all made me happier than I've ever been in my life. I had ten years that kept getting better and better. Made me feel like I finally belonged somewhere. To somebody. I don't want anybody blaming themselves for what happened. The people who did this are all dead. They can't hurt anybody else."

Suddenly, the need to know once and for all overpowered Vivian, and she impulsively asked, "Did you kill them, Adrena?"

Unburdening her soul now would place a permanent noose around Doc's neck. Adrena knew she had to give Vivian as much peace as she could. She owed her that and so much more.

Adrena gave Vivian a feeble smile. "No, Doc. I didn't kill a soul . . . I guess you know I wanted to, though. There was something else I wanted to tell you, Doc."

"What's that, Adrena?"

"I love you."

Hearing those words, after so many years of mending, molding and prying, stripped the final vestiges of Vivian's strength. She wept openly as she said, "I love you, too."

With a deep sigh, Adrena said, "Good. Junior already knows I loved him. He told me so."

There was a deep rattle in Adrena's chest. Her body twitched. With Vivian lovingly stroking her hair, Junior holding her hand, and surrounded by the people she loved most in the world, Adrena's eyes closed for the final time. Every eye in the room closed with hers for a while. Tears fell, but there was no yelling or screaming. They napped briefly with a loved one who had moved on.

Epilogue

Six months later, Vivian, Max, and Junior still struggled with the loss of Adrena. She represented something different to each one, and each of their lives was permanently altered by her absence.

For Maxine, Adrena had been a gutsy, bold little sister. She loved teaching her all of the quirks of being a woman. She really loved the way Adrena absorbed her every word and refused to do anything to the contrary. Maxine saw in Adrena the opportunity for someone to have it all, before they turned thirty. If she was crazy, then maybe a woman needed to be a little crazy to get it all.

For Junior, Adrena was his first true love. They had three years of learning, laughing, and loving. Everything Junior did revolved around being with Adrena. For months, without his motivator, he sat. Junior would never take a shirt out of the hamper again without remembering her. He would never make love to another woman and not remember her.

In sharing his memories of Adrena with Vance, Junior told his father everything. He included the shattered car window on prom night, the apartment at school, and Adrena's house. Vance sat staring at Junior in total disbelief. Not because so much had transpired between the two. Rather, because his beloved, precious daughters were keeping secrets from him. Vance expected anything from a teen-age boy. He expected more from his mischievous, intelligent, pillar-of-the-community daughters. Vance swore he would live long enough to assist Aria, Scooter, and the newest addition, Connie, in their endeavors. See how Vivian and Maxine would like that! Junior had to laugh at his father.

For Vivian, Adrena was a firstborn. No one would ever replace her. Not even the two precious children to whom she had given birth. If God was kind, Vivian knew her own children would never need the kind of love, nuturing and understanding Adrena needed. It came to them naturally. Absolutely nothing normal people take for granted came to Adrena naturally. Not even the basics of how to wash your face, or eat a meal at the dining room table with utensils. Sleeping in a bed and using a wastebasket were as foreign to Adrena as a butler or a handmaiden to a homeless person. It broke Vivian's heart to find that Adrena had never been formally toilet-trained at the age of ten. That wasn't revealed until they removed all of the hospital aparatus. Vivian literally had to oversee the total programming of the human being . . . to do that and not love . . . Vivian never mastered.

Adrena's scars ran so much deeper than the ones reflected on her body. Emotionally, they ran deeper than the horrible rape she endured. Adrena was a person with no sense of self. She had no identity. She only existed in the eyes of others. All Vivian had done was draw Adrena's attention to her reflection in other people's eyes. It was a small accomplishment, but it brought Adrena some happiness and gave her a semblance of pride and accomplishment.

As a doctor, Vivian knew she had done all anyone could have done for Adrena. Yes, she could have institutionalized her. Perhaps, Adrena would still be alive. In Huntingdon, Adrena's life would have been a long, neverending exercise in futility. Because she lacked so many of the social amenities taken for granted, eventually Adrena would have adopted the warped posture of the truly insane. No one would have troubled themselves with teaching Adrena to read and write. The laughter they all became accustomed to would never have touched her heart.

Outside of Huntingdon, she became educated, sophisticated, and strong. In the end, Adrena felt. She even knew she loved and expressed it. That was the most important thing to Vivian Matthews-Shaw. Adrena knew she was loved and loved back.

Everyone recovered from their injuries in time. Howard handled his end of the business from home, after being bedridden for three weeks. He loved being home with Vivian, Scooter and Connie all day, but life beckoned and

Howard answered. With Clayton complaining it was too soon, Howard was back at work after only two months. He insisted his hand was good enough to drive and push a few keys, although there was some limitation of movement in it. Howard just thanked God it worked at all and that there was still feeling in it.

Vivian still cried about Adrena every once in a while, but her mood swings stopped after a month. Howard and Vivian's relationship mended slowly, as they lay in bed together talking for hours on end about everything that had transpired. Howard gained a better understanding of the bond between Vivian and Adrena. After getting to know Adrena, Howard came to know why Vivian loved her.

Vivian decided to take a long sabbatical. She wasn't sure she wanted to return to psychiatry. Being a wife and mother meant so much more to her now. Vivian clung to every precious moment of it, and Howard liked knowing she was there with the children all day, every day.

They named their new daughter Constance Adrena Shaw, in memory of Vivian's mother and Adrena - two people who didn't get a chance to live life to its fullest. Connie would have to do it for them, and she was off to a good start. Connie looked more like Howard than Scooter, but she already had her mother's hair and zest for life. The little girl seldom slept and demanded constant attention, and Howard saw that she got as much attention as humanly possible.

Mr. Lewis called Vivian and told her he would be reading Adrena's will, and when everyone was well enough to attend, he came to Vivian's house for that purpose. Like her grandmother, Adrena left her immediate family members one hundred dollars each to satisfy any legal obligation she might have to them.

Adrena left the portion of her estate handled by Williams and Shaw in trust to Howard Devon Shaw II and any other offspring of Mr. and Mrs. Howard Devon Shaw, Sr., to be divided equally among them. To Aria Williams, in trust, fifty thousand dollars. To Mr. and Mrs. Stanley, twenty-five thousand dollars. The remainder of the estate, including her home and car, went to Vance Matthews, Jr. To Dr. Vivian

Matthews-Shaw, Adrena left her most prized possession . . .
her doll, Max.

Vivian wept over Max for months. Finally, she took the
doll to be encased in glass and placed her on the mantle over
the fireplace in her bedroom. Flanking Max were Adrena's
graduation and prom pictures. Behind her was Adrena's
diploma which Adrena had given to Vivian for safekeeping.

Junior returned to school in the fall. He decided to follow
in his two elder sisters' footsteps and major in medicine,
although he hadn't yet decided what his specialty was going
to be. He moved into the apartment for the first semester, but
felt it would be better if he gave it up; without Adrena, it was
too lonely. He resided in the dorm for the remainder of his
stay at college.

Clayton and Maxine married when she became pregnant
for the second time. Vance thanked God she had finally come
to her senses, although he didn't understand why Maxine
refused to take Clayton's last name - but Vance was a smart
man, and he didn't ask any questions.

Vivian and Howard's life was as full and rich as it could
be. Whenever Vivian wanted to talk about Adrena, Howard
listened, and Scooter would point to her picture. Connie had
no idea what they were talking about. She looked at the doll
longingly though.

The greatest change in their lives was Lula, who moved
in with Howard and Vivian for two months after that tragic
night. Lula took care of the children and Howard. Vivian
didn't know if she trusted Lula's motives until they began to
talk. Lula had what she needed in Vivian - a full-time shrink.
Vivian had what she needed in Lula - a sister-in-law she could
trust with her family, while she recuperated. And Howard
had a sister who wasn't trying to be his mother anymore.

After two months in the Shaw household, Lula packed up
and moved out. She called often to make sure everyone was
all right. She dropped by occasionally, to sit and chat with
Vivian and see her niece and nephew. It was easy to see that
Lula was taken with the children; Vivian constantly found
ways to remind Lula they were *her* children though.

If Vivian had any wild ideas about having any more children, she would have to do it with her second husband. Howard asked about birth control before resuming their sex life. Said he wanted to make it perfectly clear, there would be no more babies anytime soon.

Vivian asked, "Does that mean we can have another one later on, Howard?"

Howard gave Vivian an emphatic "*No!*"

The End

USE THIS FORM TO ORDER ADDITIONAL COPIES OF DAMAGED!

FILL IN THIS FORM AND MAIL TO:
Waverly House Publishing, PO Box 1053, Glenside, Pa. 19038
For information call: 1-800-858-2253

Method of Payment

☐ Check   ☐ VISA [VISA]   ☐ Mastercard [MasterCard]

☐ American [AMERICAN EXPRESS]   ☐ Discover [DISCOVER]

Card Account No. Please list all numbers on card.   Exp. Mo.   Exp.

_____   _____
Customer Name   Customer Signature

_____   _____
Street Address   City   State   Zip Code

_____   _____
Day Time Phone (include area code)   Night Time Phone (include area

Your name and address must be filled in even if you're sending to another address.

Order #1 - Please send the following to the address below:

Qty	Description	Price	Subtotal
	Damaged!, softbound	$14.95	$
	Damaged!, hardbound	$22.95	$
	Add shipping and handling (see below)		
	Add sales tax if required (see below)		
	Total		**$**

Ship to arrive week of _____ to: Name_____

Address_____ Apt. # _____

_____ Zip _____

Card to read:_____
You may enclose your own card or we'll enclose handwritten one with your personal message..

Order #2 - Please send the following to the address below:

Qty	Description	Price	Subtotal
	Damaged!, softbound	$14.95	$
	Damaged!, hardbound	$22.95	$
	Add shipping and handling (see below)		
	Add sales tax if required (see below)		
	Total		**$**

Ship to arrive week of _____ to: Name_____

Address_____ Apt. # _____

_____ Zip _____

Card to read: _____
You may enclose your own card or we'll enclose handwritten one with your personal message.

SHIPPING AND HANDLING; For one book, add $3.00; for each additional book, add $1.